PENGUIN BOOKS
REQUIEM IN RAGA JANKI

Neelum Saran Gour is the author of six novels, four short story collections, two works of non-fiction and a translation of her own work into Hindi. She has been an active columnist and book reviewer and an academic by profession. Her most recent novel, *Requiem in Raga Janki* won the Hindu Fiction Prize (2018) and also the Sahitya Akademi Award (2023). Her other books include *Grey Pigeon and Other Stories*, *Speaking of '62*, *Winter Companions*, *Virtual Realities*, *Sikandar Chowk Park*, *Song without End*, *Allahabad: Where the Rivers Meet* (edited), *Invisible Ink*, *Allahabad Aria*, *Three Rivers and a Tree*, and *Messres Dickens, Doyle and Wodehouse Pvt. Ltd.*

REQUIEM *in* RAGA JANKI

a novel

NEELUM SARAN GOUR

PENGUIN BOOKS

An imprint of Penguin Random House

PENGUIN BOOKS

Penguin Books is an imprint of the Penguin Random House group of companies
whose addresses can be found at global.penguinrandomhouse.com

Published by Penguin Random House India Pvt. Ltd
4th Floor, Capital Tower 1, MG Road,
Gurugram 122 002, Haryana, India

 Penguin
Random House
India

First published in Viking by Penguin Random House India 2018
Published in Penguin Books by Penguin Random House India 2024

10 9 8 7 6 5 4 3 2 1

ISBN 9780143467342

Typeset in Minion Pro by Manipal Digital Systems, Manipal
Printed at

www.penguin.co.in

To the memory of my father, Sitawar Saran, and his guides,
Ustad Rehmat Hussain Khan of Etawah and
Pandit Purushottam Mishra of Allahabad,
and all those ragas, stories,
that formed the soundtrack of my childhood

'If there's a book you want to read and it hasn't been written yet, then you must write it.'

—Toni Morrison

1

You want me to talk about her after all these years? So be it. Maybe you can get a book out of all this. Me, I'm content to turn this raga into a requiem. Isn't that what Vilas Khan did? Tuned his Todi to a note of grieving, sang it to the corpse of his father, Tansen, and the corpse raised its hand in benediction. Some years back you might have heard that raga on All India Radio every time the country went into state mourning for a leader. What, another story? Patience, it shall come. Somewhere in my rambles when its time is ripe.

And since it's my stories you're after and since you are my patrons, promoters and paymasters, I'll let loose some on you right away. But please don't think me your chattering relic. I'm no hireling of your museum, understand this. I am an artist and we artists had our pride. Let not our shifts and rags mislead our hosts into imagining that we were subjects of lesser empires, for the sovereignty of excellence was our cause, that others could only gawp at, yes, even the most powerful, excuse my grandiloquence. This I learnt from Rajab Ali Khan Sahib, a friend of my family who used to be durbar musician at Dewas.

He once received Rs 2500 from the maharaja of Indore. This Rajab Ali Khan was a man of whimsies, famous for the way he dealt a severe shoe-beating to a tonga-wallah who had cruelly whipped his horse and then commanded the man to drive to a mithai shop, bought two seers of jalebis and personally fed them to the whipped animal. A rare eccentric, the story ran in my family. One other weakness he had, apart from music, and that was itr. How many of you have experienced those Kannauj perfumes? Inhaled the ether that rises out of those cut-glass vials of floral oils, those visitations of rose water and rajnigandha, mimosa or acacia, sandalwood and camphor, musk or first-rain-on-parched-earth? By all accounts, an expensive taste for a mere musician, you would say and I would agree. A taste for the raees, not the poor artist. But the money that warmed his shervani pocket, earned by an evening of music, had kindled his longing. So he hailed a tonga and told the tonga-wallah to drive to the best itr shop in Indore on his way back to Dewas. He chose the best perfume. The shopkeeper looked doubtfully at him, his humble clothes, his well-worn shoes, and sized him up. When Rajab Ali asked the price he received the surly answer: 'It is much too expensive for you, sir.' Rajab Ali was stung. He well understood that fine semitone of disdain in the merchant's response, he who dealt in the tiniest shifts of inflexion in a human voice.

'I asked to know how much it is, sir?' he repeated in a louder voice.

The merchant felt the bristle of indignation and said: 'It is Rs 150 a vial.'

'And how many vials have you in stock?' asked Rajab Ali.

'Ten, sir,' was the baffled answer.

Rajab Ali took the banknotes out of his pocket and laid them before the dealer. 'Then,' he said, taking off his battered footwear, 'be so kind, janab, as to take the whole accursed lot in your shop and pour them into my shoes!'

Pray do not gasp. I have heard this searing shocker narrated many times in our courtyard. And there's more of the same for you.

Can you endure another one? Then listen. There was a poverty-stricken Lucknow maestro, Haideri Khan, whose only demand of the unknown raees, who'd driven up in his carriage to his dank and lowly lane with a request for a song, was a filling meal of malai and puris, enough for him and his wife, when he finished the recital. He was taken away in the carriage to an opulent mansion and the poor fool didn't realize who his host was. Yes, none other than the heir to Nawab Saadat Ali, Ghazi-ud-din Haider himself! Later, when he'd become a court performer, at the beck and call of the young prince, he gave his employer such a piece of his mind that it thrills my heart just to remember and repeat it. The prince had summoned him on a caprice and commanded: 'Sing to me, ustad. Make me weep today. I am in a mood for plenteous tears. Sing, and if my tears should fail to flow, be assured you shall be beheaded, make no mistake.' The terrified maestro sang and was relieved to behold his patron's eyes moisten and presently overflow. When he finished he was asked by a mellowed master: 'That was stirring, ustad. Speak. How may we reward you?' 'Then, huzoor,' replied Haideri Khan, 'I beseech Your Highness never to lay such conditions on me. If you did commit the folly of rashly beheading me, think what a loss it would mean to your state. A mere princeling like you, when dead, is easily replaced, but never an artist like me.' I can still hear Janki's dense, throaty chortle as she removed the hookah from her mouth to laugh at this one.

When I work myself up into a state of flaying contempt they fall over their feet to soothe my ruffled feathers, bring paan and supari for me, fuss around with rooh-afza or chai. 'Sahiba,' says one of the organizers, 'what we pay you is a small token. Who can ever calculate the worth of what we receive from you?' Sahiba! That's quaint. As though I am an antique Baiji, kohled and hennaed and betel-chomping, my voice squelching with grainy

tunes and my manner as imperious as that of an ancient mistress
of a music chamber. A Baiji I am emphatically not, never was like
Janki, though like her I am subject to fits of ungovernable fury, so
mind your step, sirs. I am, by your leave, that other thing that you
historians make so much of, a lore-mistress of the mehfil. We've
got you cheap, sahiba, they slaver at the institute's office. For
where else shall we ever get to hear all these fine accounts? What a
service to posterity this shall be. I relent, nod graciously, switch on
my benign old woman's smile. We know the threadbare truth of
the situation. Like shrewd tradesmen we have been measuring our
outlay and our profits. If I tell them five more stories now, it shall
consume an hour and earn me this week's allowance. I sing for my
supper, yes, even as I seem to scorn payment, but it's my stories
that make up my song.

However I must warn you that at my age things crowd in
unbidden. Memory overreaches reality. And there's something
like false recall. Memory is its own insular dimension. Alauddin
Khan Sahib—God rest his soul, sage that he was—in his old age
lost his earthly memory and wandered about the alleys of his inner
chronologies. If asked his age he answered with great simplicity
that he was fifty thousand years old. Artificial memory might just
be imagination intensified. When I start telling one story I often
end up telling another. I may begin on one and end up telling a
score. Because I carry in my memory not just the stories but the
ancestors of stories too. Is that hard to understand? That stories
have their parent stories and grandparent stories? I have lived long
enough to have known many generations of stories with the same
bloodlines, so when I tell you one I must tell you its kindred ones.

But they are keenly interested in it all, they've assured me.
They want to record it. They want information about a forgotten
woman that only I seem to have. They might even get a respectable

institute publication about her at the end of the exercise. What
is my stake, you might ask. In the old days royal musicians were
gifted a gold anklet for the left foot by their patrons. A thousand
rupees an hour every Tuesday and Thursday for three months is
my allowance. Privately I cannot pretend I don't need this cash. I
am not like Janki who squandered her earnings on others. Or like
our venerable Bande Ali Khan Sahib, that carefree anchorite of the
veena, who often gave away all that he received. From the maharaja
of Nepal he once received a divan made of solid silver (the same
divan on which he had sat in the durbar and played Raga Sankara),
gorgeous silken robes and gold mohurs. All of which he distributed
among his pupils and relatives and friends. There were those two
dhrupad maestros, Shadi Khan and Murad Khan, who were given
a dais strewn with silver coins, a lakh and a quarter of silver coins,
and everything covered with a costly carpet, and an elephant
provided by the maharaja of Datia to carry away this largesse. But
our two merry maestros (cap-exchange brothers, for when two
musicians were the greatest of friends they exchanged their caps to
seal their friendship, becoming topi-badal brothers), riding atop
the swaying elephant, had lifted handfuls of coins and tossed them
among the scrambling populace! And further back in time, at the
court of Kumarapala, there was that celebrated musician, Solki,
who was gifted 116 gold coins for his magical singing and who
went and spent it all on sweets for crowds of children he met on
the way. The relation between artist and patron was a delicate one,
a duet of competing vanities. Two different registers of gallantry.
The patrons weren't amused but the maestros always had ready
answers. Shadi Khan sweetly pleaded the cause of the deserving
poor and his own mission of spreading the good word about
the maharaja's spectacular generosity. (Which elegant argument
earned him a further Rs 10,000 from his impressed patron!) But

Solki was banished and his home and property attached and he
had to earn back his king's favour. Far and wide did he perform, in
other kingdoms and courts, earning enough money to purchase a
pair of elephants, which he then humbly offered to his estranged
king and was forthwith received back into his good books. Does all
this extravaganza of gold and silver strike you as overly medieval?
The stuff of fairy tales? It wasn't. I have personally witnessed Janki
seated on a platform beneath a peepul tree in a crowded Attarsuiya
square, singing, and in a very short while the concrete platform
was completely hidden beneath heaps of silver coins. They said the
silver amounted to more than Rs 14,000 and the event came to be
called her 'chaudah-hazari', event of the fourteen thousand. But
she didn't appear to be happy. She seemed ineffably weary, sad.
This I have seen. I was a tiny child then.

I should have written all this down but I didn't. Music took
up all my time. I'm pushing ninety now. There was a time when
I could hold a high note without a tremor for as long as it takes a
man of ordinary stride to walk across the Naini Bridge from end
to end, but that was a long time ago and breathlessness overcomes
me. Still, if they think my shambling tales worth this much, if I'm
to be paid a thousand rupees an hour for my fuzzy memories of her
and others that I have known or heard of, then so be it. My brain
is sagging under this overload and it's getting hard to carry them
to the summit or the pit, whatever lies ahead. Time to offload this
weight. I have given away my porcelain and my furniture, though
the china was discoloured and the wood warped. I have given
away my silks and georgettes though the fabric was falling apart.
Burn down my costumes for their gold or silver thread, I say—as
Janki's were. Four seers of gold and seven seers of silver they got
out of her lehngas and drapes and embroidered peshwazes. My
own jewels I sold long ago. It's my stories that will not fade. Take

them. Help yourselves, feel free. By the grace of Saraswati and the Sayyad of Mausiqui, I am here to share what I remember of things told to me by my ustads and their ustads. Stories of musicians and songstresses and conquerors and patron benefactors. Of love and art and betrayal and loneliness and God, and especially of this woman, Janki Bai, whom I feel such an affinity with, who lived in this city exactly a hundred years ago. I will tell you what I know. Bear with me, please. I am a rasika of the remembered word and a hoarder of treasured tales. Do not nudge me awake if you see my eyes close upon a mood. But should you find the story arresting, then let us go with the flow, meandering along the modulations and variations, wandering into the unexpected and the contingent and the serendipitous, like listeners lost in the ample labyrinths of an Indian raga.

2

Her name lingers in certain locations still—Bai ka Bagh, Liddle Road, Rasoolabad. There is a godown on the Jawaharlal Nehru Road that is used to store Magh Mela tents and other equipment. There is a large field at the Police Lines. And a crumbling monument in the Kaladanda cemetery called Chhappan Chhuri ki Mazaar. I will tell you what I know of her and also what I guess and imagine.

Chhappan Chhuri was Janki's nickname—she of the fifty-six knife gashes. I don't think that that figure, fifty-six, is to be taken literally. She herself wrote somewhere that the number of stabs far exceeded the proverbial fifty-six which was a mere metaphor, an attractive alliteration endorsed by confusion and inaccurate reportage. With time it assumed other cloaks of innuendo so that 'Chhappan Chhuri' suggests someone armed with many weapons of assault, a woman of lethal witchery, of potentially heart-piercing beauty—such the devilry of words. But really she was none of these. She was just a woman who'd survived a murderous attack and who carried on her body dozens of scars which would become her signature of identity, conjoined to her name, Janki Bai.

There are three different accounts of the stabbings and no one knows which the authentic one was, and Janki's own account is a carefully constructed fiction, challenged by other concurrent versions. In one account a crazed fan, spurned, worked his rage on her. But that does seem unlikely. She was barely eight, according to this account, when it is supposed to have happened and her protective mother could not have turned away a besotted lover from her mehfil simply because she hadn't started entertaining audiences that way. That's just one of those romantic stories that attach themselves to people as image enhancers for posterity. It seems that Janki herself initiated this account in the introduction to her diwan of verses, little realizing the transparent inconsistency of it. I can understand her reasons, though. She was a marked woman, quite literally, her skin torn in crumpled gullies of stitched together flesh, lines which the decades had failed to erase. That was the very first thing people saw, the disfigurement. It followed her everywhere. I can't say if she ever really accepted it. It's possible that it had sunk into the grain but it did not surface in her voice as any obvious ache. Nothing so trite. Rather, there was the powerful swell and soar of overcoming. But for purposes of history some subterfuge was in order, especially in times of circumspect and censored telling. And especially in situations of family shame. What is stated as an authentic truth is not so much a deliberate lie but a carefully composed face-saving fiction to answer the disquieting personal questions that are bound to crop up. Like all the plasters of lentil paste, soaked and buried in earthen pots, the unguents of sandalwood and turmeric and flour, the masks of clay-of-Multan and honey and lime, the story doesn't quite camouflage or convince.

But desperate efforts to conceal what has clearly remained unhealed must be respected. There was a second version in circulation, that she was attacked by a rival singer whom she had outsung at a durbar soirée organized by the maharani of Benaras.

There is even a name to this shadowy assailant—Raghunandan Dubey. She was eight years old, a singing prodigy, and she defeated a much older and far more established singer, and consequently she was the victim of a jealous attack. She did not die but underwent treatment generously paid for by the maharani, who took an interest in her. And when she recovered, her mother, afraid to stay on in Benaras with all its vicious intrigues and rivalries, brought her to Allahabad and they made a life for themselves quite different from the earlier one.

Let me first recount the concocted history, the version invented by Janki as preferable to what did happen. Let us place it all as Janki would want us to, the music chamber, the crowd of connoisseurs, the shy loveliness of the little songstress, who'd trained under Koidal Maharaj of Benaras himself, rendering 'Jamuna tat Shyam khelein Hori', and the man who came as just another one in the crowd, accepted the paan, acknowledged the itr and the proffered wine and lolled back on the bolster and listened intently. He wasn't old and he wasn't young. They noticed him the very first time when he produced two banknotes from his achkan pocket and beckoned to Janki. She had only just finished a song. Obligingly she slipped up to him, smiled and sank to her knees in a graceful swirl of silk and tinsel and a cascade of tinkling anklet chimes. He circled the notes around her head and tossed them into the ornate silver dish that lay alongside his bolster. They were all taken aback at the amount though they did not show it. Janki raised her jewelled fingertips to her brow in a salaam, a shy flush playing on her young face.

He raised the standard of payments, that much was sure, and for that Janki's mother Manki Bai was grateful. Other visitors were obliged to offer larger amounts as nazrana in virile competition and Manki counted each evening's takings with satisfaction, tucking away the wads of money, the gold mohurs, the ropes of pearl, the rings, in grain barrels and rice urns and old chests and quilt linings. But then he sought an interview with Manki and came up with the most outrageous suggestion.

'Malkin,' he said, 'it cannot have escaped your attention that I am taken with your daughter. I know she is yet unripe and has not had her nath-uthrai and I would like to present myself to you as a nath babu. I'm in no hurry. I can wait till she comes of age. It can't be long now. She must be twelve . . .'

Manki's surprise had stupefied her temporarily but she soon recovered her wits.

'Just a minute, sahibji,' she interrupted. 'Do I understand you right? You wish to pay bed-money for my daughter, who is yet a child, and be her first client? You take my breath away, sir. We are insulted. But we are prepared to overlook this injury. Let me hear no more of this nonsense! And please, do not darken our doors again, we beg you.'

He drew in his breath. 'You are insulted by an honourable offer, say you, malkin? Do not forget your place, my lady-whore-madam, and put on airs unseemly to your standing.'

'What did you call me?' she cried. 'We are no street women, you gutter-slime. We are performers of music!'

'Yes. Performers in the divan-khana, and the couch chamber too!' he scoffed. 'Don't put up your price, my clever bazaar-crone. I know she is a twelve-year-old virgin. State your demands. I can meet them and let's have none of this warm-up alaap.'

'Why so desperate, babuji?' Manki taunted him. 'Benaras is full of courtesans. Each more tuneful and warm of flesh than the last. I advise you to go to Dal Mandi and look up at the overflowing balconies. That's the place for you. This is the place for musicians and discerning connoisseurs.'

'I do not want any old singing harlot,' he retorted. 'I want this girl alone.'

'Why?' demanded Manki.

'You know why. Do I have to spell it out?'

'Because she is a peerless beauty? Because she is a virgin? And a singer of matchless excellence and you can pimp her about and live off her takings when you are done with her? Ah, I know the likes of you!'

'Listen, woman. Don't try my patience. I am a sipahi in the angrez police fauj and a high-class Dvij Brahmin. Were it not for your daughter, I'd have plucked out your foul tongue from the root and cast it into the cesspool!'

She put her hands together in mock farewell. 'Please', she said, 'let us not detain you any more, my brave babuji. Beni Prasad, show babu sahib the door. And please do not sully our chambers again. I warn you, sir, and for sure we here shall not mourn your absence.'

He left that day but was back the next evening. He even made a farmaish, a request for a song, asking for Janki's most popular number 'Maza le le rasiya nayi jhulni ka'.

'Come here, girl.' He beckoned to Janki when she finished the song she was singing to the gathering. And when a trembling Janki, frail and delicate, came and seated herself in front of him, he asked her to take off the earrings she wore. Uncomprehending, she obeyed.

'Put them in my hand,' he commanded.

She did so, puzzled.

Then he produced from his achkan pocket a jewel case and asked her to open it. She gasped in surprise when she beheld the contents—the most gorgeous jhumka-and-jhoomar set, complete with forehead pendant, exquisitely worked in gold.

'Fair exchange.' He smiled blandly at her. 'You give me yours as a keepsake and I give you these.'

Janki was trained in professional coquetry, well rehearsed in rejoinder and repartee.

'You are an unwise trader, sir,' she remarked in coy wonder.

'No, but I am ready to trade my iman for that little ring you wear on your nose, lassie.'

She well knew his meaning and lowered her eyes, flushing. For a man was propositioning her in full view of the mehfil.

The nose ring, as you must know, was the prepubertal courtesan's mark of virginity, surrendered to a carefully chosen volunteer as soon as she came of age, which is a polite way of saying that she menstruated for the first time. The nath-removing feast in the courtesan household was as splendid as a wedding, and for the next few weeks or months the little girl received sexual training from a much older man. It was a sort of apprenticeship, an orientation into a way of life. Also a compliment to the man chosen for his virility or prudently accepted for his wealth and generous endowment to the household for the delectable function of deflowering a virgin. There was room for terror, for cruelty and pain, for delight and, who knows, maybe even for romance in the transitory connection between a small girl and a seasoned man.

That day Manki called her daughter sternly from the doorway.

'Jankiya, come here immediately, bitiya!'

And when Raghunandan Dubey was leaving, she barred his way to the staircase.

'I shall trouble you, sir, not to trifle with a child's unformed heart. Janki is too young and untried to fathom your ill intentions.'

'She is to be tried sometime or other, no?' he asked, leering.

Something in his insolent air provoked her beyond the limits of discretion. She drew herself up and called into the music room—'Paraga, bring me a mirror, girl. And bring Janki with you. Now Jankiya, take this mirror and hold it up to this fine babu sahib's face.'

Which Janki, trembling, did, not daring to lift her eyes to look the guest in the face.

'Repeat after me.' Manki's voice was imperious. 'Babu sahib, I have danced the Shagun-Nek for the angrez laat sahib at the raja of Benaras's kothi. And I am the famous beauty of the city of Benaras that people come from distant places to behold.'

Manki intoned the words like a high priestess pronouncing an incantation, pausing after each clause. Poor Janki, red with shame, repeated each segment of Manki's scornful declaration in a timid monotone.

'Tell him—I am the disciple of the glorious Hassu Khan Sahib of Gwalior and Lucknow and the venerable Koidal Maharaj, and I shall be empress of the world of music very soon. But you, sipahiya, what are you? Look at your face and tell me. A mere jamadar in the police fauj.'

It got too hot for Raghunandan to take. With a mighty blow he struck the mirror out of Janki's hand. Brow steaming, a nerve pulsing wildly in his temple, he gathered the spittle in his mouth and spat with such force into Janki's face that she staggered back against the wall, the gob of spit spattering her cheek, streaking a trail down her betel-reddened lips.

'You dare hold up a mirror to my face, gutter-slut!' he shouted, his voice cracking in rage. 'You will never ever be able to hold a mirror to your own! I promise you that, on oath, or my name's not Raghunandan Dubey!'

And with that he thumped down the stairs and was gone.

He slipped into the courtyard one afternoon when Manki was on the terrace, minding the pickles and the papads, and Shiv Balak out on one of his wrestling events, and Lakshmi asleep in her kothri. Janki, busy applying henna to her feet, froze at the sight of him. She'd heard a buggy drive up and the door creak on its hinges, and she thought it was Beni Prasad back from flying his kite. Then she turned and saw Raghunandan. In his hand he carried a sword.

This is how Janki might have wanted posterity to imagine the episode. We cannot change the events of our lives but we can script them differently for our peace of mind, internalizing our fictions until they turn into our irrefutable realities. She wanted to be remembered as a famous sought-after beauty, an irresistible object of desire.

For this business of beauty and ugliness is an old one in the domain of art, falsely divided as it was then into sacred and secular, temple and durbar. And because her kind of music was saturated with the sap of sensuous love, soaked through and through in longing and desire, it became as much a celebration of the heart's finer moments, a flourish of the body as a flight of the soul. Janki, scarred, ordinary, had to contend with her disfigurement in the full glare of public gaze and turn it into a strength. Though, I'm sure she didn't quite manage to outgrow a sadness till well into middle age, by which time she had finally managed to convince herself that music wasn't just a performance but a soul mission.

It couldn't have been easy and it was a problem that women performers had to handle. No one minded an ugly male maestro but a woman had to be easy on the eye. The beauty of songstresses is something even Amir Khusrau was constrained to write about as part of his durbar duties as head librarian at the court of Jalaluddin Khilji. We can see them, strumming instruments, singing, telling anecdotes and jokes, playing chausar and chess, riding, dancing. Their names have come down to us: Dukhtar Khasa, Nusrat Bibi, Meherafroz. I don't know if Khusrau enjoyed writing verses in praise of the beauty and winsome affectations of these durbar nymphets but he entered into the spirit of the thing, celebrating shringar with shringar.

Whenever Hassu Khan, in his expansive tales, went overboard with his stories about the celebrity songstresses of Muhammad Shah Rangila's court, Janki flinched inwardly and sulked. She did not know whether he was provoking her to greater efforts or giving way to senile ecstasies of male adoration. The lovely names promised visions of bejewelled, gauzy, tuneful houris in a glittering durbar tipsy with music: Noor Bai, Ramjani, Mani Chakmak, Gulab, Uma Bai, Tanno, Zeenat Bhajji. But he looked at her crestfallen face out of the corner of his eye and added that of them all only Rahiman Bai of Charkhari's stunning looks remained in historical memory—of the rest, only their skill. In fact, said Hassu craftily, nothing is said of the appearance of the two most famous songstresses at Muhammad Shah Rangila's court. Panna Bai and Kamal Bai were urbane and soft-spoken and artists par excellence, not tawaifs. And since he was on the subject, there was a child prodigy, a singularly unattractive little girl, daughter of a singer at the Jaipur court in the nineteenth century, who was trained by the famous Bairam Khan, quite as meticulously as she, Janki, was being. The little girl grew up to win the title of Bharat Kokila Gauki Bai and was one woman widely respected even by the greatest of ustads. Here and there a name might crop up of a singer who was also a famous beauty. Like Nanhi Bai Khetriwali, disciple of Tanras Khan, court poet and musician to Bahadur Shah Zafar. And another one, the same Rahiman Bai Charkhariwali. And the celebrated Chandrabhaga Bai, royal favourite of the Scindias of Gwalior, but she is remembered more as the mother of the well-known Bhaiyya Sahib Ganpath Rao, illegitimate son of Jiyaji Rao Scindia, though some said he was the son of Daulat Rao himself. What Janki had to remember, said Hassu, was the great tradition of female maestros to which she belonged, and Hassu recited the roll call of names that set Janki's pulse beating. Chitra Bai, Imanbandi, Sukhbadan Nartaki, Gulbadan Nartaki in Benaras in the early half of the nineteenth century. In Agra Khursheed Bai and Chanda Bai; in Kanpur that mistress of khayal and thumri, Amani Jaan Gayika; in Rampur Zadi Gayika and Mammi Gayika who were specialists of the tappa. Forgive me, Hassu cleared his throat in an access of emotion, we old lore-masters get carried away. I love the very names, the scent of them, the sound, so bear with me. I could recite them from memory like the syllables of a new musical raga: Sundar Bai and Latifan, both sisters of Rahiman Bai. Sharfo Bai and her mother Sedhu Bai. Jeesukh Bai, Dhooman, Kamla Bai, Hira Bai, Khajur Bai, Bandi Jaan and Lazzat Baksh and Jaan Baksh and Ballo and Vazeeran Dhrupadwali.

Janki wished to ask whether in this rain of names there were any who were ugly like herself. She put her question with timid deference: 'Are there any pictures in any nawab or badshah's tasveer-khana, sir?'

Hassu just might have divined her trouble for he hastened to add that all he knew was that they were women maestros of khayal, dhrupad and tappa, not just the thumri, and respected as maestros, not as durbar women alone, for even God and His angels must surely honour music, Allah forgive him this impiety!

Janki's brain plucked its own consolations and turned them into personal parables. At the monastery at Sarnath where the Buddha preached the worthlessness and impermanence of the body, she'd heard a bhikshu tell a story and never forgot it. There was, say ancient Pali chronicles, a maestro named Guttil who lived at the time of the Buddha in the city of Ujjaini. Once, smitten by the overpowering beauty of a kul-vadhu, a city courtesan, he approached her handmaidens with an amorous proposition. Now, those ganikas were high-profile women of great class and affluence, enormous style and sophistication, and so an ordinary musician's overtures made no impression on the lady, who scornfully turned down the maestro's offer. So Guttil picked up his been, which is a string instrument and ancestor of the veena, and began serenading the haughty beauty. The music worked such enchantment on the lady's senses that she forgot herself and sped down the steep staircase in the direction whence the outpouring melody came. In her haste she lost her balance and fell through an unbarred window, plunging to her death at the musician's feet. Thus much the pride of the foolish body before the power of music!

And at the temples of Benaras Janki had heard pandits discourse on form and name and essence. And how that celestial minstrel, Narada, maestro to the gods, learnt bitter lessons on the truth of the body and the truth of music. Once, singing and making merry, he found himself in an unfamiliar city, a city of palaces and the most beauteous citizens, all lotus-faced and clad in divine raiments. What was most puzzling to him was that, prepossessing though they were, they were all deformed in some way or other. Some lacked feet, some had no thighs, some were without a waist and some were throatless. There were hunchbacks, toothless faces and beautiful bodies without arms. Struck by the spectacle of so many lovely forms in such a dire state of mutilation, Narada addressed them with great reverence: 'O marvellous beings of divine beauty, lotus-faced and divinely dressed, who may you be? Be you gods, gandharvas or rishis? You sit immersed in song, playing on celestial instruments, but how came you by this mutilation? Who ruined your sweet forms and brought you to this sorry pass?'

Said the divine creatures: 'Sir Sage, our bodies live in great affliction. Whither shall we betake this pain? Who shall relieve this suffering? Sir, we are ragas and raginis and our anguish has been occasioned by a certain Narada, son of Brahma. This Narada, rapt in music, breaks all the rules. He sings dhrupad all wrong, he wanders singing all over the earth. He sings with scant regard to the time of day, the rhythm and the season. It is his lawless ravishment of the rules of music that has broken us.'

Narada was astonished and penitent and requested: 'O esteemed ragas and raginis, where may I learn the proper rules? The proper timing, rhythm, notes? Who shall teach me? This I do ask in all humility and hope that I may, at some foreseeable future, when I am better schooled in music, heal your injuries and make you whole.'

Thereupon the ragas made reply: 'Not we, not we, O Sage. Only Saraswati, she who is the goddess of music, can instruct thee.'

So Narada travelled to the great Shubhra Mountain in the high Himalayas and sat in meditation, invoking Saraswati. For a hundred years he practised austerities, neither ate nor drank, until the goddess, appeased by the rigour of his devotion, appeared before him and instructed him in the ancient rules of music, the ragas and their families and their lineage, their countries of origin, their notes and proper paces and the fifty-six crore variations and their countless internal subvariations and modulations. And from this learning did music heal the disfigurement of the ragas and restore them to beauty and wholeness. For beauty of the flesh is a contingent thing, only the apsaras and the nymphs of the waters and the sylphs of the air possess its constant blessing. But Saraswati, in her alabaster light, awakens that other dimension, that blessedness which heals and makes whole. The mirror of the perfect note shall show you the truth of the soul, not your face.

To see the image of your truth in the slow waters of a river, something like the Benaras Ganga at dawn just after the Brahmamuhurta, when your solitary voice arches like a dark-dispelling early bird and descends into the stream and flaps its wings in joy and takes off again, ah, that was music, the riyaz that Hassu prompted with stories that thrilled Janki. The swara was the ultimate mirror, said Hassu, the shining, immaculate, perfect note, held in absolute, unwavering stillness. And this, mark you, is not the mirror that mere vanity preens itself at. This transparency comes from utter fidelity to the inner forms which exist, who knows, in dimensions beyond physical sound, as do the peaks of the Himalayas in realms beyond. That sort of thing happens in a rare and luminous moment sometimes but an artist has to strive a lifetime for it. It comes unexpectedly but it is enough to keep him or her going on the chosen path even if it is a hard and thankless one.

I have had it happen to me and I have heard it told of others far more famous. There was an instant when Abdul Karim Khan Sahib appeared to freeze upon a certain note and no sound seemed to emerge from his throat. The tanpuras went on playing, the fingers of the tabla players continued galloping on their tablas and those in the audience held their breath in wonder. And Khan Sahib's voice seemed to have just vanished. It had merged so purely, so perfectly with the tanpuras and harmoniums that an auditory illusion had been generated. Swarsiddhi—that's the word for it, to be a siddha of the swara, an adept of the note, one who has perfected the miracle of self-disappearance at a magic moment of transfiguration.

And those that have the good fortune to take this holy dip in the still waters of primal swara come up washed and sanctified like prayerful pilgrims drenched in grace. Then even an ugly woman shines with a radiance that touches us with exaltation.

It's said of Roshanara Begum, niece and disciple of Abdul Karim Khan, that she was fat and dark of skin and her most fervent admirers wouldn't have dreamt of calling her beautiful. But when she let loose the power of her lustrous voice, its smooth suppleness and overpowering strength of throw and depth, all produced with an expression of perfect tranquillity on her face, she'd turn into a transcendentally beautiful woman. That's what music did in Janki's case. So that, eventually, after the trouble had been wrestled with and conquered and dismissed, at the end of many years, she could tell the maharaja of Rewa: 'Funkaar ka imtahan soorat se nahin, seerat se liya jaata hai, huzoor.' The test of an artist is the art, sir, not the face.

But that story will have to wait for later. Let me retrace my steps, feel my way back along this alphabet of notes to where I can pick up again a different flight of this same raga.

3

But there's this third account of Janki's stabbing. Only Raghunandan Dubey's name figures in it but there are other unexpected players. It emerges from the evidence of some contemporaries that Raghunandan Dubey was no musician but a junior sipahi of the police force. He used to visit the shop in the mornings when he knew that only Lakshmi and Janki were there. They had a house with a shop in front, a tiny mithai-and-puri shop belonging to Shiv Balak, the milkman-wrestler, tucked away in the narrow lanes of Barna ka Pul in Benaras, close to the bridge on the Varuna river.

They'd be squatting before the twin clay hearths, one stirring the frothing milk in a large iron kadhai, the other bent over platters of sweetened chickpea in ghee, moulding small, perfectly round laddoos. Or Lakshmi might be circling the sieve over the cauldron, drizzling batter into its crackling sheet of oil, or dancing her pretty, smeared fingers in coils and whorls and scalloped ringlets which floated up to the surface as delicate, swimming imartis that she, Janki, gathered in the large mesh scoop and flung into baskets to drain. Lakshmi, dainty, companionable, neither elder sister nor aunt nor quite stepmother, always grew tense when he turned up. For he carried himself with all the swagger of the sarkari sipahi, in turban and puttees and coarse, noisy boots. He was handsome in a rakish way and he flirted and teased and set them giggling.

'A seer of magadh laddoos,' he'd demand, 'and a chhatak of pedas. Though, he added with mischief in his eye, 'I can't say which one I actually prefer, the seer or the chhatak.' He rolled his eyes from Lakshmi to Janki and back again.

He'd grow gallant, maudlin, grandiose, poetic. He knew, he said, what gave such flavour to the burfis. Not the saffron, not the cardamom and pista, not the silver foil or the rose water. No, it was the touch of her hands.

Her hands. Janki didn't know which of them he aimed his sallies at. He looked straight at her because she was the one making up the palm-leaf basket and then handing it across. His massive hands closed over her small ones holding the basket.

'How much?' he asked.

'Three pice,' she murmured, very softly.

'Cheap at three cowries,' he declared, his eyes boring into her face. 'But what syrup there is in her voice!' he marvelled. 'She might be a songstress or a sweet little koel. What are you, girl, koel or songstress?'

'A parrot,' snapped Lakshmi. 'She loves eating chillies. Beware or you'll find yourself eating chillies with her. Be off, will you!'

He laughed. 'Parrots that feed on chillies sing that much sweeter, lassie,' he remarked. 'Look,' he said, turning to Janki, 'let me feed you a laddoo for a change. Open your mouth, chilli-child.'

It seemed to Janki that Lakshmi bristled in indignation. There was a faint smart in her voice as she retorted: 'Is there nothing better for a sarkari sipahi to do than this foolery?'

'Ah no,' he answered, guffawing. 'I'm only a sipahi part of the time and my sarkar isn't there in Kulkatta but here.'

Even Lakshmi couldn't help relaxing. 'God help the sarkar if they have louts like you in the force. Why did you become a sipahi, sir, if the jingling bangles of women find more favour with you than the handcuffs of your calling?'

He looked deep into Janki's eyes and said: 'I became a sipahi so that I can come and arrest you some day, lady. Come, open your mouth, parrot-fairy.'

It became quite the regular thing between them.

The language they used was unlike the refined Urdu of Janki's later years. This was the patois of the cobbled alleys, an earthy language of honey and sawdust that had the spice of the earthen hearth and the banter of the village well. The language spoken in the dark, winding lanes of Benaras, where sarees hung down three floors of trellised balconies to dry and the shadows were lit with the glitter of brocade embroidery or the goldsmiths' firelight or the smoke-light of rain-slicked stone.

They actually began looking forward to the sipahi's visits. Each time he came he flirted, teased, called them the seer and the chhatak, and fed Janki a sweet. He grew bolder. He looked longingly at the milk-dough that Janki and Lakshmi kneaded and spoke softly: 'What must it be like to squeeze that way? Bhagwan kasam, if I wasn't a police-wallah I'd be a halwai.' He was staring meaningly at Lakshmi's breasts. She pulled her saree across them and smiled a mysterious smile and there passed through the air a sudden vibe that Janki sensed but didn't quite understand. For Janki was eight, the vague shapes of fantasies just beginning to flutter. She wondered if this gallant sipahi would make a bride of her, as he joked. But no, he was a Brahmin. But, truth to tell, she wouldn't mind ending up like Lakshmi in their home. A wife about the house but no marriage in anyone's recall.

Once her mother Manki came into the shop and chased Raghunandan away.

'Who are you? What do you want here?'

'Same as everyone else, malkin,' he answered with easy impertinence. 'Sweet things.'

'Then take the stuff, pay up and be off!'

'I wish I could,' he leered and Manki stiffened in rage. A customer was a customer but Manki was a stern and bitter woman. She turned to look at Lakshmi with misgiving. Lakshmi, her saree-anchal pulled over her head, was working intently on the malpua batter.

'Sahibji,' said Manki, 'you are a sarkari sipahi, true, but my husband Shiv Balak is a well-known wrestler. No doubt you know that. And he will not take kindly to sipahis doing lup-lup with the bahus and betis of his house.'

Raghunandan went off smirking roguishly. He delivered his parting shot over his shoulder. 'That's your beti, bhauji, but who is that other one to you and to your wrestler man? You tell me, bhauji.'

He didn't wait. He turned a corner. But Manki stood stock-still. She turned and went back into the courtyard.

He came again. Popped a scoop of rabri-malai into Janki's mouth, making jokes about Shakkar Khan and Makkhan Khan, the famous qawwals of Lucknow and how they probably owed their skill to the sugar and butter they consumed. For this Raghunandan, sipahi though he was, knew somewhat of music and had been to the soirées of the local raeeses, the Shahs, the Rais, yes, even to the princely home of Bhartendu Harishchandra, that legendary man of letters. He dropped names. He had enchanting stories to tell about the magically lit-up boats on the Ganga's waters at the Budhwa Mangal festival, about the festive tents, the flowers, the gleaming drapes, the big brass lamps. He offered to take Janki there if she wished to go to hear the fantastic singing. He made it all sound as though he'd been one of Benaras's pleasure-loving merchant princes and not one of the sipahi guards hired to mind the gates. A sipahi has privileges that musicians can't dream of, he told them. He could gain admittance into the havelis of the Shahs and the Rais as even the stellar Mauzuddin, that young prodigy, could not, when he started out. Had they heard of Mauzuddin, the thumri singer? They had. If only from their halwai fraternity. For Mauzuddin, that lightning flare of genius, was hailed by the sweet shops in the lanes of Benaras, the incense makers and flower sellers, and asked to sing, even when he was a small child. The halwais gave him their choicest confections in exchange for a song. He was a mere boy—and not an effeminate one either—no, rather noble looking, but he sang of the longings and aches of women, the horis and chaities of spring, the kajris of the monsoon, and he sang with eyes closed. Everyone said that a celestial power descended into his voice as he sang, for sure he was utterly unlearned in music and sang from instinct alone. Yet even he, Mauzuddin, couldn't gain an entry into the Rais' haveli and had to hide in a bush outside and sing as loud as his powerful lungs could manage, in the hope of attracting the attention of one of the Rai brothers. Which did happen presently. But all this only proved the superior standing of the sipahi, declared Raghunandan. Even if his only source of power derived from this uniform he wore, given by the British sarkar, a cohort of arse-wiping, pig-and-cow-eating firangees justly put in their place by the gadar. Whereas Mauzuddin's power came from the Sayyad of Mausiqui himself, so they said.

The Sayyad of Mausiqui. The holy soul of music. Words which stayed with Janki all through her life, quite like the jagged scars of the knife which this man was to inflict, this very Raghunandan Dubey, this lecher and possible paedophile, who courted her and told her stories and fed her sweets and once brought two little bottles of rose fragrance for them and a couple of jasmine garlands for their hair.

When Manki saw the gifts she broke into screams of outrage, grabbed hold of Janki and dragged her across the old stone-paved courtyard, hauling her by her hair. She snatched off the affected little rope of flowers and hurled the perfume bottle into the swilling drain. To Lakshmi she said nothing but her lip curled in contempt. The next day she took her seat beside Janki in the shop, imperiously minding the large earthen rabri bowl, and waited for Raghunandan to arrive.

When he did, she challenged: 'You bring your foul face here again, wretch! I marvel at your shamelessness!'

'Not shamelessness but the pull of love, bhauji.' He smiled his lazy smile and stood lounging against the mildewed wall.

'I shall put your love under my pestle and make panjeeri of it to feed the curs of my lane!'

'Oh, come, bhauji. Shout at me all you like. Your cursing doesn't trick me a cowrie. You're like that old crank of the Jhakkad khandaan who spits his paan down on people one minute, then scoops up his gold asharfis and rains them down the next. Come, abuse me all you like—your good-bad words don't affect me. I'll wait. Patiently.' He cast his eyes on the two girls.

Tears of fury prickled Manki's eyes. 'Go, send in your arzee for leave, sipahiya. Because you're going to be laid up soon. I'll ask *him* to break every bone in your body!'

'Who, your Shiv Balak? First your heart, now my bones. Breaking is what he's mastered, eh? Ah well, you should know.'

Here Manki's self-restraint gave way. She sprang to her feet, flung the nearest thing she could grab—the pot of white malpua batter. It caught him full in the face, broke, its clammy white slime crawling down his sneering face, blinding him momentarily.

'Get out!' shrieked Manki, now reaching for the bowl of scalding syrup. 'If I see your vile face here I shall go sit on Kashi Vishvanath's threshold and starve myself to death if the Lord does not take the skin off your buttocks!'

He ducked, ignominious, to avoid the bowl. He looked ridiculous, his face a clayey mess with asymmetrical slits for eyes and even his lashes oozy white. But his words were still provoking as he staggered away and his voice was fiendish: 'Oh, Shiv, Shiv, Shiv! That the Lord be summoned to skin my buttock when his own bull rump's been left behind in Kedar, bhauji.'

'Gutter-snipe!' Manki shrilled after him, her voice cracking in rage.

They closed the shop for a day.

So there might have been many un-simple reasons behind his manic attack. Beyond the obvious one of being interrupted mid-thrust astride a woman, as one narrator of Janki's story claims. Whatever happened as a consequence took on the vestments of a legend that clothed itself in a nickname: Chhappan Chhuri.

One afternoon, happening to blunder into the shop, Janki was puzzled to find the heavy green doors closed to the alley outside and also to the courtyard within. She'd been napping in the upstairs room in the cool of the drenched khus screen, Manki gently waving the palm-leaf fan in fits and starts between spells of sleep and waking. The shop closed for two hours on summer afternoons because no customers ever appeared during that time.

She found the carved panels of the door merely pulled close, not bolted. Drowsily she pushed it open and stopped short in puzzlement. In the half-light of the enclosed room, down on the floor, and between the row of earthen hobs and cooking vessels, she saw a huddle of grappling limbs. Heavy, muscled buttocks pumping atop the fair, splayed thighs of a woman, heaving and plunging, her ankles tensely locked in a tight clinch, her head thrashing from side to side, pinned down by the pulsing weight. Lakshmi's saree was rucked up and Raghunandan's khaki shirt was the only thing he wore, which emphasized the brute nakedness of it and the shocking shuffle of the action, which startled Janki into a loud gasp as the door groaned and banged to behind her. A sound that sealed her fate. Because with a mighty lunge Raghunandan hauled himself out of Lakshmi and swung round, inflamed, engorged, in full, furious tumescence. Like a bull in a rage. He bore down on Janki, picking up the burfi knife on the way. He thrust it into her again and again and again, continuing the charged rhythm of his thwarted thrusting. Breathing hard, eyes bloodshot, the knife mangling Janki's flesh in a gale of gashes until she slumped, a ragged mop of bloody flesh until—and I wonder how I am saying this to a hall-ful of people, decorous old crone though I am—until a jet of exploding man-sap shot out of him and trickled down his thighs and he ceased his thrusting and looked down at its slow, gummy crawl in bafflement before he became aware of his hand which held the burfi knife.

I don't say it happened exactly this way. But three inconsistent accounts of the event, all mutually contradictory, leave room for the endless play of inference and intuition. At any rate this embraces all three official versions and accommodates them in a plausible configuration. Some accounts have it that Raghunandan Dubey was an earlier paramour of Lakshmi's and the two were playing along all the time. Some state that Raghunandan was arrested and jailed. A third account holds that Lakshmi ran away with him some time after all this happened, vanishing into the narrow lanes and pilgrim crowds of the Benaras riverfront, the way she'd come. Manki screamed, tore her hair and beat her breast, rushed Janki's limp, butchered body to the Mission Hospital, clasped the feet

of the English doctor, wept before the maharani of Benaras who
had once appreciated Janki's singing, and passed out on the floor
when the maharani said she would pay for Janki's treatment. The
maharani kept her word. And when years later Janki sang 'Mo pe
daar gayo sare rang ki gagar', a popular hori in Raga Khambaj,
the image of blood spouting in a drenching flood sometimes rose
unbidden in the minds of feeling members of the mehfil who loved
her music and knew her story.

4

People who knew Janki and her family confirm this last version, neighbours, disciples, old tawaifs, relations. Their names are now enough to conjure images of bleary old-timers vibrating with memories. Much like me. There is Mahesh Chandra Vyas and Sobrati Mian and Rambhajan and Rehmatullah Sahib. Bechoo Aheer, Lalman Bhant and Chhabile. The relatives of Janab Abdul Haq. Mirza Habibullah Beg of Sabzimandi. And Rajkumari, Kesbai, Saloni, Raziya and Savitri, all vintage Benaras tawaifs. It's from their accounts that I gathered that Janki was born in the Barna ka Pul moholla in an aheer family, that her father's name was Shiv Balak Ram and her mother's name was Manki. But there was also a stepmother whom Janki called 'chachi', aunt. A convenient obfuscation, this ready use of a guileless category of family kinship to camouflage the illicit connection. This 'stepmother', who wasn't actually married to the father, was a Brahmin and she was young and light-skinned and by all reports very personable. Unlike Janki or her mother, who were dusky and unremarkable. There were no children from this relationship so Manki's children were Lakshmi's too. Yes, that was her, Lakshmi. Janki's own account, in her *Diwan-e-Janki*, mentions siblings. It's clear from most accounts of her Benaras life that between Manki and Lakshmi there was a keen appropriation of loyalties at work,

31

a complicated staking of claims. Because Lakshmi wasn't just attractive and upper-class, she could read and write and she had some idea of music. She directed the ceremonial worship in the household, organized the hygiene and aesthetics of the home, tried to teach Manki recipes and rituals and lived up to her, and Janki's father's, image of being the upgrader of their family culture. I don't think Manki bought any of this but Janki apparently did.

How Lakshmi came to stay is sensational and owes its retrieval to the inherited gossip of neighbours and it has all the ingredients of a garish film script. You have the scene—the thickset wrestler out on a binge. He often went to fairs and wrestling matches, won money, got doped. It is the evening of Shivratri. He is walking along the Ganga bank. He's a bit high on bhang, the kesariya booti. He hears a splash and realizes, to his horror, that someone has just leapt into the Ganga from a tall balcony. He is a riverman. He plunges into the water and rescues the person. He perceives that it is a pretty young woman, distraught, benumbed. And, knotted up in her saree-anchal, is the corpse of a babe three or four hours old—so the local lore-masters say. He brings her home. I don't know whether it was the unusual circumstances or the lore-master's manner of telling the story that make its credibility open to scepticism. But this may be my own bias against the overly dramatic, for God knows, life can frequently upstage the extremest drama we can conceive. We have no way of knowing what really happened—all our sources are dead and there is only the vague contour of a residual rumour.

When the heavy iron knocker-chain clanged on the old teak door neither Manki nor her children knew what husband and father had brought home from the fair. They'd heard the clip-clop of a horse's hoofs on the cobblestone flags of the lane and they'd expected the tonga to trundle past their door, as so many did. But when the coachman and Shiv Balak carried in a drenched and raggedy woman, streaked in river scum, and laid her on a charpai in the courtyard, they gathered round, at a loss for words.

'She was drowning,' was Shiv Balak's brusque report.

Manki drew in her breath, then got to work with warm milk and turmeric. Spoonfuls of syrup that she coaxed the stranger to sip and rose water that she gently dabbed on the closed eyelids. For long she did not open her eyes and when she did it was to look on Shiv Balak in pure hate. 'Go away,' she hissed. She looked to her anchal and tears started up in her eyes. They slid out of the corners of her eyes and coursed down her temples, frail tears vanishing into sweetly draggled hair. They studied her face carefully. There were dark circles round her eyes, her kajal and roli had smudged her cheeks and forehead and in her grief she uttered low moans of pain. For a second she opened her pain-sodden eyes a second time and stared blankly at them, before rage convulsed her face and with an impatient jerk she tugged at the beads she wore round her neck, wrenching at them with fists clenched tight until the string cut a deep graze round her neck and Manki had to grab hold of her manic wrists that seemed to have acquired a life of their own, intent on sawing her throat right through. The string snapped and the beads spilt over.

'Please,' begged Manki, 'won't you have a sip? Please.' But the stranger kept her eyes resolutely shut. Manki did what she could, rubbed her feet with mustard oil, whispered that life was hard for everyone and that one must not break. She climbed on to the string cot and took Lakshmi's head in her lap and ran her fingers through her hair.

'Janki,' she called, 'go to my sandukchi and take out my blue Bangla saree, the one with the red border. Bring the chameli-scented hair oil.' Then she softly questioned the inert woman. 'Speak to me, sister mine. Where do you come from?'

There was no reply.

'Where is your home? What are you called?'

No answer.

Maybe she'll speak after a day or two, thought Manki. She's not married—this I can tell. She wears no toe rings. But her tall nose and her pale colour, for sure she's of Brahmin blood.

When, after a week, the stranger hadn't still spoken, just lain around with dead eyes, occasionally stumbling to the privy or listlessly gulping down whatever it was that she was entreated to eat, Manki told her, 'Now since you won't tell us your name, we'll have to give you one. I'll call you Lakshmi. You've come into our home like the goddess comes on Diwali night. Like her, such tiny feet you've got.'

They all smiled, the oafish Shiv Balak too, who found himself staring incredulous at the woman's feet.

The next day he took some money out of the till in the shop and visited a silversmith's and brought home a pair of payals, a little fancy twine of a thing, wrought of thin braided filaments of silver, with delicate festoons looped along with tiny ice-white droplets of bells.

'There,' he said to Lakshmi, gruff. 'Maybe you'll speak now, girl.'

Her dead eyes awoke from their trance and alighted on him. Ignited slowly, turned manic. But she clamped her face shut in stubborn resistance.

'Now again, where do you come from?' he persisted quiet, dogged.

Suddenly she flared up. 'How dare you torment me? I am sore sick of all this! This day-long night-long "Who are you, where do you come from, who are you, where do you come from"! Who are YOU, tell me that!'

'I am the man who saved your life, and sure I am glad I did it, Lachhmi. Now, if you'll only trust me . . .'

She sprang up and hissed at him: 'I don't remember a thing, I tell you!'

'Hush,' Manki whispered. 'Be patient. Maybe she really doesn't remember, Janki's father. Don't rush her.'

She took Lakshmi's hand. 'Try to remember, small-sister. You jumped into the river near Assi Ghat. Is that where you lived?'

'I tell you, I don't remember!' Lakshmi's voice had risen to a hysterical shriek and cracked upon the words. Tears bristled hot and furious in her eyes.

'I'll have to speak to people around Assi Ghat and thereabouts. See if anyone can tell me anything,' muttered Shiv Balak.

He sighed wearily and left. 'What is to be done with this fretful vixen?'

He came back from Assi Ghat and shook his head. No go, his look signalled to his wife.

'Then shall we take her to a ghat-side temple?' wondered Manki. 'She can earn a living making garlands for the god.'

Her husband drew a deep breath. 'No, wait a while more. Let us see . . .'

Wait they did—several days, Shiv Balak insisting that they give it some days more, Manki grown increasingly nervous and frequently cantankerous. Especially at Shiv Balak's constant, craven appeals to the stranger that she speak to him—you'd imagine he was under her debt and not the other way about, Manki muttered. He entered Lakshmi's chamber at all hours.

'Lachhmi, why do you act so difficult with us, girl?' he repeated his abject plea.

She was lying on her cot as usual, her face to the wall. He sat himself down timidly on the cot, noticed the silver payals flung beside the rolled-up bedding that served as a pillow for her tousled head.

'You haven't even tried them on, lass.'

No answer.

'Then let me put them on you.' Bashfully he reached out, picked up the small foot and looked at it with interest. Timidly he unclasped the delicate silver chain and looped it round the dainty ankle, fastened the hook round the ring. The little bells stirred and whispered together. Then, surrendering to a compelling urge, he ran his finger along the arch of her toes, curled petal-like towards the snowy cushions of the foot. Suddenly he looked up and saw Manki standing motionless in the doorway. He saw her expression, frightened, furious. She was staring at him, the look in his eyes, so shamed, so dazed. Like the mornings after the kesariya booti or after losing a wrestling match.

'She'll have to go,' pronounced Manki summarily. 'We'll send her to the temple first thing tomorrow morning.'

'Send away the goddess Lachhmi, woman?' he lashed out at this now-inadmissible idea. 'Stop this kain-kain!'

It was Manki's turn to lose control. 'Can't your butthead see I'm doing whatever's to be done?' Manki shrieked. 'Ask her a million times, she won't answer. She's pretending. And you said there was a dead babe. No one's even so much as mentioned that—we're that scared of upsetting her majesty! Her queenly majesty, the babe-killer! Where did that babe come from? Are dead babes sold at the hawkers' stalls in the lanes of Benaras, though we all know how they're begot? Yes, hit me now, you besotted man! Go on, hit me!'

Shiv Balak had let his raised arm fall to his side. Lakshmi had risen from her cot. Her face had hardened as she cast a shrewd, measuring eye on the man, this desperate captive that he now was, and the weeping woman, his wife. For the first time she spoke in calm decision. 'I won't go to any temple to sing bhajans for a dole.'

'No, lady, you'll sit here and eat us out of hearth and home while we wait on you hand and foot!' shrieked Manki.

'I'll sweep your floors and wash your dishes but I won't go.'

There was such relief in Shiv Balak's swarthy face, such a glow, even Janki could sense it. And much after all this was a thing of the past, she remembered next morning's tableau. Lakshmi had picked up the broom and the bucket, hitched up her saree well above her pretty white calves, the silver chain sparkling against her shiny skin. She swept and washed the rooms, the courtyard, the tulsi sanctum, the staircase, the threshold, until Shiv Balak, coming in from the shop, rushed to her side and snatched away the broom.

'Never!' he shouted at her. 'Never let me see you do that again!'

Lakshmi turned and looked candidly into his flushed face. His eyes were tipsy with longing.

'Never let me see these hands hold a broom.' He reached out, took both her hands in his own.

'There are floors to be washed here, babuji,' she protested with a faint tinkle of laughter beginning to sound in the depths of her voice.

'There are plenty others to do that here, bahuji,' he answered gruffly, letting her hands drop.

From her chamber Manki heard it all and her heart sank deeper into the abyss. That night she heard her husband rise, unbolt the door and go out. She heard him descend the stairs. Then she heard the door to Lakshmi's room softly groan open.

It may well have happened this way. In her volume of ghazals called *Diwan-e-Janki* which she published in 1931 through the

Israr Karimi Press, when she was already a big name, Janki glosses over Lakshmi's presence in her home with appropriate murmurs, notwithstanding the fact that the deadly attack that scarred her for life was largely to be laid at Lakshmi's door. She writes that her father Shiv Balak had, other than her mother Manki, another woman named Lakshmi Dubain, a Brahmin by caste but 'love is such a power that it surpasses the boundaries of religion and caste and the human being is compelled to renounce these meaningless boundaries'. By the time Janki would have written this she would have known all about it, love and all the rest. Her marriage would have happened and crashed, but she could go on with her overt and obviously self-censored account with composed self-assurance. 'It was as a consequence of this that Lakshmi Dubain, without any hesitation, began living happily with Shiv Balak. Since there were no children from this connection, she considered Manki Bai's children her own.'

There is no way of knowing whether Manki Bai was comfortable with this arrangement. Neighbours spoke of beatings. When Shiv Balak, incited by Lakshmi, picked up his stick and roughed Manki up, Janki took her mother's side and refused to speak to her father for days in protest, but I rather think this last bit relies heavily on uncertain alley gossip, for how could the neighbours know when Janki went silent and when she spoke?

Janki's narrative, however, mentions a detail not found elsewhere, the existence of three siblings. Three sisters named Kashi, Paraga and Mahadei and a brother named Beni Prasad, all of whom died young, not an uncommon thing in those days of large epidemics, though Beni Prasad died at a relatively adult age. Janki writes about the Benaras she remembered at length. 'In attractions Benaras, also known as Kashi, enjoys a place of excellence. Hindus consider it a holy place and, travelling from far-off and by difficult routes, come to perform their rituals The scene on the banks of the Ganga by morning is worth seeing. Some are bathing on the steps of the ghats, some are taking dips in the deeper waters. Here and there small and various boats are to be seen . . . Buildings are reflected in the clear waters of the river. Its praise exceeds description. From the small hours of the morning women bathers and priests begin coming and going and at this same time philanderers and "birdwatchers" begin their activities. Benaras is famous for this. Beautiful scenes and living images of beauty are to be seen here. Shaikh Ali Hazeen, a famous Persian poet of his time, when he came to India from Iran, after exploring the whole world, chose this city and finally decided to live and die in Benaras. Among the many fairs of the city the fair of Budhwa Mangal is extremely well known. In that age visitors, according to their means, reserved boats on hire, and tastefully decorated them according to their choice, and on these boats enjoyed themselves. Where there are countless temples, the mosque of Dharera is also a special place. Kimkhwab, bolts of brocade, embroidered sarees, "laddan-dupatte" have been exported to different countries from the early ages. Although the streets in the densely populated areas are not broad, passers-by can walk down them easily. But certain lanes are so narrow that the sun's plentiful rays never penetrate. Here it is cold in winter and hot in summer. The lower floors of houses are completely uninhabitable and the upper storeys are barely usable. Dal Mandi is the name of a famous street of brothels. At dusk the women, all decked out and full of winsome wiles, turn into instruments of undoing for young men and lure them (to their kothas). In Moholla Hakal Ganj of this city, some distance away from the densely populated quarters, near the Varuna Bridge, in a kutcha house Janki Bai was born, probably in 1889. Janki Bai's father's name was Shiv Balak Ram and her mother's name was Manki Bai. Shiv Balak Ram kept a puri-and-mithai shop. Although not a large shop, it was enough to satisfy their requirements . . .'

I don't know if Janki ghostwrote this stilted introduction, whether she dictated parts of it or commissioned someone else to write it according to her instructions, but there are things in it which unwittingly reveal carefully suppressed alter-truths. She wrote this about Benaras much after she converted to Islam but retained enough warmth of regard for her Hindu anchorings. She was also unorthodox enough to allow a wicked flash of observation to escape the sedate formality of her voice when she mentions the philanderers and birdwatchers of the Benaras waterfront, surely something no one else, overawed by the spectacle and the sanctity of engraving one's life history in an autobiography, would have thought of including. But this naughty living detail instantly vitalizes the formulaic gravitas of the description. The date of birth she supplies, 1889, is puzzling. Other records put it at 1880 and one even pushes it back to 1874. We might risk calling it an inexactitude of times unconcerned about chronologies or even a piece of womanly camouflage.

Janki's account of her training in music and her rise to fame is completely at odds with the accounts of those who knew her:

'Janki was still young when her father, Shiv Balak Ram, left Benaras for a few days, to engage in some business in Allahabad, and stayed there. And his companions also moved and settled in Allahabad. There, from observing others and in keeping with the Hindu belief that religious music was not suitable for girls, Lakshmi Dubain began making efforts to train Janki in these skills. Hassu Khan of Lucknow, then in Allahabad, was famous for his musical skills. When Janki was five, he was appointed to teach her.' She mentions his fee of Rs 200 a month. The print is blurred. It might even be two thousand. In any case the amount is transparently beyond the means of a mithai-wallah of those times. But she puts it on record with insouciance, even a calm authority.

Much of it is inconsistent with other accounts. An unknown music mentor of Daryabad also finds mention. But let us go along with Janki's narrative. 'Very soon,' she reports in her commissioned or personally penned crypto-biography, 'because she was intelligent by birth, she absorbed this education well. When she had received some education, Shiv Balak Ram grew nostalgic for his native city and the family returned to their old home (in Benaras) and Ustad Hassu Khan, out of sheer fondness for them, accompanied them and even after settling down in Benaras the business of music-making continued. From night to day and day to night, from weeks to months to years, time passed and during this time, by sheer good luck, Janab Lieutenant Governor Bahadur Sahib, who is now known as Governor Sahib, came as a guest to the house of the maharaja of Benaras. On this occasion, for which arrangements had been made for all kinds of pleasing things, there was also a lively programme for singing and dancing. Because Janki Bai was famous as an artist, she was given the honour of performing the Shagun-Nek, the opening mujra of this grand durbar. The audience was overjoyed and the maharaja gave her many fond gifts. All of it was gifted to Ustad Hassu Khan and he, after blessing her, returned home to Lucknow. And Janki Bai's mujra life began at the rate of Rs 15 a day.'

Other accounts say Rs 5 a day. This, anyway, is Janki's personal narrative and one may write one's life story as one pleases if truth holds no copyright over imagination. I strongly feel that Janki made up many things about her childhood, especially the stabbing. We may decide to respect her fictions and give her the benefit of the doubt, making some concession for her instinct for subterfuge. After all, we are arguably more than the sum of the situations that overtake us in life. We are also the denials we practise, the alternative images of ourselves we cherish, and all our alter-histories. We are also the people we wish we were and all the things we wish had happened.

So on to Janki: 'It is said that love and fragrance cannot stay hidden and by the same logic, if we say that beauty and talent too cannot stay hidden, then it will not be inappropriate,' she declares coyly. 'At this time Janki Bai may have been only eleven or twelve when news of her beauty and excellence began spreading. Discerning connoisseurs applauded her. Admirers of beauty adored her. Often philanderers began visiting. Truly, beauty and wealth are things which either protect life or endanger it. Among the visitors, a much older man named Raghunandan Dubey Jamadar became a new suitor and, with great ardour, began calling on her. For some days nobody in the house guessed the reason behind his visits. But when he began overdoing his attentions, everybody grew cautious and attempts were made to discourage his visits. Manki Bai abused him soundly and almost came to blows. Following this unexpected rebuff he became a source of torment and started troubling them in various ways. After an interval of a few days a fit of revenge seized him. The situation reached a point that, seeing his chance, he entered the house and finding it empty, he attacked Janki unhesitatingly with his sword. Up to two or three strokes she remained conscious, then she fainted and in that state Raghunandan Dubey spared no efforts to kill her. But truly has it been said that those whom God protects none can kill. When many assaults had been made and he was sure that she was dead, and if perchance she lived it would not be for long, he resolved to flee. Just then the local police arrived on the scene and he was immediately arrested. Handcuffed, he was thrown into the lock-up. After the investigations were over, the court straightaway sentenced him to twenty years' imprisonment in jail, where, after a month and a half, he died. Those who call Janki Bai "Chhappan Chhuri" from this belief that she had fifty-six gashes are mistaken because eyewitnesses are of the opinion that she had many, many more wounds on her person. In such matters we must acknowledge the mercy of God, that even after receiving numberless wounds she stayed alive. When her family and well-wishers saw her condition they rushed her to hospital and treatment began. In a few days the mercy of God granted her a new life and a complete recovery. Then she began living in her former house as before. But the situation in Benaras was not such that she could live there as she wished. For these reasons she forsook her native city and moved permanently to Allahabad. And all the fame and glory that she achieved was achieved here.'

There are two telltale clues that indicate the possibility that there is enormous narrative licence at work here. All that talk of her renowned beauty which drew admirers from distant places is more than stretching the facts. By all reports Janki was a plain woman, and it wasn't the scars alone that impaired her looks. She takes pains to describe, or commission a description, of her looks and general personality. Of medium height and medium build, and what she calls a 'kitabi-chehra', by which is meant a symmetrically pleasing face, 'Large eyes, wheaten complexion, mild manners, with a sweet voice and a slightly swaying gait, the scars of the knife . . . after the passage of time, have somewhat faded, though some remain.' But, she defensively continues, that the overall beauty of her face stayed undiminished.

I shall tell you my impressions of her. High cheekbones in a large, swarthy face, and a strong, wide Mongol nose. She has a carved, heavy-lidded look. She is hung with many silver chains, lockets and pendants. Massive, jewelled danglers weigh down her earlobes and the voluminous drapes of intricate design round her broad girth give her a look of solid abundance, asexual and commanding. A substantial woman of matronly presence. Someone who inspires awe rather than passion. But it may be argued that this portrait belongs to her later period and that it is unfaithful to her beauty as a young woman. Excuse me, even the ruined palace retains traces of royalty and an old woman some residual vestige of her youthful self, and in Janki I did not find any, only a powerful personality. Two lines of self-description clinch this impression: 'In quick-wittedness, which is a necessary distinction in this profession, she is a complete adept. To any witty, bantering comment, she can penetrate its inner folds of meaning and with such frankness make rejoinder that she can amaze, making it seem as though her answer has been previously rehearsed.' Janki would like to be remembered as a woman of compelling character. And this would indeed be borne out by the first paragraph of the introduction to her *Diwan*: 'From ancient times it has been seen that people preserve personal diaries . . . and later the same records become storehouses of information for succeeding generations.'

My strong suspicion is that the Janki Bai of this introduction is, partly at least, a fictional character in Janki's own mind. As each of us is, to a great extent, in ours as we dream or imagine ourselves into being our ideal selves. A burfi knife won't do as a weapon. It isn't romantic enough, so it has to be a sword. A grand passion has to be the motive behind the assault, not the thwarted lust of a paramour of one's father's mistress. Janki in her *Diwan* was creating a life story, not recording one. That's why the contemporary accounts of others differ so radically from hers.

Of one thing, though, there can be no doubt. Janki may have been 'nihayat badsoorat', as one authority on her life candidly puts it, but music made an entrancing woman out of her. The instant she began singing the audience felt itself lifted on the crest of a sumptuous emotion that kept them afloat or capsized them at will.

5

In an Indian raga we are free to undo the design, retrace our course and weave another texture. The raga does not change, as the sea does not, no matter what altering shapes the waves take on. It's the same with life. If something had happened differently, would the outcome have been different? I suspect that in the end we'd be exactly in the same interior location where we find ourselves now. But this is just an unexplained hunch. So I have honoured Janki's account even as I remain unpersuaded by it, recounting what didn't happen, a variant adopted by Janki as preferable to what did happen, a fabricated history alongside the relatively authentic one. She probably came to believe it was her truth and she endorsed and fostered it with ringing authenticity. We choose the stories that we inhabit. We are made up of what did not happen as much as what did. What we believe happened, what should have, what almost happened but stopped short and our flinching selves denied. Our fantastications, our edited, pruned and pared memories, our lies, yes, our comforting, sheltering distortions in which our realities take refuge. That was how it was with the history of the fifty-six stabs.

But to come to what most surely did happen: when Manki burst into the shop and grasped the situation—Janki lying bloodied in a dead swoon, Lakshmi in a flap, clothes in disarray and bodice unbuttoned, and Raghunandan's agitated step fleeing across the threshold, the door to the lane ajar, Manki had it figured out. Then Janki's condition made her break into a scream and run, beating her breast and tearing her hair, and gather up her daughter, calling down the maledictions of the gods.

But later. After the crowd had rushed in and the buggy came and the Mission Hospital reached somehow, and Janki attended to and a flustered Shiv Balak arrived on the scene. After the outcries and lamentations against the wretch, that son of Satan, that son of the pig, and the shudderings had died down. Then a cool, practical piecing together of the episode happened in Manki's head. And Lakshmi all the while hovering cravenly around, overly anxious to please. And as Manki's intent gaze began resting longer and longer on Lakshmi's crestfallen face in challenge and contempt, Lakshmi shrank into herself, and both women knew who now held the whip and was restraining her hand by a supreme effort of will, biding her time. Increasingly, as the days passed, Lakshmi's dainty hands, those hands made for painting ritual murals on walls or tinkling with glass bangles as she swirled the wooden whisk in the curd pot, those fragile hands now wrestled with grindstone and grinding-wheel and pestle and coconut husk and ash in mute appeasement of Manki's cold retribution. Still Manki sat, stony-faced, only breaking her silence with a sigh and words addressed to Janki: 'When will you sing again, my koel child? When shall I hear you speak?'

Between Manki and Lakshmi reigned such a weighted silence, such static in the air. Manki held her captive numb in the snare of her compelling gaze, like the potent eyes of the python stun the creature it means to strangle. Her silent stare tightened its coils round Lakshmi's throat, crushed the breath from her lungs, made her heart jump and her mouth go dry in panic. When the English doctor came to check up on Janki, lying sedated, all stitched and

bandaged up, Manki's eyes would fill and she would entreat him
for a definite answer.

'When will my Jankiya speak, Daktar Sahib?'

The question sent a frisson through Lakshmi's slight frame,
left her face stricken and paralysed with dread. It made her fumble
with vessels and jars, made her drop things. An issue hung in the
air in a stillness stretched to cracking.

Until one day Lakshmi rose speechlessly from her mat, went
and knelt before Manki, stooped in abject shame, and clutched
Manki's feet.

Manki's face kindled. She drew her feet away, disdaining
Lakshmi's touch. Her voice was hard.

'No need for all this nautanki. Don't think I did it for your
sake. I said what I did to save his face—that thankless wretch I'm
married to.'

For Manki had told Shiv Balak what she'd told the rest—that
Raghunandan came after Janki and attacked her in vengeance, that
Lakshmi heard, rushed and raised the alarm. It was an account
she'd steadfastly maintained. Until the time approached for the
stitches to be removed from Janki's gashed and swollen face. Then
Manki artlessly remarked: 'Poor child! What she's been through!
At last now she can unburden her heart.'

So when the last bandage had been removed and Janki looked
feebly into the English doctor's face and he asked her to smile
again and again to test her face muscles, and the tears prickled
her eyes each time she tried, the pain was so sharp, and the doctor
said in his stilted English voice: 'Bahut achchhe. Now speak, my
dear. Kuchh bolkar dikhaaiye.' Janki whispered, 'Ji achchha,' and
Manki dabbed at her eyes with her saree-anchal and thanked
Kashi Vishvanath Lord Shiva for his blessing—that very day
Lakshmi vanished.

No one saw her go. The gram lay half-ground on the grindstone. The fire had gone out in the hearth and her clothes were missing from the clothes line.

In two well-spaced communications Manki broke the news to Shiv Balak.

'Oh, Janki's father, Bhagwan be praised, our Jankiya has spoken two words today!'

He was in the act of ritually washing himself for the evening worship, cupping his hands for the water that she poured out of a large earthen pot in the courtyard and splashing his feet and arms and face before mopping up with his shoulder cloth. He'd only just come in and asked, as he always did, 'O Lachhminiya, where be you, girl?'

Today Manki's hands shook and the brass lota she held tilted and sent a jet of water, all over Shiv Balak's grey head. Then she repeated that Janki had spoken and that Lakshmi was not to be found.

It wasn't the shock of the water that made Shiv Balak gasp and freeze a moment before his flushed face unlocked and he stood stock still.

'What did she say?'

'She said "Ji achchha",' answered Manki.

He knocked the brass lota out of Manki's hand in a frantic fit.

'Not her. The other one. Lachhminiya. What did she say?' He was roaring now.

Here Manki took a long moment to answer. She stepped up to where the brass pot had fallen jangling to the ground and lifted it, checking it carefully for dents before turning to confront him.

'What do I care? Shame on you, you less-than-sane man! Your daughter has spoken for the first time in weeks, your daughter that might, but for the grace of Kashi Vishvanath, be dead and burnt at Manikarnika Ghat. She is alive and has spoken and you—you have thoughts only for your Brahmin whore!'

But Shiv Balak paid no heed. He was in a daze. His voice shook: 'The river . . . She said she'd go to the river again!' He grew desperate, fearful.

'She said many times she'd go to the railway line too. Or hang herself with her saree. I wish she'd gone and done it long ago! Drowned herself in the Ganga before casting her blight on my courtyard. I pray she's really gone and lain down on the railway tracks! I'll offer up a chunariya to the Devi, I will, yes, and hold a havan and serve prasad to the whole city, if she has!'

Manki's rant had risen to a shrill harangue. And Shiv Balak's rage took a quick turn into panic. He seized his outdoor clothes, pulled on his long shirt and hurriedly knotted his dhoti round his waist. In a few moments he was out of the house, rushing down the lane in rapid strides. Manki sprang to the main door and shrieked after him in tearful fury: 'Wait till my Jankiya can speak more! Wait till you hear what she has to tell you!'

As it happened, Janki did not betray Lakshmi to Shiv Balak. She turned her face to the wall and acted as if she had no recollection of what had happened. Manki never forgave her for this. So it was Manki's initial account that survived, supported first by Janki's refusal to speak up, later by her willing adoption of the version. The truth was buried by Lakshmi's disappearance and Janki's silence. But of this later.

Shiv Balak did not return that night. Nor the whole of the next day. He dragged his feet into the house late the next evening and made his way to the lone cot in the courtyard and sank into it.

Manki towered over him. 'Well?' she wanted to know.

He looked away.

She was satisfied that Lakshmi hadn't been traced. Then a closer look at his face filled her with consternation. His features were distorted in grief, his chin trembling, his eyes red. Tears streamed down his stubbled cheeks. The lines on his dusty forehead had deepened. There was such despair in his sagging state that Manki could not hold back her outrage.

'For shame, man!' she screamed in disgust. 'Weeping like a child! Like a little lass leaving her father's home and going to her sasural in a palki! Is this how a pahalwan finds himself? That lion of the wrestling pit? Have your wits died? Have you no sense? And all for a slut! All for a deceiving whore!'

She pounced on him, shook him violently, hauled him to his feet and dragged him to Janki's bedside in the inner room.

'Jankiya,' she commanded, 'speak! Tell him what you saw. Tell him why that sipahiya attacked you. Don't be ashamed. Speak the truth, bitiya.'

But Janki turned away, sickened, and would not oblige.

Manki was bitterly disappointed. 'I don't know if this muhjali has forgotten or her tongue has been struck dead in her mouth. That woman has worked her magic on this one as well, a curse on her! But I—I am not afraid of your magic spell–wali kept whore! I'm pretty sure she was there, the hussy, down there on the floor among the vats and bowls and pans, dancing the raas flat on her back with that whoremonger. Yes, exactly that and no less! Like a bitch in season! Jankiya surprised them at it. Saw everything. So he tried to kill her. To stop her tongue. But I have no fear. I shall shout the truth from my rooftop! Shiv Balak, the halwaiya, the great pahalwan of the akhara kept a fancy woman who was caught fucking with a two-cowrie rascal sipahi in Shiv Balak's own shop! And here's her fond lover boohooing like an abandoned bride in a fair! And what I still haven't told you is that she's raided my trunks and carried away all my gold, yes, the nine-tola waist-girdle, the earrings, the solid kangans, everything, and all the gold mohurs and money we kept in the big iron chest, that we'd saved up these many years!'

There were sparks crackling in her voice. Her temples pulsed, her pupils snapped, crazed, in her bulging eyes. She was possessed. It was one of those less-listed items in the catalogue of grief, to see your man weep brokenly over the loss of another woman, to grow unstrung with mourning, and sit sagging before her. What comfort could she offer him, or herself?

'Get up,' she hectored. 'Wash up! Eat! The evil has passed. Look to your daughter there, only just escaped dying from your slut's tricks. Look to your other children and your shop. Get up and stop wallowing in your folly like a buffalo in a filthy pond!'

But he neither washed nor ate. She heard him pace the terrace by night. Before the first temple gongs and conchs sounded in the morning sky and the first calls to prayer began in the minarets of Benaras's mosques, she heard the heavy wooden door to the alley groan softly open. When she ran down the steep stone stairs and burst upon the dim courtyard, Shiv Balak was gone.

If Janki had spoken, then or later, the account might have been different. But Janki chose not to, for reasons she knew best or did not know yet. What is significant is that old neighbours would carry the unwritten story forward, alongside and at odds with the official written record, the sordid and sorry human tale of Lakshmi and Raghunandan and Shiv Balak's grief and Manki's breaking, and the way she put herself together again and morphed into someone else. As Janki did too. Later Manki would accuse Janki of being partial to Lakshmi, of being under her spell, as Shiv Balak was. But by then Janki had chosen which account to adopt and that became her declared history.

Shiv Balak never came back. For days Manki combed the ghats and bazaars, the wrestling pits and bhang joints, the temple courts and fairgrounds, the boatmen's mooring stands and the empty, muddy stretches of riverbank, even the lanes of Hira Mandi where the prostitutes crowded, and the mutts where the holy men lived. She returned, miserable and bone-tired, to her house every night, to tend the convalescent Janki.

On Parvati's shoulder she rested her head and wept, and to Parvati she spoke of what the astrologers had told her, and what the parrot with the card, and what the wild-eyed augurs of the burning grounds. She discussed the forbidding cost of the rituals that guaranteed Shiv Balak's return and the difficulty of arranging the bizarre and frightening black-magic items that the ash-covered, bloodshot-eyed ascetics on the cremation grounds asked for in order to look into the mists of time and say where Shiv Balak was, dead or alive, alone or with someone, sane or maddened.

The mithai shop closed, Kashi, Paraga and Mahadei caught the pox that swept across the city and died. It was Parvati who arranged the litter-bearers and the obsequies because Manki by now was good for nothing. Janki caught it too but lived. A few pock scabs did not add further disfigurement to her already marked face. Still Manki wandered the ghats, jostling shaven widows and sages and street women and fierce stud bulls.

It seemed to Janki in later years that this desperate, tireless search for someone gone away, someone lost in the crowd, turned into the theme song of her life. It was the one subject she wrote no ghazal on, set to no thumri tune, for no words or notations could render it. First her father searching, agonizing, for his lover, then her mother searching for her father. And she herself would live to share the same fate. Like Baiju for Gopal in the old music lore that Hassu Khan interlarded his teaching with.

This Baiju, whose eminence in music had reached most of the royal courts in north India in the early sixteenth century, could

get an emperor to withdraw his command to put a whole city to
the sword. In 1535, the history books calculate. Humayun had just
defeated Bahadurshah Gujarati and conquered Mandu and, as was
the engaging practice with conquerors, the victory was followed
by the dreaded decree of *Qatleyam*, genocide or kill-all. Blood
ran down the lanes and squares, pooled in gutters, streamed into
the river and soaked into the earth. Men, women and children,
all were seized and slain. A horrific hubbub. Cries of agony and
fear, shrieks, prayers for mercy, gut-wrenching howls filled the
air, while the emperor, otherwise a mild man but here merely
following a military custom, stood, sword raised, for the execution
of his imperial orders to be completed. The story goes that Baiju, a
Mathura Hindu and a celibate devotee of Krishna, sang a Persian
verse that so charmed the emperor that he ordered the massacre
instantly stopped. Baiju had been taken prisoner by a Mughal
soldier, then recognized by one of Humayun's Rajput braves
and led to sing before the emperor. Which he did, melting the
emperor's heart. Humayun had gifted him a horse and fine clothes
and offered him a position at his court, but Baiju, who belonged
more to the other-world of temples and mystical longings, had no
use for these things. The gifts he'd passed on to his Mughal captor,
the court position he had politely declined.

To such a one came the harrowing fate of wandering the earth,
searching for a lost son. His music rusted, his feet grew sore and
blistered. With matted locks, ragged clothes, overgrown beard and
crazed with grief, Baiju turned into a mad fakir, sifting the ash
of woods and fields and cities and villages, calling out his son's
name—'Gopal! Gopal!'

Naik Gopal was a boy he'd adopted, fed and clothed and
trained to sing dhrupad and dhamar of a high order at the temples
of Mathura. In some accounts Gopal was a son-in-law, married

to an adopted daughter, Meera. Baiju lost his mind, combing the earth for his lost Gopal and his cry reached that other Gopal, that celestial one, Lord Krishna himself, one of whose names was Gopal too. And as he lay like a wasted and weary beggar at a wayside temple he overheard the conversation of two travellers, and from them he gathered that someone resembling Gopal was court musician to the maharaja of Jodhpur. In some accounts Kashmir—but as we know, legends enjoy the flexibility of having many optional versions. Baiju, baffled that one whose music was consecrated to God alone should have succumbed to the pomp and show of a court, managed to reach Jodhpur, mingled with the crowds and heard Gopal sing at a royal gathering. Then, unable to control himself, he rushed forward and threw himself on the ground before his son, crying: 'Son! Gopal!' Gopal refused to recognize him, breaking his heart. But, as the saying goes, in God's world there are delays but never denials of justice, and events transpired to shame Gopal and vindicate Baiju in a wonderful way that has become one of the sublime stories in music lore.

Baiju was saved by the powerful poetic licence of a five-hundred-year-old story but Manki had to work out her destiny—and Janki's—all by herself. One evening Parvati said to her: 'Enough, Mankiya! I can't go on sitting silent, watching you wear yourself out like this.'

Parvati was large and broad as a banyan tree. She came all the way from her home in Chaitganj to buy sweets and savouries from Manki's shop. Later they became shopping companions at the Budhwa Mangal fair. Together they compared prices, haggled, made scathing remarks about the worthlessness of the merchandise they'd secretly planned to buy, for the benefit of the stall keepers. They picked up bangles and iron skillets and ladles and tongs, tinsel-lengths for head scarves and candied musk melon seed for the children. As their acquaintance grew they went to temples together on holy days, shopped for fast and puja things, held up a saree length as a screen behind which the other changed into dry clothes after a Ganga dip, sang away entire nights at keertans and weddings and childbirths. Parvati knew scores of songs and was clever at the dholak. She was such a mine of energy. The greatest problem-solver that Manki had ever come across. She was the one who arranged for a buggy and coachman with admirable speed when Janki had to be rushed to hospital. She even knew how to read and write and had scribbled the desperate letter to the maharani of Benaras and pushed the holder-and-nib into Manki's fingers and made her scrawl her unformed signature. And she had carried that SOS to the maharaja's kothi and argued persuasively with the sentries at the lion gates and the women retainers at the staircase to the maharani's chambers. And, on being granted an audience, she had thrown herself at the maharani's feet and sobbed out poor Janki's plight so feelingly that the maharani sent her back to the Mission Hospital with a note for Richardson, the English doctor, and a purse of money, and also promised to come in person to the hospital. Parvati carried back many assurances of support from the maharani to the mother of the child singer she'd heard once and liked.

Parvati was always amazing. She knew people everywhere, had answers for everything. And when Shiv Balak disappeared she flew to Manki's assistance with an energy that was the marvel of all. When the Great Maata swept into the lanes and homes and laid waste large swathes of the city so that hundreds died of the pox, Parvati brought fronds of neem leaves and sat for hours waving them in the air near the sickbeds of Manki's three children, fanning them gently, lifting brass tumblers of cooled neem water to their parched, whimpering lips, putting a finger to her lips when any loud voices spoke as they slept the fitful sleep of the delirious. For hours she sat, her lips moving in silent mantras to the Devi, until the fever broke and the first beads of sweat appeared.

And when Manki came back, haggard and deadbeat, after another long, useless trudge through the city's labyrinths, Parvati rose and fetched buttermilk for her which she'd set in an earthen pot and placed in the way of the hot, searing summer winds in the doorway to cool.

'What would I do without you?' Manki often sighed and said. 'You carry the name of the Devi and you are the Devi Ma herself come to cast her anchal over my face in my evil time.'

But Parvati shushed her up. No Devi, she said wryly. 'The Devi could be far more merciful, but what mercy was it to take away three such angel children as Kashi and Paraga and Mahadei? How wasted their bodies were! How quickly they burnt upon the pyre. Ah, poor mother!' Well could she understand the trials of a grieving mother, a single mother with a good-for-nothing vagabond for a husband who'd made the storm burst on the poor bowed head of his helpless wife! All this Parvati said when Manki tried to thank her.

As the days passed Parvati began gently counselling Manki as a well-meaning friend should.

'He's dead and gone for you. If I were you, I'd go light a lamp for him and hang up a pot of water from the nearest peepul tree. If I were you, I'd summon a priest and perform the death rites for his wicked soul. It must be wandering about without any peace. And it will still go after that woman, never you, poor Mankiya.'

Manki reacted. 'Oh, don't speak like that of him. My heart tells me he'll surely come home. The palmist at Dashashwamedh Ghat read my palm and said: Sister, your suhaag shall survive.'

'But with whom and where?' Parvati was sceptical.

Manki winced. 'The priest at Harish Chandra Ghat read my chart and said my man had gone westwards and is alive and well, and one day he'll turn east again.'

'Ha! He's gone to vilayat then and one day he'll go to Cheen!' scoffed Parvati. 'You are a believing fool.'

'I have a big fear here,' said Manki, indicating her chest. 'I'm afraid he'll come, open the trunk and find that the gold is still there. Ah, sister, I lied to him that she took it all away. And when he finds out, he'll take the stick to me. How will I look him in the eye? I couldn't save his children from the maata and I lied about Lachhminiya making off with the gold!'

'Nonsense,' said Parvati. 'You saved your Jankiya's life, and as for the ones the maata took, what d'you think he cares a fake cowrie for them? They'd as soon drown in the well, as far as he is concerned. As for the gold that's bothering you, you're free to hide it in my house. I'll lock it up fast in my big sandook and you can take it back whenever you need it.'

So Manki, much relieved and grateful, tied up the nine-tola waist-girdle, the heavy wrist kangans and fine-wrought neckpieces and chains and earrings and pendants, the finger rings and toe rings, all in a tight knot in a quartered and thrice-folded cotton saree, and put the bundle in a clay curd pot and handed it to her friend to carry home with her, telling herself for the nth time what would she ever do without Parvati.

Then when Manki couldn't go on running the kitchen on credit that the grocers and grain merchants now embarrassedly refused to continue giving, Parvati thought fit to do some plain-speaking.

'How long are you going to sit on your chaukhat waiting for that fox's grandson? Till you are bent double and have lost every tooth in your head?'

'He'll come back some day for sure,' protested Manki feebly.

'He'll not, understand this and drink a glass of Ganga water on it!'

'So what else can I do but wait? How long can I put my creditors off? I owe money to Bachau Mahajan and Bindeshwari the oilman and Ramji the milkman—oh, so many others too. Parvati, there was a time when milk flowed like water in my shop but who would think it now, to see my hovel?'

'Sell it,' suggested Parvati.

'I can't sell it or this house either. It's in his name, not mine.'

'What else can you sell then?'

'All the shop's cooking vessels are sold. Some of my belongings too—whatever I could sell. All except my gold which, thank Ishvar, is safe with you else who knows what I might have done? But Bachau and Bindeshwari might drive me to do something drastic—part with my gold or something—to pay these debts, and then where will I be, sister?'

'No,' said Parvati firmly. 'A woman must never, never part with her gold. Don't let anyone force you into such a thing. Gold is the Goddess Lakshmi.'

Manki's face flinched. 'Don't utter that name.'

Parvati realized her mistake. 'No matter,' she said in soothing tones, 'don't give the goddess the curses of your heart. The goddess and that Lachhminiya are poles apart . . .'

'But for that slut I might not have seen this evil day,' muttered Manki. 'Her shadow follows me everywhere, creeps into my every thought.'

'It is an illness of the mind,' said Parvati. 'Leave it all behind you. Go elsewhere.'

'Where can I go?'

'Come with me then,' Parvati finally spoke her mind. 'I'll take you to Ilahabad. I have many friends there. Benaras will drive you mad. I can see it coming. Besides it isn't safe for your daughter.'

Manki looked at Parvati in wonder. 'This house?' she ventured timidly.

'Lock it up. Leave in the middle of the night. No one will know. Least of all the ones you owe money to.'

Here Manki hesitated a moment, then asked, 'And my gold, sister?'

'Don't worry. It's safe with me. I'll carry it along and return it to you when we reach Ilahabad.'

That's how Janki left Benaras for Allahabad which was to become her home the rest of her living days. With Parvati and her mother and brother and some scanty belongings she travelled by boat to Allahabad, a hundred and thirty kilometres upriver.

6

Maybe she grew up with the belief that no one had ever desired her. Raghunandan had been that first and last illusion. Other women were objects of desire, never she. Only some men, fired by her awesome voice, grew inflamed with sudden lust, maybe a higher lust, if there was such a thing, as her defensive heart prompted. More likely it was a sudden thrum of nerves, the resonation of some other lust elsewhere or some unachievable imagining when a stirred man trembled to the thrill of achieved perfection and forgot the scarred bodiment of that voice. Sex was an act of self-forgetting, even at its most self-conscious, as for a tawaif it had to be, and it had its atavistic percussion and progression, its own alaap, gat, jod and jhala. Then, after the choreographed, climactic flourish, there was the bleared moment of return, the gathering up of the garment.

She usually tempered the shock of the moment by murmuring a thumri beneath her breath so that the poor client's instant of reality wasn't too abrupt. She usually turned away to spare him any glimpse of her face. As she grew older, sex grew less and disappeared, for she could afford to turn away clients with courtly quip or robust repartee.

In her memoirs she obfuscated the truth that she had indeed 'practised', until it became a blurred and doubtful matter, masterfully evaded. She relied on her reputation as the scarred woman to protect her story from posterity.

But it was Manki, just a few days into their Allahabad arrival, who had had to take the great plunge. For a long time Janki and she didn't refer to what Manki's 'work' was, even when the subject cropped up. As when Manki asked Janki to teach her some songs she'd learnt in Benaras. She needed to learn a few 'of that kind' as a professional requirement.

'Some of them want a bit extra. A song or two sometimes. Makes them feel royal, I think. They even say they'll pay a bit extra, which I can keep back from Naseeban Bua. But I don't know any, except the songs we sang at keertans and festivals. I sang a banna and he . . . he said it was something the women in his family sang, his mother and sisters and bhabhis and wife and daughters and would I please stop it. He wanted another kind of song. Bitiya, is there some other kind more . . . more suitable to my kind of . . . work?'

Janki had turned to look into her mother's face, shamed and confused. She taught her a thumri in Raga Bageshwari. Manki did not have a singing voice but she seemed enthralled by the experience. It seemed to take away the sting of her position. Frequently Janki heard her humming or singing that song under her breath as she went about her daytime chores. It was the only time she looked happy after all that had happened since they arrived in Allahabad—Parvati's deception and disappearance and their finding themselves in this situation, in this old, crumbling, many-storeyed house in its dingy lane where sunlight never reached and the only thing that relieved the dank surroundings was the sound of overflowing music from the rows on rows of old stone tenements, the liquid sounds of sarangis and tanpuras, the brisk thump of tablas, the trilling ascent of practising female voices and the jingle of tintinnabulating anklet bells. From late morning onwards till evening there were intense rehearsals, then after sundown a lull for rest and a readying for the night, and a little before midnight the nightlife of the lane really got under way. It was like Hira Mandi, the balconies full, the gauzy girls in full twitter, the visiting gentry perfumed and pomaded, reclining against bolsters in the dance halls and Naseeban Bua, the Chaudharain, as the madam of the house was called, at her most benevolent and gracious, greeting the guests with queenly patronage, the discreet little cabins on the top floor in a state of continuously changing occupancy, and the paan, itr, cigarettes and liquor going round in the halls and chambers, and also poetry, giggling coquetry, and whispers and rustlings and creakings, and hawking and spitting into silver spittoons too. Gruff groans and sometimes a man's drunken babble, sometimes a man's muffled sob or a snore. Manki could never, never grasp how she found herself in the thick of it all.

Shiv Balak's desertion, followed by Parvati's craftiness, had affected Manki's sanity for a while so that she took to her bed in a state of dire depression and Naseeban had to send for the house hakim, and the girls, scores of them it seemed to Janki's baffled eyes (though there were only about two dozen in fact), took turns to bathe her head with rose water and rub her feet with oil in a sort of familiar empathy that indicated that this was a common and understood plight, something remembered well.

For Parvati was no friend of Naseeban's, as the girls told Manki. For would a friend vanish just a day after, as Parvati had done? Surely she'd left an address, surely Naseeban knew more of her than she'd cared to reveal . . . No one could satisfy Manki's endless, hysterical questionings. When Manki refused food and raved and went into fits, Naseeban herself ascended the stairs in all the majesty of her authority and sad wisdom to answer Manki's fretful demands with experienced patience. No, she said gently, Parvati had left no gold ornaments with her, as she'd given Manki to believe. No, she said again, Parvati hadn't indicated whether she would return for them, whether it was Benaras she was going to or some other city. And yes, this she revealed with the utmost delicacy, Parvati had charged a sizeable sum from her, Naseeban, for what Naseeban tactfully called board and lodging and protection under her roof. So you see, my poor sister, you paid her and I paid her too, she broke the news quietly while the girls stood around, quiet as mice.

Manki had shrunk into herself as the full knowledge of her plight dawned upon her mind. Still, she hoped she'd got it all wrong.

'Did she pay our rent then?' she asked. 'How much?'

Naseeban looked at her in silent pity.

'I can cook,' said Manki earnestly, 'I can sweep floors, do the wash, for what else can I do, Baiji? I am a mithai-wallah's wife and I worked in the shop we had, me and my daughter.'

But Naseeban thought fit to overlook this assumption, this pitiful display of a woman clutching at a straw.

'This house is yours to live in. You are welcome to join our household.'

Manki looked at her, wide-eyed. Naseeban returned her gaze with a level, unblinking gaze of her own.

'I charge 4 annas in the rupaiya,' she said calmly. 'The rest you keep. I am known to offer the most generous rates in this trade, ask any of my girls here. The ones who join me don't ever want to leave. Come on,' she rose to her feet, looking Manki over, 'you're a fetching enough woman. There's still the juice of youth in your limbs and a nice saltiness in your features, dark as you are. And the grief in your eyes has a certain melancholy lure. Study it, girl, learn to use it, this look of desolation that you wear. It tempts the kind client to tenderness and the unkind one to finer cruelties. You are a beautiful thing, though you've never known it yourself.'

It may have been that subtle tribute to Manki's unsuspecting and starved self-esteem that made her stay. For Naseeban had a protective and kindly dignity, even at her shrewdest. It may have been the relative safety of the impending profession, compared with the imagined dangers of a life on her own, without means or shelter and two children with her. The most probable reason, humanly imaginable, was that Manki was soul-dead tired and had lost the fight and could only let herself drift, come what may. But Janki heard her last feeble bargainings.

'Only me, Baiji. Not my daughter.'

To which Naseeban answered, with that great quietness of manner of which she was mistress.

'That one, ah no, we shall see, poor marked creature, but time will tell . . .'

So maybe it was that 'poor, ugly, marked creature' factor that Manki grabbed and inflated to the level of a tiresome refrain, and that injured Janki more than anything else before, coming as it did from a mother gone strange. For Manki did indeed morph into someone alien and bewildering. Manki herself scarcely knew herself. The first time, clad in the tinselly costume of her new occupation and as timidly, selectively unclad, in her performance of it, she was paralysed with terror and with her eyes clamped shut, she saw the locked door of her Benaras house, its three-linked chain and heavy padlock, and she saw Shiv Balak returned to that door and standing perplexed to find it locked and his family gone no one knew where. A shudder passed through her as she converted the thrusts of the stranger hoisted above her body into the blows of the hammer that laboured to smash the sturdy lock. Blow upon blow fell on the old Aligarh lock until a catch or cog in its complicated innards gave way and the chain, released from its hooked notch, fell, jangling against the old discoloured wood. He entered the darkened courtyard just as the client gave one last heave and splurged his hateful scum into her, but her gasp of sorrow was a clenched sob for Shiv Balak's lonely return which the client took for orgasmic ecstasy. Later, putting the technique together, she learnt the trick of manoeuvring imagination into regions of old grief or recalled rage and found that the mind's interjections could easily be confounded with the body's reflexes, and no one was any the wiser.

Janki saw her mother change, saw her dress the part she'd been assigned, oil and wave her hair into impossible forehead curls, powder her face and redden her lips, wear low-cut lace blouses with puffed sleeves and flashy sarees in shimmering colours and paste jewellery to deceive the discerning eye. Sometimes she dressed as Muslim women did, in long, loose pajamas and flowing shirts and wide swathes of shiny odhni draped around her head and shoulders. Janki was too young to grasp that her mother was costumed in an improbable optional self, mocking while avenging herself at the same time. She, the one rejected, the extra of the second place, the woman outgrown, had herself outgrown the garments of her class and identity and was proving herself a likely object of many men's lusts. It was both love and hate of oneself, salvage of worth and sentence of worthlessness. All Janki saw was a transformation of manner, voice and gait, and she saw the door close many times a night behind her mother and her shifting concourse of anonymous men. There seemed to be nothing left of the mother she had known except an ironical remark or two about the slut Lakshmi and the wretch Shiv Balak. Then, even with her young baffled sense, Janki understood that her mother could never escape her memories or replace them with glaring substitutes of present and busy demand. For all our lives, she learnt, we're dealing with our demons, contesting issues within, even when their contexts have passed and their actors departed. We fight on, desperately obsessed and alone, still examining old challenges to self, still arguing our case in captive obedience to old patterns. Janki wanted to tell her mother—let go of that woman and father as well—but she couldn't say a word. Especially on the subject of Lakshmi, whom Manki had decided to remember bitterly as Janki's favoured ally. For she still recalled, in great indignation, how Janki had remained silent and not recounted what she had seen. Were it not for your silence we'd still be there, making mithais respectably in our shop. Your father wouldn't have gone and I wouldn't be here, doing this, this! Now see the destruction you've brought on me—see it well! Manki's every stance and posture threw this reproach in Janki's face.

But she overdid her animosity to suspicious limits. She kept Janki dressed in the shabbiest, filthiest clothes, throwing a fit when she saw her clad in a bright, clean borrowed outfit, making her change back instantly into her rags.

'Know your place, you scaly-scabbed ugly thing!' she shrieked. 'A crow dressed in peacock finery?'

To a client she explained Janki's identity as her servant: 'This dark-as-night horror whose face I have to look on first thing every morning, no wonder my days are blighted by misfortune, babuji.'

And when she lit upon Janki singing in the kitchen—for Janki spent much of her time doing heavy-duty jobs in the clammy, dark kitchen and away from the brilliantly lit, carpeted and cushioned outer chambers of the haveli—she came up close and hissed: 'Chup! Silent! At once! Before someone hears you! One line of song out of you and I'll pull out your tongue, maati-mili!'

All Janki understood was that a demon had possessed her mother and that she was working out an old revenge, a woman-for-woman thing, potent enough to undo even an umbilical tie. And she was only just tasting the hot revolt of a thirteen-year-old. 'I will sing when I please!' she hissed back. Then louder: 'I WILL SING! Stop me if you can! Who are you to tell me to shut up? I taught YOU to sing. I taught you!' Her voice had risen to a shriek and could be heard all the way down the corridor.

Manki stepped up to her quickly, clamped a firm hand on her mouth and with her other hand held her in a tight cinch and pulled her away. All the way up the stairs, pulling, shoving, struggling to break loose from this witchlike mother who, true to her devilish transformation, had grown invincibly powerful.

Manki dragged Janki into her chamber, flung her in and bolted the door from the outside.

'Cool off now, spitfire!' she called through the door. 'Stay there till you learn to do as you're told!'

Janki heard her mother's footsteps die away down the stairs. She howled her rage into the quilt and the musty-odorous coverlet. She stuffed the oil-fragrant pillow half into her mouth, biting it in a fury too hot to contain. She banged her head against the headboard of the bed. Then, when the bone-juddering hiccups had stopped, and the words of manic rage slowed to a stop in her head, Janki drifted into tired sleep.

It may have been an hour or several. She was roused by a cautious tap on the door.

'Open the door, Manki,' called a low voice. 'Ah, I see it is bolted from the outside . . .'

It was dark. The lantern hadn't been brought in. Someone entered the room. 'But who locked you in, Manki, my life?' he asked, concerned. 'Does this ogress Naseeban lock in her girls, tell me? Tell me, please. I will kill her for this, I promise you. I'll strangle her with my bare hands if she's treated you ill, my Manki . . .'

There was a thick slur in his voice. He was staggering drunk. But something in the way he called her his life, his love, made Janki's heart beat loud in her ribcage. He took her into his protective embrace with fervour, stroked her head, murmured in her ear, melting her into trembling eagerness. The darkness was dense around them as he drew her down alongside his own body, sprawled across Manki's bed, whispering her mother's name: Manki, ah, Manki! He was well into the act when he noticed her flinching, her quick intake of breath and her gasp of pain. And much before the end he'd realized what there was to realize—that this wasn't Manki, this was another one, and an untried virgin too. He couldn't, he wouldn't give up on this bounty he'd come to possess so miraculously, so unaccountably. He lunged deeper into her, holding her in an iron grip, his drink-sodden mouth heavy on hers, squelching in his own scum and her wet blood, until a shriek sounded outside the door and the shock of sudden lantern light broke into the room and for a second she felt herself violently jerked out of bed by arms that were insanely furious before she was blinded by the sharp crack of a slap that stung her face and made her reel and fall back on the floor in the middle of what sounded like an explosion of screaming, abusing, shrill cursing, and an inrush of vague forms and a babel of voices followed by the sudden stillness imposed by Naseeban Bua's imperious presence.

That night Manki begged to be let off. Janki lay quietly on the bed, Manki cross-legged on the floor. And the little oil lamp on the ledge burning too low to betray any expression on either of their faces. But even in that diffused half-light Janki could see how crushed Manki seemed, how defeated and unstrung, no demon. And when she spoke at last, it was in a very small voice.

'Did he hurt you, my Jankiya?'

'No,' answered Janki, then, 'Yes-yes . . .' She turned and hid her face in the smelly musk of the pillow.

'A beast, that one!' spat out Manki.

That wasn't the impression Janki had come away with. Initially he'd been rather sweet, later he stopped being a person but only a sort of avalanche, bereft of self or choice. An immense weight that had thrashed, pounded, mangled, bruised and then, just as suddenly, become one with the night and the chaos. She wished, secretly, that she'd seen his face at the very least.

'He thought I was you.' Her words came flat, halting.

For some reason that made Manki crumple up in tears. Shamble up to Janki's bed and hide her face in the pillow under Janki's tousled head.

'That you were me! God forbid that you should ever be me, my Jankiya!' Here was Manki smothering Janki with her sobs. 'This is what I prayed should never, never happen, and it has!' grieved Manki. 'This is why I kept you away in the cooking-quarters. This is why I dressed you in old, ragged things! This is why I never let them forget how scarred you are.' She ran her hand on Janki's thin body. 'Are you hurt, my daughter? Was he rough with you? Was he too . . . too large for you?'

Janki caught her mother's hand and brought it to her mouth. Carefully she did what she remembered doing as a child when Manki came in, hot and sweating after an afternoon of laddoo- or peda-moulding. She licked the fingers one by one, savouring the memory of syrup and ghee and the scent of cardamom and rose.

'Mithai-Amma,' she said. Sweet mother. 'Nanki meeth mai.' Little, sweet mother.

If there was a touch that could purify and heal, this was it. Manki had no words after that. But the next morning when

Naseeban Bua expressed her anger at what had happened, saying sarcastically: 'Mubarak on your daughter, Manki Bi. Henceforth she's worth nothing to anyone. She might have been something, if only her nath-worth for a night. Now with her grindstone-pocked face she's only a mouth to feed.'

Then Manki bristled and drew herself up and retorted, most unlike her usual mild self: 'May my offence be forgiven, Bua, but you little know what magic lies in my little one's throat. Far from a mouth to feed, hers shall be the mouth that'll feed your entire kotha!'

Then, turning to her daughter, she commanded: 'Sing, bitiya. Sing and show them. Sing.'

And, as though mesmerized by the command in her mother's charged voice, Janki sang and the room grew silent.

For days afterwards Manki implored her various clients: 'Babuji, this isn't business but will you have the kindness to suggest some tutors for my daughter? She's clever, take my word, babuji, and has a way with languages. And will you have the kindness to suggest some great ustad to groom her singing. I shall pay, babuji, whatever his fee.'

Every biography of Janki Bai tells us that she'd been tutored exhaustively in Sanskrit, Persian, Hindi and English, there in the kotha itself. Tutors had been found, and found well. And who should teach her music but the great Hassu Khan himself.

7

If music was likened to the great rolling stream of the Ganga in the rains, Hassu told Janki, then the ragas might well be compared to the ghats, the landings our ancestors have built along its banks. Remember, water is always and ever water as the Ganga is always and ever itself, whether at the source or at the confluence or at the mouth. Still, Draupadi Ghat wasn't the same as Balua Ghat and Balua Ghat wasn't at all like the Saraswati Ghat. The river looked and felt different at each. Did she get what he was trying to explain? he asked. She looked uncertain. She was still new to the city of Allahabad and hardly went out and these were just names. Very well, Benaras then, he said. Did she remember the great Benaras ghats? Of course she did. Who didn't know the character and scale of each one? Manikarnika with its soaring towers of flame, Dashashwamedh with its immense spectacle of trumpets and conchs and cymbals and its circling firelight, Harish Chandra with its crowds and bulls and parasols. Janki remembered them all. Good, said Hassu. Sur, or note, is like that quintessential element water that makes up the river. But where you enter that stream, at what time of day, in what state of self, how you experience the differential between water and light and the rippling reflections of the stars and the temple spires and the floating breath of the chants, the pang of the bells and the throb of the drums in the water, makes of one river a thousand. Also remember, just in case you haven't noticed, sound too casts shadows and there are the souls of colours playing in the stream. The ragas are registers of being, taught Hassu, who loved discoursing. They are the river known in discrete tones of light and mind. You can step gently into the water, receiving its chill or stillness or turbulence, lowering yourself slowly into its depths and letting it circle around you. Then you let yourself sink and let it take possession of you, spreading your limbs athwart the upholding stream, swimming along its current. Then you drift your way through its aqueous lucence to its very floor until you become water, shining, pliant water, reflecting, as a glass does, as a diamond does, the sanctified light of its being, until the whole universe resonates in your head with this rendition of knowing. And do you know when this happens and why it happens? Because you have bathed in the primal element, Nada, the Divine Vibration. What falls on the ears, the sages said and our ustads taught us, is Baikhari. What vibrates in the brain is Madhyama. But that which surpasses these is called Pashyanti, the Soul of Sound, the Anahatnada, the Parabak or Beyond Utterance, the Nada-Brahma that yogis and pirs and darveshes hear in the deepest trances.

Hassu Khan's musical lineage went back to the great Ghulam Rasool, the foremost khayal maestro of Nawabi Lucknow. His two celebrated disciples, the legendary brothers, Shakkar Khan and Makkhan Khan, after receiving intensive training in the Lucknavi style, travelled to Gwalior, which was to become the parent khayal gharana, giving rise to Kirana, Jaipur, Patiala, Agra and several other smaller ones. By some accounts, these family centres of music existed much earlier, from the time Aurangzeb banned music in Delhi. Then the musicians of Delhi, deprived of a calling, disbanded in large numbers and went seeking new homes and new patrons. They settled down in towns surrounding Delhi—in Gwalior, Agra, Ambeta, Sonepat, Atrauli and Kirana, places which gave their names to ancestral schools of music.

'There is a story,' said Hassu, 'about the time the musicians of Delhi took out a juloos-e-janaza, a funeral procession, through the streets of Delhi when the emperor's decree banning music was made public. When asked who it was who had passed on to the next world, they answered: Good sirs, it is music that is dead. It is music whose cortège we bear on our stooped shoulders. There is a story,' continued Hassu, enjoying his pupil's rapt attention, 'that when the emperor heard of this, he wryly remarked: "Ah, to those that mourn, this do I say—my royal condolences, sirs, but do me this extra favour. Dig that grave deeper." Thus did they bury music in Dilli but, mash-e-Allah, who can bind a stream or a vine? The stream shall find secret channels beneath the earth and emerge, a few paces or a kos or a mile away. The vine will spread its roots beneath the selfsame earth and thrust its shoots into the air and burst into flower when its season comes. Thus it was with music, daughter.'

'But why did the emperor ban music? Who can hate music?' Janki wondered aloud.

'He did not hate music. He only pretended to,' answered Hassu, 'and he had personal reasons. Of that I shall speak later. Be you patient awhile. A shagird must cultivate the great grace of sabr, patience, when a teacher speaks and not interrupt.

'So Shakkar Khan and Makkhan Khan journeyed to Gwalior. They were brothers but they soon fell out, as did their progeny. One of Makkhan Khan's sons was Natthan Peer Baksha and this Natthan Peer Baksha was my Bade Baba Jaan, grandfather to us three, my revered elder brother, Haddu Khan, and my younger brother, Natthu Khan, our father being Qadir Baksh of hallowed memory. It was Natthan Khan Peer Baksh and Qadir Baksh, peace be upon their souls, who taught me all I know, unworthy as I am,' said Hassu, touching his rosary to his eyes, dropping it into his loose shirt-neck again.

'Fortunate was I to be vouchsafed such teachers. Ah, wash out your mouth with rose water before you utter their names! It is by destiny alone and the benevolence of God that great teachers are granted us. They never come cheap, either in money or in reverence. For they are the custodians of inherited compositions, ancestrally preserved skills that they will never, never impart to a stranger. Unless that stranger is worthy. Unless that ustad is noble.'

Hassu stopped and let his eyes rest on Janki in a meaning manner. 'In the old gharanas the real taalim, the precious teaching, was only for sons. The next best was for the sons-in-law, so that they could earn a living in music. What remained was for outsiders, those not of kin, those that hung around, anxious for crumbs from the master's table.'

'But wasn't there anything for daughters?' was Janki's timid query.

'How could there not be?' Hassu laughed his throaty laugh. 'Can anything be hid from you prying women? They will catch things from beyond a three-foot-wide stone wall, from behind a heavy shisham door. Sitting coyly behind their veils, their nimble brains will hear and memorize. Fanning at the hearth or pounding at the pestle or beating the clothes on the stone, they will try out what they have learnt. What knowledge can be hid from you women, bibi? Then they have such dire threats. Sing this for me or the fire shall not be lit and where will my lord-maestro-husband be without his meal? Sing that for me, or I shall mix sour mango in your sherbet and you shall croak through your riyaz and all your shagirds shall snigger. No,

bibi, you women are the undoing of us all! To answer your
question, daughter, the heritage passed from father to son and
from son to grandson but the dower of daughters wasn't small.
Compositions, jealously preserved, were passed from family to
family as wedding endowment. Or even pawned for years. But
to return to what I was saying, there were few teachers who
imparted their knowledge to outsiders—with noble exceptions
like the illustrious Bairam Khan of Jaipur who taught even the
children of weavers, such as were promising, but few others
besides. In fact there are tales aplenty of the desperate ways in
which disciples courted maestros for acceptance as pupils. The
legendary Alauddin Khan, craving to be taught by Ustad Wazir
Khan, court musician and resident music guru to the nawab of
Rampur, was turned away every time he tried appealing to the
teacher's mercy. At last he was driven to throw himself before
the nawab's carriage in supplication and the nawab, touched,
allowed him into the teacher's circle of disciples. Still more
remarkable is the case of one Imam Baksh of Farrukhabad, a
pakhavaj drummer of great skill, who longed to train in tabla with
the famous Haji Vilayat Ali of his city. Now Imam Baksh wasn't
at all sure of having his request granted were he to approach Haji
Vilayat Ali. So he grew a beard and, donning worn and shabby
clothes and a mien of the utmost submission, produced himself
at Vilayat Ali's household and begged to be taken in as a servant.
The teacher asked: "And what can you do, fellow?" To which came
the humble answer: "I can sweep floors, huzoor. I can go to the
bazaar for the kitchen requirements. I can prepare the hookah.
Anything you command, this lowly one shall willingly do." He
was taken in. For months he hung around the master, sweeping
and dusting, scouring and washing, fetching and carrying, and
all the time keeping his attention riveted on what the master was

teaching his regular pupils. He'd go home every night, to his tiny house on the outskirts of the city, and practise hard. Then one day a guest arrived at Vilayat Ali's home, a famous dhrupad singer. The guest's eye fell on Imam Baksh, busy at his menial jobs, and he exclaimed: "Ah, I know this one. Many a time he has been my accompanist and we have made great music together." 'Vilayat Ali put the visitor right. "You're mistaken, janab. This is our family servant who dusts and sweeps and shops and prepares my hookah."

"'It is you who are mistaken, sir," persisted the guest. "This, may the offence be forgiven, is the famous pakhavaj player, Imam Baksh, and I am ready to swear on the Holy Book. Summon him and he'll bear me out." But Imam Baksh, seeing the game was up, fled. The master grew troubled, wondering why a famous performer should have resorted to such a step as to pose as a servant for so many months. He set off to search for the runaway and after many days and many inquiries he came to a small house beside a mosque on the outskirts of the city. From its window came the sound of tabla-trot, briskly prancing, thunderous as the crackle of monsoon lightning, an intricate cantering of masterly fingers on the two drum faces. Someone was practising. The master halted in surprise. "But that is my style entirely!" he exclaimed to himself. "Such energy and finesse, such symmetry of pace! Who is this?" Thoughtfully he pushed open the door and walked in unannounced and stopped short. For it was indeed Imam Baksh, his servant. The tablas fell silent as the shocked disciple stared horrified at his master. But the master advanced and embraced Imam Baksh and asked him: "Why ever was this necessary? Why the pretence?" To which Imam Baksh faltered: "I was afraid you would refuse to teach me if I came and asked you." The master conducted this new—and best—pupil home and displayed him proudly before his class. "See this fellow." He smiled. "Hear him play. He's one of the best, is he not?" The other pupils were jealous. "How is he a pupil at all? He hasn't even had the ritual ganda tied!" challenged one. The ganda, as you well know, is no small thing. That ordinary-looking strip of black cloth with its knot of jaggery and Bengal gram, tied to the wrist at the time of initiation, is sacred to both teacher and pupil, the jaggery standing for the sweetness of the art, the Bengal gram representing the severity of the discipline and the black cloth wristlet serving as a talisman and a covenant of honour between maestro and initiate. But Imam Baksh had ignored this mandatory ritual, hadn't he?—protested some. Where then was the rightness of it all, the sanctity of the tradition? Hearing this, the master's wife, herself the daughter of a famous Lucknavi musician, came quickly forward and pulling off her bangles, slipped them on to Imam Baksh's wrist, saying: "Here is the ganda. There now, the ritual is over. Are you satisfied?" Ever afterwards, there has existed a school of percussion named after Imam Baksh of the Bangles.

'But of course some teachers there are who are the soul of generosity. Like my noble kinsman, Bande Ali Khan, son-in-law to my brother, Haddu Khan. Now Bande Ali Khan spotted a poor lad singing at a theatrical. The boy had a voice of gold, ah, such a gifted one he was as would shame the angels to let his divine talent go waste for want of money or a proper teacher. So Bande Ali Khan calls the boy, provides the black-cloth wristlet and the gram and the jaggery and ties it round the lad's wrist and says: "Now take this rupee, son, and this paisa, and put them in my hand as your sacred offering to me and I forthwith take charge of you as my pupil and you don't ever have to pay me anything any more." That was him, our great-souled Bande Ali. Not many like him in the old days and never more shall be, say I. For teachers have been who have had to be terrorized into teaching wicked pupils who were as menacing as they were ingenious and as inventive as they were stubborn. Let me tell you what that hot-headed young Nawab of Rampur, the younger one, the son of the one I spoke of, did to the frightened Bahadur Hussain Khan when he refused to take him on as a pupil. The junior nawab, Sahibzada Haider Ali Khan, son of Nawab Yusuf Ali Khan, had set his heart on learning to play the sursingaar from the maestro, Bahadur Hussain Khan. But would the latter agree to waste his time on that whippersnapper of a piffling dandy-boy? Not one whit. For peevish maestros have often held their own against mere rulers of little states. The young prince tried everything—flattery, threat, temptation—but nothing worked. So he invited the master to a feast at his pleasure house in Bilsi. He put him up in a splendid chamber, offered him every courtesy and the choicest hospitality and the evening went in music and poetry and wining and dining and after much revelry the party ended and the guest retired to his chamber for the night. Lo! What should he find there but a nestful of serpents. Yes, real live snakes let loose into the room. Is this hard to believe? I speak only truth. The mischievous young nawab had sent for half a dozen snake charmers and paid them to release their creatures into the chamber. True, the beasts had been defanged, but can you spend a night sharing your bedchamber with an army of serpents? Can I? Can anyone? The maestro was on the brink of a mental collapse when he realized who he was up against, the sort of wily, wilful mind he was vainly striving to oppose. In the dead of night Bahadur Hussain Khan fled the young prince's estate and made his frenzied way to Rampur and sought an audience with the nawab's father. The senior nawab learnt of his son's misdemeanour gravely, and summoned him into his presence. "What do you have to say in your defence, sir?" he demanded to know. The young nawab made reply with due deference but great obduracy: "Beg pardon,

Highness, but I'm clear on one point. Ustad Bahadur Hussain Khan Sahib shall not stay alive, should he dream of refusing my entreaties to accept me as his disciple. He knows this well—that I shall stop at nothing."

'The maestro knew when he was beaten. Sighing, he gave in, though he made some tough conditions—a handsome sum of money at the time of initiation, a promise that the prince should consent to being treated exactly like the other pupils and that he should be obedient in every particular. The young nawab accepted the teacher's conditions, but he had a condition of his own—that he be taught in comprehensive depth and detail, and no family secret, no traditional knowledge of the veena should be withheld from him, this he must swear to before witnesses at a mosque, with his hand on the Holy Book. The weary master agreed to everything. And thus did the secrets of his family, the three hundred and sixty ways of addressing the veena strings, pass out of his safekeeping.

'The point I am trying to make, daughter,' said Hassu, 'is that betwixt teacher and pupil it is a pact of honour, iman. This is not to say that there are no departures from iman—but all is fair in art. I myself, Hassu Khan, learnt invaluable things from one Bade Muhammad Khan, the prime singer of Gwalior, when my brothers and I were mere urchins. Now we three, my brothers Haddu, Natthu and I, being blessed by the grace of Allah in being natural singers and being twice-blest in having teachers of the likes of Natthan Khan Peerbaksh, were trained in the Lucknavi style. Our grandfather Peerbaksh thought we might possibly benefit from some exposure to Bade Muhammad Khan's Gwalior style. But artists are jealous beings, this you must early learn. Muhammad Khan refused to teach any but his own-begot sons, everyone knew. So we three were made to hide in a hencoop, close to the chamber where Bade Muhammad Khan did his daily riyaz. And soon enough we'd picked up all we needed to know. When Bade Muhammad Khan discovered, ah, he had his revenge, he did! At the durbar of the great Scindia he besought me to sing, addressing me in the most honeyed, endearing tones. I sang. Whereupon the chamber rang with applause, especially his. Applause and a rain of blessings. I should have known better. Then he crept up to me and said, "Son, let us hear that particular taan again." That was indeed a special taan, such a throat-heaver, such a tempestuous heaven-blaster of a taan, it was even called the "kadak-bijli taan", the crackle-of-lightning tremolo. I executed it. Perfectly, let me admit. Then, said he, cautious, insidious, "Encore. Now another one." Before anyone could stop me I launched into another kadak bijli. Do you know what happened?'

'What?' asked Janki, wide-eyed.

Hassu played out the suspense.

'I, ignorant wretch, was all aflush with achievement and delight that the great Bade Muhammad Khan was actually demanding an encore from me. Little did I know that this corporeal throat, this body of flesh and bone, cannot take that breath of fire which a second crackle-of-lightning taan brings. What had to happen happened, daughter.'

Hassu sat gazing woefully into the well of his bitter memory.

'What happened, sir?' whispered Janki.

Solemnly Hassu pulled up the left panel of his loose tunic and revealed his thinly carved ribs. 'Dislocated,' he pronounced, not without some pride. 'I began coughing blood. I might have been taken up into the realms of the angels and the prophets, were it not for a hakim who was present at the durbar. So you see, madam, this music has thrashed me within an inch of my life, this I say is God's own truth. Not once but twice.'

He paused, enjoying the pregnant silence.

'When else, sir?' prompted Janki.

'At another concert, daughter, in another nobleman's soirée. In the middle of a taan the blood came. And this time no hakim but an angry hiss from my revered grandfather made the blood freeze in my throat. My noble ancestor, my murshid, Natthan Peerbaksh, descended wrathfully upon me and threatened: "If you must die, boy, finish the taan first, then die at your pleasure, a curse fall upon you! We shall not hold you back!" Such panic did his voice occasion in my heart that the bleeding instantly stopped. I finished the entire performance without a hitch. Such was my terror and reverence for my teacher.'

The first few days Hassu prepared Janki's mind by recounting tales about taalim and legendary teachers and ragas and their stories.

'Ah, teachers, they are all sorts,' he said. 'A certain maestro of Gwalior was extremely vain and mocked his new disciples by first making them crow like a cock at the royal durbar. But the noble Bairam Khan of Jaipur shattered his vanity by sending a sarangi player who claimed to have mastery over 5040 taans. And this effectively demolished the vain ustad.'

If Hassu's intention was to impress upon Janki's timorous sense some idea of a teacher's claim to proper trepidation in a pupil's heart, he succeeded only too well. Janki's timid face was enough to confirm his satisfaction. So much so that he hastened to comfort and reassure.

'Nay, nay. Don't look so frightened, daughter. If teachers struck terror in a pupil, there have been those who were mother, father, sage, beloved, muse, all, all things to their chosen disciples. Consider the relationship between the sainted angel-beloved, heaven-sprung sufi-master Nizamuddin Aulia and his noble companion Amir Khusrau. They did not need to speak one to the other, no. Thought flew invisible from the bough of one's mind to the heart-nest of the other. When Khusrau went to Nizamuddin the very first time, he was petrified and dared not come into the saint's presence. Instead he sat outside and made up a prayer in the silence of his mind, which said: "You are such a king whose power can change even a pigeon on a cornice into a falcon. A poor beggar has come to your door. Do you allow him to enter or should he go back?" Wonder of wonders! The holy master received the transmission in the chalice of his soul and sent back his own sacred vibration. A little later a servant appeared before Khusrau, waiting outside, and recited two couplets written by Nizamuddin, which commanded: "In the arena of truth, if a true man stands, let him enter. But if the guest is undiscerning of truth and unready for it, let him return the way he came." Khusrau immediately went in and laid his head on Nizamuddin's feet and became his mureed. Remember, daughter, he whom the mind accepts as master, the mind casts itself in his mould. Even in the master's absence. Even when the teacher is long dead. The soul of Mridanga Rai, during visitations to his young son, Keshav Rai, taught him the niceties of mridanga playing to wreak vengeance on the dancers Kalika–Bindadeen who'd craftily made him lose a beat at the court of the Nawab of Lucknow Wajid Ali Shah and made him die of shame and a broken heart. Stranger things have happened in music. Even centuries after the passing of a great maestro. There is a tamarind tree above the tomb of Tansen that pilgrim musicians visit, yes, even I, Hassu. To chew the tamarind leaf of that holy tree is to be graced with a voice like Tansen's. Please God, some day you too shall go on that pilgrimage.'

8

For an entire year Hassu made Janki practise notes and scales only. Just sa, re, ga, ma, pa, dha, ni, sa. This eight-note scale, he discoursed, was called Malaw Gaud in south India and the Bhairav Thath in north India. The origins of this basic sound alphabet lay in the Pratham-nada, the primal sound-essence such as only saints and risen ones know. Therein resides the full palette of notes as the colours of the rainbow lie potential in primary white light.

'For music is of divine provenance. Hindus trace it to their celestial minstrel-sage Narada, who learnt the notes and scales and the ragas from the Muse, Saraswati, and by some accounts, from Shiva himself. Muslims believe that the seven notes of the musical scale originated from the sound of seven streams that gushed forth when divine rain thundered down on the sacred stone that the prophet Moses possessed. The notes of the scale are the voices of nature's creatures, such is the old Vedic belief. The peacock's call is the "sa". The bullock's is "re". The goat's "ga". The jackal's "ma". The cuckoo's "pa". The horse's "dha". The elephant's "ni". Amir Khusrau, that great thirteenth-century genius, who wove together so much of Hindu and Muslim music, used the Iranian names for the "swaras", the notes. Raast, shahnavaz, doka, kurd, seeka, girka, hijaz, nava, hisaar, hussaini, agnu and neem. He based his classification of Indian ragas on these twelve names.' Hassu taught

Janki the old gharana maxim—'Taal gaya to baal gaya, sur gaya to sar gaya'—if rhythm be lost, consider it the loss of a hair. But if the note be lost, consider it the loss of the head itself. To get one note right, just one, is the fruit of years of rigorous effort. For the finished note must glow from within and the singer's body and being must experience the vibration of this radiance. And not only must the note be perfect, its echo must be perfect too.

There was a great vocalist who was taken by his teacher to the great mosque at Lahore and made to sing facing a massive wall which tossed back the echoes to each uttered phrase of music. The teacher asked the pupil whether voice and echo sounded the same. To which the pupil was constrained to admit that the echo did not match the voice. Then the teacher began singing. The wall sent back its resonance and the pupil, paying close attention, observed that both voice and echo were tonally perfect.

'That's what a singer must strive for, the interior purity of the single note. As they used to say in the old gharanas, "ek sur sadhe to sab sur sadhe"—when one note steadies all the other notes stabilize. It is absolute rightness that we are talking of,' Hassu said, 'the essence of a note and its inner incandescence, which, when achieved, unlocks the door to real excellence. All else is mere cleverness. That pupil became one of the greatest singers of his age. You'll be amazed to learn that he made a living selling kulhars of tea at railway stations and playing the sarangi at a dancing girl's kotha. But nights he headed for the Hindu burning ghats and practised singing in those vast, desolate wastes where pyres burned and wild-eyed sages drowsed. Where else could he find the emptiness and silence except in the place of death? Later, when he was a famous man, he'd stand beside the sea at Chowpatti, in the middle of the tempestuous Bombay rains, and try competing with the ferocity of the roaring sea, taking each wild wave as his natural rival, pitting his voice against the ocean. That was one who lived his music, not just performed it. You're not an artist some of the time, remember this. You're an artist all the time, in sleep and in waking. You breathe in your medium as a fish breathes in water. It is your chief reason for existing. It steers your ears and your eyes and the coursings of your blood. Whether the world accepts or rejects you is immaterial. The element you inhabit and stay all awash in fills your days and nights with purpose, with the promise of truth. The achievement of that one perfect note is God's currency whereby you are unexpectedly and serendipitously paid. The song you sing isn't the real one, the real song is elsewhere. The one you sing is a copy, a shadow cast on the waters of the self. Try to get as close as you can to the real one. The soul of each raga is made up of esoteric alphabets, in ideal conjunctions, in transcendental chronologies. Make yourself worthy of each note, the descent of each raga in all its astral nobility.

'My friend Abdul Rehman makes his disciples sing the first note of the scale "sa" hundreds of times before allowing them to move on to the next note "re". Only seldom does anyone succeed in producing that transcendentally pure sound, but when they do, the teacher's face thrills and the entire chamber trembles with the knowledge of something surpassingly excellent. And though one's belly must be filled and one's vanity be honoured, still there is a cause aside and apart from all these, such a cause as the world's fools and saints and artists and madmen of genius know. This teacher that I speak of is the son of one of the greatest. Yet he lives in terrible poverty, supports himself by tuitions, just about Rs 5 or 10 a month. His white jacket has turned yellow and his dhoti has been darned so often and grown so threadbare that he carries a needle and a length of thread stuck in the lining of his cap. Poverty is a wretched thing and no one must ever valorize it, but there are marvels that lay claim to our wonder, that a man should carry, in the thick of sweat and struggle, in hunger and illness and exhausting, demeaning chores, the fastidious striving for one excellent note and the pursuit of that possibility of perfection. You may call it compensation but you cannot call it illusion.

'So be patient,' said Hassu, 'and go on practising the notes, individual and in their proper order. Then in paltas or prescribed combinations. Ascend and descend, run down the staircase, skip, overleap, alight and take off, land on your feet and fly up again. Others have done it before you—for five, six, seven years. This is what gives "taseer" to the voice, bloom and body. Timbre and flexibility. The grandson of the venerable Ghulam Abbas Khan who, take my word for it, will one day rule the world of music, has not been allowed to sing any raga, much less attempt any taans or venture into the forbidden terrain of a song. No, it is just the notes of the scale for young Faiyaz Khan, with wrestling and push-ups as part of his grooming. Once when the mischievous lad climbed a tree and let loose a loud burst of song in Raga Yaman, of which he was very fond, he was immediately hauled down and given a right royal thrashing by his grandfather, for breaking rules and singing a raga with all the melodic trills and other tricks of the throat, much before his voice was pronounced ready and ripe to go ahead. But you, daughter, are now ready, as I behold in the greatest satisfaction. So that very raga it shall be—Raga Yaman, and we shall begin with its particular scale.'

Hassu demonstrated. Janki replicated. Raga Yaman it would be for months.

'My close kin, Bahadur Hussain Khan, yes, the selfsame maestro who found serpents in his bedroom, taught Inayat Hussain Khan only one raga for years and that was the Gaud-Sarang. Each raga has its own character and personality, its hour and estate, and must be realized in profound communing with it. And there are individual histories too, bearing the signature of teachers both divine and human.'

After Raga Yaman Hassu moved on to Raga Todi, of which there were eighteen different kinds.

'Some time back you asked me why the emperor Aurangzeb banned music and I commanded you to be patient, which you most admirably were,' went on Hassu. 'The moment is come when I shall answer your question, and to that end I shall speak of Raga Todi. There is a whole extended family of Todis. The one invented by Tansen, Akbar's durbar singer, fondly called "Mian" by the emperor, has the name "Mian ki Todi".

'Tansen didn't come willingly to Akbar's court. He was compelled to leave his original patron, Raja Ram Chandra of Rewa, and move to the Imperial Mughal's capital at Agra. Which he did most reluctantly. He was seventy years old and wanted to retire and renounce the world, but he had no choice. But once established in the Great Mughal's durbar he shone like the brightest star in the firmament.

'When the time came to depart the earth he wondered which of his four sons should succeed him as first musician. Surat Sen, Sharat Sen, Taranga and Vilas Khan were each singers of skill and distinction, so it was hard to choose. His time approaching, Tansen summoned his four sons and told them: "It is time for me to leave this life, my sons, and my heart grows faint. Just a few moments remain to me, after which the breath shall leave my body. Then, when that has happened, sing to me, my sons. Sing one by one beside my lifeless form. He that shall sing the best shall move my corpse to raise its hand in benediction. He shall be my successor." So it transpired. It is said that when the youngest son, Vilas Khan, sang his own version of Todi, Tansen's lifeless hand rose of its own volition and blessed the lad. That Todi is called the Vilas Khani Todi and its notes are saturated with the grief of loss and bereavement. Vilas Khan's descendants inherited the position of court maestros at the Mughal durbar. Two generations later, the emperor Shah Jahan faced a quandary similar to the one faced by Tansen long ago: how to choose a successor between four contending sons. Once again the Raga Todi made history. In the war of succession between the sons of Shah Jahan, the chief vazeer, Ali Mardan Khan, predicted that whichever of Shah Jahan's sons had the services of a particular official, Murshid Quli Khan, that son would succeed him as emperor. Shah Jahan had intended attaching him to Dara, his eldest and noblest son. But Aurangzeb, the youngest son of Shah Jahan, bribed Khushal Khan, who was Vilas Khan's son-in-law and court musician then, with a lakh of rupees. Together they hatched an ingenious plot. Everyone knew of Shah Jahan's love for Raga Todi. It was said that the emperor always grew rapt, on listening to Todi sung or played, that he grew quite heedless of the world. On the Nauroz festival, while Khushal Khan outdid himself singing Todi, Ali Mardan Khan quietly slipped the document regarding Murshid Quli Khan's transfer to Aurangzeb in the Deccan before the emperor, who, without so much as a glance at it, promptly affixed his signature, while immersed in the mysteries of the raga. Later, on discovering his gaffe, he was deeply embarrassed. But an emperor could not show himself up as so careless as to sign a document without reading, nor could he withdraw his orders on that plea. So Aurangzeb, the fourth son, by craft and design, acquired the general who would help him seize the throne. Khushal Khan was disgraced, allowed to retain his title of "guna-samundar", or "ocean of merit", but prohibited from ever singing in the future. For Aurangzeb, once he ascended the throne, grew acutely suspicious of music, which was always associated in his mind with Khushal Khan's treachery and Shah Jahan's carelessness. If a maestro could betray his master's salt with a song for a lakh rupees, if music could turn an emperor so irresponsible as to make him sign an important state document without looking at it, then music was a most pernicious influence. But Aurangzeb actually did not hate music, no. Banning music was a political decision, an eccentric reaction, that's all. See, had Khushal Khan's Todi not impaired the emperor's wits, the history of our land might have been otherwise. Maybe the saintly Dara might have been emperor and what would Indian history have been then? That's Todi for you.

'And our next object of study, Malhar. Of course you know the story of Tansen singing Raga Deepak that invoked the celestial fire and found his body in flames and that two women instantly sang Raga Megh Malhar that called down the rain from the clouds and doused the deadly flames. But in truth that's just a doubtful old wives' tale. For Raga Deepak was created not by Tansen but by Haji Sujan Khan on whom Akbar bestowed the title Deepak-Jyot—Light of the Lamp. And Raga Malhar, for some reason, you'll be interested to know, has several avatars mostly associated with women. Like Todi there are several Malhars—Meera ki Malhar, Birju ka Malhar and, my favourite story, the one about the courtesan in Gujarat. She, it was said, was the greater maestro, far surpassing the legendary Tansen. She'd slip off her nose ring and drop it into a dry well. Then she'd start her song, and as she sang, the mighty clouds burst and the rain roared down and filled the well to overflowing, and the pretty little nose ring came floating up to the surface, and she ceased her song and retrieved it with an artful smile that threw a triumphant challenge to the awestruck Tansen. It is said that he learnt how to sing Raga Malhar from her, though her name is lost and his is writ large in the history of music.

And there was another Malhar, this one invented by that saintly madman, Baiju, contemporary to Tansen, the one whose singing stopped a massacre. The one who went seeking his adopted son, Gopal, who'd basely run away and refused to recognize him. There are various accounts of Gopal's desertion. In one account Baiju had arranged a match for him with a girl named Prabha, a disciple of his. A daughter was born to them and they named her Meera. Then Gopal disappeared and Baiju went in desperate search and eventually traced him. He'd been appointed durbar singer at the Kashmir court (though a parallel account would have him in Jodhpur) and on Baiju's appearance there, he strongly denied that Baiju had ever been his teacher. A contest was organized by the maharaja's orders and Baiju sang a poignant composition in Raga Bhimpalasi, the words of which were: "Wherefore this fake vanity, oh ye that are called virtuous?" The composition ended with a direct address to Gopal's conscience: "Sayeth Baiju, the music-crazed, O hear me, Son Gopal, what availed thee thus to deny thy teacher?"

'The song left Gopal deeply disturbed and he sprang forward and fell at Baiju's feet. It is said that Gopal perished of guilt, so violently did his heart beat in shame and penitence. His body was cremated in Baiju's broken-hearted presence on the banks of the river Indus, and his ashes immersed in the waters of the river. Neither his wife Prabha nor his daughter Meera were there and when they learnt of Gopal's death, they hastened, frantic with grief, to Kashmir, and wept bitterly on discovering that no trace remained of Gopal, not even his ashes, that they had had no part in his funeral rites. If only we could have performed his last rites, they mourned. Baiju was moved by their distress and he taught Meera a special kind of Malhar. He asked her to seat herself on the riverbank and sing the raga he'd taught her. She obeyed. She closed her eyes and sang and lo! The river Indus stopped flowing and listened. Then it began flowing upstream, reversing the way of nature. It returned Gopal's ashes to the bank from which they had been cast for Gopal's wife and daughter to gather in an urn and perform the rituals they so much longed to do. That raga is known as Meera ki Malhar. For the next six months, daughter, we shall practise the various kinds of Malhar. Hear me demonstrate the basic scale.'

Hassu guided Janki through a lengthy and intensive course. There were ragas which had their origins in folk tunes, he told her. Like Raga Tilak Kamod, for example, created by the master Pyar Khan. Once, travelling through a village, he heard a woman singing at her grindstone. He was taken with the melody, the way it was configured, the way the notes were strung along. He returned home and tried them out. And created a new raga, Tilak Kamod. 'There are hundreds of ragas, daughter,' said Hassu. 'The names of their creators are oftentimes writ in ancient and medieval texts. Hussain Shah Sharqi, king of Jaunpur, was a musician. Remember, kings were often maestros in their own right, and tutored musicians. Babur played the veena, which was then called the been, and Akbar played nagara-drums. And we aren't even looking further into history which has conquerors like Samudragupta strumming the strings. Hussain Shah Sharqi is said to have invented twelve ragas—the Gaur Shyam, the Malar Shyam, the Bhopal Shyam and four Todis of his own, including the Jaunpuri Todi. And Ibrahim Adil Shah of Bijapur is believed to have invented Bhopali, Bhairav, Asawari, Desi, Poorvi, Kalyan and Kedar. Amir Khusrau, Man Singh Tomar, Nemat Khan Sadarang—there are many shining names that come to mind. Other ragas there are whose origins are misted in mythology. Pleased with Sage Narada's austerities, Shiva is said to have bestowed five instantly created ragas, one from each of his five mouths. These ragas are Bhairav, Hindol, Megh, Deepak and Shree. Then his consort, Parvati, awoke. She'd been fast asleep and Shiva, meanwhile, had created the rudraveena in her slumbering-woman's shape. Waking, she contributed a sixth raga to Narada's store, the Kaushik raga. Mark you, the same raga has multiple traditions of origin, depending on which text is consulted. Mark also that several ragas may have identical notes but the manner of singing and the style of rendition distinguishes them one from the other. Take for instance Bhairavi, Ramkali and Kalingada. What distinguishes them is fine points of rendition, shifting raag-bhaava, by which we mean the disposition, the sensibility of the raga, its temperament, its soul-shade.

'After the ragas, the forms. Raga-sensibility and rhythm-artistry—ragadari and layakari—are like the two streams of the Ganga and the Yamuna meeting and blending in a mighty single stream at Allahabad. They blend in various time-honoured forms developed over the centuries. Dhrupad is the one every serious student of music must begin with, yes, even women I say, though it hasn't been traditionally regarded as a women's mode. Dhrupad has thousands of ancient compositions that exercise the singer's range. Stylized songs in praise of the gods. The sixteen varieties of dhrupad have their syllabic rules, their ruling rasas and their fruits, which include longevity, prosperity, progeny, fame, joy, sexual fulfilment, victory and enthusiasm. Khayal or a meandering exposition of a raga, exploring, improvising, along certain conventional routes, taking certain customary variations of pace and design. Thumri, or the plaint of longing cast into verse and refrain. Dadra, which is a faster-paced poem of the heart sung as a raga. Ghazal, or the cry of the gazelle in unrequited yearning. Bhajan, which is prayer. For each there are thousands of ancestral compositions, or bandishes, brief lines of verse redolent of the seasons of nature and the ardours and agonies of the human heart. The more bandishes a singer practises, the better is one's training. Those compositions were the treasured property of the music clans, the feudal gharanas, and maestros were possessive about their rich collections, gifting them as wedding endowments to favoured daughters, or bestowing them as precious trophies to deserving disciples. Alladiya Khan was made to practise all night long, and he had ten thousand to twelve thousand bandishes in his repertoire. To address the bandish from eight angles, the ashta-disha, that is the classic grooming of a true singer, and to adhere to its integrity in every particular, that is the test.

'And there are devices of the voice to be mastered, tricks of the vocal cords to add that many delightful dimensions to what a human voice can do. Melodic trills, taans, those whirlwind ladders of notes that the voice races up in vibrating circuits and spirals and plunging cataracts of descent. And delicate traceries of tremolo, smooth, pliant glissandos. There are many kinds of taans, daughter. The deep, ground-quaking boom of the halaq taan, the throaty reverberation of the gamak taan which sounds like throbs of water pouring out of a broad-mouthed earthen pitcher. The swift elasticity of the fikra and firat taans. The mukh-bandi taan that is performed with mouth closed, and the jabra taan that is executed with tongue hanging out. The larazdar taan is grand and steady with a rhythmic pulse in its grain that weaves in and out in clever tanglings and untanglings. The hikka taans move in pulsating shocks of hiccupping jerks. Then there are chhoot taans and sapaat taans and taans with awesome names—the crackle-of-lightning or kadak-bijli taan, the haathhi-chinghar or the trumpeting elephant and the nangi-talwar or the naked sword. Aside from taans there are the embellishment or alangkars, the harkat or vocal sleight, the khatka or quick toss, the murki or fine ripple like the breeze blowing along a woman's silk headcloth. The kampa or tremolo, the murchhana or modulation, the andolan or stir of pleasing complication, the sooth or slide and the meend or deep glide. The zamzama which creates the shimmer of a celestial stream glimmering in the noonday sun. All this the voice must be trained to do, aside from vistar and behlawa, expanding and diversion. And dum-saans or breath control. We used to hang earthen pots from the ceilings of our riyaz chamber. They gave a nice resonance to the rooms we practised in,' said Hassu to Janki. 'Also, we were careful about what we ate or drank. Never you drink the water cooling in a new pitcher, a kora matka. It is vile for the vocal cords. Eat lots of desi ghee and almonds. Do you know what my elder brother Haddu Khan's diet is? Half a seer of milk in a bucket with four jalebis aswim in it. That's his morning meal on waking. He has korma and rotis for lunch, the rotis piled up and measured in hand-spans. He does a hundred sit-ups every daybreak and then practises for hours, producing taans fit to rattle the arches of heaven! Another maestro of my acquaintance always has finely ground almonds in the mornings, and once, when his sprightly young daughter-in-law ground in peanuts instead, he spat it out in deep disgust, declaring: "My business is to tell the true note from the false, Bibi. I know a peanut from an almond!" So eat well, I say, and exercise well, for music needs power and endurance, as every singer knows. Then put in your best, practise and practise and practise till absolute virtuosity is yours and the Sayyad of Mausiqui is compelled to visit your chamber in the dark watches of your sleep and bless you. Do not be discouraged, though, when you can't. Many of the best have been awful when they started out. Khuda Baksha, the son of Mian Shyam Rang, had earned the nickname of "Ghaghghay"—his voice was so hoarse. He received his taalim under my reverend grandfather. Fourteen years he put in and lo! His voice turned so sweet that people sat with bedewed eyes when he sang. And there was a sarangi player named Mirach Khan who'd practised so hard at his sarangi outside the shrine of Hazrat Nizamuddin Aulia in Dilli that his arm had grown bent along the shape of the bow. We need commitment like that.

'But most of all we need God's grace. When all the labour has been put in and all the concentrated will, remember that the ultimate shine is a gift from Allah, if He so pleases. The old dhrupadiyas used to sing Pratham Man Omkar, by which is meant "The first honoured is the sacred om syllable". And the Muslim dhrupadiya Haji Sujan Khan adapted it to "Pratham Man Allah". Do not forget, daughter, that human effort alone won't do, you need the descent of grace. Be sure that shall come when you have submitted your best for divine acceptance, making of your music an offering, not an achievement.'

9

Janki's biography mentions four siblings, Kashi, Paraga, Mahadei and Beni Prasad. Kashi, Paraga and Mahadei died before the relocation from Benaras to Allahabad but Beni Prasad came along. Janki mentions him fondly.

Life in a women's kotha couldn't have been comfortable for Beni Prasad. There were a few boys in the household but they had been born in the kotha and grown up there, having known no other identity save that of 'our boys about the house'. Beni Prasad couldn't fit in, couldn't stomach the transformation that came over his mother and sister or unlearn his former existence as a respectable householder's only son. Manki was mindful of his torment and arranged for lessons.

Tutors had been hired for Janki. A maulvi sahib came from Daryabad to teach her Persian and Urdu. A panditji came to teach her Sanskrit and an English-knowing master sahib had been appointed to impart lessons in English. Janki was an apt and eager pupil and uncannily quick to learn. But when Manki suggested that Beni sit in at the lessons the experiment failed. Beni had no interest and seemed wanting in basic intelligence. Bored, he stole away and flew kites on the terrace with a bunch of kotha lads. He was older than them all and usually kept his distance, maintaining a surly aloofness in his dealings with them. They mimicked him behind his back and made up nicknames for him but behaved with reserved deference in his presence. If the Sahib Bahadur, as they called him, was a snob and thought himself superior and separate, there was at least one thing about him that they genuinely respected—his kite-flying skills. This he taught them on winter afternoons and when the first rains came and a little team of kotha boys came up who excelled in stalking and assaulting every kite in the sky, cutting off their strings and sending them reeling across the horizon like wing-shredded birds, teetering to a fall in one of the narrow lanes, attracting a horde of screaming captors, who tore down the backstairs and scampered down the alleys, tracing the drifting descent of the unmoored kite.

Manki persuaded the percussionists to give Beni lessons in tabla, dholak or pakhavaj, but Beni had no sense of rhythm. As for the sarangi, Beni's fingers turned to thumbs in every skill save kite flying. Naseeban then suggested ironically that a young lad, an almost-man, should not sit and eat off the earnings of women. That rather than be an idle parasite he should serve the kotha in some capacity.

There were two possibilities open to Beni, to help with the household accounts, the takings, the cuts, the advances and the repayments that had to be zealously recorded. Or to be what she daintily called a gentleman usher, a word-of-mouth narrator of the girls' beauty and gifts to prospective clients, in other words a pimp.

Beni had a shot at both. The girls of the kotha were graded in various professional categories, as Beni was instructed to bear in mind. There were the superior bais and jaans, the former being primarily singers and the latter being singers as well as dancers. There were the somewhat inferior mirasans, the lower-classed domnis and lowest in the ladder, the randis. There were those descended from senior performers and those who were, in

Naseeban's kotha, girls sold, abducted or abandoned, who could rise in the profession as they proved their talents. It was a strange and depressing thing to sit at the low floor-desk, dipping his holder into the inkwell and entering details into the large ruled ledger: Samiran Bano—five full sessions with Shri Gorakh Nath at Rs 2 per session plus three half-sessions with Janab Asghar Ali at Re 1 per session. Total Rs 13. Minus advance of Rs 2 and 8 annas. Total Rs 10 and 8 annas. Amount payable to Begum Naseeban Jahan—Rs 6 and 8 annas. Amount payable to Samiran Bano—Rs 4.

Hasina Bi—eight full sessions with Kunwar Roshan Singh at Rs 2 per session and three half-sessions at Re 1 per session with Shri Radhe Shyam and 4 mujras at Rs 4 per mujra. Total Rs 35. Minus advance of Rs 5—total Rs 30. Amount payable to Begum Naseeban Jahan—Rs 17. Amount payable to Hasina Bi—Rs 13. Manki Devi—six full sessions with Janab Mahbub Khan at Rs 2 per session, four half-sessions with Shri Jagdish Prasad at . . .

It is not to be wondered that Beni refused to be accounts-person for the kotha, fudging up the figures so abominably that he was relieved of his services.

His achievements as procurer and pimp were scarcely more successful. For a week or two he walked along the alley and down the broad street that the lane opened into, shadowing shifty-eyed men, murmuring: 'Young, fresh-as-flower items, sir, skins white as milk, limbs supple as silk, voices like the koel in mango-flower times, anklet-tinkling feet showering silvery chimes. Visit our perfumed garden, sir, taste of beauty that shall madden, sir, songs that shall gladden, sir. Music, laughter, love are our affairs, sir. We guarantee satisfaction and freedom from cares, sir.'

He was so bad at this job that the other pimps, touting rival kothas, jeered at him: 'Ho, hawker-boy! What have you there? Basketful of tits and clits at 2 annas apiece?'

It flayed poor Beni's wincing soul raw. When it was time to go pimping next evening, he just lay in bed, feigning illness, and no one insisted. He went back to the only thing he was passionate about—flying kites. And after about six months, when the Makar-Sankranti kite-flying festival came, Beni's kite soared higher than all others, slashing at competing upstarts, sawing away at the taut strings of veterans, circling swiftly out of the reach of chasing kites, floundering into tree-snares and terrace-tops, and winning Beni the handsome prize of Rs 50. It was enough to salvage all of Beni's wilting self-esteem, quite enough to give him a swagger in his walk and a challenging glint to his eye. Triumphantly he returned to the kotha and laid Rs 49, 8 annas on Manki's cracked old dresser. For 2 annas he bought a thick jasmine-braid garland, strode up to Shaheen Bano's door, knocked on it, and when she appeared, drowsy from her much-needed rest, he held it out to her and said: 'For you.'

She took it, baffled. Then understanding awoke in her seasoned eye and she broke into a sparkling giggle and rushed back into her room.

'See here, Hasina! See what our Beni-boy has brought me!'

Behind the closed door he heard Hasina exclaim, and then the twinkling cascade of their combined laughter.

That laughter followed him everywhere he went in the kotha. It spread to the other girls, to the boys, the musicians, to Naseeban herself.

'What, Beni-boy, nothing for us? You break our hearts, as Allah is our witness!'

'Have a heart, my rajaji. What does Shaheen Apa have that we don't, Sahib Bahadur? Would you like to check us out, say?'

'Uf, this scent of jasmine, I'll surely faint, sister! Where d'you think it's coming from?'

'Oh-ho, so it's Shaheen you've set your sights on, my laat sahib. Ah, I might have known. But you're a sly one, you are!'

Beni endured all. And begged a rupee from Manki and bought a cheap Kanta scent for Shaheen.

She took it coolly. Raised her fine arching eyebrows mock-seriously, unstoppered the bottle, sniffed at it and sprayed it all over Hasina, who stood laughing by. She thrust the empty vial back into Beni's bashful hand.

'There, now. Take that and be off!'

Beni mooned away and the kotha rocked with merriment. Then one day Shaheen strode angrily up to Manki and hissed: 'Bua, keep your spoony son off me, will you! He's getting on my nerves. I can't stand the sight of him!'

Manki bristled. 'Too good for him, are you, my hussy?' she snapped.

'Listen, Manki Bua,' retorted Shaheen, 'I've nothing against you or your son. He's just a dimwit who's got buttons for eyes. But you, surely you know what's what?'

'What?' demanded Manki, incensed.

'Between Hasina and me?' said Shaheen in a furious whisper.

'Of course,' said Manki drily, turning away. 'Yes, of course. Who doesn't? Except maybe your precious clients. And suppose we let slip something here or a hint there? Whatever will Naseeban Bua have to say, I wonder.'

Shaheen's defiance seemed to fall away. Her crestfallen face grew desperate, beseeching.

'Manki Bua, I beg you, I clutch your feet. Don't tell your son anything. Just keep him off me.'

'How d'you suggest I do that? He's a grown man. Shall I tell him you bathe in hog swill? That you are a viper-woman with poison fangs? No, girl, I'll have to tell him the truth. That you and Hasina lock yourselves in together when the clients have left.'

'Hush!' whispered Shaheen. 'Not so loud. Naseeban'll hear!'

'As if Naseeban doesn't know.'

'I swear to you she doesn't!'

'Then you don't know Naseeban. She's a wily one with more brains than a nursing she-fox that knows exactly what each cub is up to.'

'Thanks very much indeed,' spoke up Naseeban from behind the shade of a chik. 'You do me great credit, Manki, my jaan, and you have my salaams. As for you, my little frolicsome filly, don't for a moment imagine that I don't know the kind of carriage that you and that Hasina draw together! God willing, some day I'll have your au pair act up for the delectation of some perverse old nawab with outlandish tastes. But till that happens, my lasses, if a word of this gets out, if so much as a whisper reaches the clients, then, as God is my witness, I'll take a strap to your dainty buttocks till not a cowrie-width's skin is left! And you . . .' Here Naseeban swirled her heavy gharara round and fixed her scorching eye on Manki. 'Kindly explain to that wimp of a son of yours that no lovering goes on under this roof except by my grace and favour. Understand. Everything, everything is done for a price and there's nothing left over for fooling. There's bread to be earned.'

'What to do, madam?' stammered Manki. 'The young are foolish and he's of the age when . . .'

Naseeban shut her up with an imperious wave of the hand. 'In that case I'll have to put him to work again and I think I know how.'

The next morning Beni was called into Naseeban's audience chamber where she sat, leaning back on her bolster in queenly amplitude, the long silver-tipped hookah pipe resting on her lips. She let the silk-tasselled pipe fall on her lap.

'Be seated, mian,' she commanded. 'I have more work for you.'

He shuddered. He'd been a flop at Persian and Sanskrit and English, a flop at the sarangi and the tabla. He had failed as an accountant and as a pimp. Now he had failed in love. But Naseeban was a master psychologist. She couldn't send either Shaheen or Hasina away though she'd long known about them. They were perfect actors and the clients loved them. They could feign the sighs, the agonies and raptures of young love with subtle and brilliant emoting and they were good songstresses and pleasing dancers and experts at witty wordplay and had a good memory for poetry too. And more, they were very young and had good, productive working years ahead. No, she couldn't spare them and neither could she afford to allow this lovesick young lad to hang around them and find things out for himself, as he was bound to, sooner or later. He would have to be manoeuvred away and she knew how to do that.

'My lord patang-baaz,' she smiled, 'my king of the kites, I want you to do me a favour. If you can teach the little Subuhi how to fly kites, I shall be greatly obliged to you.'

He stared. Subuhi was a chit of eleven or twelve, a new entrant to the kotha, and he'd taken no notice of her. But Naseeban spoke with a mysterious smile.

'I have no doubt you'll teach her well. Teach her on the terrace.' She leant forward. Her eyes narrowed. 'Then teach her to fly kites in bed.'

He took time for it to register.

'You've taught boys to fly kites, haven't you?' said Naseeban, smiling softly. 'Well, you haven't ever taught a girl. Teach her to hold up the kite and toss it up in the air as you wheel out the string. Then let your hand close over hers as she clutches the string.

Encircle her and breathe in the musk of her hair. Let the kite go but hold on to the girl. The rest I leave to your blood and hers.' Naseeban softly put the hookah pipe back on her lips.

Beni was terrified as the full import of this assignment dawned on him. He was being asked to break in this fresh little girl, initiate her.

'But why me?' he stammered. 'I mean, begum sahiba, that there are rich clients who'd gladly, I mean . . .'

Naseeban waved aside his feeble protest. 'Not with this one. She's moody. Cries all the time. Has to be force-fed. Is ready to kick and bite. She'll slap her nath babu and send him flying back to his phaeton, believe me. And give my house a bad name. It might cost me goodwill built over years. No, mian. What we want is a gentle thawing. What we want,' Naseeban smiled, malevolent, knowing, infinitely shrewd, 'is good, old-fashioned love. The way you proved your instincts at understanding the language of love, lad, I knew you were wasted in any other kind of work. Go to her, boy. Teach her to fly kites.'

She put the hookah to her laughing lips and took a long, lazy drag. Beni left the room without a word.

None of Naseeban's formulas proved effective on the terrace. Subuhi didn't let Beni encircle her but shrugged off his guiding hand. She tore up the kite and burst into tears. It was Beni's special kite, a beautiful flamingo and banana green, with a long ruffled tail. And seeing it in shreds, Beni burst into tears too. The thaw was anything but slow or gentle. But Subuhi hadn't ever seen a young man burst into tears and he made such an unthreatening spectacle as he gulped and swiped his sleeve across his streaming eyes, that she relaxed in his presence, brought flour-jelly gum and strips of paper and needle and thread and sat on the terrace floor, trying to paste up the shreds.

'There, now,' she said, offering the patched and crumpled, criss-crossed-with-paper-tapes, salvaged kite.

'It won't fly,' he said, sulky.

'It will,' she said in her child voice. 'Try. Look. Hold the string—like this—wheel it out. I'll hold it up. Like this. And let it go . . .'

Unconsciously she had encircled him and was breathing softly down his back. He smelt of sweat and camphor. And something else she could not place and she didn't know it was desire.

She ran to the other end of the terrace, held up the kite, flung it into the air. It fluttered up, askew. He adjusted the string, tugged. No good at all. The battered kite took a crazy curve, came dashing down and lay on the terrace's paving stones.

'I told you it wouldn't,' he moaned.

'I'll get you another,' she said.

But of course she couldn't. She had no money of her own at all.

He smiled wanly. 'Never mind,' he said.

There was much laughter downstairs. Beni's progress with Subuhi was a matter of keen and general interest.

'What, Sahib Bahadur,' tittered the girls, 'we hear she's left you with a ragged kite and a torn heart.'

'No, she tried very hard to glue it up, we hear!'

'How many stitches in your heart, laddie?'

They teased the little girl too, no better way to kindle romance.

Beni avoided her for a day or two, so heartbroken was he about his kite.

One day she beckoned to him from the room she shared with Samiran. 'Won't you teach me any more?' she wanted to know.

'There isn't a kite,' he said curtly.

'Buy one,' she insisted.

'How?' he wanted to know.

'Take this.' She held out a little jewelled hairpin. 'It's silver. Will buy a whole lot of kites for you.'

'Who wants a whole lot?'

She smiled shyly. 'I do.'

It was his turn to be startled at the idea of a woman courting him. He opened his eyes wide and flushed to the roots of his hair.

When a dozen kites arrived and some reels of string and paper bagfuls of powdered glass and bottles of glue, more merriment resulted down below.

'Our Beni is planning to wed our Subuhi and set up a kite shop! What, Beni-boy, it's hearth and home for our lad now, is it?'

No one recalled how the wedding joke started but it caught on fast. One evening Subuhi gashed her fingers on the razor-sharp kite string. She let out a little yelp and Beni rushed to help. The blood burbled out of three fingers and stained her white chikan dress. She brushed her hand on her white headcloth and stained it too. Then Beni tore off a length of cloth from one end of his linen kurta and proceeded to bind up the small hand, forgetting kite and kite-string and all else in the act. How the girls of the kotha pulled Subuhi's leg.

'Blood on your chunri and blood on your dress, girl? What's he been doing to you, say?'

Subuhi wasn't any longer the temperamental creature she'd been. She was pert and sprightly and quite transformed.

'See what I do to him, see!' she challenged.

Beni they plagued on his torn kurta.

'Aha, there goes Majnu, tearing up his clothes for love of Laila!' they teased.

Next day Beni appeared with a bottle of lal-dawa, the red medicine, Mercurochrome.

'Has the wound healed?' he wanted to know.

'It hurts still,' she said, extending her paw.

'Let me dress it again. I've brought medicine.'

There was something in the way he undressed the hand, undraping the fingers of their swaddling bands, down to their naked, vulnerable paleness, that made her tingle. He smeared red Mercurochrome on. It stained her palm scarlet.

'Like the mehndi ceremony, isn't it, Beni?' she asked shyly. 'Like henna on a bride's palm?'

He stiffened, tensely sopping up the extra trickles. She was provoked to mischief. Her hand shot up and left its red imprint on his cheek, then on the other cheek, then on his chest.

'Holi hai!' she said, giggling, hysterical. 'Bura na mano, Holi hai! Don't mind me, it's Holi!'

In her practice chamber Janki sang out: 'Aaj Braj mein ho rahi Hori' in Raga Sohni. Following it up with 'Mo pe daar gayo sare rang ki gagar' in Raga Khambaj. Her sisterly teasing had confined itself to songs, and by the time Beni descended bashfully down the staircase and made a dash for the bathhouse in the courtyard Janki's rich contralto came resounding down the corridor. 'Hori machi hai saiyaan ki nagariya' in poignant Pilu.

The girls were in splits when they saw Subuhi's red palms and his red-stained face.

'Ah ha ha ha! Now the mehndi is over. It's time for the baraat! Bring in the elephants-horses-palanquins! Bring on the fireworks and the flowers!'

Beni asked Manki's and Naseeban's permission to take Subuhi to the doll-mela. Manki hesitated but was overruled by Naseeban.

It was the day of the swing festival, high monsoon-time and the doll-battering fair. The monsoon sky, for days a dank pigeon-grey, had cleared and spilt runnels of foamy sun-drifts, crimson, primrose, saffron and violet. The August light fizzed, trees and bushes sizzling in a green blaze and the air polished as glass. Beni took Subuhi, veiled from head to foot, to the doll-pond fair.

It was a fair of the usual kind where you could buy bangles and trinkets and kitchenware and palm-leaf baskets. And special to the day was crunchy Bengal gram seasoned with tangy lime juice and spices, which Beni proudly bought for his girl and which she fell to, lifting her black veil expertly to one side. He bought her a palm-leaf bugle too as a joke and she promptly applied her pretty little lips to it and blew a trumpet blast into his ear, deafening him and making him jump. He bought her danglers and peanut candy and guided her to the doll pond where children had come with rag dolls and sticks. This centuries-old custom was one of the city's folk eccentricities. Rag dolls were made out of sticks tied crosswise. Two outspread arms, two scissor legs, a scarecrow thing. A head fixed atop, a foolish rag face. Then dressed in a skirt and a top and headcloth, ready for meaningless martyrdom. She was flung into the pond, flat on her back, and a crowd of howling children, roaring with rage, fell upon her, battering and bashing her sorry body with sticks, disemboweling her with fearsome, bloodthirsty shrieks. The pond turned into a graveyard for mangled dolls. The pounding went on and on, the howling mob of boys swinging their sticks in the air and thrashing the doll to shreds as it lay, a pummelled, ragged mess in the muddy water. The girls, the sisters, stood back with bagfuls of Bengal gram for the valiant heroes. It was a terrifying and disturbing thing.

No one more terrified and disturbed than Subuhi. Beni heard her gasp and, turning quickly round, was surprised to see her face twisted, sobs retching up her throat. It frightened him.

'What's the matter?'

'Let's go!' she sobbed. 'I can't bear this!'

Later, sitting in the tonga, her tears wouldn't stop. 'It was just a doll,' Beni reasoned. 'A wood and cloth and paper thing. It's just a custom.'

The shudders were beyond control. 'Their faces!' Subuhi shivered. 'The way they . . . they attacked the poor little thing. As though . . . As though they wanted to believe it was alive. As though . . . As though they made themselves into beasts because . . . because they were allowed to . . .'

He was not a man of strong imagination by any means but he had some glimmerings of what had agitated her. Beneath the hood of the tonga, he put his arm round her shaking shoulders and held her close. The support unnerved rather than fortified. She wept all the harder.

'I thought . . . I thought for a moment . . . if that was me, alone, lying there where the poor gudiya was . . . and dozens of men pounding away at me, cruel as devils . . .'

'That won't ever happen,' he said with strange surety in his voice. 'You forget whose gudiya you are.'

She lifted her tear-sodden face to look wonderingly at him. His face was shining with unaccustomed elation and his voice, when he spoke, held a tremble. 'You are . . . and always will be . . . my doll and nobody, nobody, will be able to hurt you.'

In the shade of the tonga and the dusk, they clung to one another like children huddled together, tasting some filched delight. Her veil flew over his flushed face, her lips flittered open as his mouth took hers in an overpowering clench. They closed their eyes. It was only a second, though it felt like an age, before the tonga-wallah clicked his horse and said something to it and they sprang apart.

He took her to see the tonga and ekka race but both were stricken dumb, moving stiffly as puppets. During the return ride back to the kotha they sat primly side by side, saying nothing.

Janki opened the back door and let them in. She was busy at her practice and had no time to waste. But through the corner of her eye, on her way up the staircase, she saw them pause at Subuhi's door. She saw Subuhi draw Beni in. And the door close behind him. She knew that Subuhi's roommate was away at a wedding performance. She went up the staircase, shrugging. It was none of her business and this was no place for squeamish disapproval. Still, he was her brother and she hoped he knew what he was about. And if it was love he'd found, she wished him well, she who knew, or thought she knew, all there was to know about love. She'd been well mentored by her music, the old compositions she sang that charted the changing map of a woman's mind, the grammar and notation of love, all its coded desires and the complex prosody of its plaints:

'Tu mat ja, gori, paniya bharan ko.
Prem ko jaal lagaaya hai.
Shyam Sunder ko marrhwa garaya hai . . .'

Maid, go not to draw water from the well.
A love-net has been cast for thee.
Comely Krishna has pitched his tent-post there . . .

Janki had for months sung her chants to love as her daily riyaz:

'Pun gun ke din chaar, sakhiri,
Apnon balam mohey mehngu,
Dher pun gun sona main dungi rupaiya,
Moti anmola,
Jo kuchh mangey sabhi kuchh dungi,
Balam na dungi udhar, sakhiri . . .'

The days for charity and merit are but four, my friend,
And my lover, he's costly to me.

Heaps of gold shall I give thee,
Money shall I give thee,
Priceless pearls aplenty,
Whatever thou asketh that shall I give thee
Sure,
But never shall I my lover lend,
For the days of love are numbered
But four,
My friend.

During the next three months Beni and Subuhi were mostly locked in, appearing only at mealtimes or on their way to the washrooms and bathhouses. Beni was spotted, sneaking in with jasmine garlands, leaf bowls of jalebis, pakowries and chutney. Which the mischievous girls snatched at, roaring with wicked laughter. They ambushed Beni and put a flowery turban on his head and marched him to Subuhi's room, beating brass platters with brass ladles and spoons, parodying a wedding procession. They ground up henna leaves and drew patterns on Subuhi's palms and their own, twittering like a thousand birds. They beat up an unguent of flour and oil and itr and water and plastered Subuhi's face with it. They strung up jasmines in a groom's veil and tied it on to Beni's ducking face, two of them holding his head straight despite his wriggles and pleadings. They mixed up the ceremonies of all the faiths they knew, held a Holy Book over his head as they circled his face in an arati with a lighted diya and a plate of jalebi and sherbet in mock welcome. They swirled their hands round his head and snapped their knuckles against their temples and pronounced him purified of the evil eye. They hid his sandals and wouldn't let him enter until he'd coughed up rupee and eight-anna bits for his 'sisters-in-law'.

Then they hauled out the blushing Subuhi. Brought garlands
of roses and playacted a shaadi. They sat the couple down to a
game of grab-the-ring-in-the-platter, presiding over the match
like a horde of crowing mothers-in-law and prompting the bride
and the groom not to let the ring be snatched up by the other,
else complete servitude in marriage would result. And when,
by one of those telepathic vibes that connect minds in lightning
decisions, neither of the two would grab the ring, offering it in
silent surrender to the other, they shouted: 'Aha! What have we
here? A pair of oh-so-nice Lucknow nawabs? You first, sir. Nay,
you. Nay, after you, sir. Nay, after YOU! Such love, oh dear, we
swoon, such love!' Then they sprayed rice all over the couple.
And when the two had managed to escape and bolted the door
on their laughing tormentors, the girls brought a dholak and sat
outside the bridal chamber, singing the bawdiest of bridal songs
in raucous rejoicing, celebrating the shy, tremulous secrets of
new marriage.

'Maza le le, rasiya, nayi jhulni ka!' A song which would,
in later years, become one of Janki's most popular numbers,
its innocuous words camouflaging the wickedest of innuendoes:
Enjoy, enjoy the pleasurings of a new swing, oh sensuous one!

And still naughtier songs, ancient as man and woman and the
land:

Ah, the monsoon-green groom doth come, fresh as new foliage,
Riding a saucy mare, comes he.
Oh learn, laddie, learn how mares should be ridden.
Don't let her throw you off, young master mine.
Saddle her well, and ride then, ride,
Oh, my monsoon-fresh one!

And Janki sang loudest: 'Khub khushrang bana hai yeh banna praj ki raat!'

And the girls chorused:

'Laddoo, peda, balushahi tikia tumhe khilobain,
Toshak, takia, lal palangiya tumhe sulaubain!'

There was something heady in the air as the intoxicated girls, drunk on their fantasies, shrieked in celebration, enacting a live dolls' wedding like grown children. The joke lasted many days and leavened many leisure hours. Even a box camera was arranged for a wedding photograph.

And that proved the turning point. Beni and Subuhi were herded up against the pillars of the courtyard, arranged in stiff ceremonial solemnity, Subuhi sitting decorous on a stool, Beni standing stalwart behind, baton in hand, like a valiant warrior. There was something in the way the little girl turned a little and leant into the warmth of him, something in the way the 'bridegroom's' protective arm embraced her thin shoulders, something in the look in their eyes that made the jokes turn edgy and the laughter cruel. For everyone knew, with or without a pang, that in the middle of the masquerade and the mischief there was something happening here, something heart-wrenchingly real, and it cut them to the quick.

Harmless banter changed to simmering contempt. For this couldn't be allowed. It was an obscene transgression of the rules of the kotha. As obscene as filling one's belly with delectable food in full view of a cage-ful of starving captives. Again, in one of those speechless turns of collective decision, a crusade emerged to put an end to the nonsense. They were sick of it. Enough was enough. Subuhi was a stupid creature and no good to anybody, they knew, but Beni, ah, he was a man and they knew too well what men were and how they should be worked on. They knew the extent of their power and were playfully keen to put their skills to the test with this lovesick oaf, this nincompoop Beni. It was the sheer sport of the thing and the smell of blood. And Shaheen the chosen one to execute the plan.

So when Shaheen, the same Shaheen who'd earlier been the object of Beni's devotion, smiled winsomely on Beni and said: 'Beni, my boy, do bring a hammer and some nails up to my room, will you? The latch on my window won't close and the window keeps flying open and the other day I was, you know, changing, had just lain my kurti and ghararas aside, when who should I see but a batch of wretched oglers salaaming me from the window across. That window's got to be fixed or the whole lane will be painting my bosom red!'

Whether the lane would or could is besides the point, but Beni found himself suddenly blest with unearthly visual imagination.

Obediently he fixed the latch on the latticed window and was just about to leave when Shaheen lilted across the room: 'Beni, my boy, and are you as good at hooking up bodices from behind as you're at hooking up latches?'

This was the woman who'd turned him down. And she was flirting with him. Pride ignited in Beni's bruised heart. Sullenly he fixed the hooks on Shaheen's bodice, noticing the heavy weight of her breasts lifting in answer to the pull on the hooks of the cross-hatched back-straps.

Subuhi saw less of Beni from that time forth and could not know the reason. Until the laughing kotha girls, of sheer kindness and concern for her well-being, thought fit to tell her.

'We hear, dear child, that your Beni has taken to chewing paan. That too straight from Shaheen's mouth. But don't you know? You don't? Oh really? Oh, we're so, so sorry. We wouldn't have dreamt of mentioning it, had we known. Don't think about it, dear. It's nothing, really nothing. These things happen, you know. Part of life.'

'We hear, Subuhi-child, that when Shaheen drops her odhni, no man can look away. You're young, you're pretty, but Shaheen, ah, Shaheen's got that extra thing to madden men. And now we hear it's Hasina too! Three to a bed, your Beni in the middle. Oh men! Everyone knows they carry their brains between their legs, that's really all they think and feel with. Hearts they lack.'

In her riyaz Janki sang:

'Kanhaiya naahin morey basko,
Shri Vrindavan ki kunj gali mein
Gwaalin sang atko . . .'

My Kanhaiya is out of control.
In some bower or lane of Vrindavan
He's stuck with some milkmaid lass . . .

The little girl sobbed into her pillow. Pushed Beni away, vainly tried to slash her wrists. Then Naseeban decided it was time to break up the tableau she'd designed.

She descended upon the girl, her voluminous silks rustling around her. She towered over the cot on which the little girl lay.

'Get up, this minute!' she thundered. 'Get up, I command you!'

The girl lifted herself feebly, sat up in bed. Naseeban laid hold of her bandaged wrists, turned them up and surveyed them grimly.

'Die, is that what you want, girl? For a worthless, feeble-headed, fickle fool of a man?'

Subuhi's tears began to fall. But Naseeban was merciless.

'What did he promise you? That he'd be there for you for life? That he'd look at none other? That you were the most beauteous thing he'd ever beheld? That you were angel, goddess, celestial fairy, queen of his heart?'

Subuhi hid her face.

'Know this, my child. It's the same script we've all heard, from some man or other. It's burnt into our bitter hearts. Ask any woman here. It doesn't mean a thing, believe me. One month in your bed and he's already looking around. That's the way, child. Learn it now, rather than later. Learn it early and learn it well.'

She laid her arm on Subuhi's tousled head, smoothed back her matted locks.

'Look at you,' she said. 'As pretty as a diamond in beaten gold. A prize for any king and twelve years old, all your life ahead of you. And you want to die for love, because this first big-lover of your little life has mounted the willing hips of another one? Where is your anger, girl? Where is your spirit? You're wounded, I understand. Then you go hurt yourself more. See these pretty wrists. But surely you're not as poor-spirited as this? While you pine away and go mad with grief he'll go exploring skirt after skirt. Is that fair? Why don't you return the blow? Let him get it where it hurts the most. His pride. I know what I am about, have faith in me, girl.'

Two days later a decked-up, bejewelled Subuhi received her first customer, a forty-five-year-old merchant princeling of the old city, and he swept her off her feet, by Naseeban's grace and favour. The night was such a success that he bid for Subuhi, paid Naseeban a handsome sum and sent round his phaeton to the kotha.

As the carriage began moving Subuhi glanced up, dry-eyed, and saw Beni's expressionless face at an upstairs window.

He appeared in Naseeban's chamber as she sat at her hookah.

'Begum sahiba,' he said, 'I must talk to you.'

'Do,' she urged, smiling faintly.

There was a wild look in his eye, a desperate boil in his voice.

'You planned this,' he hissed. 'This is all of your making.'

'What is, boy?'

'You, you married her to me! You've sent her away!' His words fell crumbling at her feet.

She turned her blazing eye on him. 'Don't talk nonsense, boy!' she spat. 'That was a game the girls were playing.'

'It was no game!' he shouted. 'It was no game for me. Or for her . . .'

'Enough!' thundered Naseeban. 'Was there a maulvi? Was there a pandit? Were there any ceremonies? Now be quiet and let's have no more of this fooling. And anyway,' she called after him, 'you a Hindu, an aheer at that, and she a Sayyad Mussalman. How can any marriage be?'

He swung round to confront her. 'It was no game for us, this I assure you. And you'll pay for this, I promise you. We were married, body and soul . . .'

'Oho!' she sneered. 'Married body and soul! Where was the soul then when the body lay wallowing in Shaheen's bed? Or Hasina's? Go away!' She rose to her feet. 'It's men married body and soul that make our kothas run. I can't stand them! They make me sick! They make me rich! Let me not see your face, boy, or I might do something I'll regret.'

Soon afterwards Beni found a job as a store supervisor in a grain warehouse in a distant quarter of the city.

'If I don't visit often, Amma, please do not mind,' he told Manki before leaving.

Manki inclined her head sadly.

Janki could say nothing. All this while Hassu Khan had been tutoring her on thumris and the many moods of a woman's love. Nayika-bhed it was called in the Sanskrit classics. There is the woman adorned in all her finery, waiting for her lover. There is the woman disappointed and yearning in her hour of separation. There is the furious one who will not have anything to do with her lover after a flaming row. And the one blazing with rage when she learns of her man's infidelity. Then the deep grief of the woman betrayed. The long, sad remembering of a lover far away. The leaping joy of journeying to his side. The knowledge of power when she has subdued and quelled. Love that forgives but forgets nothing. And the ever unrequited lonely thirsting of one without love. The thumris sang of love in its many ragas and rhythms, taught Hassu. Always a woman's aches. Seldom a man's. Of love that gives mortal injury, then seeks desperately to heal. Love that is craven and full of lies, forgetful and unfaithful. Love that is penitent and grieves over its fall.

This thing was not for her, never for her, thought Janki to herself. It had better not be. It was enough to sing of it alone.

10

Hassu had special news for Janki and he imparted it with much preamble and ceremony. From the pocket of his shervani he then produced an envelope which held a thick, folded sheet of elegant paper edged in gold with a fine illumination in green and red and embossed with a royal coat of arms.

'His Highness, Maharajadhiraja Bandhresh Shri Maharaja Sir Venkat Raman Ramanuj Prasad Singh Ju Deo Bahadur sends Ustad Hassu Khan his salutations and invites his assistance in this important particular, that Ustad Hassu Khan suggest the name of some songstress of proficiency and personality to sing at His Highness's Dashera celebrations following the Gaddi Pujan ceremony of the Royal House of Rewa. Every care shall be taken of the artist's comfort and for that of her accompanists and retainers and suitable remuneration shall be granted, in keeping with His Highness's pleasure and the performer's merit. His Highness awaits Ustad Hassu Khan's answer, well-assured of the quality of his choice and the fineness of his discernment . . .'

Hassu watched the play of expression on Janki's face. He saw her catch her breath and lift her gaze in wondering inquiry. He nodded.

'Did this come by the dak, sir?' she asked.

'His Highness disdains the common postal service. He has his own couriers. This was delivered to me this morning. What say you, bibi?'

Janki had no words.

'I've never sung before royalty, sir.'

'Not so. You have sung before the maharani of Benaras.'

'That was as an untrained child, sir. Not as . . . as a . . .'

'A finished performer? You proved yourself then.'

'No one judges a child severely, sir. But a . . . a songstress, a tawaif . . . I don't know what exactly I am,' she faltered, vexed.

'You are a musician, no more and no less,' said Hassu. 'And a very good one. And if Hassu Khan recommends your name you had better justify the ganda I tied round your wrist. You had better be not just any good musician but a surpassingly great one!'

There was such a ring in Hassu's voice that it brought a little shiver into Janki's throat as she bowed her head in deferential submission.

'And should you pass this test, daughter, then Hassu Khan can consider himself amply rewarded and can betake himself back to Lucknow or Gwalior, content in the knowledge that the ripe fruit no longer needs the bough.'

She looked up, stricken, as his meaning got across to her.

'I shall do my best, sir, to be a credit to your name,' she said quietly.

The first big question now was—how was Janki to be got up for the great event? There wasn't enough money to buy a suitable costume befitting an appearance before royalty. The girls offered their best outfits but Manki politely declined, finding them all a trifle tacky and over-garish and all too revealing of their low profession. Naseeban offered to alter one of her good ensembles but she was broad of girth and hip and shoulder, and taking in the entire flank of the dress wouldn't work.

An answer to the problem suggested itself as an inspiration in one of the girls' inventive minds. Why not go to a costume-lending store, the kind that theatre companies and vaudeville shows rented costumes from for the Ram Dal procession and pageant and other performances? This seemed a viable possibility and Manki and Janki returned from a costume store with a Begum Hazrat Mahal costume, suitably hemmed and tucked to Janki's measurements. A popular play had been doing the rounds in the United Provinces towns, *When Begum Hazrat Mahal Met Mallika Victoria*. A highly political play, written to coincide with the Indian National Congress's fourth session at Allahabad which the district administration had done everything to scuttle. There had been raids on the 'black town' side of the railway line and the play had been reinvented as a comedy *When Noor Jahan Met Mallika Victoria*. It did not matter that the two eponymous queens had lived three centuries apart, for neither actors nor audience were overly inconvenienced by history. The old Hazrat Mahal version was still performed in private gatherings. But its wardrobe came in hugely handy in Janki's case. At Rs 12 a day the outfits, four of them, would see Janki through several public appearances at the Rewa durbar. And if Janki was privately mortified by this circumstance, she more than made up for it in later life by indulging in the most expensive clothes that money could buy in the city of Allahabad.

The next big question was who should accompany her. It was decided that Hassu would not go. Neither would the ailing Makhdoom Baksh, who was her usual sarangi accompanist, nor Rahim-ud-din Mian who played the tabla best with Makhdoom. This time Ram Lal Bhatt and Ghaseete would be her accompanists

on the tabla and the sarangi. The two cooks Bhaggu Mian and
Baddu Mian were also included although it was altogether likely
that the hospitality of the royal court at Rewa would dispense of
their services. For good measure Jallu Mian, the accountant, went
along, as a sort of events and legal manager. This was to be her
standard troupe for years to come.

The twenty-ninth scion of the Solanki–Chalukya clan of the
Baghel Rajputs, Maharajadhiraja Bandhresh Shri Maharaja Sir
Venkat Raman Ramanuj Prasad Singh Ju Deo Bahadur ruled over
the princely state of Rewa. Tiny as it was, Rewa was the largest
independent state in the province of Baghelkhand with a British
Resident stationed at Satna. The Bombay–Nagpur Railway touched
its southern reaches but Janki went by buggy, making a stopover
at Manikpur and at a dharmashala at Maihar where she prayed,
like that other great maestro, Alauddin Khan, to the goddess at the
Maihar Temple. The pale ochre dust of the Gangetic plain changed
to rocky, scrub-coloured wasteland and then the road to Jabalpur cut
through undulating stretches of red earth and softly humped hillocks
growing steadily greener and more densely wooded until at the end of
a day and a half it was carving its way through thick forestland.

It was an exhausting ride, the horses thirsty and slow, despite
their frequent restings. There could be no travelling by night. The
thugs of this region had long been eliminated but the extensive
forest was the haunt of tigers, the famous tigers of Bandhavgarh.
Janki was glad that the durbar performances were still a good two
days away.

She was to spend a day resting in the palace and witnessing
the Dashera festivities. The royal Gaddi Pujan, the annual throne-
worship ceremony, was the high point of the celebrations. All
valiant Kshatriyas cleaned, polished and worshipped their swords
and shields and lances and guns on Dashera morning, the day

of Goddess Durga's victory over the demon Mahishasura. What more suitable day for a king to worship the prime symbol of his pledge and power than his gaddi, the throne? In the evening there would be illuminations, fireworks, a royal procession, a banquet, followed by the nightlong music soirée ending at dawn.

The Baghela rajas belonged to the Agnivanshi line—the fire-lineage clan—and were Gurjars in stock, descended from the original founder of the Anhilwara dynasty of Gujarat who, in one of those great cycles of migration, had travelled eastwards and settled down in the wooded Baghelkhand region some time in the early sixteenth century. Tigers were their royal insignia, their first king having adopted the title of Vyaghradev, Lord of the Tiger.

As Janki's troupe went up the rocky road, the medieval fortress swam into view, a grainy, earth-brown sandstone edifice surmounting a hill, the citadel of the princely state of Rewa left incomplete by Salim Shah, son of Sher Shah Suri, and occupied by the Baghelas in the sixteenth century. It took them a good hour and a half up a steep incline to draw up before the thick, massively carved pillars of the main gateway overlaid with its heavy carved lintel which had, emblazoned centrally on its crest, the royal coat of arms, two tigers, their tails curling up in stylized flourish, holding between their paws the forked flag of Rewa. Beneath a cusp of carved scroll the words which Janki, craning out of the buggy window, identified as 'Mrigendra Pratiwandtam Mapayut', which later inquiry informed her, translated as 'Beware the Tiger'. From the tallest flagpole fluttered the swallow-tailed red-and-green-banded flag of Rewa.

They alighted in the first forecourt where liveried retainers awaited them, and were conducted to their quarters, Janki's in a separate wing in the palace's premium guest chambers and the accompanists housed in a different section of the palace.

It was a large octagonal chamber, a corner suite. It was done up in the best of High Victorian decor. Vast mahogany bedstead with brocade canopy and velvet drapes and a lofty carved headboard with the tiger crest in low relief. Massive mahogany chest-of-drawers with heavy branched candle stands on either side. A tall, lace-draped mirror.

Floors carpeted in the green and red colours of Rewa. There was a life-sized marble Cupid drawing his bow on a wrought-iron pedestal and across the room a vast painting depicting a lavish Mughal hunt. A large mock fireplace, tiled in onyx and, on the mantelpiece, a row of porcelain dogs, shepherdesses, milkmaids and tiny bonneted and crinolined, knickerbockered, doublet-and-hose clad English figurines. The windows had a triple row of velvet, brocade and lace curtains. There was a bathing chamber attached with a deep, sunken marble bath. But for her convenience a copper bucket and pot had been thoughtfully arranged on a marble shelf. In a closet adjoining were large wardrobes of Burma teak with full-length panels of Belgian glass. All the chambers had something Janki had not seen before—tulip-shaped crystal lampshades hung from the ceilings with real electric bulbs that cast a mellow, buttery light at the flick of a black-and-white switch on the panelled wall behind the polished folding doors.

A soft, deferential voice spoke up.

'My name is Rukhsana, Baiji, and I have been entrusted with your comfort.'

Janki turned and saw a pretty, mild-faced woman, pleasingly dressed in pearly silk, a silver-spangled odhni draped over her head and shoulders.

'Thank you,' murmured Janki.

'Should you require anything, I am here to answer your every command. To help you dress and bejewel yourself. To oil and arrange your hair and henna your feet and hands. I am trained in all the ministrations that noble ladies require. And my companion Rabia here shall carry your instructions to the royal kitchens and provide you with whatever you may wish to enjoy.'

'You are most kind,' said Janki. 'I only ask that my accompanists and attendants are looked after.'

'They are provided with every comfort, Baiji, and lodged in the east wing of the palace.'

'How may I communicate with them? I'd like to practise for a few hours tomorrow morning.'

'A chamber for riyaz has been made ready in advance, Baiji. Your attendant, Banwari Singh, shall be posted outside your suite at all hours to carry messages and to conduct you to the practice chamber, should you wish to be led there. And now, Baiji, we leave you to rest.'

It seemed to Janki, as the door closed after them, that a sort of whispering flutter overtook her temporary retainers, a stir that impalpably communicated itself to her on the other side of the heavy shisham doors.

She laid her headcloth on the dresser, took a turn round the room, paused at a window to look on the pavilion and steps leading to a rock-hewn lake outside, then had barely taken in the view when there sounded a polite knock on the door again. She opened it to find a tall, suave princely form, in achkan and churidar pajamas, turban and tinsel-edged cummerbund.

He uttered a gentle cough.

'Maharaj Kunwar Sri Kundan Singh Baghel at your service, Baiji. As master of the estate and kinsman to His Highness Sir Venkat Raman Ramanuj Prasad Singh Ju Deo Bahadur, I bring you greetings and come to ensure that every comfort attends your gracious visit.'

She could not divest herself of a misgiving. There was in his eyes a look of such disconcerted probing, an expression of such peculiar unease, completely at odds with his smooth words, that she took a long moment to reply.

'I am grateful to His Highness for extending this welcome to me and I assure you that I find myself in comfort far exceeding my humble needs.'

He bowed his head in a slight, deferential gesture and said, 'It is our pleasure, Baiji.'

She saw him turn and stride away down the carpeted corridor and there seemed to be a certain haste in his movements that mystified her.

The mystery was soon cleared when, half an hour afterwards, there sounded yet another knock on her door, a knock more urgent and restless than the last. When, sighing, she opened the door, she saw an elderly man dressed in a cream silk dhoti and ornate, brocade tunic, who appeared to be in a state of severe agitation.

He uttered no formal speech of welcome but stood in front of her with hands clasped in a pleading namaskar.

'Baiji,' he said, 'I come to beg your forgiveness. A great mistake has been committed, for which I am engulfed in more shame and misery than I can utter.'

She could make nothing of this and stood silent in surprise.

'I am His Highness's chief steward, Munshi Manohar Prasad. I was given the assignment of arranging a durbar soirée on the occasion of our Dashera Gaddi Pujan, and to this end I approached Ustad Hassu Khan of Lucknow and he suggested your name. But a most terrible error has occurred, Baiji, and I shrink from uttering it. So base is it and so unworthy, but I have no choice . . .'

'Please don't hesitate,' she said. 'Speak your mind.'

'It is like this, Baiji. His Highness is fastidious and disposed to quick displeasure. He has a fine ear for music and also ... also a ... finer eye for a woman's appearance.'

'Oh, I see,' said Janki, instantly grasping.

'Whispers reached me, Baiji, that ... that you ...'

'That I am unpleasing of face?' completed Janki calmly.

She understood that stir among the retainers, that visit of the princeling and his strange, disturbed air. She understood that this moment had been waiting for her all her life.

'You shame me indeed, Baiji,' he whispered in misery. 'But such it is, and I tremble to imagine His Highness's reaction.'

'Now that I am here,' said Janki drily, 'I put myself at your disposal. Tell me how I should help you out of this troublesome situation, short of changing my appearance by mantras or magic.'

'Is it possible . . . is it asking too much, Baiji, that another songstress be arranged, someone more ... more personable?'

He was in a cold sweat, ready to sink through the floor.

'I wish that were possible, Munshiji, and I'd do anything to be of assistance, but I regret that I am the only singer in my group.'

'It's much too late to engage another,' he fretted, distraught. 'The journey alone . . . Ah, you cannot imagine His Highness in a right royal rage. Ah, the ignominy of it! And the sorrow and mortification I feel before you ...'

'I think I have a solution,' she said coolly. 'You'll have to do with my poor self, sir, whether you like it or not. But you can tell His Highness that this songstress lives in strict purdah and never goes unveiled. Tell His Highness she begs to be allowed to perform from behind the privacy of a curtain. Beseech him, as a gracious accession to a lowly artist's prayer. Can you carry my appeal to him and bring me his answer?'

He looked at her, uncertain. 'Go,' she prompted. 'There is no other way.'

In an hour he was back, relief writ large on his harried face. 'His Highness grants the lady's prayer and says he shall gladly oblige the vagaries of an artist if her art warrants it. Oh, Baiji, how can I thank you enough!'

'It is no matter. Go, arrange for thick curtains, Munshiji.'

The accidental grace of invisibility and the mock solitude of the curtained dais afforded such soaring spaciousness of play to her voice that Janki felt her body fall away as she became her song. She travelled through nebulous realms of mind lit with the light of the subtle worlds. After dusk when the sun has sunk there rises an indeterminate unease of the soul, caught between movement and fixity. To render it she sang Raga Shree. Then, in the second watch, between nine and midnight, with the progress of the evening, came the hour of longing consecration, and she slipped into Shuddha Kalyan, following it up with an expansive thumri in Jhinjhhoti. When the night had thickened, her voice rose in a Kaafi bandish. Navigated itself smoothly away towards a regal Darbari Kanada. And finally settled into an esoteric Malkauns trance. On her curtained platform she relaxed completely. With no eye contact and no witnesses, alone with her music, she sang to herself, appeasing every flourish, indulging every flight, expressing every whimsy, in deep converse with the ragas. And so through the remaining praharas of the night to the tremulous stirrings of a dawn raga, Lalit, before coming to rest in a resonant finale with a glowing Bhairavi.

After the climactic tihaii, the three-spiralled coil of notes that ended her performance, she awoke from her spell when a rude disturbance broke in. The curtain was abruptly flung aside and a massive brocaded form stood before her. His Highness Samrajya

Maharajadhiraja Bandhresh Shri Maharaja Sir Venkat Raman Ramanuj Prasad Singh Ju Deo Bahadur, maharaja of Rewa. If the maharaja's seventeen-gun-salute princely state had the motto 'Beware the Tiger' it had to be said that his personal expression did much to enforce that warning. She felt the piercing ferocity of his riveting gaze bearing down on her from eyes that brooded over an aquiline nose and the dense upsweep of a bushy fan-beard. Whether this was a consciously cultivated expression of ancestral authority or a natural inheritance of feature, it was hard to tell. He stood there, poised to open fire, an elaborately robed and turbaned form, as she rose to her feet, bowed and namaskared him.

'So this is the mystery unveiled,' said the Presence. 'The coy lady who might wilt under a king's gaze, so she chooses a purdah to protect herself?'

'Begging pardon for the presumption, Your Highness. But my purpose was entirely in His Highness's interest.'

'How so, lady?'

'I feared lest the sight of so drab and disfigured a countenance might trouble Your Highness's pleasure in the music.'

It would be too much to say that Sir Venkat Raman Ramanuj Prasad Singh Ju Deo Bahadur flushed because he was incapable of flinching or flushing before a mere woman, but there came over him a moment's pause, an instant of kingly deliberation between chivalric denial and gracious concession. Then his right royal pedigree prompted the proper courtly rejoinder: 'What countenance, lady? I saw none while you sang and I see none now while you stand here before me. The faces I saw were the beauteous forms of Malkauns and Lalit and Bhairavi and Darbari, and they came to me gracefully unveiled as never before.'

'Then what more can this lowly one ask, Your Highness?'

'Baiji,' he said, 'how may I measure your worth?'

'My lord,' she replied, 'an artist is measured by her seerat, not her soorat, by her art not her face. My soorat is worth nothing, my seerat I leave you to judge.'

'Ah, do not make mock of me, Baiji . . .' And this time Sir Venkat did indeed come close to flushing. 'Just allow me to thank you with this small acknowledgement of your worth, which far exceeds anything that I can offer.' He took off the rope of pearls he wore round his high-collared bull neck and put it in the large silver platter that his Munshi stepped up with. It held a velvet pouch and a jewellery box.

Later in the day the Munshi brought a missive to her chamber. He appeared to be in a state of great excitement.

'Madam,' he exclaimed, 'you saved my face, else no curtain on earth could have concealed my shame!'

She smiled and said nothing as she reached out to take the gilt-edged envelope.

'His Highness wishes it be made known to you, madam, that he invites your permanent residence at the royal durbar of Rewa which you shall adorn with your stellar performances as court musician . . .'

She unfolded the gilt-edged letter and read:

His Highness Samrajya Maharajadhiraja Bandhresh Shri Maharaja Sir Venkat Raman Ramanuj Prasad Singh Ju Deo Bahadur wishes to impart to you the information, which you may or may not already possess, that the royal house of Rewa has been patron to many great maestros of music, one no less than the illustrious Tansen himself, durbar musician to His Highness's royal ancestor Raja Ram Chandra of Rewa,

before the peremptory decree of Emperor Akbar summoned
him to take his place at the Mughal court at Agra. That His
Highness wishes to confer on you this signal honour reflects
credit no less on His Highness's munificence than your own
abilities as an artist of which His Highness is now, and shall
remain, a fervent admirer.

She thought awhile, read the letter over, then turned to face the
Munshi.

'Tell His Highness I am honoured and shall ever be indebted
to him for his grace and favour, but I seek his indulgence in this
regard. My music thrives in the soil of my beloved city, Allahabad,
and without its air and water shall lapse that taaseer that charmed
His Highness. I beg to be excused.'

On the morning of the day that Janki was to start on her
return journey to Allahabad, she received an invitation from the
maharani to have tea with her in her private suite.

The queen's chambers were furnished in an eclectic European
style, predominantly Louis XV, with chaise longues, claw-
footed tables, enamelled and découpaged sideboards. To Janki's
unpractised eyes it all seemed strange and sumptuous. On a
carved wooden swing sat the slim young queen, swaying ever so
slightly backwards and forwards in tiny, languid movements. She
wore a rich, velvet jacket, puffed and padded on the shoulders
and frothy with fine, flounced lace down to the elbows. She wore
a Benaras brocade saree of deep purple. A large gold pushpahar
with multiple chains and studded medals hung round her neck.
Heavy, encrusted gold bangles weighed down her tiny wrists. Her
head was decorously covered by the anchal of her purple brocade
saree which swept down her back like a royal train. In her lap slept
a little white kitten.

Janki bowed and was warmly offered a chair drawn up close to the swing. The kitten blinked, opened its pink eyes and yawned and the maharani patted it to sleep as a mother might pat to sleep a baby or a little girl her doll.

'I thank you, Highness, for this invitation,' said Janki.

'I thank you for accepting it.'

'How could I ever refuse your kindness?'

'I want to tell you how deeply you touched my heart with your singing that night. Even His Highness, the maharaja, was profoundly moved.'

Janki bowed her head.

'You know how it is—a fierce tiger, they say—and who should know about tigers better than we here at Bandhavgarh—will grow still before a bulbul when it raises its voice and sings. I instantly gave you a name—excuse the liberty.'

'It is my honour and pleasure, Highness.'

'I began calling you Bulbul, and Bulbul you shall be in my mind.'

Janki smiled. 'It's a pretty name. I wish I could be more worthy of it.'

'Oh come, we've all heard of your soorat–seerat repartee. It's doing the rounds in palace circles. No, the reason I wanted to meet you is that I wanted to confer with you on a matter of some . . . some eccentricity. Do you think, if tiger cubs are made to listen to classical music of a peaceful kind, it might leave an impression on their nature?'

Janki started. Her eyes darted to the tiny white kitten on the maharaja's lap.

'Tiger cubs?'

The maharani smiled and ran a gentle hand along the little creature's snowy back.

'Yes, indeed. This is a specimen of our famous Rewa tiger. Found only in our hills and jungles, nowhere else. His Highness shot this little one's mother—last week when he went out on a shoot with the English Resident Sahib from Satna. The hunting party brought back the three little cubs. Look here . . .'

Janki's eyes followed the maharani's pointing finger and saw, beneath the round onyx-topped table, a rattan basket, painted white and covered with a thick cotton circular mattress on which slept two more kitten-like cubs.

'One male and two females,' said the maharani. 'I trust no one with their care and keep them in my own chamber, and I plan to breed them for the palace and more, soften their natural ferocity from infancy by making them listen to music and play with kittens and pups.'

'It will be an interesting experiment, Highness. I have heard many accounts of what music can do. My ustad told me how he heard Ghulam Rasool sing Raga Bahar on Khwaja Basat Sahib ka Tila in Lucknow. The words of the bandish were: "Rangraliyan kaliyan sang bhanwar karat gunjar / Bolat mor, koyal ki kook sun hook utthi." The words were about the cuckoo and to everyone's surprise a cuckoo came flying out of the trees and came to rest on Ghulam Sahib's turban. And remained there as long as he sang! They say that a singer named Solki could charm herds of deer from the woods, could make dry branches sprout leaves. Tansen too, I have read, could perform the same feat, charming deer out of the woods with his Todi. He draped his pearl necklace on one of them and let them vanish into the forest, after which Baiju charmed them back with his ragini Mrig-ranjini.'

'Amazing!'

'And I have read that Baiju could calm an elephant in musth, melt stone and drive his tanpura into it and challenge Tansen to melt it again and extract his tanpura.'

'How very very interesting,' exclaimed her hostess. 'Tansen must have learnt much of his music in Rewa then. Won't it be possible? It shall test whether we're creatures of native disposition or made into what we are. I hoped you would accept His Highness's invitation to stay on at Rewa. Then we might have worked something out. But you must return to Allahabad and we respect your choice.'

Some mischief prompted Janki to say, before she could bite back the remark: 'Mrigendra Pratiwandtam Mapayut, Your Highness, is a warning that struck terror in my heart. One tiger was enough for me to face, that night. But several, even if cubs . . .'

The maharani looked closely at her, then threw back her head and tinkled out a pretty peal of laughter.

'Do you mean him, His Highness?'

Janki looked acutely embarrassed. But the maharani, far from taking umbrage, showed every sign of responding to the jest. 'Tigers are an acquired taste, my Bulbul Baiji,' she said, lowering her voice. 'As tea is. I took time to accustom my palate to their flavours.'

Janki had never drunk tea. No one she knew drank tea though some of the better class of visiting gentry at Naseeban's kotha had mentioned the new fad. Lately tongas with large Lipton boards astride their hoods and down their flanks had begun moving up and down the Allahabad streets at a fixed hour daily, distributing hot tea for free, and people had begun running up with pots, pitchers, jugs, dekchis, whatever they could lay their hands on, to receive the sweet, unfamiliar brew that was fast beginning to appeal to native tastes. But the tongas did not come down Naseeban's lane so Janki found herself behind the times and confessed it.

When the bearers entered with the silver tea service and tray-loads of scones, English muffins, pastries, pretty cucumber and watercress sandwiches and a large array of nuts, Indian sweetmeats, Lucknow kebabs and crisp croquettes, the maharani handed the cub to an attending retainer and, rising from the swing, led Janki to the ivory-inlaid table on which the repast had been laid out. Waving aside the bearers, she chose to pour out the tea personally, the fragrant steaming brew bubbling rosy against the delicate porcelain cups.

'It's a good smelling leaf that's allowed to soak in hot water,' she explained, adding a silver spoonful of sugar, then a bit of milk from the ornate silver milk jug. 'A Chinese thing actually though the angrez companies are growing it all over Assam and in some places in south India too, I hear. See if you like it.'

She passed the cup and saucer across the inlaid tabletop to Janki, who waited for the maharani to prepare her own cupful in due deference to form, before taking a sip. It had a strange taste.

'How do you find it, Bulbul Baiji?'

Janki wondered how to describe it. Not overwhelming, definitely. Sweet, scalding, with a strain of woodland breath mingled somewhere in the taste like a surprising and pleasantly alien modulation to a note that turns the raga round completely.

'It's . . . It's like the "re" of Raga Poorvi,' she said at last.

The answer obviously caught the maharani's fancy for she sank back into her velvet-tapestried Louis XV armchair and looked long and reflective into Janki's face.

'You are a complete artist, Bulbul Baiji,' she said softly. 'A real one, I see, and I'm honoured to know you.'

'You embarrass me, Highness.'

Bade Ghulam Ali Sahib, I have heard, standing in front of an aquarium of fish, watched their movements, enthralled, exclaiming how they darted about in exact consonance with the raga in his head. Art converts all experience into the medium it works in. Janki did it all the time.

The maharani told Janki, 'I have a villa in Allahabad which I visit very often. I hope we shall continue meeting one another.'

'With the greatest pleasure, Your Highness.'

'I shall look forward to our meetings then. Maybe you shall sing to my tiger if I bring him along.'

By now Janki felt comfortable enough to risk the jest again.

'Which one, Your Highness?'

And when a delighted smile lit up her hostess's face she knew this new association had exceeded the borders of courteous protocol and entered the realm of personal friendship.

That friendship was to last. As was the nickname 'Bulbul' that the maharani of Rewa gave her, taken up later by the maharani of Darbhanga as well. As was also the strange question the maharani asked—can a savage tiger change its nature if it is brought up listening to serene music? Janki answered that one a lifetime later in one of the driest, saddest verses she wrote and set to tune in Raga Vilas Khani Todi, the raga of mourning.

When Janki rose to go two retainers stepped up, holding between them a large, silver platter on which lay two beautifully wrapped parcels which, from their shape and size, Janki guessed to be some rich fabric and a jewellery box. She wondered what the correct form would be, in this new unclassifiable friendship, whether to unwrap the gifts as some codes of courtesy prompted or to merely offer conventional thanks. Her problem was anticipated by the maharani who said, 'A small token of my regard, Bulbul Bai. Open them when you reach home and if they agree with your choice of colour and design, a small note to that effect will more than gratify me. Also, it shall initiate a correspondence between us which I shall greatly welcome.'

'You overwhelm me, Highness,' murmured Janki, touched.

The buggy trundled behind its horses through a muslin rain, drumming hoofs crunching shingles of the moonlit path underfoot. An inlay of puddles glittered on the hilly track. The words came unbidden to her as though a voice spoke up in her head: 'O Janki, the heart is a sheltered cavern that the rain may not breach. Even so, this spray slants in and fills my goblet with pearls . . .' She felt herself exclaim with the ecstasy of the visitation, and repeated the lines to herself countless times till she had committed them to memory. There could be no writing them down till she got home, for neither holder nor inkwell formed part of her luggage and Jallu Mian, the accountant, was travelling in the buggy ahead, but the resonance which the lines stirred in her brain filled her with an excitement she had never known before. The leaves of the trees meeting overhead swarmed around the buggy, like clusters of gemstones iced with light, and Janki's mind, caught in a flashflood, overflowed with the poems ahead.

11

When Janki and her entourage reached Allahabad they found the kotha in a state of uncontainable excitement. Not only on her account, which was to be expected, but on account of an altogether unforeseen and stupendous occurrence. Naseeban had married. Yes, the bitter-hearted, scathing-voiced Naseeban had had a secret beau, none other than the corpulent seed and oil trader, Mewa Lal Kalwar, who had been a frequent visitor to the kotha and who, other than accept gilloris of paan and glass goblets of angrezi liquor from the hospitable girls, had been content to lean back on the bolsters in the dance chamber and close his eyes wearily against the demands of trade and tiring labour. It was even giggled among the girls that his manhood was a myth, that maybe he only liked to look in through door chinks and keyholes and paid Naseeban for that dainty experience.

But now the astounding truth struck them speechless at first and then provoked an outburst of shrill commotion that Naseeban did nothing to order into disciplined silence, so detached had she overnight become from the affairs of the house.

She received Janki with businesslike cordiality.

'I was waiting for you.'

'We all were,' added Manki, beaming with pride.

'No, I more than others,' said Naseeban, brusque. 'Because, by now, you alone may be in a position to accept my offer, considering that from all reports you have given a good account of yourself at the Rewa durbar and have come back richer of pocket than anyone else in this house.'

'How do you know?' asked Janki.

'Word travels fast, girl,' said Naseeban with a mysterious half-smile. 'Faster than your buggy horses or these new steam engines of the angrez sarkar. My offer to you is this: I'm about to wind up this establishment. All these girls and lane-boys and musicians and cooks shall be out of a job and will have to disperse. But should you be interested in buying the place, complete with all its employees and appurtenances, I shall be happy to hand it over to you.'

This was something neither Janki nor her mother had anticipated and it took a long moment to register.

Then Manki said slowly, 'Let us think it over, Bua. Janki is only just back and we need a day or two to consider your kind offer.'

'Take a week,' said Naseeban with newly mellowed allowance. 'I shall give you first priority among all other parties.'

Janki unpacked the maharani's gifts, carefully deferring the decision. The parcels held a heavy length of maroon kimkhwab, dense with gold embroidery, and a companion length of gold-trimmed silk for an ample gharara, the ensemble to be completed by a voluminous length of maroon-and-gold odhni to crown her elaborate coiffeur and cascade down the shoulders and swirl in rich gathers across the basque and hips. Yards and yards of opulent silk awaiting the artistry of a master dressmaker. But the smaller parcel outshone the first. A velvet jewellery case containing a finely wrought gold-and-ruby choker with large ear pendants to match, hung with delicate ruby clusters.

These gifts were by no means excessive, going by the standards of the times. The way singers were feted at the princely durbars is the stuff of fantasy. There have been times when maharajas have dressed as waiters and waited at tables at which star performers dined, as the raja of Himmatnagar did in honour of Faiyaz Khan. When Ustad Nasir Khan happened to be singing, with rare brilliance, a composition in Gaud Malhar which contained the words: 'Motiyan meha barse'—it's raining pearls—Maharaja Jaswant Singh of Jodhpur sent for a large platter of pearls and had them rained on the artist as he wove his way through the monsoon raga.

When Janki displayed the maharaja's pearl necklace and the pouch with the hundred gold mohurs Manki sank slowly into the only chair in the room. She trembled. Her voice, when she managed to speak, was threaded with sobs. 'What did you sing to them, my daughter?' she managed to say at last.

Janki lifted the jewellery box and the pearl necklace and held them out to her mother.

'For you, Amma,' she said.

But Manki's reaction was surprising. In an instant her speechlessness fell away and disdain kindled in her voice.

'Jewels, bitiya? I have no use for gold and jewels, don't you realize? There's no depending on them. No guarding them. Have you forgotten that treacherous one, Parvati? The one who took all my gold into her safekeeping and then made off with it? Who sold, yes, sold, us to Naseeban and reduced us to this! No, beti, these baubles are good for just one thing, as far as you and I go. To buy a roof over our heads—our very own house. And this I most strongly advise you—buy houses, daughter, buy land, fields. Remember this all your life. Buy things that perfidious people cannot steal from you so long as there's court-kutcherry in the country and a sarkar to enforce the law. Do not be overfond of gold and gems, which any highwayman or false friend can make off with.'

That Janki took her mother's advice to heart is witnessed by the fact that over the years, as her singing career soared, she came to own many villas and bungalows and tenement buildings all over the city. Even a whole village some miles out. Some properties she earned as largesse from wealthy patrons, some were mortgaged and subsequently acquired by her when the cash-strapped owners found themselves insolvent. But Parvati's betrayal long ago had consequences that turned Janki into a substantial real-estate baroness.

As of now she sagely decided to accept Naseeban's offer and within a fortnight of her return from Rewa she found herself the patroness of a kotha with Manki acting as the manageress. The marvellous dress material that came from her new friend, the maharani, initiated her rise in fortune. For it was sent to the brocade and tailoring firm of Manni Lal Anandi Lal Gotawale, designer-experts in exclusive costumery and destined to be Janki's dressmakers for years to come. Fine clothes became her passion and her trunks and wardrobes overflowed with extravagant ensembles created by the Chowk Gangadas firm. An uninterrupted succession of orders continued, one outfit no sooner delivered than another ordered. Whether this interest in rich apparel had its roots in those dark days in the kotha kitchen when her mother had made her dress in rags to put off possible clients is open to speculation but Janki Bai became famous for her sumptuous clothes, each more expensive than the last and each the product of fine craftsmanship from a firm that catered to many royal houses of Benaras and Avadh and even beyond.

The house, now theirs, was remodelled to their taste. To the three-storeyed structure were added stables, a gari-khana, dens for domestic animals, external bawarchi-khanas. The two main reception chambers for guests were her pride. One was designed in a modern style with a couch, beautiful easy chairs, tables, a silver bedstead, large mirrors, colourful pictures on the walls. The other had a floor arrangement with costly carpets, chandeliers and beautiful urns.

When that first brocade outfit came round from the dressmaker's, Janki in her new role of kotha-patroness, tried it on for the benefit of the excited girls in whom the recent changes had unleashed strange new flutters and fantasies. Naseeban's marriage had left them all of a twitter for marriage, and a settled home was an enduring dream they played out in wishful thinking, in delusional temporary liaisons with a floating population of clients, in jest as with poor Beni and Subuhi, and in bitter parody. But then, coming close on the heels of one sensational episode was Janki's meteoric rise to wealth and eminence, and this suddenly activated a possibility so far utterly unimaginable.

They fawned on Janki, envied her, sought to draw her out, teased and complimented, turned sycophantic or satirical, striving to reinvent a relationship that had incarnated in a new and unfamiliar avatar.

'Ai hai! Here's Noor Jahan come again!' cried Hasina as Janki tried a gracious, gliding gait in the silk gharara. Hasina bowed low in mock salutation and brought her fingertips to her brow in a slow, choreographed triple salaam.

'Who's this? Mallika-e-Hind?' said Shaheen with a laugh. 'Is she the Indian empress or the angrezi one, our Mallika Victoria, for sure. Except for the colour of her face!'

They brought an armchair and made Janki sit on it in regal parody of Empress Victoria on the marble pediment at the Company Bagh, putting a stick in her hand and an orb of knitting wool in the other hand. Which Janki, playing along, used liberally to thwack the ones who came close, wielding the sceptre of kotha queen on deviant members, the room ringing with laughter. Naseeban's parrot, Munne Mian, now Janki's, perched on the arm of Janki's chair, head cocked and eye bead sliding in devilish free play, as it tried to mimic the girls' voices.

Then one of them ran to Naseeban's now-empty room and came back with one of Naseeban's hookahs.

'Here, Mallika,' the girl laughed, 'I've always thought Mallika Victoria's appearance might improve with a hookah in her hand instead of that school-memsahib's bottom-whacker stick! Take this, Jankiya, and let's see you turn into our new Naseeban Bua!'

Janki did. And did it again. Taking a deep drag, little realizing then that this hookah habit too was something that would endure.

Like that voice in her head. It spoke up at odd times, when she had dozed off on long journeys, by buggy or by train. Or when she hovered between sleep and waking in the small hours. She had the sensation that her mind sang in ragas unknown to human voice, in notations impossible to chart, ragas shiningly coherent and familiar, that hung about her conscious mind for a while before fading, like itr from a garment. Sometimes there were even words, clear as day. They followed an ongoing and passionate monologue which was the inner argument circling the sum of her existence. They argued on behalf of the music that had laid siege to her life, and they argued on behalf of all those things that lay forfeited in the service of her art, and in the crossfire of claims were born many plaints, many challenging shades of questioning. This art, her captor, her saviour. To breathe free of its tyranny, to forget it for a week, a day. Not to cede so large a portion of my soul to it. For surely there were other summonings, hankerings of the body and the heart, that this austerity of art had peremptorily exiled.

Draw away, oh steal away, Janki, flee this master that you serve,
the voice transformed to an inner singing. Find that other life
that hides its face and submerges itself in deepest dreaming. But
what do you amount to, O Janki, in that unlit hour of flight? Your
soul scatters in the night, knowing not where to turn. Trembling,
I strike a match and hold it to the wick of a melody anew. My
affrighted heart seeks its home, the song. For no other love does it
know and no other home.

The voice took on the lineaments of her questioning self,
interrogating her song:

> I asked the black one on the mango bough
> Tell me why you sing, O koel.
> Looked she at me in amaze and said,
> 'Sing? What's that, sister?'
> 'This thing you do,' spake I.
> 'What thing,' asked she, 'that I do?'
> 'This flute you play in your honeyed throat.'
> 'Sister, I know not what you mean,' said she to me.
> 'I live my life, that's all I do.'
> 'Alas, I envy you,' says Janki to the bird.
> 'To live is to sing, I wish 'twer so with me.
> I need something to live by, live for,
> And that's why I must sing, know you my meaning?'
> 'No,' said the bird and I envied her more
> For her freedom from song
> Even while she sang.

Janki awoke to a finished song spelling itself out in her mind. For
a moment the miracle of it did not register. Was this a thumri,
forgotten and babbling in her sleep? Then she realized it was not.

Her mind had written its own thumri, broken free of its moorings in her waking life. As one cotton wick, nuzzling another, lights up two oil lamps, so did Janki's music ignite amorphous words in her secret ear. She heard the words happen, quite without intimation, a smattering of clouded sensations coming together in startling configurations. Ghazals and thumris alighted on her mind like birds coming to rest on a branch, preparing to flare into flight. And then one nebulous dawn, she heard the diamond-hard refrain, every word clear-carved: 'Naghma-sarai ke siwa kehti hai sher Janki / Ahle-kamal dekh lein uska hunar alag-alag.'

It was a command more than a pronouncement for Janki. The dam burst and the floodwaters of verse washed over her days and nights.

There was the inconvenience of holder and inkwell, especially on long journeys, as there is the inconvenience of the body and its obstructions. She tried to memorize the words that serendipitously waylaid her, she tried to set them to tune, so that she could hold on to them till she reached some place where they could be set down in pen and ink. Then Jallu Mian gifted her the strange implement of record-keeping that he had discovered lately, the Faber pencil! A slender stick of painted wood with a vein of graphite encased in its tunnel as is the wick in a candle. She took a childlike joy in its strokes, and the way it was sharpened to a point, as was the voice, intent upon a high note of the highest octave. And which, uptilted, like its sister, the candle, lit a trail of inspired song across the leaves of her notebook, setting the pages on fire:

Do not abandon the desire to see me,
If the heart craves life then do not give up the beloved's door.
The heart called out to him but he did not hear.
Do not abandon me to loneliness for the sake of others.

The joy of meeting can be enjoyed even in imagining.
O, my grieving heart, hold that joy in yourself.
God willing, he will come as the Messiah to heal me.
O grieving heart, have faith in your cries.
The cup-bearer of creation's grand first gathering says this to me:
Do not abandon the intoxication of the oneness of God.
Give me pain, suffering, misery,
O cruel one, do not abandon this old habit of yours.
The heart declares: Do not give up love's 'khayal',
A good tune, a good rendering, do not abandon these.
It is these things that have brought you renown,
O Janki, do not abandon the love of the ghazal, the love of the
    couplet.

It seemed to her that the pencil pierced its way through all those
clenched denials of her proscribing heart, defying the censorships
of practical wisdom, speaking what lay even beneath the crust of
dreams, discovering conflicts of allegiance and shocking her brain
into unsettling and forbidding admissions, even as it fled into the
safety of the known and the chosen. Her writing hand ranged
from unknown lover to unknown God, through the terrain of real
aloneness and conventional grief and found its nervous way back
to the song that was her sanctuary:

In temples and the kaaba I searched for him
The desire to find him was so great.
Who knows what's to happen to my failed desires and hopes?
The grief I have, none else has.
If my destiny allows we shall meet.
Why should I wander aimlessly, seeking him.
What avails hankering in a brief life?

Only grief comes from this hankering
Ere this how many misfortunes have I known.
But then, again, the same hankering returns.
From experience of the world I know the intelligent do not hanker.
This has no fruit, no result.
So there is this hankering for my heart in you.
O Janki, do not get involved at all.
He looks like a flower, in truth he is thorny.

All too often she found it slack and cheap and this enraged her and she threw it away and wrote again, inflecting each syllable as she would at her morning riyaz. And as her hand and brain grew accustomed to this new possession, as her fingers closed upon the pencil that held the reins of this stampeding stallion, mastering its power and instructing its speed, she embarked upon a story about a woman named Janki, a conquering creature she imagined into being out of the depths of her qualified memories and her self-authenticating cravings. This is how she described herself:

In appearance of medium height with a well-proportioned face, large eyes, wheaten complexion, mild manners, with a sweet voice and a slightly swinging gait, the scars of knives on her wheaten face. But these scars, after the passage of time, have somewhat faded, though some remain. Yet her overall physiognomy isn't much diminished. In quick-wittedness, which is a necessary distinction in this profession, she is a complete adept. To any witty, bantering comment, she can penetrate its inner folds of meaning and with such frankness make rejoinder that she can amaze, making it seem as though her answer has been previously rehearsed . . . In hospitality and in soft-spokenness, it is generally observable that those people

who are talented in some way are always deficient. Till today
nobody has heard her speak ill of a contemporary artist or
praise her own self. Whenever there is mention of a singer, she
always speaks well of her and remembers her or him with good
words. Whenever a cultured person comes, she rises to her feet
to welcome him and makes him take a proper seat and remains
standing as long as he does not sit. Paan, hookah, itr, elaichi,
cigarettes, sherbet, etc. are offered. From those who come to
hear her sing from great distances out of genuine shauq, she
does not charge a fee. Free of cost, she entertains him for an
hour or two. But the listeners pay her musicians something on
leaving, which is their right, because they have no other way
of earning money. Often when famous qawwals or excellent
musicians or wandering performers arrive, it is difficult for
them to leave without dining. On these festive celebrations,
prominent citizens are also invited and as situation demands
foreign visitors are also favoured with her hospitality.

She built up her story of self, stroke by stroke, believed it and
enacted it, her tales of victory, her tales of wealth:

Where at the start of her career her mujra fees were Rs 15, it
is said of her, who could say that a time would come when her
local mujra fee would be Rs 150 and in the nearby cities it would
be Rs 500 per day and at distant locations would be Rs 1000.
So in recent years this is her usual fee for her mujra. Travelling
expenses are extra and include several tickets for second-class
travel and the rest for inter-class travel, and ten or twelve people
usually accompany her. Her first contests were with famous
courtesans at the house of Janab Rai Bahadur Lala Ram Charan
Das Sahib who is one of Allahabad's exceedingly select and

wealthy raeeses, at a function related to one of his close relations, and the contest was with Vazeer Jan Karnal and Bi Bandi Patna. Then at several locations on numerous occasions, at Nasik with Sunder Moradabad, then at Calcutta, at the wedding of Babu Omkar Mull Seth Sahib's son, with Gauhar Jaan and Mallika Agra, at Muzaffarpur with Zohra Bai, at Kanpur and Allahabad with Vidyadhari Benaras and Chanda Amrohiya. At Allahabad itself with Husna Benaras and at Khaga in Fatehpur with Laali Jaan Delhi, at Bahraich with Achchan Bai Lucknow. But in comparison with them all, her own fans and connoisseurs of music, if they did not rate her higher than her rivals, neither did they rate her less. Rather, they generally cast their vote in her favour . . .

She wrote of rajas, maharajas, zamindars and raeeses. Of the Dashera festival at the palace of the raja of Bettiah where she sang 'Hathwa laagat kumhailai ho rama, juhi ki kaliyan', of the marriage of the son of Sir Sultan Ahmad, the famous Bar-at-Law of Patna with the daughter of the Nawab of Patna where she and Gauhar sang in that massive pandal, a veritable tent-township that had been created in a field for the elite of the city for the music that was performed from morning till night and then all through the night till the next morning! Of the marriage of the son of another wealthy lawyer of Patna, Kulwant Sahai Sahib, later a judge of the same high court and how the function was held in a field known as Guru Prasad's Son's Haata where she sang 'Rum-jhum badarwa barse' in Gaud Malhar. She wrote of Rani Dhandei of Jaunpur, her great friend, whose favourite was, incredibly, renderings of her sozkhwani. And how the connoisseurs used to say: 'Janki Bai ke kantha-swara mein misri ki dalia ghuli hui hai.' She wrote in a voice speaking to herself but also speaking to a future that she was confident would give her a place. This diary habit had come to stay. It lasted till well into the third quarter of her life, that delusional spell of ascendance that she lived through, in a permanent flush of gratification when her life had arched to its ultimate achievement, or so she believed, when her first record was played over a loudspeaker in Chowk Gangadas and a jostling horde of Ilahabadis converged on the scene, pouring into the square in wild abandon, till all you could see was a sea of heads more numerous than on the day of the Patharchatti and Pajawa Ramdal processions. She wrote of her wealth, her resounding fame, her enlarging properties. Seventeen houses in the city, a village of the name of Mauza Khizrpur in Nawabganj Pargana, bought from the sarkar, a rest house near Rambagh railway station, designed with shops in front and a garden behind, a place of shelter, both dharmashala for Hindus and musafir-khana for Muslims built on land dearly bought and thoughtfully constructed. A bagh planted in her extensive Rasoolabad property. And to oversee it all the meek and pious Munshi Sayyad Ghulam Abbas Sahib, the highest-paid functionary in her ménage of twelve, whose duties included court-related jobs, pursuit of cases, collection of rent, management and development of her estates, maintenance of her several houses and also looking after the horses and cattle.

For she had become one of the city's wealthiest celebrities and she wrote of her acquisitions with matter-of-fact pride in her judgement and her affluence, using an officious third-person mode with engaging simplicity.

She spoke of her triumphs and her trophies. The shields she won, a silver and a gold from the gramophone company, the silver one from the Raebareli exhibition and the gold ones from the Bharatpur Durbar, from Hyderabad, Sindh, from the Rana of Nepal. The watch she was gifted by Babu Omkar Mal Seth of

Calcutta. The Allahabad Police Department loved her, for she sang at each Janmashtami at the Police Lines, not for the several gold shields that they gifted her several years running but for the thrill, unconfessed but interiorly known, of being the guest of honour of a government department to which that assailant from long ago, the one who'd ravaged her looks and her self-esteem, had belonged. From time to time she picked up what she perceived to be her soul-theme, her truth, choosing the right notes that fitted her mood of self-confirmation. Paragraphs of applause to fill the empty chambers of her heart.

'A list of the places where she performed, the durbars to which she was invited, is difficult to make . . . Wherever she went she proved herself,' she declares with a grandiose flourish, innocent in its sweep. 'It was hard for anyone to compete and get the better of her. Let everyone accept that she never met failure anywhere.' It sounds just a semitone removed from the truth but it was all factually true. But still there was a missing note somewhere and she sought it. She sought it in music and in the noisy downpour of verse that filled her life. And at the conclusion of each spell of expression she knew what she had dared not approach. That poised, conventional, stylized poetry impostured the love she had never known, addressed a beloved who was imaginary and a faith she did not belong to, she a Hindu sweetmeat-seller's daughter. But the thread of pain running through it was real, uttering a void that threatened to declare itself all too transparently to her denying will.

But I have advanced her story far ahead of those times when she first started fashioning it for posterity. Let me revert to the days of her early verse and her reckless outpourings, uncontained by moderation or self-critical caution. Her audience applauded the powerful voice she sang her compositions in rather than the verse itself, though poets flocked to her soirées with verses of their own. There was Shah Aminuddin Sahib 'Kaisar', there was Mir Ali Ebad Sahib, there was 'Neesan' Sahib, and Maulvi Azizuddin Sahib 'Afsar' and Mir Akbar Heseen. And though Neesan and Afsar were not very frequent visitors, Kaisar Sahib, despite his advanced age, came often, leaning on his stick, and sat for hours, reciting his own verse and listening to hers. It was he who suggested to her that she meet Akbar Sahib Judge Ilahabadi and seek his opinion on her verse which needed, then more than ever before, a 'murshid' to mentor it and a mirror to reflect it.

12

So one day, after much consideration, she dressed and veiled herself and ordered the phaeton and the gariwan, wrapped the loose pages of her book of verse in a silk cloth, and went to call on Khan Bahadur Sayyad Akbar Hussain Sahib Judge Ilahabadi. She went like a European memsahib, with a visiting card and all, a little affectation of the angrezes that she had adopted for the style it conferred on her ceremonial arrivals. Unlike the European visiting cards she had seen, her own were ornate, with flowers and birds and musical instruments illuminated in the gilt embossed borders. She remained in the phaeton, mysterious behind her veil, with Samina fanning her gently and whispering over the tinsel-covered basket of rosy Ilahabad guavas that she carried.

Judge Sahib was in and would she drive to the veranda, murmured the chowkidar at the gate of Ishrat Manzil. At the veranda she was received by a court chaprasi dressed in long white tunic, cummerbund and turban, who salaamed and accepted, on a silver salver, the visiting card that she produced out of her English handbag. She was ushered into a moderate-sized chamber with book-lined walls, a number of well-tapestried sofas and armchairs and a central takht which dominated the room. Janki sat herself down on the sofa opposite and made Samina sit a little to the side on one of the armchairs. A court retainer appeared, bowed and drew open the curtain at the window. Then he hesitated and drew it close again. Guessing his disquiet, Janki covered her face with her headcloth in decorous modesty. He bowed and left.

In a few moments a tiny, half-stooped figure shuffled in at a shambling pace and, heading for the central takht, sat himself down on it. He had a lined and shrivelled face, like a dried-up raisin. In his hand he held her visiting card. His eyes flashed when he spoke and on his wrinkled face appeared an impish twitch as he ran his eyes up and down the card, turning it this way and that. His eyebrow lifted, his lip curled: 'Janki Bai Ilahabadi,' he read with a comic inflexion in his voice. 'The koel-voiced songstress herself! To what do I owe the honour of this visit?'

'I encroach upon your time, Judge Sahib, on the advice of Shah Aminuddin Sahib Kaisar.'

He seemed to be convulsed. With grief which subtly converted itself to laughter. 'Ah, Kaisar!' He shook his head in woe. 'What new terror will he unleash on me? With friends like Kaisar, who needs enemies, and now do but consider this latest assault of his on my hapless head. A mujra miss sahib at the house of Akbar! Ill fame follows me everywhere, madam, but never this kind. And a mujra miss sahib with a visiting card, Allah be praised! She signs herself Janki Bai Ilahabadi and I sign myself Akbar Ilahabadi. Posterity is sure to get us mixed up, so Akbar the poet might be remembered as a nautch lady and Madam Janki might be remembered as a Judge Sahib!'

She was nonplussed, offended. Then she saw he was laughing in diabolical glee and grew bolder: 'Your fame, Judge Sahib, is enough to drown out the sound of our drums and sarangis.'

'It wanted but this, lady, I stand demolished. Let me lament my sorrows. One evening in Simla it was, where I was on holiday,

an angrez came to call on me. What is your tareef, sir? I asked.
To which he answered: They call me Auckland Colvin. I shook
all over. Excellency, to what do I owe this grace and favour, that
you should light up my humble hotel room with your presence?
I am in a mood for verse, he said. My rapture knew no bounds.
I flew to entertain him. I recited verse after verse, poured him
goblet after goblet of wine. On my ninety-ninth verse when he
was well in his cups, as the angrezes say, he raised his hand and
said: Enough, sir poet. You are good and glad I am to have taken
the advice of my khansama and come to your door but now I
must sleep. It was a cold night and much too snowy for him to
go back to Peterhoff so he went to sleep on the sofa in my suite.
When morning came he awoke and asked: Where is she, the
lady who sang to me last night? I humbly presented myself. No
songstress, sir, I said, abashed, a mere poet. He rubbed his eyes.
You mean, you are not Raunak Bai Ilahabadi? he asked, puzzled.
No, sir, quoth I, I am only Akbar Ilahabadi. It seems Raunak
Bai was staying in the same hotel. Do you mean to say you are
not Auckland Colvin? I demanded to know. Auckland who? he
asked, still more puzzled. You can judge for yourself, lady, my
own trials. Even this elegant visiting card, this excellent paper
herald, outshines the hoarse heralds of the courts where I ply
my rude trade to earn my bread! For truly this dainty angrezi
hazirnama is worthy of that infamous couplet I once tossed off:
"Sheikhji ghar se na nikle aur yeh farma diya / Aap BA pass
hain, banda Bibi pass hai."

'I should thank you, then, sir, that you did me the honour of
emerging to receive me,' said Janki drily, 'if that is indeed your
practice when a visiting card is sent in to you.'

'Take no notice of me, madam, when I begin tossing around my
verses. They swarm about me like locusts. As Amarulkaiss said, when

I reach out to catch one, I find myself clutching two. A despicable habit. And do not think I scoff at your card but only at the way we are turned into gibbering monkeys aping the sahib and his ways: "Kya kahoon isko main bad-bakhtiyar nation ke siwa, / Usko aata nahin ab kuchh imitation ke siwa."

'Forgive me, Judge Sahib,' she retorted. 'Meaning no offence to you and may you not think me presumptuous but I beg you recall how Amir Khusrau first sought permission from Nizamuddin Aulia to be ushered into his presence. He made up two couplets in his mind that addressed Nizamuddin, saying: "You are such a king whose power can change even a pigeon on a cornice into a falcon. A poor beggar has come to your door. Do you allow him to enter or should he go back?" I beg you recall what Nizamuddin said to him. A little later a servant had appeared and recited two couplets written by Nizamuddin, which said: "In the arena of truth, if a true man stands, let him enter. But if the guest is nasamajh and nadaan, then let him return the way he came." I assure you, sir, that I am neither nasamajh nor nadaan and a truer woman never stood before you. Were it possible for me to transmit my appeal for an audience in thought, and were it possible for you to convey your permission in like manner, sir, no angrezi card, no herald or town crier might be needed, but as it stands you must hear me and try me in your court with clemency, milord, considering that you and I are guilty of the same crime. Only you are seated in the judge's lofty chair, holding my fate in your hands, while I stand trembling in the dock.'

He had quit his goblin mask and was attending to her words with gravity.

'What crime be this, madam?'

'I speak of poetry, sir.'

That seemed to provoke a violent reaction in him. Irritation suffused his face. 'A poet, madam? A woman poet?' There was a sting in his words. 'No doubt you spend your private hours spilling tears and ink on the passing of beauty and of love. But I am mourning the passing of an entire civilization.'

'And I, sir, am celebrating its kindling,' she said softly.

'Poetry is a long and arduous training,' he said.

'As music is, sir,' she put in.

He resented being interrupted. 'Hear me out, madam, before you commence your twitterings. Forty years of writing lie behind me. At nineteen years I was assigned a test—to compose 200 trial verses. At twenty-one I went to my first mushaira . . .'

'By that age Ghalib had almost written an entire diwan,' she murmured, to his greater annoyance. She resented his supercilious manner, his playful mockery, and had begun enjoying provoking him with tiny barbs of her own.

He glared at her. 'What be your age, madam? No, it is from curiosity about the arts you practise, not any amorous inquiry, let me assure you.'

'I am old in suffering, if not in years, sir.'

'Tush, a woman's cliché.'

'By no means, sir. For every year in a man's life, a woman knows full three years' worth of living. Enough to learn the art of poetry, I make bold to say.'

He testily desired to know whether her verse was, like her card, in angrezi. And she could not resist teasing him with the meek confession that, yes, she knew angrezi too and wished she had written verse in it too. And she had studied Hindi, Persian and Urdu as well. She said it in the abject manner of a criminal admitting to a long chain of serial crimes that he had committed and had now been cornered into confessing.

He swore under his breath. Then he drew up his tiny form in imperious majesty on the takht, as though he was about to pronounce sentence, and launched into a vigorous diatribe. 'Jannat, they say, swarms with beauteous virgins, bibi. But do you know what jahannum must be to my imagination? Beauteous women—thousands of them—writing verse in English with—whatsitcalled, perdition take it?—ah, fountain pen—under rows of electric bulbs and getting their trash, their kambakht poetry printed in that sarkari rag, the *Pioneer* . . . "Kyon koi aaj hari ka naam japay? Kyon riyazat ka jeth sar pe tapay? Kaam wah hai jo ho governmenti. Naam wah hai jo *Pioneer* mein chhapay." I am not against women getting some sort of education, no. But as I wrote somewhere: "Taalim ladkiyon ki zaroori to hai magar, khatoon-e-khana hon wah sabha ki pari na hon."

'I regret to say, Judge Sahib, I have not been brought up to be a lady of the house, a khatoon-e-khana, but only, to my shame, a pari of the gathering. But I do wish I had written in English,' said Janki mischievously. 'Maybe I should have sent it to the *Pioneer* and maybe Knox Sahib would have put in a word with Allen Sahib and that bright young whippersnapper—Kipting or Kipling— might have edited it . . .'

He was sarcastic. 'No doubt,' he pronounced. 'But you are unlike other women. You are an exceptional lady, a mujra miss sahib. A free lady who performs for Knox Sahib and Allen Sahib and all these benighted sahibs. Unburdened by the cares of cooking and keeping house.

'Khuda sent us these sahibs in their shining buggy
To deliver us from ignorance, widow-burning and thuggee.
So if your belly be empty and your shirt in tatters,
As long as Bartania rules, do you think it matters?'

By now she was incensed, charged up. She kept silent. She had uncovered her face and he noticed, with a witheringly critical glance, her kajal-lined eyes, her bright-red lips, the flash of her nose stud. A homely creature, grotesque with her made-up nautch-lady face, her pretensions to learning, her claims to writing poetry and her encroachments upon his valuable time. He lashed her with another stinging verse, designed to put her in her place:

'Wah, her high-heeled shoes, her wristwatch, her bag,
A British mem is here, no Hindustani nag.
Put aside the paan box, pick up that lipstick,
No stick to smite a dog, but to plaster the mouth slick.'

She had had enough. She let him have it. 'A woman and write verse, ah, a courtesan?' she said bitterly. 'Whoever thought of a mushaira for women?' Then she tossed her impromptu verse in his face:

'I stir no pot, no cradle rock.
No hearth do I tend, Judge Sahib, do not mock.
Allow me, sir, to write a verse or two,
Although my business is to sing and my trade to woo.
It's all to be laid at the service of milords,
The ones who hold our destinies, the ones who wield the swords,
But for every song that for a man does languish,
Grant me some lines for my secret soul's anguish.'

He seemed to be withholding judgement, his gnomish countenance weighing the question. There was a long pause. Then he said, very slowly, as in a courtroom, 'Granted.'

She bowed her head and salaamed him. And produced from Samina's custody her sheaf of verses tied in their silk cloth. She laid it before him on a table he drew up. He had weak eyes and he had gone suddenly very gruff, very crotchety. He called for his spectacles. The retainer appeared with them. He signalled for more lights to be switched on. He signalled for sherbet. He put on his glasses and asked for another light, muttering to himself: 'Barkh ke lamp se ankhon ko bachaye Allah / Roshni aati hai aur noor chala jaata hai.'

Then he leant forward, squinting at the first verse on the first page:

Nala dile majzoon ka rasa ho nahin sakta, yeh kaam bajuz
    hukme Khuda ho nahin sakta,
Ulfat teri dil se mere ja hi nahin sakti, nakhoon se bhi gosht juda
    ho nahin sakta.
Hai khana-e-dil mazhare ansare ilahi—rutbe mein koi usse siwa
    ho nahin sakta,
Zahir mein alag dono hain batin mein mile hain, mashookh se
    ashiq to juda ho nahin sakta,
Uljha hai kisi kakule pencha mein mera dil, yeh murghe giraftar
    riha ho nahin sakta.
Ai Janki khaliq ki paristish hai badi cheez,
Patthar ka jo but hai wah Khuda ho nahin sakta.

He peered at the small letters of her Urdu calligraphy, shaking his head, frowning, before he said in a puzzled voice: 'This is strangely familiar, bibi. Where have I heard these lines before?'

'May the offence be forgiven, sir, but this stanza is modelled on one of your own. Permit me to remind you.'

She recited from memory:

'Mazhab kabhi science ko sajda na karega,
Insan uray bhi to Khuda ho nahin sakte.

Azrah-e-ta-alluq koi jora kare rishta,
Angrez to native ke chacha ho nahin sakte.
Native nahin ho sakte jo gore to hain kya gham,
Gore bhi to bande se Khuda ho nahin sakte.
Hum hon jo collector to wah ho jaye commissioner,
Hum unse kabhi ohdaabra ho nahin sakte.'

'Oh, ah, yes, I do remember it,' he said, visibly mollified. 'Did madam set it before her as she wrote? I'm afraid I make a very peculiar model.'

'On the contrary, sir. Your verses are like kamrakh chutney that awakens the palate and sets it tingling. Unlike the sugary syrup of other poets that sticks to the throat.'

'Ah, spoken like a woman at last!' He smiled his goblin grimace, his eyes twinkling. 'Only a woman would use this bawarchi-khana trope.'

'If it please milord to think so, far be it from my intention to disabuse his mind.' She smiled.

'But you have, my lady, written a woman's poem. Where mine dealt with religion and science, with the despair of defeating the angrez, you have turned the stanza on its head and written of love and God.'

'You think much of the British, sir?' she asked.

'Think? I am their servant, bound hand and foot to their benighted sarkar till the day of qayamat! All I can do is write verses, more shame to me, madam!'

'Laughter punctures the powerful, sir. You do well.'

But he was dressed in a shervani of fine British serge and his carpet slippers were covered with tweed. Her eyes rested wonderingly on them. He noticed her glance, divined her thought and felt compelled to explain: 'My son, Syed Ishrat Mian brought these slippers for me when he returned from vilayat. I have to regard his feelings too, you understand. But look you, madam, at the carpet these slippers tread on. No firangee thing. The finest Kashmiri. At my lowly feet Bartania and Hind meet.'

'And one walks all over the other,' she remarked.

He seemed to like her riposte, for he broke into applause. 'Wah, madam, that calls for a verse! Ah, here it is: The feet of sahibs cannot bear Hind's taaseer / They wrap them in tweed for a carpet from Kashmir!'

It was her turn to applaud, though she found his verse silly. Then her eyes fell on the ticking clock on the wall, and she rose from her chair, apologizing profusely.

'Judge Sahib has graciously conceded me more time than I deserved,' she murmured. 'I should be leaving now. Before going, I beg leave to consign my book of poems to his custody, with the humble hope that he may some time glance through its pages and, if possible, instruct me in their improvement . . .'

She was surprised that he readily agreed. But added a stern demand: 'With pleasure, madam. But bear in mind that the British sarkar pays me a salary for the time I spend in its khidmat. I expect you to do the same.'

'How so, sir?'

'Give me a song, lady,' he said. 'That I too may boast an equal standing with Knox Sahib and Allen Sahib.' He grinned his devilish grimace.

'I shall do so, and more.' She smiled. 'I shall sing you one of my own compositions, something I have sung for no one.'

The song she sang was in Raga Malhar, a verse she had written recently:

'Every mercy my Maula confers upon me,
Every blessing and thoughtful sign of reward,

I count it as I count the beads of my rosary,
Tremble and bow down at the feet of my Lord.
Lest for every single mercy from heaven's amount
There is in hell an equal count
Of sorrows awaiting me, equal to my peace,
For such, it seems, are destiny's fees,
The abacus of fate must be counted with care,
Give me only as much fortune as my heart can dare.'

He was silent as the song ended. Then he said, 'My ustad, Waheed Ilahabadi, used to say that the two things a poem needs are sheereeni, sweetness, and sanjeedgi, gravity. This poem of yours, madam, has both and in ample measure.'

Someone had entered the room from the veranda. A tall, slender man of middle age, very personable in his black shervani. He stood beside the door till Akbar noticed him and signalled him to be seated but noiselessly, which the visitor did. By the time Janki's eyes fell on him she was well into her song, and for a moment her voice shook in self-conscious uneasiness and her voice grew tense, introducing an added stir of emotion to her lines, which only served to lift her song to an elated pitch of utterance.

'Well, Haq Sahib,' Akbar greeted the visitor, 'you see me engaged otherwise than you are accustomed.' He uttered a croak of a laugh.

'So far as I can see, pleasantly,' said the visitor in a bemused but deferential voice.

'I have been honoured to receive the famous Janki Bai Ilahabadi in my poor home, Haq Sahib,' said Akbar, 'and I am loathe to let her go.'

'I do not wonder,' said the visitor. 'Never mind me, Judge Sahib. My business is not pressing and I can wait. If I may?'

'You will have to ask the lady, Janab,' quipped Akbar. Turning to Janki, he questioned most playfully: 'What say you, Baiji? Shall we allow him into our mehfil?'

Janki was unaccountably flustered. 'It is not for me to say, sir,' she said. For an instant the usually composed Janki had been rendered speechless.

'Then, stay, Vakil Sahib, since the lady has no objection. For with women you know as well as I, when the decree is nay, the meaning is aye, when the answer be evasive, consider it persuasive.'

Suddenly Janki was desperate to get away but Akbar had queries about music that her song appeared to have kindled.

She spent the next hour discussing Raga Malhar with him, its many forms and shades. Megh Malhar, Sur Malhar, Gaud Malhar, Jayant Malhar, Ramdasi Malhar, Birju ka Malhar, Meera ka Malhar, Mian ka Malhar. She told him of Tansen's contribution, the kanhda-ang, the andolit or wavering gandhar. The story of the Gujarat courtesan who was given to dropping her nose ring into a well and then singing Malhar to bring on the rains until the waters of the well brimmed over and her nose ring appeared. The story of Meera, Naik Gopal's daughter, who made the waters of the Indus flow upstream with her Malhar. She sang snatches of Mian Shyam Rang's famous composition 'Aaye badra kare kare' that he'd sung for Muhammad Shah Rangila. For his part he told her of the article he had read about how Helmholtz had taught himself to hear the pitch of incredibly high frequencies, the ultrasonics, which were known to create fog, smoke and rain. Haq Sahib sat, quietly listening, in engaged silence.

It was almost an hour later that she left. To the basket of guavas that she had brought him as a gift he quipped, his eyes twinkling with roguish merriment: 'I used to say that this city holds nought but Akbar and guavas, madam. Now I must allow that it holds Janki Bai too. Khuda Hafiz.'

But when she asked if he had a telephone he crowed: 'My misfortune it is, Baiji, to need one. Ummeede-chashme-murowwat kahan rahi baqi / Zariya baton ka jab sirf teleephon hua.'

13

Hassu, on one of his visits from Lucknow, brought the tantalizing news that the angrezes had invented a talking machine. 'You shout out your song, loud enough to rouse the dead in their graves, into a conical, bugle-like thing. Your bawling voice makes a needle go round and round and it cuts grooves on—whatsitcalled?— ah! Zinc or wax, I'm not sure which. Their ships carry off your voice like the farishtas bear away your rooh—to their karkhanas in Germania, and there they are pressed into flat, round plates the size of a medium-sized thali, only made of shellac. You put that on another flat plate, like you put a pot on a hob, and you wind up the contraption with a handle. And wah! You can hear your own voice! You hear yourself sing and at the end you hear yourself bellow out your own name: "My name is Hassu Khan." Or "My name is Mian Shyam Rang." Or "My name is Tansen." Except that neither this Hassu Khan nor that Mian Shyam Rang nor Tansen would surrender to the indignity of reducing their khayal to a niggardly three-minute cheez!'

But though his brother Haddu Khan had first refused to have anything to do with the infernal instrument and had cursed it with brimstone and fire, it had survived and thrived, and he'd had to relent. A Gaisberg Sahib and a Hawd Sahib had recorded hundreds of songs by Calcutta singers—Miss Gauhar Jaan,

Miss Sushila, Miss Rani, Miss Binodini and also a few men. Records and phonographs had begun finding a market in Calcutta, advertised by British manufacturing firms like Western Trading Company, Harold and Company, T.E. Bevan and Company. There were even some Indian ones like Dwarkin and Sons and M.L. Shaw. They'd been selling cylinders and phonographs for houses like Pathe, Edison and Columbia. But the giant among them all was called GTL, short for the Gramophone and Typewriter Company Limited.

It was a stirring experience to be able to hear your own voice that way, thought Janki. Onstage, during riyaz and during mehfils, you generated the song, birthed it, you lived its breath and heartbeat. To watch it from afar, delivered, to be able to hold on to it, to be able to return to each note's immaculate, irreducible moment, was an unimaginable prospect. She broke the news to Hassu that she too had recorded for the Gramophone Company he spoke of. She played him one of the first recorded songs. He sniffed, shook his head.

After a discreet interval she telephoned Akbar Sahib to fix up another meeting where, she explained, she could enjoy the slings and arrows of his criticism of the poems he might have had the generosity to peruse. He bawled back at the top of his voice, almost deafening her, that she was welcome on the coming Sunday when the district court would be closed and the sahibs resorted to their churches to redeem their sins and avert their entry into jahannum. She asked why he found it necessary to shout. He answered, cursing the Satan-begotten instrument, black as its progenitor, the telephone, that he, Akbar, was not Janki Bai Ilahabadi whose voice was said to carry all the way from the Police Lines to Rasoolabad. She replied that his voice had the power to condemn a man or to acquit him, as Khuda's voice could. He answered with a bristling couplet: 'Speak not to me of Khuda, Baiji: Rakabiyon ne rapat likhwai hai ja ja ke thane mein / Ki Akbar naam leta hai Khuda ka is zamane mein!' She laughed and responded with an impromptu couplet of her own: 'Kiski jurrat ki Judge Sahib ko koi giraftar kare? Jinki zabaan se har daroga, har thanedar dare.' She heard him chuckle with merriment, then he said: 'I shall await your august presence at ten on Sunday morning, Baiji. Itwar ko dus baje aapke aane ki muhurat hai, Baiji Janki jinki door-door tak shohrat hai.'

And that's the way it started, this remarkable comradeship of wit and repartee, stanza and song between Janki Bai Ilahabadi and Akbar Ilahabadi. On the appointed Sunday she was gratified to find that he had gone through all her poems and was primed up with scorn for some and grudging approval for some.

'This, Baiji, that you call your *Diwan-e-Janki*, has all the promise of an unripe mango on the bough, fragrant and sharp, but it awaits a good summer storm to release it from the branch and fling it on the bruising cobblestones of life.'

'What good a scarred fruit, sir?' she asked.

'Only a turbulence of nature or of fate can deal the wound that educates the pen. You would not reveal your age the other day, Baiji, when I asked. Time is what these verses need. I spent . . .'

'I do remember—forty years,' she put in. 'Must I wait forty years for the fruit to ripen, sir? When like Aurangzeb's beloved, Hirabai, I would much rather leap into the air and pluck the mango on the bough than wait for it to fall into my lap?'

'Then, madam, pickle your unripe fruit in the spice of affectation and convention and hope your *Diwan-e-Janki* does not sicken and mould over in the fullness of time. For this I do predict: neither a Diwan-e-Khaas or a Diwan-e-Aam is it going to be . . .'

She started laughing at the Diwan-e-Aam pun.

'Your own poetry, sir, is both khaas and aam,' she observed. 'You excel in both, so far as I can judge.'

'Well said.' He beamed. 'Different compartments of the mind, as in these benighted trains that the angrez has brought us. Some of my poetry travels in the second class and some in the first class. Much of it travels intermediate.'

A tonga had driven up, horses' hoofs clopping on the stone flags without. There was a rustle and stir of the curtains, a movement, and someone entered the room, gently inclined his head and salaamed Akbar Sahib, and turning in her direction, salaamed her as well. She started. It was the intruder of her earlier visit.

'Ah, Abdul Haq Sahib come again!' greeted Akbar heartily. 'I might have known. I might have guessed.'

'May I make bold as to ask how and why?' Abdul Haq had a deep, suave voice.

'Your appointed hour was five in the evening. What magnet draws you here at ten?'

Abdul Haq smiled mysteriously. 'Urgencies of a case, huzoor,' he intoned in a low, bashful voice.

'Can you perchance have forgotten that Baiji was to call at ten and your own appointment with me was at five? Come, come, this senile Akbar is not so far gone in foolishness as not to know what brings you here, in such unholy haste, at ten! I see that I have underestimated you, Haq Sahib. I knew you to be a man of the courts. But that you are as subtle in paying court comes as a surprise to me.'

Janki flushed, quite out of her depth. Abdul Haq acknowledged Akbar Sahib's witticism with a gentle bow and a laugh.

'Let us then assume that it is music that is the magnet.' Akbar lifted his eyes to gaze solemnly at a fixed point above the skylight, his typical stance when he was creating a provocative verse. 'I swear it is her song that draws me to her lane / But mayhap it is her sweet self that beckons me again.'

There was something in this playful exchange, this male coquetry, that rather incensed Janki and, not to be outdone, she broke in with a protest: 'Nay, gentlemen, the voice shall be silent and the sarangi and drum / In my lane of music no stranger can come.'

That was when Abdul Haq turned and looked her full in the face. He thought an instant, then responded in his deep, suave voice: 'When last the lady sang, she beheld no danger / In my unworthy self she saw no stranger.'

'Wah, wah!' cried Akbar, 'You outdo yourself, janab!' He repeated the couplet in ecstasy: 'When last the lady sang she beheld no danger / In my unworthy self she saw no stranger. Kya khoob!'

Janki could have sworn it was all a cultured social game of riposte and repartee, words and verses.

'You have written a couplet, Vakil Sahib,' remarked Akbar with a whimsical croak of a laugh. 'Who could have credited you with the secret of consorting with the Muse, sir?'

'It is the first—and only—couplet of my life,' confessed Haq.

'That calls for a reward. A first couplet! And Baiji shall be gracious enough to vouchsafe it to you, I daresay. A song, Baiji, a prize for Sheikh Abdul Haq Sahib!'

So she sang, without accompaniment or forethought, some of her recently recorded songs.

A full five years after the very first recordings of Indian singers were done in Calcutta by Gaisberg and Hawd, a letter had arrived for Janki from a certain Mohammad Aslam Saife of Lucknow, introducing himself as one of the directors of the newly formed Hague, Moode and Company, Lucknow. He wrote not just on his own account but offered to put her in contact with the representatives of the Gramophone and Typewriter Company Limited (GTL), William Conrad Gaisberg and George Walter Dillnutt. The result of the ensuing correspondence between them was a journey to Delhi in March 1907 and twenty-two recordings. Of these, seven titles were initially released. Produced by Deutsche Grammophon, A.G., Hanover, they were re-pressed at Sealdah by GTL. Janki had been paid Rs 250 for the first lot of single-side discs. She had been amazed to learn that the total number of these single-sided discs sold was 2408. These sahibs had come, wearing their tropical suits and pith helmets, unacquainted with Indian music and uninterested in it, but with a shrewd eye on the possibility of the money to be earned, using Western technology to carry music from the mehfil to the Indian market. And they made big money. Later she did too—by the standards of the times. Her first records were reissued as double-sided concert records again and again until the number rose to 12,825 pieces sold by 1911 alone. Out of these the first seven discs alone accounted for 3746.

When she had played the first one released—'Mere hal zaar ki ai buto tumhein kya kisi ko khabar nahin'—to herself in the privacy of her divan-khana, she had felt faint with the unfamiliarity of this new excitement. It was as though she was meeting herself the very first time, her ideal self, not the musty, workaday companion-self she knew within herself but a finished and perfected being in which all that was possible and potential, all that was promised her in her best moments, had converged in a magical manifestation. It wasn't, it couldn't be her, and yet it was. The cool, half-laughing proclamation at the close: 'My name is Janki Bai Ilahabadi,' sealed her incredible claim to this miraculous avatar of self, and she had played and replayed the entire set dozens of times.

She sang four of these that day for Akbar and Haq Sahib: 'Chubh gayi jiyabeech pyari chhab tihari', 'Janeman jo nazara na hoga', 'Rum-jhum badarwa barse' and 'Ram kare kahin naina na uljhe'. She sang without accompanists or lyrics in front of her, out of the fullness of her elation, and when she finished she was surprised to see her audience of two, for she had quite forgotten their presence, and overcome with embarrassment, she apologized for being carried away and having imposed on them more music than they had bargained for.

'On the contrary, madam, you do us great honour,' murmured Akbar, 'for you offered us the true voice in its original splendour, not the one that rises from a wound-up machine. I hear there was a stampede in Johnstonganj when these songs of yours were played and the police had to be called from the Kotwali to restore order. I do not wonder.' But like Hassu he frowned and sniffed.

Abdul Haq Sahib, however, wanted to know where he could acquire a gramophone. She replied that a shop in Johnstonganj was said to have provided some aficionados, that she could write to Mohammad Aslam Saife Sahib or Dillnutt Sahib and arrange one from Lucknow or Calcutta.

'Madam is most kind. As for me, I am prepared to go to Calcutta to buy one, Bai Sahiba, believe me,' said Haq Sahib gallantly. He looked about to add something but stopped short. Akbar shot him a piercing look.

It was around this time that a new addition to their ensemble appeared in Janki's house—the harmonium. Naseeban's household had held a harmonium but no classical musician worth his salt would stoop to use it. Janki had heard of the charismatic Bhaiyya Sahib Ganpatrao, love child of Jiyaji Rao Scindia and the beautiful Chandrabhaga Devi, who was an absolute wizard on the harmonium but she herself had some reservations about the instrument. Initially she found it outlandish but Chandra Bhan Dutt argued in its favour with such persuasive ardour, sang so meltingly as he plied the bellows with his left hand and rippled the keys with his right, that she was won over. Chandra Bhan Dutt was not a musician but a dealer in musical instruments and had a shop in Chowk Gangadas. When she pointed out that she found the harmonium too firangee, altogether too European for her liking, that it could not be tuned onstage and that it was impossible to play a sliding meend on it or a tremulous andolan, he drew the gleaming new instrument towards him and after ceremonially seeking her permission, launched into a trilling Punjabi ballad that took his voice into the most terrifically intricate tappa tremolos:

'The gallant Siddha Bhog Dutt, who assumed the title of sultan,
    made Arabia his new home.
There he was called Meer Sidhani.
He worshipped Brahma and was a devotee of the Holy Five.
He offered his head for the sake of Hussain.
Rahab's seven sons laid down their lives for the love of Hussain.
O descendants and followers of Hussain, do not ever forget the
    Dutts . . .'

Janki was impressed. 'I did not know you are such a good tappa singer,' she observed. 'But what is this ballad you just sang?'

'It's a folk song sung in our Dutt homes during this lunar month of Mohorrum, Bai Sahiba.'

'But aren't you Hindus?'

'Brahmins to the core. But there used to be a centuries-old saying about us: Dutt sultana, na Hindu na Mussalmana. And a legend about Dutts having a vision of Hussain's horse during the days of Mohorrum. My own grandfather did, though the vision has now left us, it seems.'

Janki was keenly interested and asked about the legend. A Brahmin community, cherishing its interior lore, belonging to two faiths without abdicating either. This was an idea that had been growing on her lately.

'It's said that we are descended from Ashwatthama, Dronacharya's banished son,' Chandra Bhan told her. 'We are traders. Business took us to Arabia in the seventh century—to the port of Al Hera near Basra. We were admirers and supporters of Imam Hussain, though we were orthodox Brahmins, and some of us fought in the battle to avenge the death of Hussain. My grandfather told me the name of the Arab general on whose side the Dutt Brahmins fought but I can't remember it now. Later our families turned east and migrated back to the Punjab over a period of time and settled down in large numbers near Sialkot and in Rajasthan. There are plenty of us here in Allahabad and Benaras.'

'Well, Dutt Sahib, your singing and your story far exceed the attractions of this newfangled harmonium that you have brought, which can never, never compete with the sarangi. I am sure that neither Makhdoom nor Ghaseete will approve.'

'Madam,' argued Dutt, 'take my word for it—the harmonium is the instrument of the future. It is loud enough for a large concert hall. It is easy to learn . . .'

'Rubbish,' said Janki, silencing him. 'Since when did something loud and easy endear itself to audiences over real art?'

'Beg pardon, sahiba, you are about to see that happen. With the coming of the gramophone your music has already left the mehfil and the kotha and moved into family courtyards and living

rooms. Soon good wives and dutiful daughters will begin singing
and they will need something easy to learn.'

'Ah, I see our days are done, if that is what you are threatening
me with.' Janki laughed. 'You are a true trader, as you must surely
be if your ancestors were traders in Arabia. All right, awful though
this tuneless, braying creature is, I shall buy one, for the sake of
your song, though I dread the look on Makhdoom's face when he
sees it.'

After he had salaamed and left, she tried running her fingers
over the keys while trying a rhythmic motion on the pleated bellows
and regretted the rash purchase with all her heart. It was Dutt's
song which sank to the bottom of her mind and lodged there. For
though she never thought of it again, bits of the conversation must
have taken possession of some empty recess of self.

It must have been around this time that she first contemplated
converting to Islam. Initially it was not so much a spiritual impulse
as a matter of social belonging, of espousing and making official
a comfort zone of the mind. Inhabiting the music world in cities
that possessed a culture of rich coexistence and exchange, the
social category of the artist was somewhat irrelevant since the
art itself was the faith. Still, faith often indwelt the art. Religion
both mattered and did not matter. Hindu mythology had
interestingly enough consigned performers to the Shudra domain.
The Natyashastra, that divine textbook for actors, dancers and
singers, conceived in the mind of Brahma as the fifth Veda and
materialized through the agency of Bharat-muni, was taught
by the latter to his hundred sons. But, goes the story, the sons,
grown arrogant with time, took to ridiculing the rishis in their
compositions and performances, whereupon the rishis laid a curse
on them. Henceforth all this singing and dancing and acting would
be the business of Shudras and women. Abul Fazl lists various

musical sub-castes—Dhari, Qawwal, Hurakiya, Dafzan, Natwa, Kalawanth, Kirtaniya. Musical function defined a performer's sub-caste. But religion was different. Tansen was a Kalawanth but whether he was a Hindu or a Muslim was an issue hotly debated for long. Whether he was the disciple of the Hindu saint Haridas or the Muslim saint Sheikh Muhammad Gaus was a question that provoked furious disagreement. He had two Hindu sons and two Muslim sons, but multiple marriages were common. But what's more interesting is that he had two graves, one beside that of his pir, Sheikh Muhammad Gaus in Gwalior, the other in Vrindavan, and no one knows which, or if any, is the real one. It was latterly held that his real guru was Muhammad Adil Shah 'Adali'. Some sources claim that he was a Brahmin from Gwalior, others that he was a Telang or a Gour. A compromise position states that Haridas was his kavya guru and Gaus his music guru. But whether he was Hindu or Muslim remains unproved and in musical tradition he is both. As to his funeral, it is not even known whether he was buried or cremated. The Persian word used in the *Akbarnama* is 'supurdekhakh', which only translates as consigned to dust.

As for Amir Khusrau, the great achievement of his life was to build a profound cultural connection between the Indian and the Turkish–Iranian streams. His father was Turkish, his mother a Hindu from Braj-country and he was brought up by the Hindu side of his family, which explains his remark that Hindi was his mother tongue. Among his ninety-nine works in Persian, Arabic, Turkish and Hindi is one about Bhagwad Bhakti, the *Matul Anwar* of 1298. To bigoted Islamists who called him an idolater, a 'but-parastha', Khusrau responded with an indignant Persian verse: 'Khalaq mi goyad ki Khusrau, but-parasthi mi kunad / Aarey-aarey mi kunam, bakhalko aalam kar neste', meaning: 'The world calls Khusrau an idol worshipper; yes, yes, I do worship idols,

I have nothing to do with the world!' Khusrau's living blend of Persian and Hindi reflects the great cross-pollination, the fusion and flowering, never more manifest than in the realm of music. His tender lament, on beholding his murshid Nizamuddin dead, exhibits what came of this difficult harvest: 'Gori sowai sej par / Mukh par daarey kes / Chal Khusrau ghar aapney / Raine bhayi chahundes.'

Despite the tortured relationship between Hinduism and Islam during the days of the Delhi Sultanate, violent repulsion at its peak and an indeterminate ambivalence at its mildest, and alongside all the genocide, parricide, fratricide of the times and the escalating tension between Hindus and Muslims, Shias and Sunnis, Lodis and Sharqis, Turks and Afghans, Muslims of Indian origin and those of foreign descent, music prospered, albeit at a high cost. The frenzy might have cooled by the Mughal times but in the domain of music Hindu reaction appeared as the dhrupad form, with the Braj-country around Agra and Mathura and the Malwa of Man Singh Tomar as the nucleus, pitted against the khayal-qawwali forms centred in Delhi. But the Mughal kings became enthusiastic patrons of the dhrupad form and the location of their capital at Agra informed their inclination. The dhruva-pad was the musical worship of Hindu gods and goddesses and liberal Mughal emperors encouraged their composition and performance. A certain dhrupad verse declares that only he with whom Saraswati is pleased is fortunate enough to find favour with Shah Jahan. Shah Jahan commissioned a collection of dhrupads for the Persian Sahasrasa. Another dhrupad states that by the grace of Brahma, Vishnu, Mahesh, Ganesh and Vyasa did Aurangzeb become king. Aurangzeb is said to have liked this particular dhrupad immensely. Yet another dhrupad extolled the guru, Saraswati and Parabrahma, by whose grace one acquired a master like Aurangzeb. So while a proxy-war between singers of dhrupad and khayal mimicked the animosity between Hindus and Muslims, with dhrupad singers mocking the intricate affectations of the 'turushkapriya' khayaliyas, and khayal singers declaring that only those whose voices had grown coarse and stiff took to dhrupad singing and 'bhajananandi music', it is equally true that music served to bridge the divide through a refined synthesis. Of Akbar, Emperor of India, we know. But even minor kings like the Subedar of Kara, Malik Sultan's son, Bahadur Malik, invited famous pandits from Prayag and Benaras to work on histories of Indian music like the *Sangeet Shiromani*. So that a king like Ibrahim Adil Shah of Bijapur could dedicate his 'navarasa' with a stuti to Saraswati, defying the mullahs of the time. The Avadh nawabs, being Shia, weren't interested in the Sufi qawwalis, rather they patronized local forms like the thumri, chaiti, kajri. Hindustani music was a gorgeous, intermeshed fabric so closely knit that to pluck at the strands and undo the weave was to irreversibly ruin the entire tapestry. And this was the air that Janki breathed.

One night she too dreamt of a horse. In a state of tremendous mid-sleep thirst she sighted a stately, jewelled beast, draped in ornately embroidered velvet, and waking, she told Samina of her dream. Samina stared at her, awed.

'And you say you felt great thirst, Baiji?' she questioned.

'More than I can tell,' answered Janki. 'I felt my throat would crack with thirst.'

'Do you know what I think, Baiji? You have had a soul-vision. That was Imam Hussain's horse, none other, and something is being said to you. The martyrs died thirsty and great thirst in your dream is a sign. It is the first day of the month of Mohorrum, recollect.'

Samina was a devout Shia Muslim, as were Jallu Mian and Makhdoom Baksh and in deference to their sentiments a sombre hush pervaded the household during the ten days of Mohorrum. No bright colours worn, no joyous songs sung except those of professional necessity. But Samina's words must have worked on Janki's mind because on the fourth day of the ten, in the middle of her morning riyaz, she experienced a profound depression that overcame her like a dark cloud, blocking her song.

'Samina,' she said that evening, 'take me to the Imambara with you tomorrow.'

14

Living among Shia Muslims she was familiar with the wealth of exquisite literature and songs mourning the martyrs of Karbala but the sozkhwani at the women's majlis left her stunned. The high syllables of ancient pain kept alive in the hearts of generations, like a lamp kept burning for hundreds of years, overcame her as she joined in the old dirges, swaying to an arcane rhythm of grief, her streaming eyes, like those of the others, swollen with weeping. She lived Karbala in her throbbing brain, felt her throat grow parched with the desert's thirsting, felt her heart break with the anguish of betrayal, a cosmic treachery of all nature against the innocent. Some incurable ache in her soul found its ally and rose agonizing in keening lament, feeding on its own mortal wound. It seemed a high celebration of suffering. She felt she could seize the keenest of knives and deal herself the same fifty-six stabs that the old enemy had done, if only to find herself fatally bloodied beneath that revelling groundswell of grief that surrounded her on all sides. Grief that was holy for it drained the mind and left it empty in the sacred presence of the Holy Five, the Infallible, Immaculate Ones, the Twelve Exalted Ones, the Holy Masters.

Back home she made arrangements to install a tazia in a corner of the courtyard and cancelled all soirées for the remaining days of mourning. Borrowing Samina's Holy Book, placing it deferentially unwrapped before her, she browsed it in tentative exploration and read of goodness, justice, gentleness and charity, and what virtue was meant to be.

'Virtue lieth not in bowing to the east or the west. Virtue lies in having faith in God. Believing in the future day. In angels. In the Law and in His Envoys. In lovingly expending wealth in spite of one's own needs, on those of kith, the guardian-less, the handicapped, the homeless, those who ask, those who are yoked in helplessness. In ever-readiness to do one's duties and to fulfil one's every obligation. Those who keep to promises, when promises they have made. Those who persevere amidst adversity and pain, as long as these do last. These are the genuinely virtuous.'

She read: 'There is a guide for every people. We make no distinction between any of His apostles.' She read: 'The entire creation is the family of God and he is loved by God who loves His creation.' She read: 'He who does not pity the denizens of the earth, the angels in Heaven have no compunction for him.' And she read: 'The Deity of all of you is the One Deity. No other deity is there but He, the Rahman, the Rahim. Your different peoples are indeed one single people, and I alone am Lord of all! Therefore fear ye only Me.'

There are stirring examples of enormous individual bonding in the world of music, of Hindu and Muslim maestros living together in common households. Bade Nissar Hussain Khan lived as a member of Shankar Pandit's orthodox Brahmin home in perfect reciprocal accommodation, but for the absence of meat in his diet, for which and for opium a silver coin was placed under his pillow every morning by his host. The guest, for his part, put on a dhoti after his daily bath, and sandal paste on his forehead and even carried on a recitation contest in Sanskrit slokas with his hosts. He was given to saying that in his previous birth he had been a pandit named Nissar Bhat. The two visited the Jagannath Temple in Puri and the Kalighat Temple in Calcutta and sang bhajans there.

There is the example of Bairam Khan of Jaipur who lived for twelve years disguised as a Brahmin so as to learn Sanskrit and study the ancient musicology texts, applying tilak on his forehead and even engaging in rituals like the sandhyavandam, which was the Hindu temple's evensong. But all the while honourably keeping out of those temples which denied entry to Muslims; and at the end of his stay, having studied texts like the *Sangeet Ratnakar* and the *Sangeet Kalpadrum*, confessing the truth of being a Muslim at his guru's feet, giving his reason for the pretence and asking his forgiveness and blessing, which was readily granted.

Most striking is the example of Abdul Karim Khan singing a Marathi bhajan before Sai Baba at Shirdi, the words of which were: 'Lord, I ask only this of thee, that in my heart thou may forever be.' Sai Baba is said to have told those present: 'See how yearningly this Muslim lad renders this hymn, and with what softness he prays to receive the Lord's grace—unlike the lot of you who pray as though you are hectoring the Lord to grant your prayers!' Sai Baba invited Abdul Karim Khan to live in Shirdi with his Hindu wife and children, which he did for a time. When he left he was given a silver rupee with a blessing and asked never to spend it but keep it as a talisman. Abdul Karim sang in Hindu temples and Muslim shrines with the same deep devotion, urging his Hindu pupils to visit Hindu holy places and bearing all their travel expenses. His 'Hari Om Tatsat' in Raga Malkauns and his Ram Dhuns were appreciated by Lokmanya Tilak and Mahatma Gandhi, and the latter even expressed a desire to take Abdul Karim with him on his tours to various Indian cities so that Hindus and Muslims, growing increasingly hostile to one another again by British machinations, could hear him and be recalled to their senses.

There have been of course instances of bigotry and partisanship as in the case of the Marathi singer Bhaskar Rai Bakhle, originally groomed by the large-hearted Bande Ali Khan but subsequently entrusted to the tutelage of Fayez Muhammad Khan by the Baroda state. Fayez Muhammad neglected the boy because he was not a Muslim, making him work as a servant, sweep floors, go to the bazaar, cook meals and massage his feet. Once even, it is written, sending him to buy beef and cook it according to his recipe. Which the meek Brahmin boy, who did not eat even garlic and onions, dutifully did in obedient service. The master is said to have tasted the beef and blessed him, declaring that he was only testing his loyalty. Bhaskar Bakhle's next guru, Nathan Khan, was scarcely more liberal. He preferred to train his own sons and his Muslim pupils in the advanced techniques while contriving to send Bakhle on domestic errands. But he had not reckoned with the fierce opposition of his wife, Jasia Begum, who loved Bakhle like a son, and who personally taught him rare compositions of the Agra–Atrauli gharana. She quarrelled with her husband, refusing to light the fire and cook meals for the family, if he neglected to include her adopted son from the 'khaas taalim'. In later years Nathan Khan had a change of heart and began regarding Bakhle as his eldest son, even assigning the training of his other children to him. Bhaskar Bakhle continued to look after Jasia Begum in her old age, building a house for her in Dharwad, handing over the greater part of his earnings to her and personally washing the dishes in which she and her family ate to spare the feelings of his Brahmin wife. Such an authentic khayaliya did Bhaskar Bakhle grow into that when the idiosyncratic Rahmat Khan of Indore heard him sing he exclaimed: 'Not Bhaskar Bakhle but Khan Sahib Bhaskar Khan! Henceforth that is your name!'

It is not to be wondered that Janki, inhabiting such a climate, should have become a divided soul. In the last years of her life when she surveyed the choices she had made, her voluntary embracing of Islam found the same consistent reason that she gave to her mother in that turbulent termination of relations between them.

The fact that all her immediate circle was made up of Muslims, that she had lived and breathed the ambience of Islamic Avadh in her music, in her friendships, in her reflexes of behaviour, in the very slope of her thought processes is what she recorded in her memoirs. But it could not have been an easy decision, nor was it a simple changing of ways.

For her mother, till then the most flexible of women, turned suddenly rigid.

'All your friends, did you say?' she demanded caustically. 'Do I and your brother count for nothing now, my great Bai Sahiba?'

'How can you ever think that? You are my mother. To whom I can confide that all my life I seem to have stood outside. Outside temples, outside mosques, outside family, outside home. Longing without belonging. The only time I belong anywhere is with these my friends, my staff, my musicians, my poets, and all of them are of a kind—except me. Do you think it shall make me anything less than your daughter? If I were merely to say in front of a mullah that there is no God but Allah and that Muhammad is His Prophet? Amma, I feel alone. There are so many different kinds of believing, I want something simpler . . .'

'Listen, you.' Manki swirled around to face her. 'I am no fool. Longing without belonging, indeed. Fine words! Nonsense. We were women of the kotha, singers and dancers. We practised in our cabins. A kotha-woman did not choose her clients by religion. When I was a mithai-wali in Benaras, did I choose my customers by religion? Life places us where it will, what can we say? But understand this—you are the daughter of an aheer from Barna ka

Pul in Benaras, whatever else you may have become. And you are
a Hindu. You can't see that . . . it is too much inside . . . like a
mother you quarrel with. Like me whom you scarcely remember
when you live out your days among your poets and your singers.
You might forget who we are, what went into our making, but you
will remain a Hindu nonetheless. As I did, though half my clients
were Muslim, some of them good people too.'

'We are poles apart then,' said Janki.

'The problem with you is that you are grown too big for your
own good. You imagine you know everything. Soon I will turn
into an infidel to you.'

'I have been reading. The Quran doesn't exclude earlier and
later apostles . . .'

'Oho, so you are now turned into a mullah preaching to me.
Soon you will be sitting on your rump facing holy west and reciting
the namaz! My own daughter!'

Anger surged in her heart. 'You are right, Amma. That is
probably what you shall see me doing.' She turned and walked away
in the direction of her room. Manki limped after her, trembling: 'I
know! I know what it is. You can't deceive me. Most likely it has
something to do with some man somewhere who has caught your
foolish fancy!'

Janki made it to her room, slammed the doors behind her. She
heard Manki shout outside: 'Go, then. Go your own accursed way
and may the blight fall on your head! But never, never call me
mother again!'

She needed to discuss this with someone. Janki thought of
conferring with Akbar. But Akbar Sahib shruggingly dismissed it
all. He was in a mood for laughter.

'As to Allah, Bibi, Allah is my private business and I have
sworn to hold my tongue.'

'But what makes you a Mussalman, Akbar Sahib? If I may take the liberty of asking?'

'Arey, madam, mazhabi bahas mainey ki hi nahin / Faltu aql mujhmein thi hi nahin!'

She gave up. The only other individual she could rely on was her lawyer Hashmat Ullah. This Hashmat Ullah had been hired by her to manage the affairs of her ever-expanding properties, her several houses and the village she owned, her taxes to the sarkar, her village tenants and their matters and more recently her new project for setting up a hospice and rest house at Rambagh. From respectful professional advisor and legal representative, he'd slowly changed to protective guardian and vigilant friend, a man of few words who concealed beneath his remote manner a sincere determination to pre-empt the sentimental excesses of his lady client. As when she insisted on setting aside a sizeable sum devoted to marriage expenses for girls of indigent parents, and he'd argued with that soft tenacity which was his manner with her that too many of the indigents who vied for her largesse shied from furnishing proofs of their indigence. As when he opposed, with all the compelling force of his personality and legal experience, that it was much too soon for her to appoint trustees for her properties, she being still of an age when, he delicately hinted, natural successors were not outside the bounds of possibility. She had been stung at that veiled reference to her unutilized fertility and had haughtily put him down. Now she braced herself for yet another trying confrontation with him and on a subject that would demand explanations that might prove awkward in the extreme for both.

He proved extremely touchy. 'Am I to be a procurer of mullahs now, madam?' was his sarcastic query. 'To make you read the kalma?' But she thought she saw a fleeting flash of pleasure in his eye before being subdued to its customary crabbed grimness.

He did what was required, even arranged for the quick ceremony to be held in his house, stood by as she repeated that there was no God except Allah and that Muhammad was His Prophet and, on her request, arranged for a maulvi, Janab Reza Ali Shah of the Sambhal district of Moradabad, to visit her house every other day to groom her in the faith. And when it was over he awkwardly gifted her an elegant prayer mat and a Benaras stole of green brocade.

Her voice was unsteady but she quipped, 'Honestly, Hashmat Ullah Sahib, you look as though you expect that you and I are likely to stand beneath this stole soon. Let me advise you to entertain no such rash thought.'

That eased the solemnity of the occasion. 'Baiji thinks too highly of herself, if I may make bold to say. And far too poorly of my intelligence, that she should imagine me capable of such complete folly.' He turned away, irritable.

When she entered her house, carrying the prayer mat, with Samina bringing up the rear of the little procession of staff and accompanists, a dark silence lay upon the courtyard. Manki sat on a cot, her eyes fixed on the door. She stared at Janki, she stared at the rolled-up prayer mat and she buried her face in her hands and sat very still. That evening she set up a separate kitchen for herself and Beni. But while she cooked for Beni, she herself went on a rigorous fast, denying herself even a drop of water, until after twenty-four hours, she lay wan and enfeebled in bed with her face to the wall. Janki had striven to ignore this protest initially but as the hours passed she grew anxious. At last she plucked up courage to force her entry into her mother's room, carrying a glass of sugared water. She strove to make light of it all: 'What on earth is all this, Amma? Or have you turned Mussalman too, like me, and plunged yourself straight into a Ramzan fast?'

There was no reply. She made place for herself beside Manki on the bed and held the glass of water to her mother's lips.

'You will make yourself ill. Come, sip some water, do.'

Manki shuddered. She knocked the brass glass out of Janki's hand. 'Don't ever,' she whispered fiercely, and brought up the next word in a vicious hiss: 'you mallichhchha!' Mlechhchha—the filthy, the ultimate word of insult in Manki's vocabulary.

Janki sprang to her feet: 'So that is how it is going to be? I seem to remember that you had no objections to eating the food cooked in Naseeban's mallichhchha kitchen not so very long ago!' She quit the room, shut herself up in her own, to deal with herself.

She failed to understand what had happened to Manki. Ever so liberal, so accommodating, so actively sharing in the little ceremonies of faith that were observed by the other residents of the house, her recent inflexibility shocked Janki to the core. Beni was quiet but he undertook to pacify their mother, coax her to eat. He made no mention of her change of faith and for that she was grateful.

She thought she would abstain from all lavish food, clothes, social visits, even music, and give herself up to understanding her new faith. She prayed five times a day, facing west, and immersed herself in the Book, copying verses from it as a spiritual discipline, as medieval emperors had done to earn their pocket money. She read the *Seeratun Nabi* and the *Sahih-al-Bukhari* under the supervision of Maulvi Reza Ali Shah. And as the days passed she felt a large peace descend on her, a quiet fulfilment in the certitude of belonging to a sacred fellowship and soul-simplified. Oddly, she felt that her Islam had only extended her original Hindu self, added something while uprooting nothing, that there was nothing antithetical in her successive registers of belief, only a fulsome continuity. It was another matter that Maulvi Reza Ali Shah was a devout Sunni Muslim and made his disapproval of her Shia leanings only too obvious, grooming her slowly and surely away from them. If there were certain simmerings in the household, a line drawn between her domestics and the maulvi, his overpowering personality and intensive theological force masterfully dominated her pliant heart.

It was Maulvi Reza Ali Shah too who administered a jolt when one day he cleared his throat and said ever so gently: 'Bibi, this is something I have been meaning to speak to you about and it is serious. These pictures of Hindu worship, this Krishna and Rama and Hanuman and Ganesh and whatnot that you retain in your house must go.'

It took a moment for that to sink in as she cast her glance at the framed prints of Hindu gods hanging on the walls of her veranda. 'But this is my mother's house too,' she said. 'And, for all you know, these pictures might have been painted by Mussalman artists.'

'No matter,' he said. 'There are strayed heretics everywhere. Their presence shall be distracting to your mind. You need to keep your mind pure of forbidden things. Untainted.'

'But what harm are they doing, if my own belief and practice are pure?'

'You will not understand,' he swept her protest aside. 'It is written.'

'But, begging your pardon, Maulvi Sahib, is it not written that Allah raised among every people a messenger, preaching in the language of that people and through their own holy books? And did not Allah say: "We sent some messengers whom We have already mentioned and some messengers whom We have not mentioned to thee"? I have read this myself.'

'You may read a million things for a million years, Bibi, but it is possible that you still will not understand,' he retorted.

But she would not be silenced. 'Hazrat Shah Mirza Mazhar Jan-e-Janan has even suggested that Rama and Krishna might be described as Indian prophets.'

He rose in his seat, incensed. 'You are yet new in the faith and hence deserving of concession for your presumption. All I seek to remind you, Bibi, is that there is One God, as you repeated in your kalma. There cannot be several. And that is the first, the fundamental truth you have sworn yourself to. Now, excuse me, there is nothing more for me to say. I shall not come again until you have done as I have advised and you may consider your faith and practice wrong if you entertain things that are patently Kaffir and haram.'

He had the last word and it left her disturbed. She could find no answering argument in her mind and the more she sought to go round the argument, the more frequently she found herself up against that finality. After a day's agonizing, she saw no prospect of escaping the issue and steeled her mind to do the unavoidable—to shift the pictures quietly to the tiny room in the corner of the veranda which was their puja nook. If it was done very unobtrusively, preferably while Manki was out in the bazaar or on the terrace, maybe the matter would lie silent between them. With this intent she waited for the hour when Manki drew on her outdoor clothes, summoned the little chokra-boy with his basket, and called for the phaeton.

As soon as she heard the horses' hoofs clopping away on the cobbles Janki called Makhdoom Baksh and asked him to fetch a hammer and drive some nails into the walls of the worship room so as to transfer the pictures there. He had hardly begun on the third nail that the phaeton was heard approaching the front door of the kothi. It stopped. Manki had forgotten to carry her purse and had returned to fetch it. She stepped into the courtyard, surprised to hear the sound of hammering coming from the direction of the puja room.

Then she burst into a loud tirade. 'What is going on in my puja room? Do you think I don't understand. Nails being hammered into walls to cast out evil spirits! Are the gods of my puja room evil spirits now to this she-maulana? Who gave you permission to enter my puja room? You have no business there now!'

Makhdoom stood irresolutely, hammer in hand. He put it down and looked to Janki for succour.

Janki sped forward and pushed her way in between her mother and Makhdoom.

'You're mistaken, Amma,' she said. 'They are not those sort of nails. We are only trying to hang up your pictures in your puja room.'

'So! My pictures and my puja room only now, are they? I get it. They are nothing to you now. I am being pushed into a corner in my own house by these Mussalmans. In my own house! No, I forget—it is her house, this she-maulana's! It is that mullah who comes here these days who is turning her head. Soon she will kill me for a Kaffir. Yes, she will halal me for her Bakhreid and I will have no one to save me from these Mussalmans!'

Manki had sprung to the pictures on the veranda wall and, running from one to the next, unhooked them from the wall, clasping them to her bosom in a paroxysm of furious tears.

Janki sought shelter in her own room where the wry Makhdoom followed her.

'It is not my place to advise you, Bai Sahiba, but if I may say a word.'

She had sunk into her couch. He stood hesitantly in front of her.

'Do,' she answered, tired and shaken.

'In the way of the faithful there will be obstacles, Bai Sahiba. But you must surmount them to grow in Belief. In the Book Hazrat Nooh says of the idolaters—that they have devised a plot and they have said to each other: Do not renounce your gods. Do not forsake Wadd or Suwa or Yaghuth or Ya uq or Nasr—they have led numerous men astray . . .'

'What, another plot? This house has too many plots circulating in its rooms. But hasn't Hazrat Nooh also said that because of their sins the idolaters were overwhelmed by the Flood and cast into the Fire. And that not a single unbeliever should be left on the earth for if Allah spares them, they will mislead the Faithful and beget none but sinners and idolaters? So what do you suggest I do with this idolater-mother of mine, Makhdoom? Cast her into the Fire or will you arrange a Flood?'

He frowned. 'Bai Sahiba misunderstands me. All I meant to convey is that Bai Sahiba has done well and has my appreciation.'

'What a good Mussalman you are, Makhdoom,' she replied, shrugging. 'If only you felt the same way about the harmonium I purchased.'

He saw that she wished to change the subject. 'That,' he responded, expressionless, 'is another matter.'

She had done as commanded but she felt far from satisfied. There was still the hardest bit left. She had to dispose of her Saraswati. The pretty, precious white Muse, seated on her swan, with her veena and her book, that she had kept on the shelf in her room for years. She could not see how the presence of that innocuous image could impair her relations with Allah, but she was early in her new faith and direly earnest and it was much too soon to be an excessive interrogator. In Maulvi Reza Ali's eyes, keeping her Saraswati in her life was a fundamental transgression and so she resolved to immerse the icon in the Ganga. After all, Hindus routinely immersed their clay deities in their holy waterbodies, so it was nothing more than a sacred rite of passage from one state of faith to another, she told herself.

It would have to be done at dawn, before the household was up and awake. And she had to go alone, unidentified. Manki had barred and bolted herself in her part of the house. Storm clouds hung about the air, the household silent, dining early, retiring to their quarters. She awoke early, offered the dawn prayers, placed the Saraswati icon devoutly in the old puja basket in which her mother carried flowers and worship items to the temple, drew on her dark cloak and veil and stole out into the lane and the street. An early tonga stood at the turn, as though beckoned by some destiny, and she hailed it.

'Take me to the boat jetty on the Yamuna, please,' she told the tonga driver. 'Behind the Fort.'

The sky was a cool pigeon-grey over the twin rivers and a soft breeze blew her veil about as she alighted near the boat jetty behind the Man-Kameshwar Temple on the Yamuna front. It was still early for the pilgrims and the pleasure boats but, like the tonga, a single country boat was ready to sail. Relieved, she hastened towards it, only to find someone else there, arrived just a moment before she did. A young man of about twenty, looking distraught, who wanted to be rowed right across the river to the other bank. 'The boat ashram of the ascetic-raja of Raebareli,' he told the boatman.

'Do you mind if I come too?' she stepped forward. 'I have to immerse something at the sangam.'

He agreed, though the boatman said the trip would cost more and they would have to row to the ashram first and on their return route take in the sangam since the sangam 'had shifted far to the east'. That was no matter, she assured, she would pay. The young man said he would pay, though he hardly had enough to cover the entire distance. She insisted that she would do the paying since her direction was a little removed from his. He insisted that he would contribute his mite since the money for the fare had come to him by mysterious destiny, which made her wonder. Finally the boatman helped them step into the boat, unmoored and swung it around with a few deft heaves at the oars and they floated away, borne on the river tide towards the far bank, a good mile away.

She questioned the young man about the ascetic-raja of Raebareli who had set up his ashram on the far bank. He told her that the ascetic-raja was a man of rare learning, educated and well travelled, who had chosen to live on a boat and devote himself to meditation and the pursuit of liberation. She was surprised to learn that the young man had never met him, that this was to be his very first meeting with him. This fact, together with the troubled appearance of the youth, perplexed her. For his part he timidly wanted to know her business and she indicated her basket and told him that she had undertaken this river expedition to immerse her Saraswati icon. He nodded. It is proper to immerse our old icons when we get ourselves new ones, he remarked, obviously thinking no more of it.

It took them the better part of an hour to achieve the crossing to the Ganga end and well before they reached the bank the ashram hove in view. It was really a cluster of boats moored to a makeshift jetty. There were bamboo huts on the sandy bank and on a few of the boats wooden cabins had been erected. Flags fluttered on bamboo flagpoles and there were also a couple of mud and straw-thatch shanties behind the jetty and a cowshed. A row of clay hearths lined the frontage of the structure at which, she guessed, the ashram's cooking was done by the disciples. On the largest boat, before a simple sanctum shaded by a gunny-covered bamboo canopy, the morning discourse was in progress. About a dozen disciples sat around the guru, a man clad not in the customary vestments of religion but in an ordinary white dhoti and bare-bodied save for a white shoulder-cloth. He had a low voice with a hint of song.

'When Krishna vanished, all of a sudden, the gopis, a hundred and ten crore gopis, the Bhagwat tells us, were overcome with longing. Like a herd of cow elephants without a tusker, the Bhagwat describes these milkmaids. Thus, abandoned by their lord, they wandered, unstrung, among the forests, begging the trees—"O aswattha, nyagrodha, chuta, palash, bakula, bilva, kadamba, O have you seen our Krishna?" They gathered on the Yamuna bank and called to him in song. The *Gopikagita* tells us their plaintive appeal. "Friend," they addressed him, "you are no son of a milk-woman. You are the sakshin, the inner witness of all beings, born to a milkmaid to bring succour to the world. Friend, grant us the nectar of your lips that banishes from our souls the taste for all other worldly joys." Krishna heard their plaint of love and reappeared amongst them. They clung to him. One held his sandal-fragrant hand, one clasped his lotus feet in an embrace, one twined his arm round her shoulder, and so they lost themselves in the rasakrida, the dance and sport of love. And such his lila that each one imagined she alone beheld and possessed his loving presence, each one blinded to the one hundred and ten crore Krishnas sporting in their midst, each one believing he was hers alone. So the One became many, and danced the rasakrida in the moonlit night on the banks of the Yamuna. The *Bhagwat* describes their love dance, the One-in-Many shining like a myriad emeralds strung between nuggets of gold, the gopikas like flashes of lightning in a heap of clouds. Now when Raja Parikshit asked

the sage Suka how Krishna, who had come down into the world
to renew dharma, could dally thus, the sage replied that when
there is no ahankara, no sense of the I, there is no good or evil.
It is the lord dallying with himself alone, for in the sport of god
there is but a single player, all else is mithya, illusion. Surrender
to the lord is all. "Sarvadharman parityajya mamekam saranam
vraja"—Abandoning every other dharma come to me for refuge,
the Gita tells us. For the lord shall be by your side whenever you
require his presence. Again and again he shall descend to the earth
for the protection of humankind. "Sambhavani yuge yuge." Our
mortal eyes may not behold his effulgence, for he is the Param-
Atman, the World Soul. All that our human vision can hope to
hold is the little butter-thief Krishna with the feather in his hair,
the playful dancer, the flute-player of Vrindavan. Om Namo
Bhagwate Vasudevaya!' He lifted his hands and held them before
his closed eyes in a devout namaskar, before he announced in a
more conversational voice: 'For this morning's arati we shall sing
a verse from the *Swetashvataropanishad*.'

And as the ritual plate bearing the sacred flame was circled
before the image of Hanuman, the guru's voice rose in elated
song, with that of the disciples following: 'Not of Him is there any
master in the world. Nor ruler, and verily of Him there is no sign.
He is the cause, the creator of all physical lords. And of Him there
is neither progenitor nor lord.'

The discourse had been on Krishna, the hymn was to the
Formless but the arati was to neither. Behind the rough cotton
hanging stood the vermilion image of Hanuman, divine monkey-
warrior, devotee of Rama, scholar, musician, protector. The joss
sticks spread a sandalwood ether around the boat, bells rang, the
conch blew, then the ritual plate with the sacred fire was brought
round to each one. Sandalwood paste applied in a cool upward

stroke to the forehead, hands receiving the warmth of the flame and lifted to the head, and this for Janki was the most difficult moment, to resist the call of her former self. She placed a coin in mute offering in the ritual plate but backed away from the sandal tilak and did not circle her palms over the flame or place the warmth to her forehead as the others did. She raised her eyes and saw the guru's eyes fixed on her. In that instant of wordless withdrawal her abdication was grasped by her and by him. The boy with the flame passed on.

Then while prasad was being distributed, the guru signalled to them to approach and be seated in front of him. He addressed her boat companion first.

'What have you come seeking, my son?'

The young man answered in timid confession. 'I cannot lie, master. I came without any intention of coming.'

The guru looked closely at him.

'Explain,' he prompted.

'My name is Bhola Nath Bhatt. I had heard of you. That you help mendicants and musicians—and now I happen to be both. Actually I came to the river to end my life but I was interrupted by a family friend—a Muslim friend of my late father's—who came upon me and asked me what I was trying to do. I told him I was trying to cross the river. He asked—Are you mad? The river is deepest and broadest here and you will surely drown. He asked me why I was trying to cross the river. I lied to him, master. I said I had no money to hire a boat and I was trying to get to the saint who lived in a boat ashram on the Ganga bank and I thought of swimming across. So he insisted on giving me the boat fare and sent me to the jetty, and by then dawn had broken and I had lost the courage to drown myself.'

'And you, lady?' The guru turned to Janki. 'What brings you here?'

She bowed her head in submission and said simply: 'I too
have come by chance. There was only one boat and there were
two passengers. I came to immerse my Saraswati idol in the river
because I have converted to Islam and have been commanded to
do so by my maulvi.'

Her simplicity made the guru pause in reflection. He
regarded her without comment. After a pause he said, 'I spent
a month reading the *Majjhima Nikaya*. The Buddhist text. The
boat-discourse. Earlier, I had spent a long night meditating the
Buddhist axiom "Gate, gate, parasamgate, bodhi swaha". Which
means "Gone, gone, gone, bodhi, to the other shore". Which
means different things to different people. But first, why did you
want to end your life?' He turned to the young man.

'Because my uncle threw me out of the house when my father
died. Because he refused to teach me any more music . . .' brought
out the young man.

'You wish to learn music?'

'I wish to be a better singer than my uncle!'

'How may I help you, son?'

'Help me to go away from this city, master.'

'Will it bring any relief to you if you sang something now?'
asked the master.

'If such is your command, how can I refuse?' whispered the
young man.

He thought a while, then closed his eyes and uttered the
opening notes of a morning raga, and even a few lines of song
were enough to convey the certainty of his being an exceptional
singer, one absolutely beyond the rank and file. His voice carried
across the water with sureness and unalloyed perfection. Janki had
not heard the like of him before, not since the days of the young
Mauzuddin in Benaras.

'Main moorakh teri, Prabhuji more,
Jo chali tej nadiya-neer pachhore.'

Thy fool am I, O Lord of mine,
That I try to sift
The river waters swift . . .

Janki held her breath and listened. She closed her eyes and learnt the composition, the words and notes, until they lodged themselves fully in her memory. While the young man sang, a disciple had moved silently to his side and placed a palm-leaf casket of fruit and batashas, the guru's benediction, in front of him. A similar casket was placed before her. When the song ended, the singer opened his eyes, his face transformed. The agitation had left him and the despair in his expression had cleared.

The guru spoke: 'One who has earned by his karma the grace of such music must never be tempted to end his life. It is the tapas of many lives that has brought you this gift. In his kriti Sri Rama Jaya Rama Tyagaraja sings of the mighty force of tapas—that of Kaushalya and Dasharatha to have such a son. That of Lakshmana to have been granted the grace of being with his brother, that of Ahalya to have the touch of the lord's lotus feet, of Janaka who gave Rama a bride like Devi Sita and that of Sage Narada who sang of them all. You do not know your own tapas in previous lives to have achieved the grace you now possess and you have a world to serve with song. As the *Ananda Sagar* says, "The soul that does not float on that ocean of the ineffable Bliss of Brahman, which we know as music, is an encumbrance to this earth." Do not think yourself an encumbrance to this earth. Dedicate yourself to naadopasana, the worship of musical sound, and remember that he who understands the secrets of naada, the srutis, the jatis and the talas ascends the path of moksha without effort. So says the Yajnavalkya Smriti. In the prasad basket you shall find enough money to travel to places where Mother Ganga shall take you, living and singing, not a lifeless corpse—to Benaras, Calcutta. Spare not yourself the tapas which life demands of you.'

The young man lifted the palm-leaf casket to his forehead, then prostrated himself before the guru. But the guru had now turned his attention to Janki.

'Lady, what be your trouble, that you sought another faith?'

There was a faint hint of severity in his voice.

She repeated what she had explained to her mother—that she felt she belonged naturally among her Muslim friends, that she had always felt she belonged nowhere, that she stood outside.

'As to praying from outside a faith, there are examples aplenty. The worshippers of Vishnu and those of Shiva have ever been at loggerheads. Once Adi Sankaracharya visited the ancient temple of Vishnu at Kaladi but the factious Brahmins, who hated his teachings, locked the doors of the temple and told him that it was a temple to Shiva. So Sankara prayed outside the temple and left. When the doors of the temple were opened, lo! The image had changed to that of Shiva. God shall come to you in the form your soul desires. Ekam eva advitiyam Brahma. The same Tyagaraja of whom I just spoke once lost his image of Sri Rama. His brother had thrown it into the Kaveri to spite him. He wept and entreated the lord to return. Saint Haridas told him not to grieve but to offer a hundred songs to the lord. So Tyagaraja sang to the lord in his cottage. One day, as he sang, rapt, he heard a knock on the door. Opening it, he beheld Sri Rama and Devi Sita and Hanuman standing there! It was not the image but the lord himself who had come in answer to his call. But you say you have to immerse your Saraswati?'

She nodded.

'Omar, one of the your Prophet's companions, and later a noble Caliph of Islam, refused to pray inside the Church of the Holy Sepulchre when it was time for his namaz. Jerusalem was conquered from the Christians by the Muslim armies and he had entered the city, victorious, and the Christian priests had invited him to offer his prayers anywhere he liked but he chose to go out and pray in a field. His reason—that he had instructions never to destroy a place of worship, no matter of what faith, but, he explained, not all his followers could understand this and were he to pray within they were capable of destroying the holiest church in Christendom and turning it into a mosque, which was utterly against what the Prophet had taught. I do not mean to offend you, lady, but even Islam's wise men knew what its followers were capable of. No one knows this better than us, we who being Hindus, allow all the faiths to speak to us, who can be anything we desire, any faith on earth. I earnestly believe that you have made a mistake. You must return to your mother faith. A simple rite of return and a dip in the holy river shall be enough.'

She could not meet his eyes. If she stayed any longer in his presence her will would break. 'Master, I have made my choice. There is no going back for me.'

He looked displeased. 'Then go where your karma takes you, lady.'

As her boat pulled out and swung eastwards in the direction of the sangam, riding the river waves, she did not look back, not once. She was conscious of the young man watching her intently as their boat wobbled precariously on the rising crescents of the ridge of colliding streams that marked the confluence. There she laid her Saraswati in the rapids, just at that joint or fracture in the stream where the Ganga met the Yamuna, and watched the snow-white image sink and vanish in the roiling deep where boats, it was said, always went out of control and boatmen prayed to the river's deity to save their craft. The spot where urnfuls of ashes of the dead were emptied, to dissolve and mingle in the flow. Then, dead and reborn, she turned her face to the other bank and covered her face with her veil. 'Dheerey baho nadia,' her mind chattered its songs like a runaway beast. And 'Balam naiyya dagmag doley,' it chattered on, an interior bandish she could not stop.

They parted in silence on the Yamuna jetty, she and the young man. Neither knew who the other was. He did not know he had shared the boat and the morning's experience with the famous Janki Bai. She did not know that she had heard the future sage Bhola Nath Bhatt sing. When Bhola Nath Bhatt returned to Allahabad in 1935 Janki Bai Ilahabadi had been dead a year and buried in the Kaladanda graveyard and had a mazaar in her name named Kaisabiniya ki Mazaar. Maybe the domestic name she came to acquire as a devout Muslim woman was Kaisabiniya, though that is a street distortion and there is no evidence of any other name save the one she signed herself and the one she announced on her records—Janki Bai.

When Janki returned home she found her mother packed and ready to leave. Her possessions had been put in two metal trunks and her bedroll lay ready on its side in the courtyard. She had made Beni pack up too.

'Where will you stay, Amma?' Janki asked her mother.

Manki turned burning eyes on her. 'My wealthy daughter builds shelters for homeless women, what do I have to worry? There surely is a corner of the floor for this homeless woman, Baiji.'

'And what will you do?'

'I don't know. Maybe beg in some temple yard. Till I earn my way to Benaras or Vrindavan.'

There was no holding her back. Janki, frantic, sought out Beni. 'I beg you, my brother, take the keys of my Johnstonganj kothi and take her there. Reason with her. She listens to you.'

Manki's empty room reproached her for days and she wept in her prayers that her mother might forgive her and be persuaded to return. She found that changing one faith for another was anything but easy. Some mornings she awoke with thumris about Krishna and Radha blowing about her head somewhere on the edges of sleep. She tried harder, became driven and desperate. She prayed, fasted, read the Book. She took to writing devotional verses, sang them to herself until God and His Prophet, Peace Be upon Him, came to reside in her heart and locked its doors securely against the intrusions of other visitations. Then, whenever she was called upon to sing a bhajan to a deity her vocal cords pulsed in sharp grief and when she composed and sang a naat to the Prophet tears choked her voice, and like those boats on the sangam that went out of control on the crashing currents of two mighty rivers and left the boatmen helplessly praying, she too lapsed into incoherent appeals that her prayer be heard. Until she resolved to keep away from devotional songs altogether till such time as her soul had settled. When that happened she made a surprising discovery. She found that she could sing 'Raghubar aaj raho more pyare' as well as 'Madina mein mor piya vala hai re' with equal fervour. She found that despite her having opted to become a Sunni Muslim she retained enough of the Shia in her as to sing a soz like 'Balake ban mein jo sograka naamabar aaya' with deep emotion.

15

In early 1908 she recorded for a Frenchman, Henri Lachapelle, at Lucknow for the Pathephone and Cinema Co., Calcutta, acting through the agency of the Hague, Moode and Company of Lucknow, which had come to be established there. Along with her Wazir Jaan of Benaras and Ladli Jaan of Lucknow also recorded. These were eleven-inch discs, pressed in Belgium, and they came to be known as Disque Pathe. But the Hague, Moode and Company soon collapsed.

Then in late November 1908 she was once again recording for George Walter Dillnutt in Calcutta. Rs 900 for twenty-four titles seemed handsome enough. Though, as often happened, a song or two went missing and she mourned for it. All through 1909 and 1910 these records were steadily released into the market and the number sold rose to 8827. The gramophone companies held back many titles, to announce and advertise them gradually when early titles had circulated sufficiently. Her songs of this period include the popular 'Main kaise rakhoon praan shyam madhuban gailona' and 'Ab kaise jobna dikhaoongi'. In the same lot were 'Rukh-e-gulshan ki dekhi bahar', 'Pyare Ahmed-e-mukhtar, tumpar Allah ka hai pyar', 'Ek Kaffir par tabiyat aa gayi', 'Hamne to jaantak na pyari ki, Kanha na kar mosey raar' and 'Dar kharabat-e-mughan noor-e-Khuda mee beenam', one of her best-loved Persian ghazals.

By late 1909 she demanded twice her former rate from the Gramophone and Typewriter Company Limited and the price she quoted was accepted: Rs 1700 for twenty-two titles. These were double-sided discs and they sold out rapidly. In another year a cautious proposal arrived from GTL. There were rival companies competing with them in the Indian market—Beka Records, A.G. Berlin, the Pathephone and Cinema Co., Calcutta, the International Talking Machine, Berlin, representing Odeon. Three of these had offered Janki Bai Rs 5000 a year for exclusive recording rights. GTL offered a three-year contract for forty titles. She refused to be tied down to any such agreement. Her concerts were fetching her more than enough.

At several of her performances in the city, she spotted Abdul Haq in the audience. At the Hardinge Theatre in Bahadurganj, at the Mayo Hall, at the Police Lines, at the Kotwali, at the Ram Bagh Baradari, it warmed her secret heart to pick out his handsome face in the sea of faces. The very first time she threw him a charming bouquet of lyrics, a lilting provocation, singing:

'Ek Kaffir par tabiyat aa gayi.
Parsai par phir aafat aa gayi.
Humdum, isko dillagi samjha hai tu?
Dil nahin aaya, museebat aa gayi.
Yaad karke tumko ai jaan ro diye,
Saamne jab achchhi surat aa gayi.
Chupke-chupke ro rahe ho kyon samad,
Sach kaho kis par tabiyat aa gayi?'

That was one of her most popular numbers and it brought the house down.

The song passed like a signal between them that she had registered his presence, that she acknowledged it and welcomed him, that she was gladdened that he was there, and that she also knew why he was there. At the next concert she was pleased to find him in the audience again and even more pleased when a farmaish from him, scribbled on a shred of paper, appeared before her, requesting that first song: 'Ek Kaffir par tabiyat aa gayi.'

Gratified, she obliged, but added a song: 'Phadkan laagat mori ankhiyan', a dadra. A delicate slip of a song, a suggestion more than a statement. He acknowledged it with a salaam, sitting in the audience. At the next mehfil a farmaish came for the song 'Phadkan laagat mori ankhiyan'. She sang it with a smile playing on her lips. And added another: 'Mumkin nahin ke teri mohabbat ki bu nahin', a ghazal in Bhairavi.

So it went. If he asked for 'Jabse us zaalim se ulfat ho gayi', sung in Jhinjhoti, she complied and offered him also 'Dil ek hi se laga, hazaron khade' in Pilu. If he requested 'Kaffire ishkam Mussalmani mara darkar nist' in Bhairavi, she tossed him 'Tum hi kufr ho aur iman tumhi ho' in Jogiya.

It was a game they were playing and they played it with zest. Then suddenly for her it wasn't a game any more. For just as suddenly he stopped coming. At the riverside performance, at the Magh Mela, she sought the audience in vain as she sang: 'Gham raha jabtak ke dam mein dam raha'. Then, at the soirée at Ram Krishna Seth ki Bagiya she missed him again. She had to travel for a recording with Gaisberg's Company. When she returned to Allahabad and performed at the Balua Ghat Baradari and at the Jamuna Tat, he still wasn't in the audience.

She felt an unbearable oppression, the sensation of being trapped in a story, her story, the predictable and ordained script of it, and she longed to discover some welcome fault line in the safe narrative she had so far inhabited without question, and escape into the unexpected. It was a time of obsessive writing for her.

Verses flew from her pen, of an intensity and abundance like some
sweet and heady possession.

What or who I am, you know me
You meet me after an age, do you know?
Laila lives in the heart, not in the camel's 'mehmil'
O Majnu, that you seek her in wilderness and forest.
A blink of your eye is sufficient to kill,
Why do you draw your sword against me?
This is a great judgement and a new justice,
That you implicate your friends among your foes.
You draw your sword repeatedly,
Have you vowed to slay your lover?
I am oblivious of past and present.
Why do you turn epochs in your head?
I may plead a thousand times, do not meet my rival in love,
When do you ever heed Janki's word?

What perdition has wounded me,
This injury I have suffered, jesting.
Only he has enjoyed life whose heart has known love's wound.
My wound has stopped hurting but meeting him has exacerbated
    it anew.
You tore apart my heart and looked into it.
But did you spot my pain anywhere?
Did you see the effect of my love
That this injury engendered that injury too?
O Janki, I tell my heartache to that cruel one.

When she showed them to Akbar, on one of her visits, he read
them with a quizzical eye, then took off his glasses and regarded
her with interest: 'Allah bachaye marz-e-ishq se dil ko, sunte hain

ki yeh aariza achchha nahin hota. Baiji shows symptoms of a classic illness, I perceive. Who, I wonder, is the happy object of these flights?'

'Love is a classic subject, your honour, and needs no mortal object,' she quipped. 'Consider your own verse, sir.'

'True enough,' he conceded, 'for were you to count the multitudes of phantom maidens that crowd the mind of a poet, you would out-populate the harem of Suleiman!' He breathed a verse into the air like a ring of hookah smoke: 'Bahut raha hai kabhi lutf-e-yaar hum par bhi, guzar chuki hai yeh fasl-e-bahar hum par bhi.' He turned on her a look of infinite pity and did not question further.

She returned home and wrote more of the same:

I remember that time when love began
My heart was beside me, your secret was in my heart.
The eyes of the beloved held both enchantment and wonder
I beheld both things and the secret became known.
The one whom I gave my heart to was formidable indeed,
No wonder I suffered grief at his tyrant's hands.
Was my appeal a veiled one's secret?
Till today it did not emerge from my heart on to my lips.
Do not ask me, ask only your own heart
What was the origin and consequence of love.
In the valley of love each one takes his own path.
I had only my heart to console me.
How many cruelties did he inflict on me, how many griefs,
That beloved whose beneficence Janki took pride in.

She wrote late into the nights in a sort of frenzy:

I had not known the riotous to become a sacrifice,
That my heart from my bosom shall move away.
If the condition of love be visible to the eye
Then my heart shall grow oblivious of self.
Ever since he has taken my letter his address is not known.
How could it be known that the letter-bearer shall grow
      forgetful?
How should I believe that he shall stay indifferent to me?
Shall my restless heart have no effect on his?

The more poems Akbar Sahib read through the higher did his eyebrows climb up his forehead, but though he darted his sharp, ferret eyes at her, though he raked her face with his knowing expression, he held his tongue and said nothing.

Finally one day, taking her courage in both hands, she asked him with seeming casualness: 'Has Haq Sahib left the city?'

'Why do you ask, Baiji?'

'I do not see him here. Or . . . Or anywhere else.'

'Meaning your own celebrated performances, Baiji? For which Haq Sahib turned heaven and earth upside down to arrange passes and invitations? Madam, Haq Sahib is very busy and somewhat caught up with a problem.'

'What might that be, sir?'

'Haq Sahib is busy with the coming municipal elections,' he answered, his face expressionless.

She was puzzled. Her eyes mutely sought to know more.

'Haq Sahib has been trying to move the collector sahib to relax a particular clause in our municipal laws regarding our election candidates, and to that end he has been canvassing around, gathering support in a signature campaign.'

She had to know more without revealing excessive interest.

'The collector sahib is known to me. Is there anything I can do to help Haq Sahib?'

'Madam,' said Akbar ironically, 'there are matters of law that a song from a koel or a baiji like yourself cannot wish away. Haq Sahib keenly wants to contest the municipal elections but he is not technically a resident of the city.'

She was still more puzzled. 'Not a resident of Allahabad? I fail to understand.'

'Haq Sahib owns no property in the city. He lives in Mehdauri village outside the city. He cannot contest these coming elections, not until he can establish his residency in the city. That is the clause he is striving to have revoked but I see no prospect of his succeeding.'

She returned home, her mind in dire confusion. The question that kept her awake that night found resolution in the small hours of the morning, at the hour for the best riyaz or the hour when she believed that the light of one's impending truth shone for a few seconds in the mind, and it required an urgent summons to her lawyer, Hashmat Ullah.

When she consulted Hashmat Ullah as to which of her houses could be suitably gifted away to a deserving friend, the exasperation simmered in his eyes, though he kept his voice level.

'Might I ask, madam, who this deserving friend is?'

'We are discussing the house, not the friend, Hashmat Ullah Sahib.'

'As your lawyer, it is well within my rights to ask, may I respectfully remind the sahiba?'

'You are my lawyer, not my conscience keeper, Hashmat Ullah Sahib.'

'Before your conscience I have my own to consider, madam. And I would be failing in my duty were I to give my professional consent to many of the rash compulsions of your oversensitive conscience.'

She saw that he was adamantine in his insistence, and sighed.

'There is someone who wishes to contest the municipal elections, Hashmat Ullah Sahib, and is disqualified from doing so simply because his house is a rented one.'

A look of excruciating annoyance sprang upon his face. 'May the liberty be forgiven, madam, but you need scarcely say more. The courts are places of much gossip and exchange and there is some such rumour afloat . . .'

'You do astonish me, Hashmat Ullah Sahib,' she said coldly. 'This thought has entered my mind scarcely this morning and the city has already got wind of it! Are my thoughts as distantly audible as the sound of my voice is said to be, sir?'

'Not the sound of your voice, madam, but the sound of gold mohurs ringing in your coffers. They have been known to have reached the ears of a certain unworthy gentleman of the city, yes, one who frequents your mehfils affecting to like the sound of your voice when all he can hear is that other sound which impresses, excuse my bluntness, far more than even your famous voice can do!'

Despite his composure, she could tell that he was close to losing his temper. Speaking in the tones of a censorious father to a wayward and wanton daughter. It annoyed her, made her voice rise.

'You strangely forget yourself, Hashmat Ullah Sahib.' She snubbed him in the most faultlessly ornate Urdu at her command. 'I have not shared my plan with you, but now, since you betray such astute prescience of my intentions even before I speak, let me discourage you from any further remonstrance. My mind is made up and yours has conveniently forgotten that the properties you protect are earned by the very sound of my voice that you rate less than what it encashes.'

He was sullen, resigned before her wilful obstinacy. 'I did not mean to insult you, madam.'

'Then let us revert to the matter in hand and decide which of my houses it shall be. I expect you to have my papers ready and I shall sign them when they are prepared. Yes, and in the company of the gentleman whose signature shall also be needed.'

With that she swept out of the chamber.

And all of it done without so much as mentioning a name.

That evening, she ordered her phaeton but when Samina asked where the coachman be directed to go she only said, 'Mehdauri village,' in a voice that discouraged any further inquiry. And when Samina made preparations to accompany her, as she always did, she said, 'No, not today, Samina.'

'Sahiba means to go alone?' asked Samina in wonder.

'Yes. Alone,' said Janki and turned away from the light lest Samina notice her face.

Months later, when they had been married and living most of the time in her own Sabzi Mandi house, married in the teeth of opposition from Manki and Hashmat Ullah and surprisingly even Akbar Sahib, the mist of that lit-up night refused to leave her senses, continued to waken that flush of disbelief.

To the coachman she had said, 'Drive to the river first, Ramzani. I need some fresh air.' As if that were enough and the utterance of the destination used up all her remaining courage and left none to utter with decisive finality the name of the man she had chosen. And when they passed the river and she felt its cool breath upon her face, her shrinking brain broke into an involuntary prayer to it, her Ganga still, invisible in the night but running alongside her like an inexorable fate, a proceeding karma. Like the invisible blood coursing in her veins. Circulating in an inevitable direction and continuum that was her life. When for it to stop or turn back could only be death.

And when the firelight from the hearths of the riverside ascetics mingling with the glimmer of kerosene lanterns and the smoking oil beacons of squatting hawkers who lined the riverbank fell upon the dark hem of water, she felt a tremor pass into her throat as she told the coachman to stop at a footpath spread with silver, a fish stall, lit by a single earthen oil lamp. She made him turn the horses and head for Mehdauri and ask the way to Vakil Sahib Sheikh Abdul Haq's house.

She had chosen to call late, much after sundown, to avoid attention. She had refused to step down from the phaeton or to announce her identity. To the old family servant who opened the gate she had merely said: 'Tell your master, a lady who has something important to tell him respecting the municipal elections is here.' That had made it seem practical and regular in the servant's curious eyes, in the coachman's too.

Why have you united your heart with mine after an age?
Did he remember the past that he came again?
The trapper took away the bulbul captive with him
In the garden why did the trapper create this riot?
I too have waited to see this sight,
Why did Allah show such a sight to Moses on the mountain of Tur?
Why did someone look this way with tender guilefulness?
Why did he take aim at my heart?
O Janki, I am trying hard, intently,
But why he should have forgotten me, what is the reason?

When she heard rapid steps on the paving stones and heard his
cautious voice hushed to a perplexed undertone, asking 'Who is
it?' she refrained from lifting her veil and kept her voice brisk and
even.

'It is I, Janki Bai Ilahabadi,' she had said grandly, as she did
at the close of her gramophone recordings. As though she were
the empress of the city or the city itself, conferring a gracious
visitation, granting a prize to one of its minor but favoured
citizens.

Even in the darkness she had seen him start.

'Baiji,' he had exclaimed, 'is it really you?'

'No.' She had laughed, an arch, bemused laugh. 'It isn't me but
someone resembling me . . .'

> Think of the consequences of the beginnings of love,
> O failed heart, reflect on this.
> The result of this enemy love is nought,
> If it occurs, then one is defamed for nothing.
> Oh, restless heart, so restless am I.
> What is to be the consequence of my beloved's love, think.
> Who was it who brought on the swoon on Tur?
> Who was it or what, what is his name, think.
> O Janki, it is hard to escape with my life from him.
> Now the message of love has arrived, now think.

'It isn't me,' she had said, 'but someone resembling me. For can
you imagine Janki driving up alone at nine in the night? And yet
this is someone who answers to my name . . .'

He had stepped close to the side of the phaeton. 'My good
fortune, whoever it is. I invite you to grace my threshold, Baiji.
Will you not come?'

'I invite you to grace the kutcherry tomorrow, Haq Sahib. Will you not come?'

She signalled to the coachman to turn the horses round and click them on, calling over her shoulder her imperious command: 'At eleven o'clock sharp, Haq Sahib. The kutcherry.'

Without any transgression of mine why do you torment me?
For God's sake, tell me why?
Did you ever have the kindness to ask how I was?
Even my rivals grew amazed at your interest in me.
If somewhere I met the Messiah I would ask
Why I am not healed?
Why are you angry when I complain of your cruelty
That suddenly you grew aloof and apart?
O Janki, people wrongly consider Allah a foe,
Who knows why he was given this grand place!

She made over the house in Hashmat Ullah's stiff and sullen presence, signing her name in her impeccable Urdu calligraphy alongside Abdul Haq's shaken masculine scrawl. It felt more like an outlandish nikah of destinies than a transfer of property.

She drove him in the buggy to the address now entered in the municipal documents. It was not a new house and she apologized for its condition. It was old, scarred, unrepaired, ugly. Yet it was solid and large, and of course it was not to live in, merely to supply an address, as she spelt out.

They stood beneath the peeling paint of its crumbling arches. My address, Baiji, is where yours is, he whispered, overcome. If you will allow me, he added in humble submission. Then she threw back her veil and turned her proud, scarred face to his gaze. He understood and hastened to add: A house is precious because

of the way it makes us feel, the comfort and shelter it gives, not
the way it looks to the eye. He respected—and honoured—the
scars left by time and by trouble. He caressed the cracked wall, the
fissured trellis and she came to him, saying: Do not look on me
thus, Haq Sahib.

That you should have come to me in the darkness of the
night, like an angel of mercy . . . No, she whispered, I came in
the dark that you may hear my voice alone, not see my uncomely
form. I came on a moonless night lest you see how pitted my face
is, more so than the moon herself. I am henceforth sightless, he
whispered in reply. Lying in his arms, she chided him, playful:
Oh, you are a lawyer, not a poet, sir. What argument stronger
than love's appeal? Milord, I charge you with the larceny of my
soul. For shame, Vakil Sahib, you make of me both defendant and
judge, and what may your fee be? This, he said, and she knew no
more. Till, spent, she could summon breath enough to whisper: I
plead that you adjourn this court indefinitely, milord, just so that
I can go on arguing my case forever, before you. It is you who are
my judge, my lady, he whispered. It is you who shall advance or
adjourn . . .

> You are the killer, beloved, oh perdition!
> You behead me, oh perdition!
> Scores of offences are his, oh perdition!
> And here there is my lone endurance.
> The heart is being drawn that way,
> What is his power of attraction, oh perdition?
> He never comes this way even by chance, even after promising
>   daily, oh perdition!
> In my heart there is the ache of love,
> And on my lips are sighs of agony, oh perdition!

The songs of her riyaz put words to her desire. She knew exactly
what it was to be taut as a bowstring ready to snap at a touch: 'Mori
angiya na chhuwo, karungi kapolan lal. Yeh angiya nahin, Janak
dhanush si / Chhuwat tootey tatkaal . . .' Touch not my bodice,
else I shall smear thy cheek red. This is no mere bodice but King
Janak's bow. A touch can instantly snap its string . . . She closed
her eyes and immersed herself in the overflowing excess of her
imaginings. All shame cast aside, the conniving surrender: 'Ab toh
tihari ban aye, chhaliya. Bahiyaan pakad mukh malat gulalwa. Ab
toh sang ki saheli door nikas gayi / Hum hi akeli dar pe aye . . .'
Now I am all yours, O prankster / Who grabs me by the arm and
slathers my face red. My handmaidens have wandered afar. I alone
have come to your door . . .

Soon after their marriage, Abdul Haq moved in with her.
And when, as a mark of her protest, her mother sent across an
envelope containing rent for the house she occupied with Beni—the
Johnstonganj kothi, another of Janki's several houses—Janki sent
it back, knotted in a garland of jasmines. For these days and nights
were perfumed ones for her. She seemed to be inhabiting a dream
and all those other faces that existed outside the circle of her lighted
heart—Manki, Beni, Haq Sahib's other family, his wife and two sons
and large extended family—seemed altogether insubstantial. She was
intoxicated by this groundswell of emotion. For some weeks at least.

She couldn't be sure when, in the flight of octaves that was her
life for a brief interlude, the first false note appeared. She thought
it was an error of the ear, a play of wrong acoustics or a lost beat.
But it reappeared to shock and pain her and fell her in high flight
like the shot that grounds a bird.

Tonight he, whose beauty even the moon envies, has come to me.
Tonight is the good consequence of the day's love.

The night of the full moon brought this trouble.
Tonight his memory returned whose beauty the moon envies.
Tormented in the night's grief my heart says but this:
Let us see how long this night's dawn does not break.
Perhaps my cries have no effect on him,
Else why does he stay uninformed of me?
Remembering his pearly teeth weep I, then
My tears turn to pearls as they fall.
If you do not keep your promise to come, beware,
Because tonight I shall spend weeping, agonizing.

When he forgot himself and rebuked her sharply for humming a thumri in bed, saying: 'Stop, begum, you'll waken the whole household!' she felt her ecstasy fall away even as he bestrode her, even as he pierced her. It was a small thing, but she felt rebuffed, insulted, she who was used to being entreated to sing. She had begged her husband to come to her bed in complete darkness lest her old shame come between them. But silenced by his urgent voice, absorbed in its own grasping gratification, all she could register was an unsettling memory and squirm beneath his thrusts. She had no words save what she sang in her riyaz, suddenly an unshared, private matter: 'Aisi chatur Brajnaar rang mein ho rahi babri / Ek man udat gulaal, sawa man kesar rori / Radhe pe chhirkat Shyam, Shyam par Radha gori / Radhe chali muskaat, Shyam ne bahiyaan marori . . .' A saucy Braj maid giddy-washed, colour flying, a maund of vermilion, maund and a half's saffron-cinnabar! Krishna splashes Radha, fair Radha drenches Krishna. But as she smiling moves he grabs and twists her arm! She grew cold at the memory.

Janki's mind had ever swarmed with fantasies of an ideal love. Fed on songs and stories of perfect partnerships in which marriage was one continuous companionship of musical converse. As that of the maverick Bande Ali Khan and his beloved Chunna. He nearing fifty, she barely eighteen, he a maestro of the veena, she a singer par excellence. For a brilliantly executed performance at the court of Jiyaji Rao Scindia he'd been asked to name his reward and he had asked for Chunna Bai, the court singer. The Scindia was astonished when the girl had immediately agreed. On their wedding night some village pranksters had hidden themselves on the roof of the nuptial chamber, planning to take a peek into scenes of what they expected to be interesting carnal intimacies between an ill-assorted pair, as unmatched in age as in their faiths. To their great surprise the bridal chamber was soon welling with music. The young bride sang all night, her elderly groom outdid himself on his veena until dawn broke. Unknown to the happy lovers, the peeping Toms had spent a tormented night cramped on a narrow ledge beneath the tiles, forced to listen to a night-long recital they had no stomach for. Years later when a Pune medicine man named Bapu Sahib Menhdale cured a chronic sore on Chunna's head he'd asked for an unusual fee for the treatment—that Khan Sahib stay back in Pune and be available with his music whenever he was asked. A request that Bande Ali Khan granted. The idea that love between a man and a woman could be transmitted entirely in the currency of music, that a medical fee too could be paid in music, had fired Janki's imagination for years. She had also nourished her soul on the songs of adoration composed by Roopmati, the Sarangpur prodigy, for her beloved, Baaz Bahadur, Sultan of Mandu. He had won her when he'd successfully figured out a puzzle of Khusrau's for her. She was a Hindu, he a Muslim, and she knew him only as her Malik Baizeed, not as the sultan of Mandu. When the proposal for her hand arrived from the sultan she was forced to give her consent. They met, separated by a curtain, and she laid down her conditions: she would not convert to Islam, she wouldn't observe purdah, she'd partner the sultan on his hunts and share his throne in court. She'd build a temple to Shiva in the inner court of her palace and have a canal dug that brought Narmada water to her, for she'd drink no other. He granted it all and when the curtain was drawn aside she was overjoyed to behold not a stranger but her own lover as the sultan. So went the legend. They made great music together, he on the rubab, she singing and dancing in ecstasy. The songs she wrote for her lover were songs that were part of Janki's repertoire.

Aur dhan jorti hain ri,
Mero toh dhan pritam ki poonji.
Kahu triya kin a laage drishti.
Apney kar rakhoongi kunji.
Din-din badhaye savayo, dyodho,
Ghatey na ekau gunji,
Baaz Bahadur ke saneh upar,
Nichhawar tan-man-dhanji.

Others amass wealth,
My lover is my treasure.
May no third covet my wealth,
In my hand shall I hold fast the key.
My wealth grows by the day, grows, doubles, multiplies,
Not a whit does it ever lessen.
On Baaz Bahadur do I shower my love,
Consecrate body, mind and wealth.

The songs remained songs alone, their words lost their charge, their promise faded.

In time she and Haq Sahib settled down to a rhythm of unquestioning ordinariness, unambitious about their love, exulting over nothing. At some crucial stage too her singing stopped existing for him and she came to accept that as well.

Beni reappeared most bashfully to deliver the message that Manki didn't want to live on in Allahabad, especially on Janki's property. She wished to go back to Benaras, open a mithai shop again.

'Why can't she open a mithai shop in Allahabad? Why Benaras?' Janki wanted to know.

'Because Benaras is her real home and Father might have come back,' faltered Beni.

'Also because she'd like to end her days in Benaras. Hindus who die in Benaras achieve moksha, she says.'

'Since when did Amma become such a devout Hindu?' asked Janki wryly.

'Since you became such a devout Mussalman. The more devout one becomes, the other follows suit. Even to madness.' Beni, the taciturn, had never delivered such a strong opinion before. Janki flashed him a look of amazement. She offered to finance the mithai-shop business in Benaras but Manki had refused to accept any more money from her. Beni didn't repeat her exact words but they were to the effect that she wanted to go away and live somewhere where nobody knew she was the mother of the shameless Janki Bai. Still Janki pressed some money on Beni.

'But how shall we repay you, Jiji?' he asked her.

'With a tokra of Amma's mithai once in a while,' answered Janki sadly. 'It's a taste my palate hasn't known for some time.'

16

In early 1911 Janki recorded between sixty and seventy titles for T.J. Noble of Pathephone and was paid Rs 5000. GTL was hot on her trail and she obliged them with twenty titles for Rs 3000, promising their recording engineer Arthur Spottiswoode Clarke another twenty-four titles. Since 1911 was a hectic year, extraordinary in many ways, the promise could not be kept for another three years. A happening year for the country and for her. Allahabad was crowded with pilgrims when the Maha Kumbh Mela began in January. Thousands camped on the banks of the Ganga, ash-smeared ascetics from the great mutts of India, ordinary people come to meditate and do penance for a month, tradesmen, artists, acrobats. What made this particular Kumbh Mela special was that part of it coincided with the great industrial exhibition of the United Provinces (UP) held at Allahabad, designed to be the greatest Indian show of the century.

Janki was as excited about the crowning event of the exhibition as the rest of Allahabad's citizenry. The 18 February event, when a Frenchman, Henri Pequet, would pilot a two-seater biplane across the Ganga, flying from Allahabad to Naini, carrying the first-ever cargo of airmail in the world! It would take off from Allahabad's Polo Ground and land near the Naini railway station in a field cleared by convicts from the nearby Naini Jail. The event was highly publicized. Letters and cards addressed to locations all over the world were invited, to be stamped with a special magenta seal for 6 annas each before being dispatched to the sack of 6500 similar envelopes and specially designed postcards that would fly the ten-mile distance between Allahabad and Naini and earn the distinction of being part of the first aerial postal experiment in the world.

Janki sent three letters, one to Haq Sahib, one to Akbar Sahib and the third to Manki. The first one carried a love poem, the second her respectful salutations and a quip or two about what the world was coming to with gramophones recording human voices and letters flying through the air, and the third some words of deeply felt apology and appeasement to her mother and brother. She drove all the way to the Oxford and Cambridge Hostel near the grand university building being constructed on Church Road. Both the grounds of the Holy Trinity Church and the hostel were filled with crowds, eager to deposit their letters and see them stamped with the words: 'First Aerial Post, UP exhibition, Allahabad 1911'. She knew William Holland Sahib and Wyndham Sahib somewhat, though she knew the former to be too pious to admit 'nautch women' into his social circle.

After its first eruption in the late 1890s, this 'nautch girl' business had raised its head again in the local papers from late 1910 onwards and only something like a flying postal service could temporarily eclipse it. But only temporarily. The great UP exhibition was a sort of trade fair, planned on a massive scale, an ambitious display of arts and crafts, farm produce, industrial goods and implements, and entertainment that would showcase the culture of north India. King George V was due to be crowned in June. Allahabad was milling with crowds, those who

had come for the Maha Kumbh and those who had poured in for
the UP exhibition. The city was one big fair, the papers bristling
with criticism of the expense, the wastage, the mismanagement.
When it had been a matter of a Congress meet, the papers argued,
objections of order and hygiene had prevented the honourable
sarkar from granting permission for any suitable site that was
proposed. When it was a small matter of Tilak and Gokhale and
Bipin Chandra Pal delivering a lecture to Allahabad citizens,
all venues were cancelled due to technical reasons. Then in
the matter of this massive jamboree, how was it that the entire
segment of land extending just beyond Government House and
Lowther Castle and all the way up to the Sohbatiya Bagh Tank
had been requisitioned? Most outrageous was the matter of the
'dancing girl' celebrity, the papers stridently declared. Not just
Allahabad papers but also papers from other cities of the United
Provinces.

Janki followed the issue with mixed feelings, reading what the
Prabasi of Calcutta said, what the *Abhyudaya* and the *Leader* of
Allahabad said, and when her curiosity had been amply aroused
she called for her phaeton on Sunday mornings and drove to the
library in Company Bagh to read the *Hindustani* of Lucknow, the
Fitna of Gorakhpur and the *Saddharma Pracharak* of Bijnor. How
could the government and the organizers of the exhibition have
the bad taste, the temerity to include a dancing girl's performance
in the list of special attractions?—screamed the papers. Was
it only for cheap publicity and to raise funds to cover up losses
incurred by gross mismanagement? Why were the young and
impressionable students of the Muir Central College and the
Anthony McDonnell Hindu Hostel being granted concessional
passes for the performance of the said 'dancing girl'? Would
Mr Madan Mohan Malaviya kindly look into this moral issue, and

what was Mr Motilal Nehru doing? And Sir Syed? Did Justice Iqbal Masud have any opinion at all? Most outrageous of all, the *Leader* decried, was the scandalous decision on the part of the citizens of Allahabad to present a gold medal to the said dancing girl, the star performer at the George Town Music Conference, the one and only Gauhar Jaan of Calcutta.

Janki read all this with interest and also—for she was only human—with some private sadness. It was so like the people of her city to fete the local artist with fulsome praise but to fall flat on their faces before a performer from the Big City. She knew Gauhar Jaan, had recorded alongside her in Calcutta studios and engaged in gajras, nok-jhonk and musical dangals with her at Patna and Lucknow. Gauhar was then the femme fatale of the music world. Her face appeared on matchboxes printed in Austria and on postcards in wide circulation. But by 1911 Janki's own records were competing with Gauhar's in every market.

Janki was generous and she well understood the power of the Big City and its easy opportunities, as well as the advantages of a physically attractive personality. If Allahabad was offering Gauhar a medal, Gauhar richly deserved it. What hurt her pride slightly was that she, Janki, along with certain other performers of the second grade, was included in the performance in the capacity of filler artists. This, her own Allahabad that she swore by!

The letter to Akbar Sahib was delivered punctually and he rang her up and showered her with his ire.

'I hold in my hand this aerial carpet, sahiba, that has flown through the air at the behest of an angrezi jinn. I thank you for it.'

'Does it look different, sir, for having flown?' she asked him facetiously.

'Only as a note held in the beak of a pigeon would, a pigeon that has feasted on crumbs of angrezi cake for want of an Indian burfi and consequent to that unloaded his bowel-mush on this air-travelled missive!'

'Sweetened for its flight, nonetheless, sir?'

'As sweet as the knife-edged string of a kite, madam, that has slit the throat of every old-fashioned carrier pigeon in the land,' he answered, gruff, though she knew him well enough to guess he was laughing.

'There is a signature behind the letter,' he said. 'Henri Pequet. The Fransisi coachman of this air-carriage, I understand.'

'You have scared away the British with your verbal onslaughts, sir. The French are now trying.' Amazing how a bit of banter with Akbar could restore her good humour.

'La haula wa la kuwate! We have plenty of Anglo-Indians in the city. Are we to have a population of Franco-Indians too? One of them is soon to descend upon us, did you know?'

'I do,' she answered. 'But Gauhar Jaan isn't French?'

'She's a number of things, or so I hear. She's to sing at this benighted exhibition that has enraged me so much that I have written a poem about it.'

'You must recite it to me when I visit next, Akbar Sahib. And I know about her show. I have been asked to sing in it too. As a supporting artist.'

He drew in his breath sharply. There was a silence at the other end of the line that made it clear that nothing was lost on him.

'It is only befitting, sir. She is a guest of the city and I am a local. Also it is her that the city of Allahabad is giving a gold medal to . . .'

He erupted into a curse. 'Not the city of Allahabad, Bibi. Only a few people who presume to speak for the city.'

'But she is very good, sir. I have performed with her.'

'I know, I know. Her mother Malka Jaan was good too. I know her well. The outrage of it is that you have been invited as a supporting artist. Could they not have avoided this gaffe, the kambakhts?'

'I do not mind, sir. Not much. Only in the beginning . . .' Her voice trailed away. But Akbar was speaking in a voice of rare sobriety, free from any of his usual perversity.

'Remember this: you are not competing with anyone, no matter how others rate you. It is what I have learnt. Do you think I write only to plume myself that I am better than the next poet? No, none of this Ghalib Zauq nonsense for me, Bibi. I know why I write. I write because some things ask to be written. I write because some people read my verse. I write because some years remain to be lived meaningfully. Nothing more and nothing less, mark you. I write because the words find me before I find them. You would do well to regard your music likewise. Also, a prophet is never appreciated in his own country. Someone outside shall measure your worth better.'

She thanked him for his counsel, promising to call soon to hear his poem on the exhibition, and hung up, wondering what the operator in the telephone exchange made of their conversation. She remembered the time when Akbar had unloaded a particularly scathing verse into the telephone receiver and they had heard a distinct chortle and a muffled 'Irshad'. Akbar had then launched into a lengthy monologue addressed to the invisible telephone operator about the indignity of his low calling, the 'peeper into boudoir and privy'. She could always count on Akbar Sahib to lift her spirits.

Especially when what he predicted happened. Someone outside did measure her worth better. A letter in an official On His Majesty's Service envelope arrived for her a few days after the conversation with Akbar. It informed her that on the occasion of the forthcoming coronation of His Majesty, the King Emperor George V, on 12 December 1911, at a special event at the forthcoming Delhi Durbar, she, Miss Janki Bai of Allahabad, had been selected to sing a song of felicitation in company with Miss Gauhar Jaan of Calcutta before the King Emperor and his royal consort, Queen Mary. The letter stipulated the kind of congratulatory song to be sung, its duration, the drift of its sentiment of allegiance and adulation, and requested an advance draft of the song to be submitted.

Excited, she wrote to Gauhar Jaan, respectfully proposing a bandish with the refrain: 'Salamat raho, sultan-meherban'. She received a formal letter penned by Gauhar's manager–secretary, Syed Ghulam Abbas Sabzwari, that Gauhar Sahiba wasn't free to write back, that he had discussed the suggested song with her and regretted that Gauhar Sahiba found it below par. And that she desired that Janki Bai Sahiba be told that she, Gauhar, would choose or compose the song. Further, that she would be visiting Allahabad to sing at the UP exhibition's event and to accept the gold medal which the citizens of Allahabad desired to present her with. If Janki Bai Sahiba was free then she, Gauhar, would take the liberty of training her in a morning's rehearsal which would, she hoped, suffice to enable them to give a good account of themselves at the Delhi Durbar in December.

Quite crestfallen, Janki realized that under all circumstances Gauhar meant to upstage her, and she happened to mention the letter to Akbar Sahib when she called on him to hear his exhibition poem. He had declaimed the verse with zest: 'Exhibition ki shaan anokhi / Har shai umda, har shai chokhi / Okhlidas ki naapi-jokhi / Man bhar sone ki laagat dekhi', and she had applauded and laughed before she happened to remark that whatever the sarkari investment was, it was expected that tickets for Gauhar Jaan's performance would cover a considerable part of the costs, and in her capacity as local artist she too would contribute her mite to the coffers.

He swore. And added, 'I hear the maharaja of Datia took her down from her high horse, your Madam Gauhar Jaan, and so did young Faiyaz Khan.'

'She is a fine enough lady. I have performed with her. Recorded with her.'

'I do not doubt it.'

'As her friend and fellow artist I shall invite her to my humble home. For a meal and then for some lessons in singing which she means to impart to me.'

He barked with raucous laughter. 'Then, Baiji, you shall not grudge me the pleasure of inviting both of you to my humble home too. After she has taught you to sing, that is.'

'I accept your kind invitation, sir, and I have no doubt that she will too.' Janki smiled. The way he rolled his eyes might have given her some inkling that this would be no ordinary visit.

To her all he said was, with his drollest expression, 'I shall now apply myself to writing a eulogium in her honour. And yours as well.'

So Janki wrote back to Gauhar that for her part, she was open to any supervision that Gauhar Sahiba might think fit. That she looked forward to having the pleasure of Gauhar Sahiba's gracious company at her home in Sabzi Mandi on the morning of the day of her arrival. And that she took the liberty of accepting, on her behalf, a generous invitation extended to them both by the well-known poet Akbar Ilahabadi at his villa, Ishrat Manzil.

She received an equally graceful reply, albeit conveyed by Gauhar's manager–secretary, Sabzwari, and in the next few days she set her household staff to preparing for the visit of the glamorous diva from Calcutta, Gauhar Jaan.

News of Gauhar's impending visit, on the appointed day, seemed to have leaked out into the immediate neighbourhood. Glancing through the chinks of the curtains at her second-floor windows Janki saw clusters of people hanging about the lane in a state of suspense. It was the same in her own household. There was excitement in the air. Her musicians were tricked out in their festive finery and so were her domestic staff. Sayyad Sahib and Makhdoom Baksh and Ghaseete were resplendent in freshly ironed silk shervanis while Rahimuddin, Mian Jaan and Ral Lal Bhatt had turned up reeking of scented hair oil and the ministrations of a fancy barber. Samina, Farida and Feroza dressed in their best, with flowers in their braids and an extra-abundant mass of shimmering glass bangles tinkling on their wrists halfway up to their elbows. Jallu Mian flitted about wearing a fur cap at a rakish angle and even the two bawarchis, Bhaggu Mian and Baddu Mian, wore fresh muslin kurtas and sashes befitting chefs of a royal entourage. Janki marvelled at the preparations her staff had made in order to make themselves presentable to their celebrity guest. She herself had chosen to wear a pale onion-pink ensemble embroidered with silver thread, a quiet, functional outfit as befitted a hostess.

There was a stir and flurry on the stairs and Jallu came rushing up to announce the arrival.

Gauhar's first words, on entering the divan-khana, were: 'A hookah. How very quaint. Yours?'

When Janki nodded, Gauhar moved impetuously forward to examine the object. 'Now I know what to send you from Calcutta. I'll send you the finest hookah with its pipe coiled round with silver. As dainty as a dancer's hair braid. They're made very close to my Chitpur villa.'

'Welcome to Allahabad, Gauhar Sahiba,' Janki greeted her guest. The guest swirled round and, advancing, put both her arms on Janki's shoulders in a warm embrace.

'I am not new to Allahabad,' she said. 'I came here earlier this year, incognito, all veiled and disguised.'

Janki was surprised. 'Really? How so?'

Her guest seated herself on the central divan, raised her eyebrows playfully and said in a mysterious undertone, 'I had unfinished business with this city.'

Her words invited inquiry but the formality of their association discouraged Janki from asking anything. Instead she signalled to Farida and Samina to bring in the sherbet and make preparations for the repast to follow.

It wasn't Gauhar's beauty but her tremendous class, her absolute exclusivity, that first struck you. She looked—and was—of indeterminate race. Dark hair, brown eyes, a European skin. No one could call her slender, yet she wasn't plump either, though just beginning to fill out and overflow. Her hair was well pomaded and rippled and coiled into a chignon. Her dress too was uniquely indeterminate—a saree which created the impression of a gown. Red velvet with large panels of lace bunched just so, concealing here, promising there, revealing at a third place. A bare navel covered with the lacy gathers of an anchal. Even a hint of bare leg glimpsed through the saucy side-lace of her net saree. Was her underskirt side-slit and lace-panelled too?—Janki wondered. The jewels she wore were tasteful and obviously very expensive, crafted specially to go with her ensemble, their gold filigree repeating the pattern of the lace she wore. She took off her large, round sunglasses and Janki saw that her eyes were finely kohled and her eyelids gently gilded. Her cheekbones were softly touched with rouge and she wore lipstick. On her feet she wore velvet shoes with high heels. The room had filled with her overpowering cologne. Janki remembered the gossip that Gauhar fans swooned over, that the diva never wore the same clothes and jewels twice to any recording or performance, that she matched her clothes to suit the mood of the concert.

'We of Allahabad are fortunate to have you with us,' Janki said.

'It is I who consider myself fortunate, my Janki,' replied Gauhar gracefully. 'It is so very kind of the citizens of Allahabad to confer this medal on me. I only wish,' she sighed, 'that Allahabad citizens had sent me a train like the maharaja of Datia did once. A special train of eleven coaches, exclusively for me.'

'Eleven coaches! Who travelled in the other ten?' asked Janki wonderingly.

'Oh, my khidmatgars, barbers, my dhobis, maids, horses and syces. Of course, my musicians. But your Allahabadis aren't royal in temperament—they might be bookish and political and talkative. I heard the whisper that went around when I mentioned the Datia hospitality—"Is she bringing a baraat?" I could tell them what's often said of me: "Gauhar ke bina mehfil, jaise shauhar ke bina dulhan." Indeed, a baraat, gentlemen, I might have said, but let that go.'

She had the most fluent eyebrows. Her voice was trained as much in speech as in song and it flowed in many registers. A perfectly finished artwork, flawlessly executed—that was Gauhar.

This was the first time Janki and Gauhar had spent so much time together. Gauhar ate and praised, took a tour of the house, met the musicians and the staff, chirped to the parrots and lowered her beauteous nose into the rosebushes on Janki's terrace. Far from being haughty, she could be warm and personal when the mood took her. Vivacious, versatile, contrary, vain, sad and self-effacing—during the course of the day Janki saw many sides to her guest's personality. They spoke of many things.

They spoke of other singers with whom they had performed. Malka Jaan of Chilbila, Badi Maina, Husna Bai of Benaras, Wazir Jaan, Suggan Bai, Mangu Bai. They gossiped about the beautiful Malka Jaan Agrewali's affair with the much younger Faiyaz Khan. They laughed over Haddu Khan's indignation when he went for his first gramophone recording. When the large bugle-shaped horns of the microphones were put before him he grew agitated that he was asked to sing for them. His rage was enduring. In later years his special ire was directed at the dog in the HMV emblem. La haula wa la kuwate!—he'd swear—What a way to compliment an artist! To offer him a portrait of what he is now become, a wretched cur in the leash of foreign machines! And the first time the recording was played back for him he was outraged that he was being mocked by the machine. This, he had fumed, is the jest of the devil! They get a mimic to mock me, may Allah smite him dead! I shall not endure it, sirs! He had hobbled out and it had taken six people to soothe him and make him stay.

'Indeed,' said Janki, 'for maestros like him it is hard to squeeze the vastness of a raga into three minutes.'

'Well, I managed, didn't I?' responded Gauhar.

'You did more than managed. You excelled,' said Janki.

They spoke of the great Calcutta soirées of Seth Dhulichand and Shyamlal Khatri. And the soirées at Lala Bisesar Das's bagiya in Allahabad, at Chowk Gangadas, at the Rani Mandi Kothi, at Babu Radheshyam Kalwar's haveli and the Pakki Haveli at Daraganj. But when Janki spoke of the time she had sung before the raja of Benaras and the laat sahib at the age of eight, Gauhar immediately spoke of the time when she was just ten and she and her mother Malka Jaan sang 'Jab chhod chale Lucknow' and 'Babul mora naihar chhuto jaye' before the exiled Wajid Ali Shah at Matia Burj. When Janki mentioned her teacher Hassu Khan, Gauhar promptly spoke of Bindadin Maharaj, *the* Bindadin Maharaj of Wajid Ali Shah's glittering durbar who had taught her.

'And, mind you, it was not the pupil that sought out the master but the other way around. It was he who approached my ammi with an offer to tutor me. I travelled to and fro between Calcutta and Lucknow for years to learn from him. What rigour, Janki. My guru practised just one gat—"Thig dha dhig dhig" continuously for three years. Twelve hours a day! And I did not have only one guru but several. Bamacharan Bhattacharya taught me Bengali songs, and Ramesh Chandra Das taught me keertans. There was Srijanbai for dhrupad-dhamar and even a certain Mrs De Silva for English songs.'

Janki noticed that Gauhar did not mention Kale Khan about whom there had been some gossip in music circles. There was something going on between her and Gauhar that made her uncomfortable. A fine edge of rivalry which in Gauhar appeared as condescension camouflaged as friendly advice.

'English songs too!' exclaimed Janki. 'You sang it before the sahibs?'

'I even recorded it,' said Gauhar, smiling. 'It went like this: "My love is a little bird that flies from tree to tree".'

She sang it in a swinging lilt and Janki clapped and said: 'Mash-e-Allah!' Gauhar sang in many Indian languages but this came as a surprise and she was filled with admiration.

'I've heard that a European conductor named Fredliss and his band played Raga Yaman and Poorvi before the viceroy in Baroda and also that Bade Nissar Hussain Khan sang "God Save the King" in Raga Hans Sarang before the Chhote Laat Sahib at Calcutta. For which the Chhote Laat Sahib gave him a huge silver watch and he now uses it to smash almond and walnut shells with! But you are no less. You are a true memsahib,' said Janki.

'Shouldn't I be?' responded Gauhar. 'After my Benaras heartbreak I swore to be one.'

'What happened in Benaras?' asked Janki cautiously.

Gauhar settled herself comfortably against the satin pillows. 'Ah, Benaras,' she said, sighing. 'I don't know whether to love it or despise it. It makes you and breaks you. It threw fifty-six stabs at you, my poor Janki, but it hurled many times that number of knife stabs on my young heart when that faithless Chaggan Rai chose his English-twittering wife above me, whom he had kept in love and in his care for three whole years! And me just seventeen years old! You should have seen him warbling English verse to me that he'd written: "Where have you gone, my beloved jaan, leaving my heart asunder?" Before his family found an English-chirping girl for him. So when the mood takes me I turn myself into Eileen Angelina Yeoward again, off and on. For I am English on one side from my Hemmings grandfather and Armenian on the other side from my father. Behold—Gauhar is many, many, many, many, many things!' She sang out the last words like a refrain. Like the climax of a thumri, thought Janki.

'It must be strange to change one's name and identity,' mused Janki.

'Strange it is,' replied Gauhar. 'Not I alone but my mother as well. Names, faiths, cities—we changed them all. From Eileen Angelina I became Gauhar, the Jewel. A French admirer used to call me Jewel, Bijou. Madame Bijou, he began calling me. "*Tu est une autre Madame B*," he used to tell me. What a rascal, Janki. I discovered that the first Madame B. was Madame Bovary, the second was Madame Butterfly . . . you know, the opera. And the book—by Gustave Flaubert, I said to him—"*Merci bien, monsieur, then you leave out Madame Blavatsky!*" That foxed him.'

Janki knew of none of this. Too dark to flush, too proud to pretend, she shook her head, saying, 'No, Gauhar Sahiba, I haven't heard of any of them.'

So Gauhar, the cosmopolitan, patiently explained to her what opera was and who Flaubert was (adding that she'd read *Madame Bovary* in its French original) and who Madame Blavatsky was.

'Now in French your name would be Jean-Qui,' said Gauhar with a comic flourish. 'Or Jane-Who in English.'

'Who is Jane?' asked Janki, by now quite out of her depth.

'Nobody. Just an English name. Often used for a plain woman. Plain Jane. Oh, not you, I didn't mean you. But whatever *does* Janki mean?'

'It's one of Sitaji's names,' said Janki timidly.

Gauhar gave vent to a tinkling laugh. 'Ah, the good wife!' she quipped. 'When you marry—if you do—your name shall be your certificate of wifely virtue, Sitaji.'

Janki bit her lip. For some reason unknown to her she held back the information that she was married and that her husband was presently at his other house.

But Gauhar was prattling on: 'Personally, I don't ever intend marrying. Shaadis are like the notorious pedas of Mathura—if you eat, you regret, if you don't eat, you regret. I don't marry my men. I make them pine for me.'

Then followed an intimate and cosy woman-to-woman outpouring of her roller-coaster love life. The raja of Khairagarh, old and dissolute, who had ceremonially undertaken her deflowering— 'Two months my keeper. My keeper, forsooth! As though I was a little tigress. I was too—let me assure you . . .' The wealthy and love-struck zamindar of Behrampur, Nimai Sen, who took her out riding, introduced her to the races—as Amrit Keshav Naik, the love of her life, did later. 'Such a man, Janki, you never saw! If I refused him a kiss he wept. If I had a headache he burnt banknotes to make a fire to make me a cup of tea—we were in a deserted dak-bungalow in the hills and the caretaker was away!'

Janki listened, awestruck. 'Good marriage-worthy creature,' she remarked, affecting a savvy, frivolous tone.

'To be honest, I thought so too. If—and it's always if with these men—he'd consented to actually marry me. But no, Baiji, not for him. Anything but and I mean anything. Gifts of gold, ivory, jewels. Me, I was overcome. I gave him my diamond nose stud as a mark of my devotion. We parted of course.'

'Did you . . . Did you never meet him again?' asked Janki, quite absorbed by this tale of Gauhar's loves.

Gauhar looked at the ceiling, closed her eyes, breathed deep. 'No. But some day when we are both old he'll need me again.'

She laid a ringed, bangled hand on Janki's sleeve. 'Listen,' she said, 'do you know what often goes on in my mind as I sing? My lips may be intoning the words of a thumri but my mind is busy, busy, busy. I imagine with such intensity that I often wonder if my thoughts travel to the ones I have loved and knock on the doors of their minds. Yes, even the ones no longer alive.'

The telegraph of inside gossip brought to Janki, some years later, that Gauhar had indeed rushed to Nimai Sen's bedside as he lay dying but she reached too late. That on arriving she was handed the nose stud which she had once given him, for he had left instructions that it be returned to her when she came. To Janki it sounded like a Sarat Chandra Chattopadhyay novel. But that was years after that memorable day that she and Gauhar spent together in her Allahabad kothi.

On that day Gauhar seemed possessed by the need to bare her heart and for a while they were not competing professionals but siblings and soulmates, despite the ambiguity of intimacy and alienness that defined their association.

Of Amrit Keshav Nayak she spoke with real pain. 'The real love of my life. Him too I never married. There was no need to. We were one in voice and thought and soul. Every time he wrote a song and I set it to tune and sang it, it was a marriage greater than any other.'

'So you might actually have married him?'

Gauhar looked away, eyes clouded. 'Maybe, if he'd lived longer. Yes, I might have. Only thirty years old he was, cut down in his flower. Drink killed him. It killed the two people dearest to me, my mother Malka Jaan and Amrit. Yes, I might have married him. I would have . . .' Her voice trailed away like a song left unfinished, like a string snapped, and Janki had not the heart to remind her of the Mathura peda. There was such sadness in her face that Janki realized, with a woman's intelligence, that marriage was a sensitive issue with Gauhar for all her feisty bravado.

The bravado was back in a flash. 'What folly if I had indeed married any of those creatures! My biological father was a knave and my foster father was a gentleman! My father married my mother and deserted her and my adopted father—who I thought was my real father—never married her but stood by her all his life.'

'My father too. Deserted my mother, I mean,' faltered Janki. It was hard for her to share such things but Gauhar's candour invited some confessions.

Gauhar pulled herself upright on the divan. 'Did he? That's another thing we have in common. Why did he desert her?'

'For the love of a woman,' replied Janki.

'Ah,' breathed Gauhar. 'My dearest Janki, lucky are you whose father left your mother for the love of another woman.

Better that than the love of lucre such as my shameless Abbajaan has! Glad I am for my mother that she was rid of the gallant Robert William Yeoward, though it was a long time ago. Listen,' said Gauhar, turning to face Janki dramatically, 'I told you I had unfinished business in Allahabad. I came here on a secret mission just a few months back. I came here to track down my long-lost Abbajaan, dear Mr Yeoward.'

'Here? In Allahabad?'

'Right here. Come on, don't look so surprised. He married my mother at the Holy Trinity Church. She was called Victoria Hemmings then, not Malka Jaan, you know. And I was baptized at the Methodist Episcopal Church when I was little Eileen Angelina. So Allahabad and I go back much further than Allahabad and you.'

'Did you find him?' asked Janki. The longer one talked to Gauhar the more eventful did her life seem.

'I did. I really needed to find him. It's this court-kutcherry business I've been embroiled in. With the bastard Bhaglu, who's been little more than our servant, my mother's and mine. Actually he's the son of Ammi's old maid. Lived on our scraps all his life. Now after Ammi's death he has the gall to announce that everything I have belongs to him because he is my mother's blood-begotten son and I, Gauhar, am a bastard! Allah rot his soul. So I swore to go in search of my biological father, who'd walked out on Ammi when I was a tiny child, and produce him in court. And I traced him here—in Allahabad.'

'Whereabouts in Allahabad?' Janki ventured.

Gauhar shook her head. 'That I can't tell you. He lives near a certain sugar factory.' Janki ran her mind over the various sugar factories she knew of but discreetly refrained from any further inquiry.

'How pleased he must have been to find that the celebrated Gauhar Jaan is his daughter,' Janki remarked.

Gauhar tossed her head disdainfully. 'Very pleased indeed,' she said, 'especially when he asked me to pay him Rs 9000 for appearing in court and declaring that he was lawfully wedded to Ammi and that I was his legitimate, biological daughter! He said he would. With papers and all. If I paid him Rs 9000!'

'Nine thousand!'

'That's nothing to me, understand. I spent Rs 1200 on my cat's wedding and 20,000 when she had a litter and I threw a banquet that all Calcutta attended.'

'Someone told me that the nawab of Junagarh spent Rs 2 lakh on the wedding of his dog. Maharajas were invited to the feast and portraits painted of all his dogs, all dressed in gold. And Abdul Karim Khan has a singing dog named Tipoo Mian who performs onstage. My own parrot, Munne Mian, can sing a thumri as well as any, I assure you!'

Gauhar tittered. 'Not just cats and dogs. I regularly toss a thousand rupees to the viceroy . . .'

'Yes, I heard that story. That the laat sahib of Calcutta fined you.'

'After bowing from the waist and taking off his cap to me as I tore past in my carriage. Six white Arabian steeds, you understand. No less in style and scale than the carriages used by royalty. The poor man thought I was a queen or a princess and bowed deep as I drove past him near the maidan. Imagine his horror when he learnt he'd bowed to Gauhar the songstress not the queen of some native state!'

'A queen of mausiqui, surely,' murmured Janki, awestruck. She could see that Gauhar was pleased at this homage. She smiled.

'That's why he slapped the fine on me. A thousand rupees for driving in a six-horse carriage. Made the rule that henceforth only the viceroy and royalty could travel in six-horse carriages, not ordinary citizens. But I do not count myself an ordinary citizen, *excusez-moi*. A thousand rupees is what I earn in a single concert. Voila! I paid the fine. And continued riding past him, all the way from the viceroy's palace to Eden Gardens. Every time I was fined I paid it and repeated the offence with the greatest pleasure. So, you see, what's Rs 9000 to me! But that it should have been my father!'

'So did you pay him? Your father, not the viceroy, I mean?'

'Not a cowrie. The court summoned him and he came. Most meekly. Produced the papers. And all the proof that I was his daughter. I won that round.'

'So that was your unfinished business.'

'I saw the sights too. All there is to see. The Sangam. The temples and mosques and churches. The garden of Prince Khusrau.'

'There's still a monument you haven't seen. And that's the famous Akbar Ilahabadi,' revealed Janki.

Gauhar clapped her hands. 'Wonderful!' she exclaimed. 'He used to know my mother. Liked her verses.'

'Your mother was a poet?'

'A very good one. Akbar Sahib admired her.'

Janki cleared her throat bashfully. 'He guides my callow pen. I write a few verses too.'

Gauhar was enthusiastic. 'Oh, so did I once. In my Benaras days I used to write as Chhaggan-piya and Gauhar-piya and Humdum. Now, tell me, my Jaan-Kee, which "piya" do you suffix your name with? Kaisar-piya, Akbar-piya? Hardinge-piya? Curzon-piya?'

She shook with girlish laughter.

'No, Gauhar Sahiba. I write only as Janki.'

'Then there is no Janki-piya?'

Janki joined in the girlish giggling and would not offer a clue.

Gauhar eyed her with narrowed eyes. It seemed to have struck her quite suddenly that while she had been most expansive about herself Janki had remained a quiet listener, volunteering no information of her own.

'Look how I run on, Janki, while you keep your lips sealed.'

'What to say, Gauhar Sahiba? I haven't had an interesting life.'

'Then go get a life, for Allah's sake! We only live once. But you're a Hindu, no? You'll get reborn. What'll you be reborn as, my Jaan-Kee?'

Again Janki withheld the information that she had converted to Islam. Instead she said, 'I don't know. As a raga maybe . . .'

'Oh, subhan Allah! A beautiful thought. A raga in which songs may be sung by a thousand voices. You're right. Maybe we're all ragas. Each one made up of notes placed just so, no two alike. And if perchance someone gets the exact placement of the notes that make you up, voila! You're reborn! Wonderful, my Jean-Qui! So when do we visit this monument of yours?'

'This evening. At five.'

'Then after lunch we'd better get down to the Delhi Durbar song,' remembered Gauhar. 'I still have to coach you for it.'

'Yes,' assented Janki and sent for Samina and asked her to lay the sheet and serve lunch in the dining chamber.

At Ishrat Manzil that evening Akbar sparkled with verse and witticism. The ladies of his family had arranged a plentiful repast, not without copious commentary from Akbar himself. Tea, now so popular through the length and breadth of the country, was served by the orderlies and bearers, with Akbar grimacing in droll despair, shaking his head: 'Gaye sharbat ke din yaaron ke aage ab toh ai Akbar / Kabhi soda, kabhi lemonade, kabhi whiskey, kabhi tea hai!'

There were dry fruits, kebabs and cake served on the finest silver and porcelain. Akbar reciting ruefully, to their great merriment:

'Thay cake ki fikr mein, so roti bhi gayi,
Chaahi thi shay badi, so chhoti bhi gayi,
Wayiz ki naseehatein na maneen aakhir,
Patloon ki taak mein langoti bhi gayi.'

He had met them most gallantly, fulsome in praise of their beauty and bounty in thus gracing his poor threshold with their shining presence. Witnessing this excess of chivalry and courtly self-abasement Janki wondered what mischief was at play in that puckish brain. But his courtesy was faultless. He made polite mention of Gauhar's mother, the gifted Malka Jaan, her book of poems—the *Makhzan-e-Ulfat-e-Mallika*—which she had once sent him and which he had acknowledged in his letter to her, applauding the delicacy of the verse and the depth of thought it contained. He expressed sadness at her tragic passing. He hobbled to a side cabinet, pulled open a drawer and displayed a stack of records that he had recently borrowed—most of them being Gauhar's and Janki's—from a friend. To try out the working of this absurd new instrument, this gramophone, he explained. The large trumpet-jawed monster sat in the ladies' quarters, he told them—the begum and the other ladies of the household had got too fond of it.

'Not,' he qualified, 'that I have ever laid claim to being the pretty parrot of a houri, but surely Akbar's face is a shade better than that of either the dog or the trumpet! But the begum prefers both to mine, alas!'

'How heartbreaking!' said Gauhar with a laugh.

'You have only yourselves to blame, ladies,' said Akbar in mock despair. 'It is your sweet voices that have seduced the begum's ear. She bade me to convey to you her greetings and her fulsome appreciation of the blessing that has descended from heaven into her humdrum life—the gramophone! She observes strict purdah and apologizes that she cannot appear in the divan-khana to meet you ladies. She has sternly chided my timid suggestion that she suspend her principles and appear before you today, you being ladies, but she is strict and she pointed out that there are bearers and chaprasis here and hence I am left to be host and hostess both! Me, I have other views both on the gramophone and the purdah!'

And he let loose a further verse that had them in splits:

'Bepurdah kal jo aayeen nazar chand bibiyan,
Akbar zameen mein ghairat-qaumi sed gad gaya.
Poochha jo unse aapka purdah wo kya hua?
Kehne lageen ki aql pe mardon ki pad gaya.'

Gauhar threw back her head and laughed heartily. Then she ventured to ask, 'You do not share your begum's enthusiasm for the gramophone, sir?'

He coughed, affected deep thought.

'As ever,' he explained discursively, 'it is not the gramophone I object to, but the infinitely richer renditions that it has supplanted. A middle-class thing, the gramophone, excuse me.'

'People said that about the harmonium, sir,' Gauhar pointed out, 'but time alone shall tell whether something is an improvement or a loss.'

'And who is this being, this Abba Time?' he turned to demand. 'Is it the hoarse voices of the hoi polloi? Is it the lying testament of the masses who know little, understand less?'

'More people can experience the joy of music, sir,' argued Gauhar. 'People like your begum sahiba, like those who could not go to musical baithaks, who did not have the leisure or the money . . .'

'Exactly,' he retorted. 'A herd of cattle pretending to enjoy a rose garden! Ah, Bibi, you do not see the cattle chomping up the roses! You strew them in their path. You cannot consult the rose that's ground to death beneath their jaws. You have broken faith with the rose garden of true art!' He was all charged up. He launched into verse: 'Wah mutrib aur wah saaz, wah gaana badal gaya. Neendein badal gayeen, wah fasana badal gaya. Rangey-rukhey-bahar ki zeenat hui nayee, gulshan mein bulbulon ka tarana badal gaya! But what am I doing? Instead of making you welcome, this old crabby Akbar has taken to his accursed rant again! A thousand pardons, ladies. And allow me to congratulate you on your latest glory—this invitation to sing at the Delhi Durbar. I saw the last one, the one Muhtaram Curzon organized in 1903. I was there. What a spectacle.'

And he proceeded to tell them about it. The fortnight of festivities, the pageantry and pomp. How a dusty plain was transformed into an enchanting city of tents, a city with its own miniature railway, its telephone exchange, magistrates' courts, shops and hospital, all lit up with electricity, you can hardly believe it! Policemen in their specially designed Delhi Durbar attire, the medals stuck, the days of polo, the military reviews, parades led by Kitchener Sahib, the commander-in-chief, the bands, fireworks, dinners, balls, even something Akbar had never beheld before—a film in which images actually moved on a screen! And though the King Emperor Edward VII and Queen Alexandra did not come, the king's younger brother, the Duke of Connaught, did, with a horde of dignitaries. But everyone agreed it was Curzon's show. You should have seen the Curzons arriving, riding elephants caparisoned in bejewelled velvet, some bearing heavy gold candelabras on their decorated tusks. Curzon with his high, balding forehead and pinched nose, dressed in cream breeches and a train of midnight blue and a jacket embroidered with dense gold sheaves. But it was Begum Curzon's sumptuous dress at the grand ball that left the beholder stupefied. She had deep eyes, did Begum Curzon. No purdah to conceal the beauties of these memsahibs. Deep eyes and chiselled nose but such thin lips. Her ball dress an exquisite affair made of chiffon and covered with zardosi work in gold and silver thread embroidered by the finest of Agra and Delhi embroiderers. A design of peacock feathers with a blue-green beetle wing studding each peacock eye. But the fabric was styled into a gown in Paris, it was said. Created by the House of Worth!

'Were you invited to the ball, sir?' asked Janki in wicked innuendo.

'What else do I do, lady, save dance to the angrezi band?' was Akbar's answer.

'But our Indian maharajas with their grand retinues stole the show. The jewels they wore, heirlooms of Hind, treasures preserved in private collections for centuries! The elephant carriage of the maharaja of Rewa alone meriting a poem!' Wait, he had written a poem in honour of the dazzling display: Akbar put on his glasses, shuffled the pages of his ledger-like volume of scribbled verse and found the one he was looking for.

'Ah, here it is. Here's what I wrote in my bedumbed delight: "Jalwa-e-Durbar-e-Dehli" is what I called it.

'Sar mein shauq ka sauda dekha,
Dehli ko humne ja dekha,
Jo kuchh dekha achchha dekha.
Jamunaji ke paat ko dekha,
Achchhe suthre ghat ko dekha,
Sab se unche laat ko dekha,
Hazrat Duke Canaat ko dekha.
Paltan aur risale dekhey,
Gore dekhey, kale dekhey,
Sangeeney aur bhaaley dekhey,
Band bajaney waaley dekhey.

Daali mein narangi dekhi,
Mehfil mein sarangi dekhi,
Bairangi baarangi dekhi,
Dahar ki ranga-rangi dekhi.
Achchhe-achchhon ko bhatka dekha,
Bheed mein khaatey jhhatka dekha,
Munh ko agarchey latka dekha,
Dil darbar se atka dekha.
Auj British Raj ka dekha
Partav takht-o-taj ka dekha,
Rangey zamana aaj ka dekha,
Rukh Curzon Maharaj ka dekha.'

Akbar shut his volume, looked up, mischievous. 'Wah! Subhan Allah!' cried Gauhar. 'You should sing it, sir, for best effects. Maybe to a keherwa beat.'

Akbar squirmed bashfully. 'The sarkar makes me dance to its tune and the lady would have me warble to hers. Where's the justice in this, O Akbar?' he lamented. 'There was a time when

Akbar thought: Sur kahan ke, saaz kaisa, kaisi bazm-e-saamai?
Josh-e-dil kaafi hai, Akbar, taan udaney ke liye. But I have since
those days of folly lost my voice.'

'Then, by your leave, I shall sing it for you,' offered Gauhar
with a flourish.

Akbar looked overwhelmed. 'Baiji, you take my breath away.
My verses shall flower on your lips and bless them.'

'And you, sir, are a poet and we ladies know better than to be
misled by the protestations of poets,' retorted Gauhar playfully.

'If sing you must, sahiba, it must be a better verse. One befitting
this honour. I offer for your perusal this lowly ditty. One I have
only just written.'

He found a loose folded page and handed it across to Gauhar
who without a moment's hesitation began singing, improvising
brilliantly, as she sang:

'Zulf-e-penchan mein wah sajdhaj, ki balayein bhi mureed.
Qadey-rana mein wah chamkham ki qayamat bhi shaheed.
Ankhein wah fitnayey-dauran ki gunahgar karein,
Gaal wah subahey-darakhshan ki malaq pyar karein,
Garm taqdeer jisey sunney ko shola lapkey . . .'

Gauhar's voice trickled to a stop and she paused a while, her lips
forming the words as she ran her eyes over them. A tiny smile
played on her face and her eloquent eyebrows arched whimsically
on her smooth forehead. She raised her head and fixed a bemused
eye on Akbar: 'I had just such a poem written in my honour,
Akbar Sahib, by the court poet of Indore, but that you should write
one for me takes my breath away. It *is* about me, isn't it?'

'Fortunate is Gauhar that she believes so,' said Akbar
provocatively.

Gauhar resumed singing:

'Garm taqdeer jisey sunney ko shola lapkey,
Dilkash awaaz ki sunkar jisey bulbul jhhapkey . . .'

'Ah,' she breathed, as though she had found in the words a confirmation of her suspicion.

'Dilkash chaal mein aisi ki sitarey ruk jaayein
Sarkashi naaz mein aisi ki governor jhuk jaayein.'

'Not the governor alone, Akbar Sahib, but the viceroy himself! It *is* for me, I see,' put in Gauhar, smiling in gratification.
'Baiji is intelligent, need I say more?' murmured Akbar shyly.
She did not sing out the final couplet but read it aloud with a resounding flourish:

'Aatishey husn se taqwey ko jalaaney wali,
Bijliyan lutf-e-tabassum se giraney wali.'

She sat looking at Akbar with an indulgent eye, as though royally acknowledging his homage. Akbar reached forward and retrieved the sheet of paper with the scribbled poem.
'It needs a final verse, madam, and I have only just created one. By your leave, Janki Bibi, I regret I have no verse for you. I do not write in honour of married women and your recent wedding to my good friend Abdul Haq, much happiness as it may have bestowed on you, leaves you permanently bereft of any verse in your honour. But for Gauhar Sahiba, here is my ultimate tribute:

'Khush naseeb aaj yahan kaun hai, Gauhar ke siwa?
Sab kuchh Allah ne de rakha hai shauhar ke siwa!'

Akbar produced the final words with just a thread of gleeful malice playing in his voice and Janki, who had been trying hard to keep a straight face throughout the foregoing exchange, burst out laughing. An embarrassingly loud peal of laughter escaped her lips, bringing a quick frisson in Gauhar's face. Akbar's disclosure about Janki's marriage had stunned her and Janki's explosion of mirth inflamed Gauhar's imperious temper. She turned to stare piercingly at Janki, eyes simmering. Then she rose, drew herself up to her full height, and confronted Akbar with a withering couplet of her own:

> 'Yun toh Gauhar ko mayassar hain hazaron shauhar,
> Par pasand usko nahin koi bhi Akbar ke siwa!'

And with that she turned peremptorily to Janki again and said coldly: 'It is late, Baiji. Be so good as to excuse me now. I shall trouble you to send for your phaeton and have me dropped at my hotel. I—and I believe you too—have a performance tomorrow.'

Gauhar never forgave Janki for that laugh. It might indeed have obliquely stoked, or at least helped provoke, the subsequent misjudgements of her life, her desperate wooing of her manager, Sabzwari, her absurd marriage and later loss of both dignity and property. Janki sometimes reproached herself for that laugh but the coolness between Gauhar and herself had come to stay. Late in life, when they were both old, reports came to Janki how Gauhar had begun charging one rupee as her fee for training students, and selling her own compositions for the same price and Janki did not know whether to believe or disbelieve or whether she should reproach or absolve herself.

At the grand exhibition event Gauhar sang with her characteristic panache and there was a stampede outside and the police had a hard time controlling the crowd. She was awarded the gold medal with great ceremony and she received it with charming deference, endearing herself to the Allahabad audience. Janki sang after Gauhar's performance and though she sang to a quieter audience her singing continued all night and far into the wee hours and till the break of dawn, her calm, strong voice floating across the silent city's temple spires and minarets and towers almost as far as the riverbank, until it turned into the signature voice through which the city identified itself, and her song a theme of timeless belonging in a language that the city's heart beat to. Gauhar had not waited. She had left as soon as her performance ended.

17

Till late October 1911 Janki had been recording for Max Hampe of GTL in Calcutta. That left her just over a month in Allahabad before the Grand Delhi Durbar of 1911 which was to last from 7 to 16 December. The first time a reigning British monarch would tour his Indian empire. A monarch who, years later, lying on his deathbed, dosed on morphine and cocaine, would put one last question to his secretary, 'How's the empire?' George V, crowned King Emperor on 22 June, at Westminster Abbey, was to perform the lead role all over again in a stupendously stage-managed coronation show at Delhi on 12 December. And to this end was organized yet another of those colonial extravaganzas that mimicked, only more spectacularly, the grand durbars of the Mughals. A stupendous gathering of 80,000 visitors, princes, military and commoners in a blaze of pomp and consequence at the glittering mini-city of Kingsway Camp created on an extensive plain on the outskirts of Delhi. A vast pageant of imperial power and princely allegiance enacted to flaunt the realized fantasy of opulence and grandeur of the empire at its height, as also to exercise the royal fiat at a particularly unsettling moment of its history. And though its scale was smaller than the previous one held in 1903, it spelt consequences considerably more far-reaching than the ones before.

To this grand carnival Janki and Gauhar had been invited, to sing a song of felicitation before the King Emperor and his queen, and though Gauhar had insisted on composing the main song and setting it to tune, it had fallen to Janki to select a bunch of minor numbers showcasing their separate styles and initiating a foreign ear gradually into the melodic cadences of Hindustani music. They would both have to be in Delhi well before 7 December, needing at least a week to rehearse together, before taking part in the mandatory rehearsals to be held at Kingsway Camp in company with all the participating nobility and gentry of the Indian Empire, as preparation for the grand event.

Janki had chosen to travel from Allahabad to Delhi on the Upper India Express, along with her musicians, rather than join Gauhar on the Calcutta Mail. After the unfortunate gaffe at Akbar Sahib's house, and Gauhar's marked annoyance, she had decided to tread with care. She arrived in Delhi a couple of days before Gauhar did and was hosted at the Maidens Hotel in Delhi's leafy Civil Lines. This graceful edifice, with its high imperial architecture, was where most of the guests who attended the Coronation Durbar hosted by Lord Curzon in 1903 had stayed. Her entourage of accompanists and staff were housed in another hotel in old Delhi close by. A carriage had been provided and on the first evening she drove out, taking the route from Ludlow Castle, north of the walled city of old Shahjahanabad towards the Lahore Gate, to see the decorations. The streets were beautifully bedecked, colourful lamps hung from the trees and something Janki had never seen before, electric bulbs in rainbow colours festooned in scallops from pole to pole, lining the entire extent of the streets. There were triumphal arches all the way from Chandni Chowk and the Dariba to the steps of the Jama Masjid. In some squares fireworks were already being lit in meticulous rehearsal of the festive week to follow. The band was playing in the hotel's lobby when she returned. Illuminations everywhere. The bar jostling with guests. Dancing in progress in the grand ballroom.

Gauhar arrived next morning, in very high spirits, her pique of their previous meeting apparently forgotten. She had with her, apart from her usual retinue, her handsome young Pathan manager, whom she introduced as Abbas. Her first dramatic outcry erupted in the grand foyer of Maidens Hotel, on learning that her manager had not been accommodated in the same hotel as her and had been put in another hotel nearby, just beyond the green avenues of Civil Lines, an Indian hotel in old Delhi.

'An Indian hotel, if you please!' exclaimed Gauhar. 'Where exactly is this one located, if I may ask? In the British Isles? At the very least, you could put him in the Cecil, so much nicer than this stiff-upper-lip dump. Nothing like the lovely garden look of the Cecil with its majestic neems and its lovely lawns. But I suppose we natives have to be grateful that we are housed at the angrez sarkar's generous expense, we who have come to sing for our supper!'

This was not quite fair on the Maidens with its graceful ivory facade, its swirling driveway and vast stretch of arches, its emerald lawns with strolling peacocks and birds, but Janki hoped Gauhar would have the good sense not to make a scene.

'We only follow instructions from Government House, madam. Only Indians who are royals or great artists like yourself have been accommodated here or at the Cecil or the Swiss,' explained the velvet-voiced usher.

That somewhat mollified Gauhar and she retreated to her corner of the foyer and flounced down on the brocade sofa, fanning herself frenetically although it was a cool December morning.

'Who, I ask, is your viceroy then?' she fumed behind her veil but taking care to keep her voice down so that only Janki heard.

'Your King Emperor's manager, is he not? And they have the impertinence to tell me that this hotel is "socially unsuitable for persons in my employ". "Socially unsuitable for persons in my employ!" Trust these British to twirl their sentences about like sugary thumri crooners at a second-rate mehfil. Well, Abbas,' she sighed, 'the sarkar has decreed that as a person in my employ you are unsuitable company for me. It makes no difference to those chameli-faced lads behind the counter and the puffy old gasbag in the hotel office if I plead with them that as my manager you might in a court of law be said to possess the management of me and then who is to decide who is in whose employ?'

'Bai Sahiba is needlessly upset,' murmured the bashful young man, obviously embarrassed by Gauhar's flamboyant coquetry in Janki's presence, 'but really, I have no objection to staying in the other place.'

'Have I asked your opinion, sir?' snapped Gauhar, meteorically transformed into the queenly employer. Gauhar was brittle, all charged up. Fluctuating between chattiness and cold reserve. 'It is not you but I who object to your being banished to the other place. But go, go, if you must. Go before you give me a headache!'

She swirled herself round, turned her back on Abbas, who waited awkwardly a moment or two, then bowed and slipped away. Janki's eyes followed him. A most unlikely suspicion had come to assail her mind.

'Is that Sabzwari?' she asked hesitantly.

'It is,' replied Gauhar. 'I often call him my Sabzwadi—my green valley. In the stark desert of my life, Janki, he is my oasis. Where would I be without this watchdog of mine?' And she broke into one of her gurgling laughs. Then, just as suddenly, her expression changed to one of extreme irritation. 'At the very least, at the very

least, they'll not object to arranging a motor car for me to drive out
and see the sights.'

'There is a carriage,' Janki told her.

'A carriage! Two meagre horses when I am accustomed to six!
No, Baiji, a motor car is what I shall demand.'

Demand she did but was politely refused. In the privacy of the
shaded balcony outside their suites Gauhar gave vent to another
paroxysm of rage.

'They've got a row of cars lined up outside, at least a score, and
they cannot arrange a single one for me, Gauhar Jaan!'

'Those are private cars, Bai Sahiba,' reasoned Janki, 'belonging
to the princes and dignitaries staying here.' They checked the
printed programme to see who else was staying at the Maidens.
The Nizam of Hyderabad, the Gaekwad of Baroda.

'Not a single petty prince here who wouldn't bow down in
reverence before Gauhar!' ranted Gauhar. 'There are at least a
dozen who know me personally, whose states I have visited and
performed in. Wait, I shall find out if one of them is willing
to allow me the use of his car. Ah, what have we here?—a
telephone! Look at the pretty brass thing. One might mistake
it for a piece of bathroom gear in a memsahib's gusal-khana.
Let me phone their office and find out the who's who of these
chambers.'

Which she wilfully did, and successfully. After a dozen
phone calls that saw her at her charming best, she hung up the
ornamented phone on its bracket and turned to Janki with a smile.
'Not one car, my Janki, but five! A different one for the next five
days. What do you say to that? I can have my pick. There is the
Waverley of the maharaja of Jodhpur. There is a 1911 model
Auburn of the maharaja of Datia. What else—let me see? A Lozier,
an Oldsmobile Limousine and a Gaylord 30! Darbhanga, Patiala,

Cooch Behar. I think I shall go for the Lozier. And which would you rather drive out in?'

Janki was embarrassed. 'I think a carriage is just right for me,' she answered.

'In that case, my sister, we shall go out separately, if you don't mind. Maybe Abbas won't object to giving me his company.'

Her mood had changed to light-hearted teasing. 'Oh, by the way,' she said as though remembering something suddenly, 'I have found out all about this marriage of yours that you were so silent about. My informers tell me that you gifted away a house as a rok-token and caught him securely by the neck.'

Her laugh of tarnished silver cut Janki to the quick. Impatience had been building up in her for quite some time. 'If that was the way to catch a husband, then Bai Sahiba Gauhar doubtless has many houses to gift away,' she retorted abruptly. A second later she wished she had not reacted.

But Gauhar acted as though it was a good joke. 'True, I should have thought of it, my Janki. Maybe I too shall follow your example. Soon.' And she turned away, flashing a brilliant smile, leaving Janki wondering what she meant, marriage or the gift of a house.

As it happened, both. As Janki was to learn, by way of her own informers. For in a little over a year Gauhar would enter into a most unsuitable muta marriage with her manager, Abbas, and sign away her massive villa at 49 Chitpur Road, Calcutta, a step which was to reduce and torment her for the rest of her life.

They retired to their respective suites to rest their voices. The remaining days were devoted to practising and rehearsing at Kingsway Camp and then they gave themselves up to the pageantry unfolding all around them, driving out to join the crowds to witness the greatest show on earth. They witnessed the arrival of the ruling chiefs at Kingsway Station. They looked on as the grand procession passed, identifying from the printed programme which was which. Then the Royal Horse Artillery firing a salute. Then, the most spectacular arrival of Their Imperial Majesties at Selimgarh Station. On the 7th there were back-to-back events: the royal arrival at the reception tent, followed by the state entry into Delhi Fort. Janki and Gauhar, in their separate conveyances, were part of the throng that watched the royal procession passing the Ridge to the King's Camp. On the 11th there was the Presentation of Colours, and, in less solemn vein, the Delhi Polo Tournament that lasted from the 7th till the 11th.

For the Coronation Durbar Gauhar wore her signature black-and-gold gauze gharara ensemble and Janki, anticipating this, opted for a white-and-gold silk chikankari-zardosi peshwaz, draped round with an elaborate gold and net headcloth. In the hectic ceremonial whirl, only stray fragments clung to her memory in later years. The delicate snow-white onion dome of the royal pavilion, set in its fine-wrought, trellised square with four smaller domes at the corners and the filigreed eaves. And in the pavilion, awash in a blaze of light, the two stately forms on their tall, bejewelled thrones placed seven steps up a pedestal, their velvet, fur-trimmed trains arranged in a lustrous cascade down the sides of the thrones and fanning out on the lavish red carpet. The peal of many bugles and the roll of drums. Mounted cavalry all around, redcoats and cream breeches astride tall steeds, turbaned Indian troops in tunics and cummerbunds astride theirs. All the royal houses of India represented by their reigning maharajas, turned out in full regalia, glittering with state jewels, bowing thrice in ritual obeisance before the carpeted pedestal, then retracing their steps backwards without turning. His Highness, the Nizam of Hyderabad, with the Resident at Hyderabad and His Highness's escort. His

Highness, the Gaekwad of Baroda, with his Resident and escort. His Highness, the maharaja of Mysore, and His Highness, the maharaja of Kashmir, with their respective residents and escorts. Then came the Rajputana chiefs with their political officers and escorts, also the agent to the governor general accompanying the leading chief. Likewise the Central India chiefs, the Madras chiefs and the Bombay chiefs with political officers and escorts. The Baluchistan chiefs and the North-West Frontier Province chiefs came with agents, escorts and chief commissioners. Their Highnesses, the maharajas of Sikkim and Bhutan came with their political officers and escorts. The United Provinces chiefs, those of Bengal, the Central Provinces and Burma came next, accompanied by their political officers and escorts. A regiment of Indian cavalry brought up the rear.

Their own performance proceeding flawlessly, ending in a grand finale with 'Yeh jalsa taajposhi ka, mubarak ho, mubarak ho!'

And then being led by an usher clad in breeches, buckled shoes, crimson jacket with a chestful of medals, towards the platform. Bowing low, raising their fingertips to their brows thrice in deferential homage, before raising their eyes to find them looking into two pairs of curiously light-coloured eyes. In later years all Janki remembered of George V was his hair, thin, parted and plastered down beneath a fur cap and a gigantic crown, obviously a heavy weight on that head for there was something in the tilt of his neck that suggested fatigue. She heard him say: 'That was splendid! Splendid.' She remembered more of the Queen's face, an elongated face, running to fullness, but very thin lips and wavy hair swept across her forehead. She seemed to radiate light in myriads of streaming exhalations from a resplendent wall of gems. A woman who held herself very erect in her chair, with her brocade gown flaring in a wide tulip bell about her. Bending forwards, a retainer in gleaming tunic and cummmerbund had lifted two velvet pouches from the gold tray held out by a costumed page and placed them in their outspread headcloths. They bowed again and again and a third time and, walking backwards, faded out of the topaz aura of light that encircled the apparitions. The blinding dazzle, the fragrance of a hundred exotic perfumes, the flourish of trumpets, the clash of luminous colours and fabrics, had left them dazed, even Gauhar, and it was only when they were back at the hotel that they thought of opening the velvet pouches to find a hundred guineas each. With the sovereign's head embossed. Their heads felt dizzy, intoxicated with colour and light, and sleep jerked about fitfully in their restless heads all night and it was only the next morning that the full impact of the Grand Durbar registered in their minds as the sovereign's ringing words, among many others about the revocation of the Partition of Bengal, the appointment of a governor-in-council for Bengal, the separation of Orissa, Chhota Nagpur and Assam, clarified into sense in their heads: 'We are pleased to announce the transfer of the seat of the Government of India from Calcutta to the ancient capital of India.'

'Isn't it strange,' wondered Gauhar, 'that Their Royal Highnesses, the Indian maharajas, were given just a medal each and we, lowly song–dance women received a hundred? I mean, just in terms of the gold alone . . .'

'On the other hand,' Janki quipped, 'our mohurs have just a man's face on them—a hundred faces. But their medals have a woman's face too. Proving that one woman is equal to a hundred men!' For this Delhi Durbar 102 gold and 26,800 silver medals bearing the faces of George V and Mary of Teck had been struck, to be distributed to officers of proven loyalty, high-ranking functionaries of governance and princes who pledged allegiance.

'Truth to tell, she quite outshone her husband,' murmured Gauhar, reverting to women's talk.

'So did the vicereine.'

'She was betrothed to his elder brother, did you know? But he died of pneumonia, poor thing, and so she finds herself married to the younger one. That's luck, if you ask me. One heir apparent dies, presto, you have another! Me, I'd marry a whole family of brothers if I could wear jewels like hers.'

'That was a very heavy crown. He looked strained.'

'Oh, that's not the real one. The real one is kept safe in England, lest some wily king or queen pawns it away on foreign soil. They were known to do that, you know, in Europe's murky past. So they made a law about it—that the Crown of England could never leave England. Funny, most of the jewels in the crown are Indian and the angrezes are insecure about their being brought to India. As though the rubies and emeralds and diamonds will pop out of the gold at the sight of Indian earth! No, that is a special crown made specially for this event. It has 6100 diamonds and that huge ruby in front and all those twinkling emeralds and sapphires and the India Office paid 60,000 pounds of Indian money for it to the jewellery house of Garrard and Company. I used to own a choker made by Garrard that an admirer once gave me. From the Royal House of Bhopal.'

'You know the maharani?' asked Janki, astonished. For the nawab begum, Sultan Kai Khusru Jahan of Bhopal, was the only woman ruler who had attended the Durbar.

'Not her. I mean her son, the one walking behind her, that Hamidullah Khan. Oh, she wouldn't have liked it, jewels being given to a singer, had she known. A real tough one. Wrote a whole lot of pious books. *Bachchon ki Parwarish, Hidayat Timardari, Tandarusti.* But sadly, none of that timardari and

parwarish could assure tandarusti to her children, three out of
the four perishing from too much parwarish!' And Gauhar burst
into a peal of laughter that Janki found reprehensible and in
bad taste.

'Oh, she looked funny, didn't she? All veiled, holding her robe
with one fat hand and her heavy crown atop her veil, peering at the
world through her mask. I thought, what if that crown fell off at
the King Emperor's feet as she bowed. As they all bowed, so low,
so low.'

'Except one,' said Janki. 'And he didn't come loaded with
jewels either.' For the Gaekwad of Baroda, Sayyaji Rao III, had not
only omitted to wear all his state regalia but had just bowed once,
ever so lackadaisically and then stalked off, turning his back on the
King Emperor, something that led to a huge outcry in the angry
British press.

'And what a resounding title the British sarkar had given
him—Farzand-i-Khas-i-Daulat-i-Inglishia! After that, the man
refuses to bow and scrape! He was, I distinctly saw, laughing to
himself as he strode away.'

'They'll find some way to make him pay for the insolence, you
bet. But I believe he is partial to the Congress.'

Their performance done, they could give themselves over to
merriment and sightseeing. On the morning after the Durbar they
drove, together for once, to be part of the massive crowd that had
come to greet the King and Queen as they appeared in a balcony
of the Red Fort, granting a sighting to the citizens of Delhi. And
on the following day they drove out again to see the Royal Review
of 50,000 troops as they marched past their king in the new capital
of the country.

It was then that a thought struck her and she risked a joke
with Gauhar again. 'But now that the viceroy is going to move to

Dilli, Bai Sahiba, how will you tease and provoke him with your six-horse carriage? You'll have to do with a mere governor-in council.'

Gauhar took it in good humour. 'Believe me, Jaan-kee,' she laughed confidently, 'it is to flee Gauhar that the sarkar has shifted base to Dilli. Calcutta was getting too small for us both!'

And so they parted on 16 December, on easier terms than before, joking till the last.

'Don't you think we should have received some sort of title too?'

'Isn't it enough that we've been invited to sing before the Presence? When it seems all the good and virtuous people in the country are up in arms against the likes of us, dancing–singing women?'

'Well, in spite of all those petitions the sarkar has still called us.'

'A title might have done us good.'

'What title do you fancy, Bai Sahiba?'

'I am no ordinary dancing–singing woman.' Gauhar smiled archly. 'I am the Queen Empress of the Durbar of Music. Gauhar-e-Taj-e-Mausiqui might do for me. Jewel in the Crown of Music. And you, my Jaan-kee, could be the Uncut Diamond of the Treasure Chamber.'

'Most gracious of you, Bai Sahiba, but *uncut* for me is unfortunate, don't you say?'

'Ah, my apologies. And be sure to give your Akbar Sahib the bad news. Tell him that to telephones and electric lights and gramophones has been added the new horror he feared. Moving images on a screen! Now definitely here to stay. Someone told me it's called Kinemacolor. Yes, I saw the Durbar being filmed. Who knows, I shall join the band. Be sure to bear these horrid tidings to your Akbar Ilahabadi. Ask him, from me, to write some of his awful verses. Blighting this new curse, this cinema, to hell!'

She was still laughing as the car moved away.

The King Emperor and his entourage went on to Calcutta and Janki returned, the following day to Allahabad, which now received her with slavish adulation.

18

War broke out in Europe in 1914 and the Allahabad papers were full of news about the Indian forces who had been shipped to France and Flanders. The 129th Baluchi Battalion fought in Ypres in Belgium, the 47th Sikhs of the Bhopal Infantry and the 20th and 21st Companies, the Sappers and Miners, fought savagely in the tiny French village of Neuve Chapelle in France. Festubert, Aubers Ridge, Givenchy had become matters of intense discussion on the pages of the *Pioneer* and also in the vernacular press like the *Indian Herald*. Janki pored over the news, her imagination fired by the depictions of fierce engagements with the Germans. Especially Givenchy where it was the Indians who had held tenaciously to German trenches in the most terrible conditions for thirty hours. The enemy had hit back by blowing up a line of mines before resorting to hand-to-hand combat. It was December 1914. By April there was a second Ypres, followed by Aubers Ridge and Festubert in May. In Allahabad native solidarity with Britain was staunch. A mammoth ticketed concert was organized at the Police Lines to raise the war fund and Janki Bai, the star of the event, happily donated the takings to Britain's war effort, in acknowledgement for which the organizer, Babu Mahendra Prasad, the deputy collector, made a speech, expressing the gratitude of the British sarkar and presenting her with a certificate of thanks.

Further commendation appeared in the form of a licensed gun, a double-barrelled, one-cartridge gun and a special security guard to escort her, this honour granted to her by K.N. Knox, Sahib Bahadur, the magistrate collector of Zila Allahabad. Janki accepted both offerings from the sarkar as she had accepted the distinction of singing before George V at the Delhi Durbar. She had come to take her favoured standing with the local representatives of the British sarkar without question.

So when she received a sudden request from the district administration to perform at the Mayo Hall on a certain evening she readily consented to do so. The performance was as usual an extraordinary one, the hall packed with dignitaries, and Janki received the applause of the audience and the commendation of the organizers with a seasoned reserve. It was only the next morning that the *Indian Herald* broke the news that a far more important event had taken place in the city the very same day. The arrival of Annie Besant and her lecture at the Hardinge Theatre in Bahadurganj, attended by a mammoth crowd of students and citizens. The *Herald* rejoiced over the fact that every attempt had been made to prevent Mrs Besant from lecturing, that her earlier fixture at the Mayo Hall had been cancelled 'due to unavoidable reasons' by the district administration and that the event had nevertheless been a colossal success, Mrs Besant arriving in a trail of glory, her carriage drawn by hundreds of Allahabad University students, and her resounding appeal for Home Rule proving to be the trigger that catalysed the imagination of those already under the influence of the Indian National Congress.

The news left Janki disturbed. She saw, or thought she saw, the significance of the gun and the guard. Was it possible that she was already being regarded as a collaborator by the Congress-wallahs? The darling of the sarkar, solicited and serenaded, a decoy of the district administration to draw away the crowds from a possible inciter? It was an unpleasant feeling. It made her take a voluntary break from her busy performance schedules and retire to the seclusion of a private existence for some time. In the form of a family visit to Haq Sahib's other home at Mehdauri. To which she went as a visitor, a celebrity guest at a family wedding. A trophy wife whose arrival was awaited with breathless speculation and greeted with an awestruck riffle and stir in the courtyard. If earlier they had looked askance at her because of her calling, the glory of the exhibition performance and the greater glory of the Delhi Durbar had put it all to flight.

They were present in full strength in the family drawing room, sons, brothers, sisters, nephews and nieces, old aunts and smoky elders, family retainers and hangers-on, when she alighted from her buggy and accompanied her husband in. They swarmed around her in slavish welcome, lavished compliments and approval, introduced themselves by their formal names and their family nicknames. The young ones salaamed and saluted, the old appraised and muttered words of stiff benediction. Such a flurry and bustle in the large household that Janki had difficulty placing who was who, which one a niece twice removed and which a cousin by marriage. The ones she looked out for were present, Haq Sahib's two grown sons, who came forward and offered their respects to this new Chhoti Ammi with proper courtesy. But that other one she was secretly longing to meet, their Badi Ammi, Haq Sahib's senior begum, was conspicuous by her absence. And when she timidly asked her husband where she, her senior co-wife, might have been, all she received were evasive answers.

Nor did she set eyes on her in the days that followed, as the wedding festivities proceeded. It was a nephew's wedding, made grand by his recently acquired government job and by the affluent family in Patna he was marrying into. Made grander still, she gathered, by her own celebrity presence. They called her Baji—middle sister—and she warmed to the sound of that endearment, until she realized that it wasn't 'Baji' they said but 'Baiji', and it came to her with sudden dismay that in their eyes she was still and ever would be, the public singer, the nautch-mehfil professional, and always different, alien. No cosy middle sister or sister-in-law or aunt or niece-in-law, but always and ever the outsider, the outlandish import of their son or uncle or father.

'Why do they not call me Dulhan or Ammi or Khala?' she complained to her husband. 'Aren't they my family now? Why must I be Baiji to them?'

'They are blinded by your stellar presence,' he said, laughingly. 'Give them a little time.'

But he spoke to them and soon enough they tried to call her Dulhan or Ammi or Khala, but the names sounded awkward on their tongues and ever so often they fell into that involuntary 'Baiji' that sealed an irreconcilable distance between them. She tried not to mind and joined in the ceremonies, taking her place among the family women and girls and lady guests, sitting in a circle round their dholaks and singing their saucy wedding songs. Little ditties of teasing coquetry and lustful innuendo and soft spitefulness. She loved those old songs, some centuries old, and she joined in with gusto, singing:

'Oh brother mine, fetch your sword and your shield,
'Tis a bride to be won and a stream and a field,
Bring collyrium for eyes and henna for palms,
Semolina and milk and ten goodly rams.'

'Oh sister, bring a steed for my evergreen prince,
And a turban and jewelled saddle and reins,
Fetch a drum and a flute and a song and a fife,
My evergreen prince goes to bring back a wife!'

Her voice rose, sterling and resonant, vibrating with indwelling power. This was her domain, this dimension of voice and verse. The song swelled on her lips, the walls of the chamber thrummed. All of a sudden she realized that she sang alone, that all the women had fallen silent. She too fell silent in mid-verse, conscious of having incomprehensibly transgressed some unstated courtyard code.

Then one of the young nieces plucked up courage to say, 'Baiji, won't you give us some of your famous mujra songs. Please.'

She might have thought it a compliment to her stature, but instead she experienced a peculiar mistrust in her own identity here. 'Hush,' she protested, affecting friendly annoyance. 'I am your khala today, not your famous Baiji.'

'Oh, we're proud, so proud, Khala Jaan, that we are family now. Or who could have ever dreamt of having you sing at a wedding here?'

'Yes, Dulhan, you have sung at the Delhi Durbar before the King Emperor. You really must sing at the wedding, when the baraat goes to Patna, and again at the walima. Allah be praised, you shall add such lustre to our feast!'

It was coming at her from every side. 'Listen, little girl,' she turned with mock irritation to the importunate young niece. 'Do any of you sing before the men?'

'Oh, perdition take me, Baiji, how could I ever dare? Even if I knew how to sing!'

'Exactly,' said Janki in wry satisfaction. 'You shall giggle behind your veil and keep to the inner courtyard. And you expect

me to unveil and come before the men and, ye God, sing for their
entertainment?'

She could see that her argument left them baffled and she did
not blame them. After all, singing at grand weddings before large
assemblies was one of her occupations. So what accounted for this
improbable inhibition?

The only possible reason that occurred to an old aunt was
scarcely utterable, but she uttered it.

'You mean you will not sing for free?'

The words left a stunned silence in the gathering. Janki turned
the blaze of her outraged eyes on the crone.

'I mean, Dadi Jaan that as a respectable daughter-in-law of this
family, I shall not stoop to entertain anyone. Not here. Not among
my own family. It's the least that I can claim.'

The old lady was visibly taken aback. 'I did not mean to give
offence, Bahu Begum,' she murmured. 'Everyone applauds your
wonderful singing and now that you belong here, so does your
singing . . .'

'Please, Khala Jaan, don't refuse us,' pleaded another. 'Mamu-
jaan said you wouldn't object. He even made a list of songs you've
been famous for . . .'

'He did, did he now?' remarked Janki, incensed. 'In that case,
excuse me, I decline to attend this wedding.' She rose to her feet
and swept away to her room.

Haq Sahib was irritated when she stormed in with her rage.
'Must you be so melodramatic and touchy, begum? They meant
no ill. They are proud to have you in the family and they want
to show you off to the mehfil and the bride's people. What's so
offensive about that? You bring izzat to the family.'

'And what of my izzat?' she demanded. 'Does this family only
regard me as a glittering Baiji, a nautch woman born to sing at

weddings? Is there no thought of my honour? No respectability as a lady of the house?'

'You are being unreasonable, begum,' he cut her short. 'And you put me in an awkward position. I promised on your behalf that you would perform your best mujra at the wedding and now your sulks have made things embarrassing.'

'On my behalf, say you? On my behalf!' It was the first time she had raised her voice with him. 'Do you own my decisions, my voice itself, that you promise on my behalf? Who are you, sir, to do so without my consent?'

His face was tight with fury. 'Only your husband, madam,' he hissed through his teeth.

'You want me to be a mujra woman beneath your roof?'

'Aren't you exactly that?'

'Not under your roof, milord, never under yours. I am a mujra singer only under my own roof and under those that honour me for myself.'

'Then,' said he, in cold fury. 'Seek your own roof, begum, and abandon this one!'

'I shall do so,' she drew herself up. 'And the sooner the better.'

She summoned her sarkari gunman, had her trunks hoisted into a tonga, swung herself into another tonga and rode away, her first visit to her husband's home concluding on this turbulent note.

Haq Sahib stayed away for much longer than she expected. She received no note from him and sent none. She resolved not to call him back, nor betray any indication of feeling his absence. The courts closed for the summer and still there came no news from him. Three months had gone by before she began feeling uneasy at this protracted stalemate in her marriage. She wondered if she should venture to ask Akbar Sahib but decided against it. It would be unseemly for the haughty Janki Bai to betray anxieties of a private nature. Moreover Akbar Sahib had left for Mussoorie for the summer. By July, when the courts reopened, she decided that some overture was in order and so she sent Jallu Mian to Mehdauri with a sealed envelope which contained a brief message: 'The fire caught in the kindling, destroying much. It has made me sing better than ever before. Thank you for this grief.'

Jallu Mian returned with the note undelivered and the news that Haq Sahib, his senior begum and their younger son had gone to Ajmer Sharif for a fortnight.

She affected withering disdain for Jallu Mian's benefit. 'Only to Ajmer Sharif? I thought he had gone on hajj to Mecca!' She wondered what her accompanists and her domestics made of her marriage and this recent alienation.

It soon became apparent that Jallu Mian knew more of Haq Sahib's family situations than he let on. 'Vakil Sahib has much on his mind, Baiji,' he murmured. 'His younger son, Yaqoob, is gravely ill.'

The news took her by surprise. 'What ails him, Jallu Mian?' And why had her husband never shared this trouble with her? She was shamed and disappointed in her own capacity for empathy, her petty, vainglorious arrogance.

Jallu Mian appeared to hesitate, then brought up the words carefully: 'Yaqoob Mian suffers from an illness of the mind, Baiji. He is said to be quite beyond control when the fit is on him.'

This was worse than anything she was prepared for.

Now that he had opened up, Jallu Mian grew expansive. 'Vakil Sahib has sought the treatment of British doctors, of hakims and fakirs across the length and breadth of India but all to no avail.'

'But when I met the lad he seemed most well behaved, very sober and polite.'

'He is so, Baiji, much of the time. But when the fit is on him he is like one possessed by jinns. Or so I have heard.'

'How long has he been this way?'

'I have heard from a very long time and Vakil Sahib's senior begum sahiba devotes all her time to him, not even venturing out of their chambers.'

That explained her conspicuous absence and Haq Sahib's evasiveness. A rush of contrition and pity for the man she had married rose in her, along with bafflement at his reticence, and a sense of rueful self-reproach that she had never guessed at his real life beyond his illusory and superficial liaison with her. Trophy wife indeed, that was all she was, and his real marriage was elsewhere, where the pain was, the horror and the prayers. She could grandly gift away houses and flaunt her soaring virtuosity in song, but it was his deep silence of grief and worry that no song could penetrate that struck her with a humbling realization of her human worthlessness. With her he had gone to performances, banquets and celebrations at the homes of the rich and influential. With his other wife he went to Ajmer Sharif to pray for their deranged son.

'Jallu Mian,' she said in a small voice, 'tomorrow you must carry another note and leave it at Haq Sahib's Mehdauri house. With anyone there who can undertake to deliver it to Haq Sahib as soon as he returns from Ajmer.'

'As you wish, Baiji,' he said.

This was no time for the affectation of poetry. What was needed here was a simple plea for forgiveness expressed in the most ordinary words. It was hard to be ordinary for one who had got used to being extraordinary. Harder to acknowledge the poverty of sympathy she had displayed alongside the flourish of affluence she had flaunted.

It took her very long to frame a letter. At some crucial moment in its composition she had the strange feeling that this was the beginning of a further chapter of self, a riyaz in some other discipline that she was now called upon to practise. She wrote:

My beloved and revered husband,

It is with great humility and concern that I write this missive to you. I am grieved to learn of our son's sad condition and have no words in which I may express my complete support of you and my honoured sister-wife in this great trouble. I hold it my own unworthiness that you have not thought fit to repose confidence of such a distressing matter as our son's illness in me these many weeks and months of our intimate association, and I hasten to assure you that in matters of service to yourself and your family, now my family as well, you shall not find me wanting in any way, whether material assistance or personal care. I beg you to indicate to me whereof I may be of help. I implore you to excuse my thoughtless lapses and grant me the satisfaction of your presence again. And I appeal to your forbearance to allow me to offer my own ministrations to our disturbed son, at our Mehdauri home or here when next you and my honoured sister-wife feel the need for another devoted hand in the comfort and care of our son. I shall put aside all other assignments and present myself at your service, my honoured sister-wife's and our beloved sons', and I sign myself, herein, in utmost humility, Janki.

She handed the sealed envelope to Jallu Mian the following day and it was duly conveyed to the Mehdauri house. Then began the lengthy wait. It lasted another three weeks, following which one afternoon, quite without notice, a tonga drove up and Haq Sahib alighted. He made for the divan-khana and called for his hookah. She made a pretence of languor, though her heart was thumping in her bosom, and carried her own hookah in to him, before the servant could prepare his, and offered it to him with a deep bow, half in jest and half in joyous welcome.

'You err, begum,' he remarked wryly. 'Mean you to tell me that in this brief separation you have forgotten which pipe is mine and which your own?' There was a whimsical smile playing about his lips.

'In this brief separation, sir, I have learnt to forget mine and thine,' she quipped. 'Besides, let this godforsaken pipe enjoy awhile what this man-forsaken woman, your wife, has long been bereft of, the touch of Your Highness's lips . . .'

He darted her a quick glance, for never had he known Janki to be so self-effacing, nor so forward in love. In the next few weeks Janki's primary exercise was in the skill of self-reduction before her sensitive husband's vulnerable ego. She learnt to make light of her performances, to stay silent about her earnings, to put aside her riyaz to attend to his tiniest needs. It was strange indeed, as she noticed, how his demands coincided with her hours of practice. She took to sending away the bawarchi and cooking meals for him as an ordinary wife would. She noticed how he seldom praised her efforts and she threw herself into this contest of wills, determined to extract his appreciation despite his reluctance or refusal. She asked how the biryani was and how the korma tasted and he said, offhand, all right. Until, like any wrought-up wife, she lost her temper or shed tears of rage and charged him with selfishness and cruelty, with withholding praise in order to spite and injure. What, more praise? he scoffed, half in indulgence and half in irony. Isn't the thundering applause of emperors and raeeses enough for my begum, that she craves applause from this lowly lawyer?

This lowly lawyer—the phrase was often on his lips now, too often. She knew his cases were dwindling, that touts were diverting his clients to other lawyers. She knew he had lost the municipal elections a second time. She suggested he accompany her to Calcutta for a season of recordings. He resisted. He could not afford to miss an active season at the court, there was money to be earned. Worry not, milord, she smiled, she would earn enough for two, no, for more, if necessary. After all, what was money for, if not for one's family? She said it in meek offering, but he looked peeved, unaccountably offended. He accompanied her to Calcutta all the same. There he sat in the lounge of recording studios, fascinated by the recording process. For a while there was perfect, blissful harmony between them. She caught him humming her songs as he tapped a beat on the arm of his chair in their hotel on the Esplanade, and that for her was proof of their reconciliation, that his unconscious will should have memorized her songs to use as a counterpoint to his drifting thoughts. But there were times when he seemed absent, frowning. His mind was elsewhere, with his other family. He waited for letters which arrived rarely. And when they did they left him distraught, though he did not share their contents with her. Once he ventured to ask if money could be sent home to Allahabad, since medical bills had mounted and he had defaulted on maintenance money for a few weeks. She had exclaimed and chided and hastened to dispatch the money, but if she expected relief and gratitude from him she found only gruff rancour, and the only way to win back a smile or a word of approval from him was further self-abasement, which by now she had perfected quite as well as her other art, her music. From Calcutta she took him and her entire entourage to Darjeeling by the Sealdah Mail. The English Planters' Association had invited her to sing for a princely payment. He did not attend her performance but spent the evening instead pacing the terrace outside their suite.

Back in Allahabad he was required at his Mehdauri house for the month of Ramzan and Eid. Janki fasted and prayed all through Ramzan, arose before sunrise to eat her frugal meal and then ate only at sunset after the evening prayers. All soirées were cancelled for the month and the accompanists sent on a paid holiday. No true-born Muslim woman could have been as scrupulous as Janki in her practice of abstinence and charity. If her husband noticed, he made no comment. And then came Eid and she plucked up courage to go visit his Mehdauri house, uninvited but well received when she arrived.

Aunts, sisters-in-law, nieces and nephews flocked around her in welcome, showed her their festival finery, their costumes and bangles and footwear, invited her to share in the cooking, to taste the flavours and to comment on the fit and fabrics. Nafisa, the pretty little niece who'd, on the earlier occasion, urged her to sing at the wedding, now teased her coyly about her widening girth. Fatima Aapa, the elderly aunt who had remarked upon her refusal to sing, requested her to help prepare something for the feast. And Ghazala, the middle sister-in-law, invited her to sit in the courtyard and help receive the women guests of the family. Janki gratefully joined in. But all through the evening she felt the absence of Haq Sahib's senior wife and the unwell Yaqoob and dared not ask after them. There was an overloud merriment in this Eid, her instincts told her, something bright and compulsively cheerful to the point of being boisterous, as though it was all being enacted for her benefit. There was something opaque in their eyes and constant curious looks being darted across at Haq Sahib, when he entered the inner courtyard. Some secret was being collectively protected.

The house swarmed with visitors, many already known to her and many to whom she was introduced, though she proudly kept her veil before the men. She kept up her famed repartee and riposte, her graceful courtly exchanges, she saw to it that their plates were refilled, that no one stayed unattended, old members reverently escorted to comfortable bolsters on the divans and their feet rested, young ones blest and complimented on their appearance and their Eidees given, old servants given their festival presents and the dishes on the dining sheets never allowed to fall empty. The evening was well advanced and the last of the guests had left when there broke out in the far quarters of the house a loud uproar. Doors banged, there was a loud crash as of crockery hurled across to smash against a wall and a sound of shrieking. In the central courtyard everyone froze and some sprang to their feet and rushed towards the gallery that connected the central courtyard with the enclosed west wing and the verandas and chambers beyond. The shrieking increased and a sort of whirlwind broke into their midst as a frenzied Yaqoob tore in, hurling abuse at the very top of his voice. In his hand he held a swinging lantern that he flailed around, tilting it crazily askew, making to take aim against the curtained doorway. Close on his heels raced three of the younger nephews, shouting, trying to seize the lantern, trying to stop his mad progress across the courtyard.

'Ah, the jinns are on him again, Bhabhi,' exclaimed Nadira, the youngest sister-in-law. 'And what a day they have chosen!'

'Alas for all Bhai Jaan's prayers and charities at Ajmer! Seize him before he sets the house on fire!'

Yaqoob's eyes were bloodshot and his face streaming with tears as a riot of incoherent imprecations exploded upon his lips. The lads wrestled with him but, powered with manic energy, he flung them aside and dashed his head against the wall. The blood streamed down his cheek and the lantern fell in a crash of metal and glass and spilt kerosene that left a trail of fire snaking across the coir matting that covered the veranda floor. In the hue and cry, someone had the foresight to run towards the bathhouse and fetch buckets of water and the fire was put out while Yaqoob flung himself down on one of the divans, overpowered by the cousins, and burst into a loud animal howl.

'Fetch Farzan Bhai, quick!' was the general cry and someone Janki had never seen before, a tall, pale man, sped into their midst from the west quarters. In his hand he held a syringe. Behind him, stepping swiftly with a kerchief in her hand and a jug of water, was a slender, worn-faced woman.

Yaqoob lay stoned upon the divan late into the morning.

'Do you know me?' she had asked the boy when she saw his eyelids flutter open. She had lain awake all night on a charpai placed alongside the boy's divan in the inner courtyard.

'Yes, Baiji,' he had muttered, keeping his eyes shut tight. His voice was tired and very low.

'No, not Baiji. Say Chhoti Ammi.'

He nodded, turning his head away from her on the rumpled pillow.

'How are you feeling?' she whispered in his ear.

'My head hurts,' he moaned softly.

'Come here,' she sat on the side of his bed and took his heavy, tousled head on her ample lap. She began crooning a soft bhajan in a morning raga, a murmurous unfolding Lalit:

'O my little lord Krishna,
My armful-of-mischief,
Will you not keep still a moment, pray?
That I may behold your blue-lotus face,
A moment, pray, just a moment, pray?'

He had grown still and his breath came deep and regular. He wriggled his head more snugly into her lap and she ran her fingers through his tangled, sweaty hair. She added an impromptu verse of her own composition and sang on:

'You have smashed the butter pots
And finished the cream.
Now, my little Lord Mischief,
Tell me your bad dream.'

He opened his eyes and looked long and quizzically at her.

She crooned yet another song: 'Hamare nabi aaj dulha bane . . .' And noticed that he was listening intently. Then, at the second repetition of the verse he broke into a childlike smile which quickly turned into a gurgling laugh.

'All night I did baa-baa-baa,' he told her in a confiding voice. 'I was a goat and Abba Jaan was going to slaughter me . . .' Here he laughed and laughed and she laughed too, peal on peal, though she felt shaken at the boy's violent delusion.

Looking up, she noticed the slender woman she had seen the night before, standing under an archway, watching them. It was too dim to see her expression but Janki thought she felt a vibration of friendship, tentative and tenuous, come at her from that direction before the figure disappeared under the veranda's arches.

'Next time your head goes baa-baa-baa come to Chhoti Ammi and I shall sing you to laughter,' she told the boy. A laughing raga, a mind-healing raga, that was what was needed for this raving child, and she resolved to spin one for him. It was what she owed this family, in recompense for her refusal to sing for them. No one had heard her that still morning except the boy and his mother but

Janki felt that never in her scores of acclaimed performances had she experienced such meaning in what she did.

She promised herself that she'd pay a visit to the shrine of Baba Tajuddin Shah Aulia in Nagpur, one of her special saints, to pray for this disturbed man-child. Abdul Karim Khan had told her of Tajuddin Baba after he had pursued him for days and caught up with him in a dense jungle. The baba had sought to shake him off, shouting, 'Go away, don't you follow me.' But when Khan Sahib had persisted, the saint had stopped—on an extremely filthy patch of land—and demanded to know why he was being pursued, whether Khan Sahib wished to sing to him, and if so, he should sit down right there in that filthy ditch and sing a song in praise of God. Khan Sahib sang a famous verse of Kabir's which overwhelmed the saint. When the song ended, the saint swayed in ecstatic agreement and gave him leave to go. But I have come to entreat the grace of your blessing, master, pleaded Khan Sahib. You are already in grace, you who possess a voice so mellow. Go, we shall meet again, said the baba. Khan Sahib had narrated how Tajuddin Baba had mysteriously vanished and when he himself arose from the filthy, wet ground on which he had sat he was amazed to behold that his own clothes had remained utterly unsmirched. At Nagpur Janki witnessed Khan Sahib singing for Tajuddin Baba his best-beloved song: 'Hari ka bhed na paayo Rama! Kudrat teri rang-birangi, tu kudrat ka wali!' She saw Tajuddin Baba rise to his feet, clap his hands and break into a dance, crying out in rapture: 'It is all the sport of God! It is God at play in your voice!' And she bowed her head and raised her moist eyes to heaven, content that she had found the song she had come looking for.

19

A week after Eid she returned to her Sabzi Mandi house, though Haq Sahib stayed on a while longer at Mehdauri. For her it was a hectic season of performances for she had deferred all programmes till after Ramzan and Eid.

'I hear your singing quietened the jinns in my sahibzada's head, begum,' remarked Haq Sahib.

'I wish my singing could quieten the jinns in yours, Vakil Sahib.'

He was pleasant, amorous. He drew her to him and whispered in her hair, 'You rouse the jinns in me, lady, if you but knew.'

After a long time a night of love. She had advanced in skill and knew better how to receive and to give and how to keep time. Together their bodies made such music in unison that its impression lasted in their two minds a long time afterwards and made of their marriage a somewhat redeemed thing. Until the cycle of events ordained to break them apart overtook them, some months later, in the shape of an urgent summons from Mehdauri. Haq Sahib's elder son, that responsible, mature firstborn, had died of heatstroke. The searing winds of June that howled and hissed, dust-freighted, around the streets and gardens and fields of the city, had struck the boy down in a dead swoon as he cycled down from the bazaar and no quantities of mango-pulp draughts and rubbings of feet and hands with mango juice could bring the raging fever down.

Janki arrived, appalled, at Allahabad, only recently back from a singing tour of the Central Provinces. She had received the news by telegram at Orchha and had immediately cancelled all appointments and rushed back. She did not find Haq Sahib in Mehdauri at the house of mourning. She found him, instead, in her own Sabzi Mandi house, where, he curtly informed her, he had retreated to mourn once the burial was over.

He sat in an armchair, eyes closed, tearless. For a moment she felt honoured that he had sought out her house to be able to weep. She seated herself on the mat at his feet and gave vent to her own tears. Tears did not come easily to her, especially those of mourning, but the thought of him shouldering the corpse of his elder son all the way down to the Kaladanda cemetery, while she, oblivious, sang songs of rejoicing at the Orchha durbar and his loneliness in that hour melted all her reserve and she wept in helpless commiseration, unable to reach out to him. But if she hoped her tears would release his, she was wrong. For he only opened his eyes and rested them tiredly on her heaving shoulders and then said: 'Leave me, begum. I came here to find an empty house, not more weeping women.'

She dried her tears, surprised at him. 'Then have you not left my sister-wife to weep alone, Vakil Sahib? Your place is with her . . .'

'Don't pester me, woman!' he cursed her. 'Go to Mehdauri and take your place there, if you like. I only want to be alone. I beg you to allow me that at least.'

Baffled, yet obscurely comprehending, she left the chamber to order the coachman to bring round the phaeton. All through the drive she marvelled at the hatred that had shone in his eyes. She was seasoned enough to know there was no such thing as lasting love. Only an accumulation of small kindnesses, many things built up into a semblance of anchorage, an intuiting and an answering of dire needs in an unstable equilibrium of compromises. There were safe areas of assured accord and a lengthening ladder of avoidances. There was above all the intense impulse to relieve aches guessed at, however small and unadmitted, in gestures however unremitting and unacknowledged. There was the making of memories together and the editing of all those paragraphs of life that were ill-written or overwritten in a co-authored work in progress called marriage. She knew she worked hard, too hard, to underscore all she saw as worthwhile and erase all she saw as discordant, for love too was a willed composition. What she failed to understand was the presence of an animosity in him when there was none in her and when she was sure she had given him no cause for it.

In the house of mourning she encountered what was a common sight. An exhausted stillness in which people lay around, asleep while others sat silent or spoke in signs and whispers lest they waken the ones lapsed in sleep after their first weeping had broken their strength. She sat herself down and gave herself up to prayer, undisturbed by the occasional sigh or sniffle or groan of grief that swept across the courtyard.

She was roused from her prayer by a sound of muffled singing that blew in from the west quarters. That faint sound called her out of her trance and drew her to it and she followed where it led, across the threshold of that old hesitation that had prevented her from entering those forbidden galleries and chambers of the west quarters. The sound came from a bedchamber that led off the veranda. Pausing at the door she saw a woman sitting up in bed, her head against the headboard, one hand clutching the bedpost.

Her eyes were closed tight, her head thrown back and swaying from side to side as she sang a dirge, a wailing strung along crumbled phrases of breath. A broken voice searching, calling out to the dead in dire denial, rising out of the pit of mortal captivity; groping, it clawed hoarsely at the dark in jerks of tear-choked retchings. She was lost in a rhythmic chanting, not of prayer but of accusation that climbed in a charged trembling, releasing a challenge in the air before it slumped and collapsed under the weight of its own grief. Thus it sang on, rising and lapsing, rising again, holding steady a long, lone plaint, falling spent. Janki stood stricken. What song was this, what raga of the beaten soul? In all her lifetime of riyaz, never had she encountered anything like this.

She might have sat down beside Haq Sahib's senior wife, her sister-wife as she called her, and joined her voice to hers in a duet of anguish, except that for once she felt herself to be the lesser voice in this pageant of grief. She imagined herself stepping close, she imagined the song ceasing and her gentle question: Why did you stop? And the other answering, I cannot go on. Go on doing what, singing or living? Do you sing, she might have asked. No, I used to. Not any more. Not in the last few years. What did you sing?

Lullabies, wedding songs, birth songs, songs of winnowing and pounding, songs of private prayer. I do not sing now. You do not sing now? Can it be because of Janki, this great, famous singer here, who took away your husband with her song? Have I become to her what Lakshmi Dubain was to my mother? Have I robbed her of her song and is this the only song now left to her by fate? And what will my penalty be, O God of Mausiqui?

She stole away unnoticed, neither having spoken nor having been spoken to. She could not endure that raga of flaming grief and she hid her head in her headcloth and hurried out in stealth, in shame, in a sadness beyond voice or word.

She remembered, to her mortification, the old story of how a vain Tansen sang before Goswamy Vitthalnath and sang his best, only to be gifted a thousand gold coins for his skill but in addition two cowries to indicate the utter uselessness of all that skill.

Before the year was out Yaqoob, Haq Sahib's younger son, was stricken with cholera and died too. Haq Sahib moved to Mehdauri where he stayed the whole of the following year. She offered to suspend her singing and accompany him but he discouraged her. He planned to go on hajj to Mecca with his senior wife, for what else was left to them both but the mercy of Allah, he said.

'Then allow me to come with you to Mecca,' she asked timidly.

He shook his head. 'That cannot be,' he told her.

'Am I less in faith, do you think?' she demanded.

'That is for Allah to decide, not me, begum,' he said. 'I go to beg pardon for my sins that brought on me this ruin. I go with her whom I wronged and whom Allah has thought fit to burden with further grief for no fault of her own but mine.'

She began to experience some glimmer of understanding. 'I share the blame, sir,' she spoke in a small voice, 'and I shall most humbly appeal to my sister-wife to be so kind as to allow me to accompany you.'

His voice had risen. 'Do so at your own peril,' he rebutted. 'I have not shared with you what people at Mehdauri say of you. Go and hear it with your own ears!'

'Hear what, sir?'

'Then listen: They say it's you who has cast a blight on the family for why else did two grown sons die within a year?'

He spoke in a cold, level voice but she found herself trembling.

'And what do you say?' She was aware that her voice shook as she spoke.

He stayed silent.

She felt herself growing hysterical. 'And what do you say, Vakil Sahib?' she demanded.

He turned away, saying as he did so, 'I do not know what to think, begum.'

For several moments she stood rooted to the spot. Then she stepped up to him and said in the voice she used when she concluded her recordings, 'Then I beg you, go. And may God grant you His forgiveness.'

20

A telegram brought her news of Manki's passing. She was in Calcutta recording for Spottiswoode Clarke of GTL which had just released a special violet-coloured Gramophone Concert Record. It had on it the image of a 'recording angel' as its trademark. A naked angel, sitting reclined sideways across the centre of the disc, wings flaring, holding a plumed stylus. The records were priced at Rs 3 and 12 annas. She was at the mehfil hosted by GTL to celebrate its launch when the telegram arrived. She cancelled her remaining dates and caught the Calcutta Mail back to Mughalsarai. Accompanied by Samina and Jallu, she hired a buggy to Benaras. With a mind swarming with fuzzy thoughts, she drove down the old Barna ka Pul lanes, now considerably tidied and broadened, but shocking her at every turn with sights that had been held in deactivated memory all her life and now alarmingly awake, disturbing. A part of her was desperate to disown it all, never to set foot in the past. The other half tugged at her, exerting an irresistible compulsion to immerse herself in it and altogether reverse the years that had intervened.

Beni sat on a mat in the empty room, the very walls of which started a shudder in her nerves. She sat on the mat opposite his, silent. The oil lamp burnt on the floor where Manki's body had been laid before being carried to the pyre.

After a long moment Beni spoke up in a strange voice. 'She had her wish. It was Manikarnika Ghat for her.'

She wept into her headcloth, blinded with pain. She could not bring herself to look upon the earthen urn of ashes that stood behind the burning lamp. She saw her brother gazing at her quietly.

'Jiji,' he said gently, 'will you accompany me to the river to immerse her ashes? I was waiting for you.'

Her throat choked at his kindness. 'Yes,' she whispered. 'To the sangam at Allahabad?'

'She never wanted to return to Allahabad, Jiji,' he said. 'So why take her there now? Any of our Benaras ghats will be fine.'

They went in the buggy she had hired for the day. They sat silent in the country boat, the urn between them. The river and its staired and parasolled banks swam before her eyes as she struggled to contain her sobs. When he asked her to lend a hand with the urn she shook her head. Suddenly the thought of Manki knocking the glass of water out of her hand had risen before her eyes. He tilted the urn. Together they watched its contents fall in a dusty downpour, rest afloat an instant on the rapid current before sinking, dissolving before their eyes. He had to take his ritual dip in the Ganga, followed by a visit to the ghat-side temple. She stood on the steps, striving to master her feelings. On the wall to the forecourt of the temple was a sign: Hindus Only. So she stayed out while he went in to pray and prostrate himself and circumambulate.

Back at the house she summoned up the courage to ask him, 'Is all well with you?'

'As well as might be, Jiji,' he answered.

'Did she ever speak of me?'

He shook his head. 'She mentioned you once or twice. She had forgotten so much lately. She said: All my children have died of the pox, my Kashi, my Paraga, my Mahadei and my Jankiya. Only you were spared by the Devi for my old age, son.'

'And father? Did she ever mention him?'

'Him never—though she remembered Lakshmi Chachi often. Even that Parvati woman.'

Janki hesitated, then managed to ask him what was uppermost in her mind: 'Had she heard any of my records? Have you?'

He was embarrassed. 'How could we, Jiji? We never bought a gramophone.'

'I shall send you one,' she promised.

He seemed to be searching for words. He brought them up with some difficulty. 'I was never one for music, Jiji. Neither was Amma. It was only you who was different, so she got teachers for you. I wasn't much good for anything. And now where's the time to hear music? The shop takes up all my time.'

She understood. More than he intended. Her heart went out to him. 'Come back to Allahabad,' she said. 'There is nothing to keep you here.'

'There is my shop.' He was stubborn. 'What will I do there, Jiji? Only fly kites maybe.'

A shadow had passed over his face and it prompted her to frame her next question very carefully. 'May I find a good girl for you?'

With a flash of bitterness he retorted, 'I married once, didn't I, Jiji? You sang songs at my wedding, I seem to remember. I am no Mussalman to go a-marrying more than one.'

'The girl you sort of married was one, sir. To wed her proper you'd have had to turn Mussalman.' It was on the tip of her tongue to remind him of their father who had had two women in the house, even if married to just one.

'That was a different time in our poor lives. As that old fox Naseeban told me there wasn't maulvi or pandit present at our marriage and thank God for that.' His face flushed.

'Suppose I find you another one like her.'

'That's impossible. There cannot be another one like her.'

She fell silent. No songs came to her mind. Nothing in her entire thumri stock could ever measure up to this thing her brother carried. Her own prolifically articulated love life paled into inanity.

'Do you have any idea where she is?'

'No.'

'I can try to find out if you like.'

'Let it be, Jiji,' he said, and abruptly changed the subject. 'I keep feeling the taste of Amma's balushahis in my mouth,' he said. 'The feeling persists night and day.'

When she left the following day she embraced him. Asked him to visit Allahabad as often as he could. Called him her 'quvvat-e-baazu', the strength of her arm. It was how she would refer to him when she wrote her *Diwan-e-Janki*, long after he was dead.

By 1916 recordings could be done at Allahabad. Dillnutt and his team arrived on behalf of the new label that GTL had assumed—His Master's Voice. All Janki's older titles were reissued as ten-inch discs. It was the only positive thing in a lonely and depressing time and it lasted three years. Then the Jallianwala Bagh thunderclap unstrung Janki utterly. From the several vernacular papers she subscribed to she'd kept up with events in Punjab. Allahabad was buzzing with the Khilafat stir, Hindus and Muslims for once united on a common platform. The crowd fired on at Jallianwala Bagh had comprised both Sikhs and Muslims out to celebrate the Punjabi new year and unaware of curfew orders. But quite besides the horror of the massacre at the bagh, what filled her mind with agitation and a stubborn self-loathing was the detail that under Dyer's orders it was Sikhs, Gurkhas, Baluchi and Rajput troops who had fired those 1650 rounds. They give us the orders and we obey them, she fumed, yes, even I. It never occurs to us to refuse. It did once, even if we lost. For a day a wild rumour had spread that in the Civil Lines crawling orders for Indians had been proclaimed but it died down as suddenly as it arose. When later she read that the English public had approved of Dyer's action, that he had been awarded a purse of 26,000 pounds and a sword, her self-lacerating conscience instantly allied this circumstance to her own, the Delhi Durbar purse of 100 gold mohurs, the benighted gun number 254 that the 'satanic government' had bestowed on her. Never before had she approved Gandhi's impassioned phrase more. When she read the resolution of the thirty-fourth session of the Indian National Congress and its dry and guarded welcome to the Prince of Wales's forthcoming visit, she knew what to expect from her city. It happened exactly as she had thought, with doors closed and windows shuttered and streets deserted and a sullen stillness in the air.

There was no peace for her so long as that velvet purse with the 100 gold mohurs lay packed in a trunk somewhere in her house. She wondered how best to utilize it. All over the city massive bonfires were devouring piles of European clothing as Non-cooperation caught on. From the *Independent* she learnt of the mammoth Holi bonfire planned in the lawns of Motilal Nehru's bungalow. He had only recently returned from having presided over the thirty-fourth session of the Indian National Congress and she knew him as one who admired her singing and collected her records. A day before the big bonfire she wrapped the velvet purse containing the 100 gold mohurs in a kerchief's breadth of khadi, along with the Coronation Song record, and placed a carefully worded letter with it, addressed to Motilal Nehru.

My respectful salutations to Barrister Motilal Nehru Sahib,
    Enclosed is a small contribution for the august organization that you have the distinction of having recently presided over. It

is the least that this ordinary citizen of Ilahabad can offer, more so since its acquisition from the hands of the King Emperor George V at the Delhi Durbar is in the present circumstances more a regret than an honour. Any useful purpose that it can serve in our common cause shall be so much more becoming to its value than a place in some meaningless corner in the vault of memory. I send, along with it, a record containing the song celebrating the Royal Coronation of 1911, sung by my friend Gauhar Jaan and myself. I earnestly submit that it be allowed to augment your auspicious Holi bonfire which shall bring singular peace and comfort to the heart of this humble singer,

Janki Bai Ilahabadi

Sayyad Sahib, her munshi, was dispatched with the packet. He returned in a couple of hours with a brief note:

Madam Sahiba,

It is my pleasure and honour to receive this valuable contribution. The gold mohurs shall go a long way in the service of our cause. The record, I much regret to confess, I cannot bring myself to consign to the flames. At the risk of giving offence to the sentiments of the sender, let me disclose that it has gone to enrich my already large collection of Madam Sahiba's records, a fact that has brought indescribable pleasure to

Yours sincerely

Motilal Nehru

She had no European clothes to burn and she didn't quite fancy a khadi wardrobe. All the same she felt easier in her mind when she read of the quickening Non-cooperation Movement activating all around in the city.

News of Akbar's death shook her to her core. He had been ailing. They hadn't met for a considerable while. Her recordings had kept her too busy for private visits and when she received news of his passing she felt orphaned, bereft beyond words. She sought his voice in her head, found it often. She kept up a conversation with him that nourished her soul. She imagined him tossing verses at her in which Death came as an Englishman and arrested him for travelling without a ticket. She didn't know if it was a deranged auditory fantasy or a music beyond the ear. She seemed to be eavesdropping into another dimension. The condition passed in a few weeks.

Two years went by before she invited Haq Sahib back, writing to him that she had a surprise gift for him. When he came she presented Abdul Aziz to him.

'This,' she said, 'is Bachcha. Salaam your Abba, Bachcha.'

Abdul Aziz did so, managing to lisp, 'Assalaamoalaikum.'

In his crisp little side-knotted Lucknavi achkan and churidar pajamas, his feet in little gold-worked velvet nagras and his well-oiled hair crowned with a tilted velvet cap and his eyes lined in kajal, he looked a tiny qawwali singer. She had embroidered his little satin waistcoat herself.

Haq Sahib had aged visibly in two years. His eyes were listless, red-rimmed, and he had lost that upright debonair form that had cut a dash in black shervani and white Aligarh pajamas in the old days. He looked a spent man. Gone that proud lift of head, that shock of wavy, raven hair over his smooth forehead and the clean-carved curl of lip, the aristocratic chiselled nose. His features had coarsened. His moustache drooped, unkempt. He did not meet her eye but seemed to speak absently to himself. A man who had lost interest in himself.

She told him, haltingly, how she had come to adopt Abdul Aziz. The night-long soirée in an Attarsuiya square when silver coins had lain heaped all around her on the paved platform beneath the old peepul tree where she sang. How the sight of that mound of silver had filled her with despair and she had prayed: 'Do not mock me with more wealth, O Lord, for what use is all this to me now? Or send me someone to serve with this.' She had donated it all to the khankhwa of the Bahadurganj daira of the Sufi saint Sheikh Muhibullah Shah, gone personally to deliver it and visited the little khankhwa alongside the shrine, when her eyes had fallen on a thin little child sitting hunched on the hempen rug, struggling with his chalk and slate, and had learnt from the sajjadanasheen of the daira that he was one of the khankhwa's littlest orphans.

'See him now, Vakil Sahib,' she had said, smiling fondly. 'Plump as a little tomcat and as mischievous as can be. Put him in a satin kurta and velvet coatee, place a velvet cap aslant on his head and put a dholak in his hands and he'll look a real qawwal bachcha at Hazrat Nizamuddin's tomb. That's why I call him Bachcha.'

She hesitated an instant, caught Haq Sahib's reluctant eye and added: 'Allah answered my prayer, Vakil Sahib, as quick as lightning. My faith is restored in God if not in man. I share Allah's gift with you and offer him to you, to us. This is the child of our old age. The child my womb could never give you. To make up for those other children that were taken away . . .'

A momentary pang sparked in his eye but died. Something like annoyance stirred in his face. He said nothing. Later he took to staying longer in the Sabzi Mandi house, sometimes bringing things for the child, which gladdened her. Once he took the boy to Mehdauri.

'An auntie gave me imartis and laddoos to eat,' the child told Janki on his return. He'd come back with a pair of kites, a wooden top, a yo-yo.

So Abdul Aziz spun his top, unrolled and rolled his yo-yo,
ran chasing the chickens outside the hen coop with little shrieks
of excitement. It warmed Janki's heart to see him marching up
and down the terrace with the oversized kite, and after a few
futile attempts Haq Sahib laid down his hookah, slowly hoisted
his portly form out of his armchair and strolled across the terrace
to the child. Janki saw him take the kite string from Bachcha's
hand, spin out the wooden reel and give Bachcha instructions.
She saw Bachcha skip across the terrace with the kite, position
himself on the tips of his toes, holding aloft the kite, then with a
jump and a squeal of joy let throw the kite into the air. It fought
the wind, flapped and sped away into the air as the reel spun
and Haq Sahib loosed out yards and yards of string. Behind
her chik she felt her eyes moisten as the memory of another
kite flier assailed her mind. And at the spectacle of the listless,
oldening man who'd lost all engagement with life, now resolutely
rekindling his interest in it for her sake. It left her gratified by the
promise of a future and the possibility of more kindness towards
one another, she and her husband.

After a gap of three years a recording session again, this time
at Lucknow. But by now she had grown demanding and it was
hard for companies to meet all her demands. But though there
were fewer recordings now, her old numbers were constantly
being reissued. She did a few sessions for new songs in Lucknow
after 1928 for Robert Edward Beckett of GTL, now HMV, this
time by the new electric method which had replaced the earlier
acoustical method. And again in late 1928 for Arthur James Twine
at Delhi. GTL, by 1931, had moved from Sealdah to Dum Dum
and merged with the Columbia Gramophone Company. It had
also introduced subsidiaries like Twin Records. Thousands of
Janki's records flooded the market, produced by HMV and Twin.

For Janki the ten years that Bachcha stayed were like some harvest of recompense for the long drought of years. The ordinary rhythm of days of blessed sameness and concerns of homely existence took up her time, although music persisted alongside like a faithful tributary. Later she would be left to wonder which was the perennial stream and which the seasonal.

But she immersed herself in the planning of meals and lavish hospitality. In the careful choice of tutors for Bachcha. In Bachcha's influenza or typhoid and what the English civil surgeon from the Bailey Hospital had to advise about the pain that kept the child whining all night and thrashing about in bed. She engaged a maulvi to teach Bachcha Islam and a sais to take him out riding in the Company Bagh on the pony she bought for him. She rejoiced when Haq Sahib accompanied them to Agra on a family vacation and rejoiced more when she saw him pick up Bachcha's history book and read to him of Ashok, Akbar or Aurangzeb. Or when he made Bachcha recite multiplication tables in a monotonous chant whenever he happened to come in in the mornings. The child's piping treble, chirping out chains of numbers and their multiples in the sweet lisp of infant syllables fell on Janki's ears like some tranquillizing balm. Bachcha's chant was like a magic riyaz, the best music in the world spelling the restful acquisition of a hard-earned concord so late in life.

But Bachcha, whatever his fetching attractions as a child, betrayed no evidence of any aptitude for his lessons, though he was a fine critic of Janki's cooking and pickling and preserving and sweet making. For, out of the reserves of memory she'd retrieved recipes from the old mithai shop of her childhood in Benaras, often sending samples of her preparations to the Mehdauri household too. In later years, when it was all over and done with, it seemed to her cruelly confessional mind to have been a willed tableau, another composition or performance, this make-believe delusional family life, as she tried measuring up to longed-for conventions of happy domesticity.

She believed what she hankered to believe—Haq Sahib's growing attachment to Bachcha and the return of humour and vitality to her husband's life. When he spoilt Bachcha with trips to the fairs of the city, with money to buy sweets, toys and fruits and vegetables made of clay, with kites and rubber balls and kulfi out of earthen pots and jalebi and kachoris at the local eateries, she loved it as proof of her husband's fondness for this child of their old age.

But when, some years down the line, this daily practice, the fatherly dole of pocket money for the day, began making her vaguely uncomfortable because of its sinister sense of secrecy and mystery, she began to wonder at what had seemed an innocent thing. Where earlier Bachcha had eagerly displayed what he'd bought or eaten in the bazaar, he now appeared to avoid catching her eye. When she asked anything he answered in curt monosyllables. There was something about his shifty-eyed expression that made her immediately think of brothels—her own past made the idea of them leap into her head, and she lectured him on the evils of 'houses of ill fame', as she now delicately referred to them.

Then she realized that he was sleeping late into the mornings, that his books stayed untouched and his maulvi sahib grown exasperated. She conferred with his maulvi sahib about activities that were ungodly and forbidden and that fell within the maulvi sahib's authority to counsel against and prohibit. But the maulvi sahib's scruples forbade discussion of such unseemly subjects with a lady.

She conferred with Haq Sahib.

'Bachcha is not himself, Vakil Sahib, or haven't you noticed?' she said. 'Have you seen how he keeps to himself and seems never to be at his books?'

'A boy will grow up, begum,' he remarked mildly.

'But he is grown deaf–mute. As though he hasn't a tongue in his head.'

'Who can boast of a tongue in his head, begum, when you let loose your own?' This said in husbandly good humour.

'This is not a matter for jesting, Vakil Sahib. I fear he has fallen into . . . into bad company.'

'Bad company?' he mimicked her pious tones. 'What company does the poor lad have save yours and mine and while I would hesitate to call us paragons of righteousness, surely we are not as fallen as you suggest? Well, he has his sais and his maulvi sahib and his angrezi and mathematics tutors, not counting the boys of the lane with whom he plays gulli-danda or flies kites and they all seem to me fairly measuring up to your high standards of virtue, if I may say.'

She ignored his lame sallies at wit. 'I don't know where he spends all his money,' she fretted.

'Well, for that matter, I do not know where I spend all of mine,' he quipped.

She decided to express the misgiving in her mind. 'Vakil Sahib, I notice how generous a father you are and how you keep Bachcha well provided, but should you not display the least interest in what your son does with the money?'

He always flinched involuntarily when she said 'your son' as though the words continued to shock and dismay him.

'Begum,' he said, 'a growing boy will not always spend his money on kites and mud pies.'

'Exactly. I'm afraid he may be spending it in the wrong places. Do you think, Vakil Sahib, that it's time we got him married?'

He looked closely at her as though the unfamiliarity of the idea with its implicit suggestion of safely monitored sexuality took time to register, before he burst out laughing. Somewhat too contemptuously, she felt.

'You women can think of nothing else save the pull of the boudoir and the bordello. Madam, may I venture to suggest to your fond matronly instincts that there are other temptations that may draw a young man?'

'Bachcha is not a young man,' she protested. 'He is still a child.'

'Believe what you will then, begum.' He shrugged with what she thought was an enigmatic smile.

Exasperated with him, she approached Zahid, the sais she had engaged to take Bachcha riding. But Zahid said that there was nothing unusual about Abdul Aziz Sahib's activities except that lately he seemed to prefer a bicycle to a horse.

'A bicycle? Where does he get one to ride?'

'He borrows mine. He says—Zahid, you take a round of the Company Bagh while I cycle down to Katra Market and back.'

'And you do so?' She could feel her temper rising.

He stood with bowed head.

'What to do, begum sahiba?'

'Why has it not occurred to you that you should go along with him to Katra?'

'A horse and a bicycle cannot ride together, begum sahiba.'

'And why have you not thought fit to mention this to me till I asked?'

'Bachcha Sahib said not to tell. But Vakil Sahib knows . . .'

'Knows what?'

'About Bachcha Sahib.'

Her head was spinning. 'Vakil Sahib knows about Bachcha Sahib? Listen, you cur, you son of a swine, will you speak plainly or shall I thrash you with my shoe?'

Her voice had risen to its highest amplitude. Her hand shot out and dealt the young man a stinging blow on the cheek.

Earlier she was apt to hit out at her accompanists when they went wrong with a note or a beat. It always filled her with embarrassment and deep repentance and she made much of the young percussionist or sarangi player, calling herself his elder sister, etc. But Zahid the sais provoked no such regret in her. If anything, he aroused another sort of regret of a practical nature in her mind. For he bowed his head, though his eyes flashed, and said in a surly voice, 'Begum sahiba, I have not joined your service to endure insults and blows. By your leave, I beg permission to quit.'

'Allah! What is this world come to when minions dare to make reply! You have my permission, you betrayer of my salt!' she shouted. 'Remove yourself from my sight or I shall not hold myself responsible for anything I do!'

The regret she experienced was that she had lost the chance of extracting information from the sais whose words 'Vakil Sahib knows about Bachcha Sahib' now filled her with terrible foreboding.

In desperation she sought out the old faithful Jallu Mian.

'Jallu Mian,' she broached the subject in humble candour, 'in all this world there is only you I can entrust this delicate task to. I want you to keep watch on Bachcha Sahib. I fear for him and I fear the worst. I need to know where he goes, what he does, who he meets. This is urgent, Jallu Mian.'

It took Jallu Mian just a couple of days to get to the bottom of things. He looked grave when he gave Janki the facts. 'I have very disturbing news for you, begum sahiba,' he told her. 'Bachcha Sahib frequents a ganja den in Katra. He has been a regular visitor there for many months now. He is, in fact, one of their important customers . . .'

Her head swam. She gazed at Jallu Mian in horror. 'So that is what it is,' she whispered. 'And does Vakil Sahib know any of this?'

Jallu Mian shook his head. 'I cannot say, begum sahiba.'

Why did the thought come into her head that Jallu Mian was holding something back? He paused and appeared to be pondering something, hesitating. Then he decided to speak: 'Begum sahiba, the dealer at the shop that Bachcha Sahib frequents said that someone once came and deposited a sum of money in advance—lest Bachcha Sahib ever lacked money to pay for his cannabis . . .'

This detail so disconcerted her that she sank into the nearest armchair and buried her distraught head in her hands. 'Whatever can this mean, Jallu Mian? You tell me. My tired brain cannot think.'

He lowered his eyes and studied his shoes for a long moment. Then he said gently, 'Begum sahiba has brains enough for ten, whatever she may say or feel. It is not for me to venture anything without proof.'

He paused, then added, 'But whatever lies ahead, it is within my power to promise that we, your musicians, are with you.'

She felt the smart of sudden tears in her eyes. 'It is your kindness. And Allah's blessing on me,' she whispered and turned away.

She decided to speak to Haq Sahib.

'Vakil Sahib,' she accosted him, 'I want to know what you meant when you said there are temptations other than boudoirs and bordellos for a young man.'

He looked up from his file. 'Did I say that? Ah, so it would seem.'

'Please do not speak in circles, Haq Sahib. Are you aware that our son Bachcha is a ganja addict now?'

He looked maddeningly composed.

'That would explain it all,' he observed casually.

She saw red. 'Do you even begin to realize the seriousness of this, Vakil Sahib? A cannabis addict at sixteen!'

'Oh well, he might have done worse. Cannabis isn't all that bad. It can even be a cure for many ills, so I have heard. A man's got to sow his wild oats, begum. It's a part of growing up.' He spoke in a tone of playful mockery.

'Do not provoke me, I beg you,' she said, bristling. 'And allow me to remind you that your responsibility as a father lies in taking control of your son, not in indulging or explaining away his vices.'

'Madam,' he said, 'it is a responsibility I neither invited nor acknowledge.'

She stared at him incredulously, the truth of the situation sinking in in all its starkness. 'I did not realize this,' she said slowly. 'Bachcha is henceforth my responsibility and I shall do what I can about this problem. The least you can do, Vakil Sahib, is refrain from supplying him with money the way you do.'

He nodded absently and turned his attention to the file he had been reading. But the ordinary circumstance of Haq Sahib handing generous amounts of cash to Bachcha that had so far seemed simply proof of his fondness for the boy now took on a murkier possibility that filled her mind with the weirdest misgivings.

She confronted Bachcha in a fit of rage. Henceforth he was to get no pocket money and was to keep to the house, sleep all day, if necessary, but never, on pain of the worst possible hammering at her hands, dare to leave the house. Bachcha looked at her in stony passivity, his bulbous eyes blank, registering no response to her violent tirade. For a few days he complied.

Then one afternoon he vanished. The same afternoon Ghaseete came, bashfully confessing that he had been unable to refuse Bachcha Sahib, that he had had to lend him money for the day.

'I do not understand you, Ghaseete,' she rebuked him.

'I was in no position to refuse him,' stammered Ghaseete.

'Tell me, is it my brain that is muddled by demons or the brains of every member of this cursed household? You were in no position to refuse, you say?'

'I was not present when Bachcha Sahib took the money from my shervani pocket.'

'When did you and your shervani part company, Ghaseete?' she lashed out in impatience.

'I was in the gusal-khana, begum sahiba. My shervani hung from a peg in the wall outside . . .'

Aghast, she scorched him with her gaze. 'You are telling me that Bachcha Sahib stole money from your pocket?'

He cringed, terrified.

She fumed as she paced about the terrace, waiting for Bachcha to return. When he slunk in, she swooped down on him and seized him by the collar, dragging him into the courtyard. He seemed witless, dulled beyond responding. He parried her slaps, turning his tousled head this way and that, but he offered neither a word nor a protest. Her hand fell to her side, helpless.

'Speak, ulloo ke patthe!' she frothed. 'Are you bent on bringing qayamat on your life and on me? What is it you lack that you go combing the pockets of our staff to go crawling the dope dens of the city?' Tears streamed down her face, the courtyard blurred before her eyes and her voice cracked in outrage. 'Speak, you beggar, before I take the skin off your buttocks! Or have you turned yourself into a Congressman and a Gandhi-wallah that takes the blows of the police and will not hit back or answer?'

The boy stayed mute. She could not decide whether this was sullen defiance or a dope drowse, whether he resisted her or merely accepted it all as a necessary evil. She dragged him to his room and pushed him in. She bolted the door from without.

'I have shut up Bachcha Sahib in his room,' she announced to the household. 'No one is to unbolt the door. I shall carry in his meals myself and escort him to the gusal-khana and the privy myself.'

It worked for a day or two. Then the boy went wild, flung himself on the door, banging on it with his fists. His silence gave way to fierce howls of entreaty that brought her down from her chambers and made her sink, sobbing, on to the divan in the veranda outside his room. She sat there, weeping silently, as the howls increased and the appeals, until, exhausted, he stopped altogether. Then, as the stillness in the room deepened, as no stirring or sounds of waking issued from the room for hours, fear clutched at her heart and the worst possible thoughts, and she unbolted the door and found it bolted from within. Then it was her turn to beat on the door and hammer on it and cry out in entreaty, and when an hour had passed there was nothing for her but to summon Haq Sahib, Jallu Mian, Ghaseete, Sayyad Ghulam Abbas and all the women staff of the kitchen and the housekeeping. They broke down the door—to find Bachcha sprawled on his charpai, fast asleep. She screamed at him, shook him, boxed his ears, until Haq Sahib stepped up and pulled her away, saying, 'Enough, begum! Take a hold on yourself!'

'Ya Maula,' she cried aloud, 'what does this child lack that he should turn to this? How did all this start and I did not even dream of it?' Then, suddenly, a monstrous thought sprang into her mind and she swung round and faced him. 'You!' she exclaimed. 'It was you who started him on this! I don't know why. I don't know what is in your envious mind but you wanted to wreck it all! You hated our little life, you hated the family I was trying to create—because you had lost your children, because you couldn't bear this . . .'

He had flushed with anger. 'You have gone mad, begum. Why should I endure your crazy excesses day after day? You have driven the lad to dope and you will drive me to the madhouse!'

'I have driven the lad to dope? Well said, Vakil Sahib, well said! I, who have never even seen cannabis in my life of forty-five years!'

'Never?' he asked in his most cutting voice. 'Never in your nautch-woman days, in your kotha days? Your clients were all goat-milk-bibbers who came sober as sages for the joy of hearing your sublime voice alone?'

'I will not be insulted, Vakil Sahib!'

'Nor I, Baiji!'

He moved back to his Mehdauri house—as he usually did after their spats. But the idea that he had somehow initiated Bachcha into ganja took hold of her mind and the more she thought of it the more she believed it.

21

She called on Hashmat Ullah one day. There had been a coolness between them for a while after her impulsive marriage but it went to Hashmat Ullah's credit that he had remained suavely professional, obligingly helpful to her at all times.

'Hashmat Ullah Sahib,' she began, when he had ushered her into his lawyer's chamber and given her a seat, and sent away his munshi, 'this is a highly personal matter. I wish to consult you in your capacity as a man of the world which I, who am only a musician and a foolish, sentimental woman, am not. Would my husband, Abdul Haq Sahib, have any interest in the ruin of my adopted son Abdul Aziz's future? I ask you to be absolutely candid with me.'

He looked at her a long moment in an appraising sort of way before he answered: 'I was absolutely candid with you once before, begum sahiba.'

'That was another matter and long years ago,' she reacted. 'I ask your opinion now.'

He chose his words carefully. 'As to Haq Sahib, I do not have the pleasure of close association with him, save formally as your husband. But legally and pragmatically, so to speak, any adopted successor of yours might possibly be unwelcome to any husband of yours, irrespective of who you married. Especially if that successor has no emotional or blood claim upon his attachment. And especially in the light of your sizeable fortune. I speak only legally and pragmatically, begum sahiba.'

Her eyes widened as his meaning got across to her. It left her at a loss for words, challenging all her instincts of denial and whatever convictions she cherished of Haq Sahib's credibility. Still, a deeper instinct prompted her next question: 'So if Bachcha Sahib's children—Allah grant him many!—were to fill my home . . . it would assure me a future other than the one I now foresee?'

'Exactly,' he answered.

'I thank you, Hashmat Ullah Sahib.' She rose to go. 'And I shall reflect on what you have advised.'

'But I have advised nothing,' he saw her to the door, 'except that you have a care about yourself and your fortune.'

'For that matter, you are there to protect that, are you not my lawyer?' She strove to end the meeting on a light note but failed, so heavy did the matter now rest upon her mind.

Her first impulse was to send Bachcha away to an expensive boarding school, but he was too old for that and too poor in studies to be comfortable anywhere. He could of course be married—he was over sixteen—but she did not think the time was ripe for that yet. Besides, who would give his daughter to a cannabis addict, even if that addict was to inherit the great fortune of the legendary Janki Bai Ilahabadi? The best course of action was to get him de-addicted first and married subsequently, and for that she had to ensure that all allowances to him were cut off. She got the English doctor at the Bailey Hospital to treat him. She confined him to the house and patiently bore his tantrums when his angry bouts led to smashed glass and violent attacks. She had to suspend her riyaz for days and the effects were present in her performances though only she noticed how stale and uninspired the notes sounded in her highly self-critical ears now. But getting Bachcha normal had become a soul mission for her, a desperate cause that would decide whether her life had been at all worthwhile. She prayed, fasted, sought fakirs for charms and talismans for Bachcha, gave away large sums in charity. And in about a year's time it seemed that life had resumed its sanity and Bachcha could be trusted out alone once more.

More, she had by now dismissed her misgivings about Haq Sahib as unworthy suspicions that left her feeling guilty and mean, and had welcomed Haq Sahib back with as great a display of wifely affection as ever before, more so if possible.

'I am of the age when the phases of the moon and the phases of the womb madden a woman's mind, Vakil Sahib,' she told him. 'Bear with me, as you have admirably done.'

'I am here to serve your every whim, madam,' he had said with an ironic little smirk.

So once again they picked up the life they had put aside, and strove to make light of the allegations and the injuries, the suspicions and indignations that had driven a wedge between them, and like most married couples, they succeeded for a while.

Then misery struck again in the form of an urgent message from the Ramkrishna Mission in Benaras. Her brother, Beni Prasad, had died of jaundice. He had collapsed one day on the ghat and been taken to the mission by the sadhus. Crazed with panic, she rushed to Benaras. Neighbours at the Barna ka Pul house gave her such details as they knew. The monks had cared for him during the few hours of coma. A sadhu had lit his pyre. She bowed her head. It is just as well, she thought. His ashes had been immersed by the time the message had got to her. At the Barna ka Pul house she came across his pathetic belongings, among them a radio-engineering kit and a metal Meccano set. She wept over them and for this neglected brother of hers who might have had a better chance had she not lost herself to her own life and her music. She wished there was a grave, something palpable to lay her head on, but there was only the swollen river, stretching to the far horizon, the river that had carried away her mother's ashes and now her Beni's. She had an impulse to take a dip, immerse herself in its waters and draw in their subtle presence through the pores of her skin. She stepped into the stream, covered her head, drew in her breath and lowered herself. The water climbed around her, closed over her head. She heard its hum in her ears and she stayed submerged for as long as she could hold her breath. Which was quite long, for her lifetime of riyaz had taught her to control her breath for prolonged intervals at a time.

As she rose to the surface a curious sight met her eyes. On a boat some distance away a cluster of women were casting into the river what seemed to be tanpuras, to the chanting of mantras. She wiped the droplets from her smarting eyes and studied them. She asked a pilgrim what was going on. 'Tawaifs,' he told her. 'They're giving up the bad life.'

More he could not tell her. Nobody on the ghat seemed to have an idea. It was left for Janki to get in touch with her Benaras friends Vidyadhari and Husna Bai to find out. Both had taken to singing patriotic songs and bhajans in response to Gandhi's call. But neither could explain Gandhi's prim refusal to accept the money the tawaifs offered to the cause. In Calcutta, they told her, Gauhar had withheld half the amount she had promised to Gandhi because he had not kept his part of the deal that he attend one of her soirées, but Gauhar was Gauhar. What did she, Janki, have to offer the cause?—they asked.

As to performances, she replied, she now gave very few and never for sarkari organizers. As to singing bhajans, she had been singing bhajans all her life, along with the rest of her repertoire. As to the saucy, teasing music of shringar now called indecent by these staid custodians of public morality, she just did not agree and was ready to defy them. There was a precious legacy at risk of extinction.

That was her last trip to Benaras.

Bachcha was well behaved and quite accepting of the marriage that had been arranged for him.

A sweet little fourteen-year-old she was, the bride, the daughter of Sayyad Shamsuddin Rizvi, who was the neighbour of one of her accompanists. Petite, fey, with a quaintly teasing laugh in her eyes even when her face was demurely composed into an expression of meek obedience beneath her heavy, tinselled headcloth. She had a ripe-guava paleness of skin with the rosiness in winter that Allahabad guavas had.

Janki had insisted on extraordinary beauty. Fairness of complexion, symmetry of features, fineness of limbs, and this little girl fulfilled all her requirements. She had also desired a girl of small education, preferably just past primary school, for she had come to believe that education prepared a woman's mind for misery. Hence this kittenish child, amusing, affectionate, a pleasure to have around, an enchanting playmate for her Bachcha.

But Bachcha seemed uninterested. He sat through the wedding ceremonies in oafish passivity, stolidly indifferent. She had seen him this way before and the shadow of an older panic waylaid her heart, but she set it aside as improbable.

The wedding was a glittering one, attended by dignitaries, British officials, lawyers, the city's intellectuals, poets and singers.

And though she did not personally sing, preferring to be the grande dame of the event, the mother of the groom, she had invited fellow performers to sing—from Calcutta, Patna, Indore, Atrauli, Benaras and Gwalior. To each guest she gave a monogrammed silver keepsake. The banquets were sumptuous and the festivities lasted five days. Cooks had been hired from Lucknow and Delhi. The sweets and paan had been ordered from Benaras and the mirasans, who sat singing wedding songs all round the clock, had been brought from Barabanki.

In the days that followed, the little bride's presence was a delight to her. Every morning she circled the stone grindstone pounder round the girl's head to cast out the evil eye and supervised the barbers' wives as they smeared the bride's limbs with honey, sandalwood and turmeric and rubbed them with rose water and fresh milk and dried her long, glossy hair over a brazier in which smoked a dozen scented herbs. The gorgeous ensembles she'd had created for the girl by her own designers in Chowk Gangadas were her special triumph, for she had chosen the silks and the crepes and the muslins and also the gold and silver embroidery down to the very skeins and the patterns of the bead and pearl inlays in the elaborate panels of the dresses. As for jewellery, she had let her extravagance go wild. The most finely crafted girdles and looped and scalloped neckpieces, the daintiest nose rings, the most heavily embellished ear-danglers, forehead pendants and hair combs, wristlets and anklets had been chosen. She felt as she had done as a little girl herself in her forgotten Benaras childhood, dressing up her doll. She drew the greatest satisfaction in standing back to marvel at the enchanting work she had created. Sometimes in the delicate, porcelain-fine girl she saw herself as she might have liked to be but wasn't. Sometimes it was the daughter after her own heart that she had always wanted. In her excitement over this toy-child that life had finally brought her, she quite forgot about Bachcha, who in his own way, was quite content with the change in his station, the fancy clothes he had received, the bagfuls of banknotes as gifts and the gold and silver coins as benedictions.

Then, one night, the little girl knocked shyly on her door and said: 'Ammi Jaan, can I sleep in your room?'

She awoke and it took her a few moments to register the presence of the little figure who stood timidly at the foot of her grand four-poster.

'Chandni Bitiya? What is it?'

'I am scared, Ammi Jaan,' whispered the little girl. 'I don't like to sleep alone, I have never slept alone in my Abba-Ammi's home . . .'

'Alone?' She sat bolt upright in bed. 'Where is Abdul Aziz Mian?'

'I don't know, Ammi Jaan,' said the girl. 'He goes out and comes back and I'm scared of . . . jinns and ghosts and snakes . . . and robbers and . . .'

'He goes out?' Bafflement seized her and a familiar dread. 'Every night?'

The little girl hung her head.

'Answer me, child.'

The little girl nodded, her face beginning to twist into tears.

'What time does he get back?'

She would not say.

'Before dawn?' prompted Janki.

The child inclined her head in assent.

Janki took hold of the girl's hands. 'You have got to tell me everything, child. I beg you.'

The girl turned away her face. A tear rolled down her cheek and she lifted an arm to swipe it off.

'Please,' appealed Janki. 'It is important. So important for him and for you.'

Still the girl said nothing, sniffling into her stole.

Janki saw she would have to put her own terrible suspicion into words, no matter how agonizing.

'Bachcha Mian got a lot of money as nek, didn't he? And so did you. Where is it?'

'It is gone,' the girl managed to bring out in a tiny, bewildered voice.

Janki felt the impact of the crushing knowledge before the knowledge struck. Her mind was in an uproar. The questions tumbled out without her conscious bidding, pursuing Bachcha's nefarious trail.

'Your jewellery? Is it all with you?'

'Only the ruby set, Badi Ammi. And the gold belt . . .'

The blood pounded in Janki's brain.

'Why did you give it to him? What did he tell you?'

The girl looked frightened. Her eyes were by now dry and she stared at Janki in shocked understanding. 'He . . . He said he would bring it all back. He said he was giving it for the country. So . . . So that the angrez people could be sent back.'

'Oho!' exclaimed Janki and the marvel of it struck her, that the dull Bachcha could be so foxy in his fabrications.

'And you let go of your jewels out of love for your country or your love for your husband?' she remarked acidly, before she realized the utter innocence of the humble recipient of this shaft, and she softened her voice and said in an altered tone, 'I am sure you meant well, child, but in your place I would not have let go of my gold and jewels so easily. I would have fought and refused.'

'I did too, at first, Ammi Jaan. But he gave me a paper from the Congress Party of Gandhiji and it said my jewels would come back to me when the angrez people had left the country . . .'

'Bachcha Mian told you that?'

The child gulped and nodded.

'And no doubt you believed him. Inquilab zindabad, eh? Bring me the paper—from Gandhiji's Congress Party—and let me look at it.'

Bachcha's ingenuity stupefied her. To think he had such gifts of invention and she had thought him slow of wit.

The girl returned from her room with a sheet of ruled paper and held it out to Janki. Janki felt the blood rise roaring to her brain, scalding every nerve. She snatched the paper from the girl's hand and read out the scribbled words: 'Khemchand Mishrilal and Sons. Jewellers and Pawnbrokers. 151 Sunehri Bazaar, Chowk, Ilahabad. Received one emerald set comprising three-string neckpiece, earrings and hair comb. Sixteen gold bangles, two kangan sets. One nose ring, forehead pendant, jhoomar . . . Child, I know you cannot read and I hate to break the truth to you but your Bachcha is no inquilabi freedom fighter but a vile cheat!'

The girl began to cry.

'This is a pawnbroker's ticket. To fund his vile cannabis!'

Then she saw the effect of her cruel disclosure and the shivering and sobbing that overtook the little girl who sank in a little huddle on the divan and hid her face in the bolster. Her heart went out to this little child of fourteen, a captive of a situation not of her making and beyond her understanding, and she cursed her own blind hopes of Bachcha's reform and a transformed future. Leaning over, she took the child in her arms and let her sob till the spell passed and was followed by an unearthly stillness. It lasted so long that Janki thought the girl had fallen asleep, exhausted by her fit of grieving, and an overpowering compassion swept over her and she whispered in the girl's ear, 'I think I know where he is and first thing in the morning I am going to bring him back to you, if need be drag him back to you by the ears. And every one of your jewels that he has pawned. Trust me, child, and don't grieve.'

Next morning she ordered her phaeton, sent for Jallu Mian to accompany her and drove first to Khemchand Mishrilal's in Sunehri Bazaar and then to the Katra den where she knew Bachcha would be.

She recovered the jewellery and dragged back Bachcha, as she said she would, berating and abusing him all the way back.

'Here is the inquilabi, the ganja-doped patriot!' She pushed Bachcha ahead of her as the girl ran out into the courtyard. 'That's what you told your little wife, did you, my sahibzade? For shame! Yes, she showed me the paper, the guarantee from Gandhiji that promised the jewels and gold back when the firangees were chased back to Bartania! If you had applied yourself as intelligently to your lessons as you do to your lies you might have become a collector sahib, mian.'

Bachcha had turned threateningly to his bride. 'You showed it to her?' he hissed in a menacing undertone. The girl shrank. Janki read his thought and threatened him in return: 'If you so much as lay a finger on this little bitiya you shall live to regret it.'

Bachcha glowered back. 'What is it to you, if I thrash her or if I don't . . .?'

This was a bit of blustering swagger to strike terror in the cowering girl's heart and Janki's head exploded in anger.

'Ah, ah, this cur! He'll steal his very mother's shroud, he'll steal the kajal off his bride's eye to make a cowrie or two! I don't trust you, you salt-betraying scum-worm, Allah knows which foul gutter you were spawned in!' Rage inflamed her temples, serrated her vocal cords. She heard a hoarse voice grazing out abuse. A voice she did not recognize but which could be nobody else's but her own. For a prolonged moment she knew only a break in the mind's continuity, heard only that blinding uproar. When she awoke from that extended absence of self she saw that Bachcha had fallen on the floor beneath the thunderous impact of her own flailing arms, wielding the stick she had seized from Jallu, and realized that she had thrashed Bachcha black and blue, that she was still thrashing him, that dust and snot smeared his face and that Jallu was trying hard to restrain her maddened fit. She saw Bachcha gather himself up, run limping to the doorway and disappear into the garden. She saw the little girl sink trembling into a chair. She saw the servants clustered in a huddle around the courtyard. She stared in incomprehension at the stick she still held in her hands, at the tall brass tumbler of water Jallu was holding out to her, entreating: 'Baiji, begum sahiba . . .'

He vanished, her Abdul Aziz, her Bachcha Mian, and vanished forever.

Initially she feigned apathy and steeled herself for the little girl's sake. But Bachcha was neither in the den in Katra nor in any of the city's other dope hideouts, nor anywhere else she could conceive of. A day passed, a week.

'Let him go drown himself in the river!' she snorted in reassurance to the girl. 'Don't eat out your heart. That one will come back like a cur when it's time for his chapati scraps. He'll come crawling back, be sure.'

But the girl's anxiety was a reproach to her and her heart relented. What could this little fourteen-year-old know of the hardness of a woman's heart when all its sap has dried? This tender vine, trusting its way up a stone column, must not be thwarted just yet.

'Don't fret, child,' she said more gently as the days passed. 'I know Bachcha Mian well. He'll be back.'

Where in the middle of all this was there space for her music? In the strident commotion of her life, she felt her art being throttled. Weeks passed without riyaz and performances fell. She felt her former magic grow tired, she ceased to grow. She declined tempting and prestigious invitations because things more urgent demanded her attention. There were times she suspected it was now the hour to put aside her music, and an ache surpassing all the immediate sorrows of her circumstance overcame her mind. Poetry had turned scarce long ago, defeated. She fervently promised herself another season of life, a grace earned by effort, when the chance to be one with her music again might be granted her. But that chance was clearly to come later rather than sooner, if at all. Enforced abstinence was to be her trial, she told herself, patience to live without music till such time as the demands of life insisted. In that testing duration she was required to unlearn all she knew, lose what youth and application and skill had accomplished, degenerate in inverse maturing. In moments of despair she wondered if that second chance would come at all. With a shock she realized that middle age too was receding. She still wanted to sing the most excellent song of her life.

She kept the child with her in the nights, sleeping on a couch in her bedchamber. But as the night advanced she heard the girl get up and patter out. She heard the door to the veranda creak open and she felt the river breeze ferret its way in. She rose and followed the child who sat pathetically on the step, her eyes staring into the dark. All of a sudden she felt the weight of a remembered oppression, a pain whose face she knew, and it brought back in a rush a horde of anarchic aches—her wrestler father waiting for his feckless lover, her bitter mother waiting for her vanished

father, and now this little unformed heart, timidly turning the first
pages of an old, ugly primer of pain, her mind stammering its first
alphabets in what would become a heavy tome of unravelling faith.
An old, familiar destiny, a refrain her nauseated heart was forced
to iterate in varying rhythms of despair.

The growing pallor of the child's face deepened her worry.
Could this child be pining? Even for a proven cheat? Could this toy
heart be sickening for love? Love was a word that provoked her to
rage. Her own marriage, she was now reconciled to think, was the
biggest error of her life and all her subsequent decades a fervent
argument against that error, but when did this child choose to fall
in love? For this too she ruefully knew—that love was a choice,
a fatal microsecond of willing that loosed all the passion and the
pain. She could no longer ignore this pining child, paying with her
misery for a misjudgement of others, living under the protection
of those who had erred. This was a colossal wrong and no wisdom,
no experience could safeguard against life errors such as this. No
matter how intensive the riyaz, life was a raga you just couldn't get
right. You thought you had the notes under control but then there
came a critical tone or semitone that tripped you up. Don't worry,
don't worry. She had tired of the falsehood of her own assuring
voice. 'Never mind if he's gone off somewhere. You can start going
to school. If you knew how to read you would have known a pawn
ticket when you saw it. Home tutors, then the great University of
Allahabad which, I hear, has now opened its gates to girls. What
can you not do if you are educated, child? And,' she added, 'you
can always count on me.'

But the child grew listless by the day. So she did what her
pride would never have allowed her to do—seek counsel from
Haq Sahib. She sent for him.

'Bachcha has not returned, Haq Sahib,' she said.

'What did you expect? To humiliate a young man in the presence of his new bride!' responded Haq Sahib sarcastically. 'Sometimes, bibi, you forget that the big world is not your mehfil. To sit in silent awe while your voice commits assault and offence.'

It was her turn to feel assaulted and offended. 'What mean you, Vakil Sahib? I was not aware my voice is in this world to assault and offend.'

'Ah, no,' he said ironically. 'It is here to sweeten our ears alone, think you, begum sahiba? Then think again and ask those whose ears it has grazed day in and day out. You do your riyaz on our hapless hearts, madam, and I don't mean music. For you are the very mistress of malefaction when you so desire, and we the poor dumb victims of your frenzy. But the world isn't made up of strings to strum along to your tune or drums to thump in agreement with your every behest, know you this!'

She turned away, mortified. She dreamt that night that a whole audience sprang to its feet, shouting, 'Silence! Enough!' and covering up its ears. Bachcha never returned. And here was this fourteen-year-old girl beneath her roof, depending on her, looking to her for a future that neither of them had planned and neither knew anything about.

When the first agony of fruitless waiting had passed, she sent for tutors for the child. And books, a radio, a kitten, a pair of chattering parrots, watercolours and paintbrushes, skeins and embroidery frames and pattern books. If not a son, a daughter whom she would school and groom into strength and grace. A new dream began forming in her mind and at the end of a year their lives settled into a semblance of resigned purpose. With wonder she noticed the little girl's growing affection for her, felt the bond deepening, felt laughter return and she felt herself wake up to a gentle contentment with her lot, never expected or experienced before. Chandni did well at her painting and her embroidery and Janki hired better teachers and displayed the girl's handiwork with pride. She was also clever with clay and her nimble fingers turned out tiny animals and miniature furniture and painted flowers that were ingenious and beautiful. She sat, quietly absorbed with needle and skeins as Janki did her morning riyaz, and if Janki so much as coughed she found a twig of mulethi instantly proffered or a glass of cardamom-and-ginger tea sent for from the kitchen. She often found her hookah hidden away and had to demand it back in mock aggression that warmed her heart and brought her rest. She sent for her accompanists and started her riyaz again. She began accepting invitations to sing. Her travels took her away from the city but she always returned home with a greater sense of homecoming than ever before. She even began teaching music at home to the bunch of pupils who gathered around her. Among them a young lad named Mahesh Chand Vyas. He'd turned up with a meek request to be tutored by her. He was a university student and a great admirer of her singing. He'd had some initial training too. If Bai Sahiba agreed to give him a few tips two afternoons a week he was prepared to pay whatever she asked. She was amused at his bashful presumption. Whatever she asked—that was a tall order, young man, she'd laughed. Are you sure you can afford my fee? And who may your guardians be? They were landowners, he answered. Be they maharajas, they might be unpleasantly surprised at my rates, she teased the young man. I never would tell them, he said sulkily. They never would allow me. Then how? she wanted to know. I would tell them I have enrolled for a law degree, he faltered. She roared with laughter. Where would this city be without its lawyers, she guffawed. Even if they spend their guardians' money at a kothawali's classes! And what would you tell them at the end of the law course? I would say I have failed, said the lad. His keenness disarmed her. All for the love of music? she asked. He nodded. It was decided that he would come to her class straight from the university two afternoons a week. She tied the ganda round his wrist, charged a rupee and 4 annas and said she would charge her fee in bulk at the end of the law course. Mahesh Chand Vyas was to become her favourite pupil, surrogate son, all-purpose assistant, even a confidant in the dark days ahead. But for the present, it was a time of meaning and peace.

Never since her childhood had such a sense of rewarding quietude warmed her life. To have blundered into this serendipitous sweetness seemed a miracle of mischance, as though a packaged treasure, sealed and stamped and addressed to someone else, had by some unwarranted error landed in her life. The softer, the sweeter for resting on a foundation of unspoken loss that highlighted the unexpected wonder of this gift. The second chance had been granted, not through satisfaction but through failure.

Chandni took the Middle exam and passed it reasonably well. Her pleasure in her report and mark sheet was Janki's delight. Janki gave her a kundan set as a gift. The girl uttered a squeal of joy on seeing it, before her face clouded and Janki dared not ask why. It was not hard to imagine the cause for dejection.

'What will I do with this, Ammi Jaan?' whispered the girl.

'You will wear it at Eid and Bakhreid and at my next performance. And we'll save it for your marriage.'

She added that last with caution and sought the girl's face for a reaction.

The girl looked shocked.

'My what?' she asked.

'Your shaadi, bitiya.'

It was something she had given much thought to, though the prospect brought a pang of unaccountable pain. Chandni had blossomed into a fine young woman and it seemed grossly unfair that she remain a handmaiden and ward all her life. And if the maulvis were unhelpful there was always the Civil Law to undo her wrong marriage and Hashmat Ullah would do his utmost. This time, Janki had sworn, the match would be made with every vigilance and inquiry. Not the way it was when Chandni's parents handed her over to Bachcha. This was her expiation, this pang of losing this late-acquired girl child, but she would do a better job of it than had Chandni's parents.

To her perplexity, the child's eyes filled up.

'You are making fun of me, Ammi Jaan,' she murmured.

Janki drew her close. 'You are so wrong, bitiya,' she soothed.

'You want to get rid of me,' said Chandni. 'Why?'

'Never.' Janki struggled to explain. 'How can I when you have brought me . . . all this . . . all this?'

The girl looked baffled. 'What have I brought you, Ammi? It's you who gives me nice things and looks after me and teaches me and . . .'

'You can't understand,' said Janki. 'But I have to see to it that you find a young man who is worthy of you, better than my Abdul Aziz, Allah protect him wherever he is.'

'No,' said the girl stubbornly. 'He'll surely be back. And I won't leave you. Not ever!'

'We are not getting you married just yet, bitiya. You will pass the FA from Crosthwaite College. Then you will go to the Allahabad University. Jha Sahib, the vice chancellor, came to my mehfil at Seth Manmohan Das's bagiya, and seems to respect me much. I shall discuss your admission with him.'

The girl began to laugh. 'No one is going to the university, Maheshji tells me. They're all boycotting it. Gandhiji has asked them to. They're sitting outside the gates and the police-wallahs

and sowars are chasing them away. What fun. Maybe I'll become
a Gandhi-woman and march in rallies and go to jail and when
will I wear all this jewellery? I will spin khaddar cloth and
dress in it.'

'You will wear it when the sahibs and mems have gone and
you can wear fine clothes again. Then we shall get you a brilliant
politician or a university professor or a magistrate sahib or a
barrister sahib.'

'Then, Ammi Jaan, I still have about twenty years with you
and I'm fine with that. I'll mind your house while you go sing, and
order the servants around and look to your tenants and handle
your dates and events and your clothes and your visitors.'

And there the matter rested. Chandni had summed up her
activities right. As the months passed and she prepared to take
the FA examination from Crosthwaite College, she minded the
house, ordered the servants about, organized Janki's performance
wardrobe and even noted down her appointments. But it could
not go on, Janki fretted. Chandni was growing into an alluring
presence, even to her visitors, and Janki felt anxious about her
safety. When she had to go out of the city on prolonged singing
tours, Chandni was left behind to manage the house and Janki
didn't like leaving her unchaperoned. She sought Haq Sahib's help.

Haq Sahib now spent most of his time at Mehdauri, visiting
Sabzi Mandi only occasionally. He consented to moving in when
Janki was out of the city, though he did it with an ill grace.

'So shall I salaam my stars on being invited to begum sahiba's
durbar again or shall I bemoan my lot on my sinking to this
position of harem guard?'

He had taken to speaking in this coarse, abrasive tone lately.
A tone Janki thought best to ignore. In recent months she had
seen little of him and she found the natural distancing of their two

lives an increasing relief. They could, it was a surprise to discover, actually sustain a courteous conversation again for minutes at a stretch. And she was grateful that he could be relied on to step in and help when she needed it.

'You are welcome in any capacity that your fancy thinks fit to adopt, Vakil Sahib,' she said in her most pacific voice. Who knew with life, the surprises it sprang? They might yet have a more or less quiet old age together, or at least a state of sustained truce, which was not such a bad thing either. Their staying apart for long periods was a most wholesome condition of matrimony, she often thought. And if they were there for each other when practical needs arose, what else was there to hope for in the complexity of a relationship permanently on the rocks?

The arrangement was not to endure. For one day, as she was about to leave for Jaipur, the girl came up to her and begged: 'Ammi Jaan, take me with you.'

'Why, what will you do there? Your master sahib will be coming and your exams are round the corner, bitiya. And here you can see that the bawarchi-khana is run right and the parrots fed and Abba Jaan's hookah filled.' The girl turned away, sulking.

When she returned from Jaipur, she learnt that Chandni was sick. She runs out of the haveli and stays in the yard, reported the servants. No, lately she climbs the stairs to the living quarters of the women servants and begs them to let her sleep on the floor, reported others.

'Where is she now?' asked Janki, a horrific misgiving throwing her mind into a panic.

She was in old Farida Bi's attic.

She saw Janki and burst into a torrent of weeping in an uncontainable fit. She shook her head from side to side and wailed inconsolably, clinging to Janki in a hysterical cinch.

Janki coaxed the girl down, sent for Davidson, the civil surgeon, who sedated the girl and left her to sleep her paroxysm off. It was forty-eight hours later that Chandni opened her eyes and stared wanly at Janki. Another two hours before she could be induced to speak.

Then Janki stormed out of the room and roared for the phaeton to be brought round. She rode hell-bent to the chamber that Haq Sahib rented near the kutcherry to meet his clients. She burst into his room, raging like a bull, her splendid voice reeling out of control in a thunderous outcry. While behind her madness, behind the passion of murderous ferocity that swept over her, the cold counterpoint of inner commentary asked—was this rage the scalding music, the high point of her shame, for which her soul was painstakingly training, her throat the beastly foundry for this devastation that scorched all it turned on, melting stone to pith and flesh to blubber? She hurled abuse in every octave, swooping up and down frenzied scales, stumbled shuddering down the pit, charring all to cinders. A roaring raga of destruction in which her throat disgorged venom in sounds no longer human, the booming soul spasm climaxing in the violent jet of spit she hurled at Haq's flinching face. She turned and fled the scene of her own convulsion, flung herself into the phaeton and tore sobbing down the roads towards her home.

Next morning she appeared early at Hashmat Ullah's office.

'I have need to speak plainly with you, Hashmat Ullah Sahib.'

He looked up, surprised. Then his face composed itself in its usual expression. 'When have you ever spoken otherwise, madam?'

'Spare me your jesting, I beg you.'

'Allah forbid that I should dare jest with you.'

Suddenly she swayed on her feet and dropped into the nearest chair. He started, stared, called frantically for water. She gulped it down, mopped her face and fell back into her chair. He fussed about, helpless.

She mastered herself and smiled weakly. 'As you see, its time I made my will, Hashmat Ullah Sahib.'

He raised his hands to heaven. 'Surely not, sahiba!'

She pulled herself together. 'Forgive me,' she murmured. 'As you know, I am never like this.' Drawing a deep breath she let slip the information: 'Haq Sahib shall now never, never cross my threshold again. This I have sworn.'

He made no comment, kept a composed face, but could hardly suppress a certain glint. He asked for no details. She supplied none.

'What I want to make sure,' she went on, 'is that not a rupee of mine, no, not a fake cowrie, should find its way into Abdul Haq's pockets. Do you understand me?'

'I understand you, madam, though what you ask is hardly feasible. Speaking as a lawyer, that is.' His tone was grim.

'You are the only one who is acquainted with the extent of my resources. Were I to will it away to my daughter-in-law . . .'

He cleared his throat. 'Excuse me, madam, but you might only endanger the young lady, as you endangered her husband by adopting him. Pardon me, I speak plainly as you desired. I do not wish to deprecate anyone without reason, least of all your esteemed husband, but Abdul Haq Sahib's intentions are open to speculation.'

She looked hard at him and whispered, 'What certainty then of my own safety?'

He shook his head. 'You're quite safe, madam. You have many working years ahead. Many more songs to record still.'

She grimaced. 'What an old cynic you are, Hashmat Ullah Sahib. But if not a will, what then? Have you anything to suggest?'

He pondered. 'A trust, perhaps,' he suggested. He spelt it out. The idea took shape. He remembered her old project and this time it made sense. It grew on her. A fund for girls—education, marriage expenses, contingencies. Yes, she felt the stirrings of an old engagement. 'I shall be sole custodian, so long as I live. But after me maybe a committee. With members like Janab Maulvi Fazle Rab Sahib, the pensions deputy collector, and Rai Man Mohan Lal Sahib, the special magistrate.'

Here he thought fit to caution her. 'Haq Sahib too might stake his claim to trusteeship, madam, which in the absence of a formal termination of your relations—in law, I mean, which of course he shall naturally contest—you shall hardly be in a position to decline. But there shall be three other trustees, including myself, to oppose misuse.'

'And misappropriation. And also,' she stipulated, 'no religion please. I'm through with Hindus and Muslims both, so no more. For the Trust's sake let us have two Hindu trustees and two Muslims. A Shia, a Sunni, and by my wish, a Bengali, a Kayasth.'

'Just as you say.'

She was relieved. 'God bless you, Hashmat Ullah Sahib. You are an answer to all my prayers. Where would I be without you?'

'Exactly where you find yourself now, madam, but maybe a lot worse.' His voice, she thought, was overly stinging, and felt confirmed in her suspicions and also deeply dejected.

'Do you recall what you said to me when I once jested about standing beneath a canopy with you? You said, "Baiji thinks far too highly of herself and far too poorly of my intelligence, that she should imagine me capable of such complete folly." I wish that you had thought highly enough of this foolish singing-woman and less highly of your own respectability and intelligence, Hashmat Ullah Sahib.'

He turned away, his face strained. 'I wish that had been so,' he said quietly. 'It's a long time back, madam.'

There was sadness between them. He saw her to the door, promising to work out the details of the Trust.

When a week had gone by Feroza announced the visitor: 'Sahib wants to meet you, begum sahiba.'

'What does he want?'

'He says he wishes to speak to you.'

'Bar the door in his face, Feroza. Tell him I said I am not at home.'

When Abdul Haq came striding indignantly in she reared up like a hooded cobra in full fury and ordered him out.

'What ill grace is this, begum? Stop this nonsense immediately, I command you!' he shouted.

She towered up before him, sizzling. 'Command, ah? A petty dependant dares use this word! Begone! Take your foul face out of my sight!'

It could not have been better calculated to sting.

'Your dependant?' he shouted. 'Heaven forbid I should ever have to live off the takings of a draggled old singing whore!'

'No?' she sneered. 'No objection had you to the walls and roofs that sheltered you when you had none in this city to call your own, Haq Sahib. And as for being a tawaif, better to be an honourable tawaif than a niggling lawyer with nothing better on his mind than gutter-scum schemes on his little daughter-in-law's bed!'

He paled. He shot off a glance in Feroza's direction. She was quick to seize it.

'Your guiles are no secret, Haq Sahib. All the household is wise of it, more shame to me! And if you do not leave my house instantly I shall make sure that the entire city, yes, your courthouse

circles, your municipality circles, everyone shall grow wise of it
and your very family be ready to spit on your face!'

He stood still a long while, then turned to go. She called after
him: 'It shall be better for both of us if your blighted shadow
does not darken my door. Ever again. Not now and not when
I am dead.'

If he heard he made no sign of protest or rejoinder. She was
still trembling when she heard the wheels of the tonga creak
into motion outside and horses' hoofs tattooing down the
cobbled path and fade away. She sank shakily into an armchair
and sat, gripping its armrests as though she feared she'd be
thrown off.

It was some time later that she summoned Chandni to the
room. 'I have thrown him out, bitiya,' she said simply. 'For all
time. There is now just you and me, child.'

Her persistent dream returned in a new rendition, a dream
that had a new refrain, that chanted that in some people the
soul too decayed, as the body did. That she was trying to stem
that rot, lifting a potful of water, she, Radha at the panghat.
And as she brings it away, balanced on her head, she hears a
voice call: Stop! The assignment she was given was to separate
the Ganga and the Yamuna from the clay pot and she finds
herself sitting with a sieve, straining the water, which escaped
continually through the mesh, mocking her efforts, while her
mind chanted a song of its own mad making: 'Sakhi-ri, main
chali thi neer pachhore'. Where had she heard that before? She
was singing 'Sri Ram kripalu', tears welling in her eyes. She was
singing a naat, her voice choking with feeling. She dreamt she
was on an oarless raft, drifting away from the Ganga bank and
never quite managing to reach the Yamuna end, her raft reeling
downstream instead and Hassu's ringing voice breaking in:

Don't struggle. You're on a mightier river, bibi. Give yourself up to it and don't worry about the banks. With sudden, superlative lucidity her mind spoke up: How right he is. My two faiths are like two different ragas of the soul and I have learnt to sing them both and I am blest.

It changed, the mad song of her mind. Till it was no longer a business of separating the water of two rivers, blue and white, but of sifting the dark waters of death from those of life, telling night from day and aversion from relief. Until it became a life-threatening wager between sickness and soundness, between her own body's excretions and odours, her retchings and helpless incontinences and the drifting of her senses into the transparencies of ragas she had never known existed in the ether, in the oblivion over which Davidson brooded like a dour dignitary and little Chandni hung around, ever present on the fringes of consciousness, feeding her, sponging her, changing her garments, spooning medicine into her parched mouth.

When she woke up in the Bailey Hospital days later Samina broke the news to her as gently as she could. Yes, it was the summer curse, the cholera, but by the grace of God and the diligence of Davidson Sahib, she had weathered the storm. But, such are Allah's incomprehensible ways, the little Chandni, who had been by her side through the worst days, had also caught it and died.

She was much too feeble to weather this storm. She turned her ragged old body to the wall and wept into her pillow for the sweet child of her oldening years, that brief lyric granted her heart by some capricious fate and as capriciously recalled just as the spent heart had known a prelude of ease. Chandni died while she, Janki, lay senseless on her hospital bed. She returned, days later, to a house so silent that no music could ever hope to fill it. What filled it now was the sound of hacking coughs. Longer than any taan could be, intricate lurchings of breath that squelched through the puddles of phlegm in her throat as her body let loose its many other voices.

22

Strings are metallic things. Fret and bellow are material. The gramophone record is shellac. The larynx is flesh. Moulded muscle, a distended loop of sore cell stuff battling a rasp, a scooping lung-grazing whoop and wheeze, and a drag and a haul of tortured breath. Interminably, till it brought up blood. This too one of the body's mad harangues. Music isn't the structure's main function. In time the brute metal or wood or flesh shall up and rebel, declaring its dominance. Bande Ali Khan Sahib knew this rage when he lifted aloft his veena and flung it on the ground to smash into many pieces. You want to hear the sound of my veena? he shouted. Here is the sound. Hear it! The sound is not just what the instrument makes when the notes are contrived together in sweet concord but equally the jangle of dismemberment when the notes crash free. Such notes that never are tamed.

One afternoon she called Mahesh Chand Vyas to her side. He had hovered around her sickbed, loyally tending her, running errands, fetching and carrying and reading out documents from the Trust's files that Hashmat Ullah routinely sent for her perusal.

'There's something you owe me, Mahesh,' she spoke with difficulty. 'Though the music classes haven't met for some time, still there's some guru-offering pending, if you remember.'

'Yes, Bai Sahiba?' He looked apprehensive.

'I want you to promise me that when I die Abdul Haq should not be allowed anywhere near me. Do what has to be done and do it as fast as you can.' He knelt at her bedside, at a loss for words. She dragged out the words, sorry for this poor lad who had come to learn music and got himself such an assignment.

She beckoned him closer. 'This that I say to you is more important than any music that I might have taught you, had I time enough. There are three things to count on, boy. One's own money, earned by one's own labour. The energy of one's own body, the strength of one's arm. And trust in God's grace. Write this down in your bandish book.'

He strained to catch her words, and did. She seemed to have drifted off again.

There was in her delusions no chronology, just a gentle time shuffle. Lying, cough-racked, she was sure she had lifted her tanpura and wheezed and gasped her way through a raga for the fakir who waited patiently listening to her laboured breaths as she picked up her creaking riyaz for him. She knew him but couldn't place him. There were notes she could not touch, new notes entirely outside any scale, and notes she had once commanded and now could not.

Singing was a travail. She took a long drag of breath, produced a trail of tortuous syllables. It was like dredging out a tune buried deep in a silted riverbed. Such an exertion. Sweat beaded her forehead, her throat felt raw. Each syllable she sang tore at it, shard-sharp, before her voice snagged on a note and splintered in an explosive bout of coughing, spattering her headcloth with more blood. She would not give up. Her cracked voice strained, tantalized by new phrases of sonic truth that vibrated just beyond her capacities. Did one have to break out of this poor wrecked instrument to reach them? In her sleep she wondered who he was. Strayed father, strayed son, or old assailant who'd dealt the wounds? Or the Sayyad of Mausiqui come at last? In delusion they merged into one. She knew him but could not place him. 'Hari bin morey kaun khabar le?' Was he the swara-soul, the sakshi, all the faces of all her audiences fused into one? Or her own soul-face, worn, hung with beads, dressed in patched and faded rags, with calloused hands and dusty feet, such a mist settled on its face? Is this fakir my accompanist or rival, challenging me to sing, or a blind lover who has eyes that do not see my ugliness, my ruin? Instead he looks past my derelict being and into the depths of me and plucks some essential bit that has stayed untransformed, like a pebble on the bed of a changeable river or a crystal note beneath an uproar of music? My blindness too, for I look past his rags and his tree-bark face and I know him and cannot place him.

Dreaming the raga in sleep. Not hearing it but living its onward flow in a music drowse. Scraps of crumbled phrases spelling themselves out in elemental successions, in essential inevitabilities. Until the mind jolts awake on a diamond-hard vein of stillness with a wisp of tune floating out of reach in the just-vacated silence. The interior diction of her life carried on in the language of her old songs as faces floated into her mind. At one time she thought she glimpsed Manki as her mind murmured: 'Usase kuchh mera bhi zikare dile nashad rahe.' Another time it was someone resembling Chandni and she heard her own voice sing: 'Jui ka fulva hathva lagat.' How it traps us. We long to sing another song but we end up singing the same one. All night the words of compositions keep revolving in the head. I sang because the song set me free, lifted me above my body and my limited life. Now my song has become my dungeon. And always that fakir outside my barred window—is he in my dream or am I in his? Is he singing me into being? I thought I'd created a raga and its name was Janki. Create is wrong. All I'd done was contrive the swaras in a certain disposition. An arrangement of units that gathered in a cumulus of self, a soul-code irreplaceable by any other and signifying I, me, Janki, this person here. What time of day would this raga belong to? 'Jabki khamosh hui bulbul bustane husain.' Sunset perhaps or the deepest night. But the way she felt an inward opening it could well be the Brahmamuhurta, the God-instant. Hari bin morey kaun khabar le? Am I a raga in his mind? Is this a swoon or have I drifted out of life and is that the singing of reality outside my window? 'Dil sahabe aulad se insaaf talab hai.'

My song now feels all wrong to me, its false notes jar. It's the politics of the self invading, but do not judge my infirmity, I was not always thus and I called to my Maula and begged: 'Take away this pain. It grows unbearable.' Said my Lord to me: 'And what shall you pay me, Janki, were I to relieve you of your pain?' 'Whatever my Master thinks fit.' 'So be it,' said my Maula. 'I take away your pain, but you must give me your song too.' 'Only let me sing my last.' She half-raised herself to sing it.

23

What is it that dies? An intensified self, sharpened to its quintessential core, though to all the world insensate. The last moments of legendary singers might well call for a separate session of my storytelling but for the present be content with these few. When Bade Ghulam Ali Khan Sahib lay dying his mind was still engrossed in notes and scales. His last words, addressed to his son, were: 'If you suppose the sound of the table fan is "sa", the dog's barking outside is the "re" and "ga" of Todi.' When Abdul Karim Khan, travelling from Madras to Pondicherry, felt an uneasiness of the heart, he immediately got off the train at a deserted village station, asked his accompanists to tune their instruments, and seated on the railway platform of a tiny station, with his face to Mecca, he managed to produce a Darbari Kanhra in offering before he collapsed. When Mushtaq Hussain Khan sank dying in the arms of a disciple, his words, gasped with his last breath, were: 'Lord, the touch of your grace made a singer of me. Forgive me my wrongs.' Janki died on the 18 May 1934. She died alone. Her body lay, unattended, until news reached her pupil, Mahesh Chand Vyas, who rushed down, called the police, stood by through the formalities of the panchnama, after which, finding no other means of transport, he hastily hired a cart from construction-site labourers and conveyed her remains to the Kaladanda cemetery

for a hurried burial. Thereby honouring the promise he had made
to her. The Trust built a small monument over her grave later.
But not before Abdul Haq had arrived to claim whatever cash and
valuables fell to his share as husband of the deceased. It is part of
the Janki Bai legend in the city of Allahabad that her vast wardrobe
of costumes found its way to Benaras where her clothes were burnt
for their silver and gold thread and four seers of gold and seven
seers of silver extracted and claimed by Haq Sahib.

There is another scrap of city lore that for a long time after
her passing a fakir was daily sighted near her mazaar, standing
motionless before the incense he had lit.

Acknowledgements

Grateful thanks are due to Madhuvrat Rai, without whose very substantial help to me in gathering primary material this book might never have reached its present form. My research was enriched by the writings of many people, chief among them being Kailash Gautam, Kumar Prasad Mukherji, Sulochana Yajurvedi, Acharya Brihaspati, Amaranatha Jha, Shamsur Rahman Faruqi, R. Gopal Krishna, Rafiq Zakaria, Pran Nevile and Vikram Sampat. I am also indebted to the January–February 1992 Volume 1–2 issue of the journal *Sangeet*, the April 1994 Volume 14 issue of the *Journal of the Society of Indian Record Collectors*, and the detailed discography of Janki Bai's records put together by Michael Kinnear. I thank Syed Irshad Haider and Ehsan Hasan for helping me translate *Diwan-e-Janki* from the original Urdu into English and Saleha Rashid for helping out with Persian. Many of the bandishes that appear in these pages are part of my father's collection. Some like 'Every mercy my Maula confers upon me', 'I asked the black one on the mango bough' and 'Main moorakh teri, Prabhuji more' are composed by me as are the handful of verses in English fictionally attributed to Akbar Ilahabadi. The Urdu verses, translated in the Notes, are original to Akbar, as is the rest of the poetry original to Janki.

Thanks are due to H.S. Saxena, Kusum and Raja Zutshi, Amresh and Neeta Mathur, Akshat Srivastava, Samina Naqvi, Kishwar Nasreen and Rafat Ullah for the various ways in which they facilitated my progress. The Can Serrat Art Residency, Barcelona, provided an ideal environment for intensive work. The strong support I received from my publishers Penguin Random House India, my editors Ranjana Sengupta and Cibani Premkumar, and the indefatigable Kanishka Gupta has gone a long way towards making this book's unfolding journey such a memorable one.

Finally I mention with gratitude my family's perennial contribution to keeping me grounded, their willingness to come to my help, whether with tech issues or with tracking down references, and their effortless accommodation of this extra member, Janki Bai Ilahabadi, who came to take up residence in our family space, invisible but insistent, making her presence felt for almost a decade while this book sought out the lineaments of her story.

Glossary and Notes

Chapter 1

Todi: a certain raga
raees: an affluent or aristocratic person
dhrupad: a genre of Hindustani classical music
Sayyad of Mausiqui: the holy soul of music
rasika: aficionado, connoisseur

Chapter 2

'Jamuna tat Shyam khelein Hori': A famous song in the Hindustani
   classical tradition, describing the god Krishna splashing colour on
   his women companions during the festival of Holi on the bank of
   the river Yamuna.
nazrana: a gift or offering, usually cash
malkin: mistress
nath babu: A man engaged, often by choosing the highest bidder, to
   ritually deflower a young girl who is to be initiated as a prostitute.
   A festive occasion in traditional brothels in former times called the
   'nath-uthrai', or removal of the nose ring.
divan-khana: sitting room
alaap: the opening phase of a raga when the essential notes are sung or
   played
'Maza le le rasiya nayi jhulni ka': Enjoy the pleasures of the new swing,
   O sensuous one.
iman: honour
Shagun-Nek: auspicious welcome offering

341

angrez laat sahib: British lord sahib

kothi: mansion

jamadar: junior rank khayal, dhrupad and tappa, not just the thumri

kothri: tiny room

shringar: the erotic essence in Indian aesthetics

tasveer-khana: picture gallery

khayal, dhrupad, tappa, thumri: genres of Hindustani classical music

ganika: honoured courtesan

gandharva: celestial being, less than divine but superior to humans and associated with music-making

ragas and raginis: major and minor arrangements of notes in traditional patterns expressing moods and hours of the day

apsara: celestial danseuse, often a temptress of ideal beauty

Brahmamuhurta: divine hour before dawn

riyaz: diligent practice

Chapter 3

seer and chhatak: units of weight measurement, now obsolete, a seer or ser being one-fourth of a kilogram. The seer was larger than a chhatak.

bhauji: colloquial term for brother's sister

qawwals: singers belonging to a particular genre of north Indian music

chaitis, horis and kajris: songs sung during certain seasons. Light classical Hindustani music.

gadar: the Uprising of 1857

panjeeri: sweet, flavoured wheat powder, ritually distributed after Hindu worship

arzee: application

Kashi Vishvanath: one of Shiva's names and the most important of Benaras's temples

'Mo pe daar gayo sare rang ki gagar': He emptied the entire potful of colour on me. Traditional song referring to Krishna playing Holi with his cowgirl companions.

Chapter 4

moholla: locality

aheer: an Indian sub-caste of cow herders and dairy farmers

bhang: hemp, used as a psychotropic drug
sandukchi: small trunk or chest
payal: ankle chain
kimkhwab: a rich fabric dupatta; stole or headcloth of fine cloth
kutcha: built of earth
mujra: originally meaning a respectful offering, a song, sometimes accompanied by dancing or histrionic gestures, sung by a courtesan
nihayat badsoorat: extremely ugly

Chapter 5

nautanki: a form of folk theatre popular in Avadh
chunariya: headcloth often ritually offered to the goddess
havan: a ritual fire sacrifice
sasural: husband's homestead, in extended families the father-in-law's home as well
palki: palanquin
pahalwan: wrestler, a powerfully built man
muhjali: burnt-face
raas: love dance, originally demonstrating the love play between Krishna and his women friends
akhara: wrestling pit
dhamar: a genre of Hindustani vocal music
keertan: communal hymn singing
dholak: two-faced drum
Great Maata: folk name for small pox, imagined as a horrific avatar of the goddess
suhaag: husband's life or a state of being married
maata: pox
chaukhat: threshold

Chapter 6

alaap, gat, jod and jhala: the four accelerating rhythm patterns that mark the progress of a raga
banna: traditional wedding folk song sung in honour of the groom
maati-mili: colloquial term of abuse meaning 'made of mud'
mubarak: congratulations

Chapter 7

gharana: hereditary school of music centred on particular maestros and
    styles and named after the place of its location
Inshallah: as Allah wills
shagird: student
murshid: master, teacher
taalim: training

Chapter 8

kulhar: earthen tumbler
rudraveena: rare string instrument
rasa: temper, indwelling mood
ashtha-disha: the eight directions

Chapter 9

rajaji: my king, said ironically. *Common apostrophe in mujra songs.*
chik: a slatted screen made of thin cane or bamboo strips
patang-baaz: ace kite-flyer
chunri: headcloth, stole
'Holi hai': popular street cry meaning 'It's Holi!'
'Bura na mano, Holi hai': popular street cry playfully uttered during
    the spring festival of Holi when colour is sprayed on friends and
    strangers with the words: Please don't mind—it's Holi.
'Aaj Braj mein ho rahi Hori': In Braj-country it's Holi today.
'Mo pe daar gayo sare rang ki gagar': He (meaning Krishna) emptied the
    entire potful of colour on me.
'Hori machi hai saiyaan ki nagariya': In my lover's city Holi's being
    (wildly) celebrated.
baraat: procession of wedding guests accompanying the groom
gudiya: doll
'Khub khushrang bana hai yeh banna praj ki raat!': How colourful is this
    groom on the night he's to become a husband.
'Laddoo, peda, balushahi tikia tumhe khilobain / Toshak, takia, lal
    palangiya tumhe sulaubain': 'Laddoos, pedas, balushahis, tikia will I
    feed thee / On mattress, pillow, red bedstead shall I lull thee to sleep.'
    Traditional wedding folk song.

Chapter 10

achkan: long tunic
Gaddi Pujan: throne-worship ceremony
shisham: teak
bandish: composition
praharas: watches
taaseer: bloom
pushpahar: a necklace in a floral design crafted in gold.
'Rangraliyan kaliyan sang bhanwar karat gunjar / Bolat mor, koyal ki kook sun hook utthi': Flower buds make merry with buzzing bees, peacocks cry, when I heard the cuckoo's coo a pang rose (in my heart).
tanpura: string instrument used as background accompaniment

Chapter 11

gilloris: cones
gari-khana: carriage shed
bawarchi-khanas: cook houses
Mallika-e-Hind: Queen of India
'Naghma-sarai ke siwa kehti hai sher Janki / Ahle-kamal dekh lein uska hunar alag-alag': Other than sing lyrics, Janki writes poetry too / See this marvel, her various gifts. (One of Janki's verses.)
shauq: interest
'Hathwa laagat kumhailai ho rama, juhi ki kaliyan': The touch of a hand is enough to wither the jasmine buds.
'Rum-jhum badarwa barse': Clouds rain like anklet bells.
sozkhwani: song of lamentation mourning the martyrdom of Hazrat Ali
'Janki Bai ke kantha-swara mein misri ki dalia ghuli hui hai': Janki Bai's voice is soaked in sweetness. (Literally, a lump of crystal sugar lies dissolved in her voice.)
murshid: teacher, guide

Chapter 12

gariwan: coachman
khansama: keeper of stores
hazirnama: proof of presence

'Sheikhji gharse na nikle aur yeh farma diya / Aap BA pass hain,
banda Bibi pass hai': Sheikh Sahib did not emerge from his
house but sent word: '(Sir), you are a BA but I am with my B-B'.
Visiting cards often had the educational qualifications of the
owner appended and B-B is a play on BA and Bibi. One of Akbar
Ilahabadi's most well-known light couplets.

'Kya kahoon isko main bad-bakhtiyar nation ke siwa / Usko aata nahin
ab kuchh imitation ke siwa': What shall I call it except the misfortune
of a country, that it knows nothing now apart from imitation. (One
of Akbar's couplets.)

nasamajh: not sensible, lacking in perception

nadaan: naive

mushaira: poetic soirée, often marked by competitive recitals and
spontaneous exchanges in verse

'Kyon koi aaj hari ka naam japay? Kyon riyazat ka jeth sar pe tapay? Kaam
wah hai jo ho governmenti. Naam wah hai jo *Pioneer* mein chhapay':
What need is there to chant the name of God? What need is there
to (submit one's head) to the (scorching summer) sun of toil and
practice? Only that work is worthwhile which has the government's
approval. Only that name is worthy that is printed in the *Pioneer*.
(One of Akbar's quatrains. The *Pioneer* was not a government paper
but it was the mouthpiece of British opinion.)

'Taalim ladkiyon ki zaroori to hai magar / Khatoon-e-khana hon wah
sabha ki pari na hon': By all means, give girls an education, but (bear
in mind) that they turn into women of the home, not into fairies of
the gathering. (One of Akbar's verses.)

'Barkh ke lamp se ankhon ko bachaye Allah / Roshni aati hai aur noor
chala jaata hai': God protect us from (these) electric lamps. Light
comes from them and light leaves our eyes. (One of Akbar's couplets.)

Janki's verse and its translation:

Nala dile majzoon ka rasa ho nahin sakta, yeh kaam bajuz hukme Khuda
ho nahin sakta,

Ulfat teri dil se mere ja hi nahin sakti, nakhoon se bhi gosht juda ho
nahin sakta.

Hai khana-e-dil mazhare ansare ilahi—rutbe mein koi usse siwa ho
nahin sakta,

Zahir mein alag dono hain batin mein mile hain, mashookh se ashiq to
    juda ho nahin sakta.
Uljha hai kisi kakule pencha mein mera dil, yeh murghe giraftar riha ho
    nahin sakta.
Ai Janki khaliq ki paristish hai badi cheez,
Patthar ka jo but hai wah Khuda ho nahin sakta.

The grief-stricken heart's cry cannot be uttered until God wills it,
My love for you cannot be taken out of my heart
As the flesh cannot be separated from the fingernail.
Nothing exceeds the grandeur of this
That the mansion of my heart is aflame with light,
Both seem apart but are one within.
Beloved and lover cannot be severed.
My heart is entangled in someone's curled ringlets,
This captive bird can never be freed.
O Janki, worship of God is an immense thing.
A stone idol can never be turned into God.

Akbar's verse:
Mazhab kabhi science ko sajda na karega,
Insan uray bhi to Khuda ho nahin sakte.
Azrahe-ta-alluq koi jora kare rishta,
Angrez to native ke chacha ho nahin sakte.
Native nahin ho sakte jo gore to hain kya gham,
Gore bhi to bande se Khuda ho nahin sakte.
Hum hon jo collector to wah ho jaye commissioner,
Hum unse kabhi ohdaabra ho nahin sakte.

Religion shall never bow down before science.
Were a man to fly he still cannot turn into God.
Someone might make connections or relationships
(But) a European can never turn uncle to a native.
Never turn native, being white, so what regret?
Even those who're white can't change from human to divine!
If we become collector, they're sure to become commissioner.
We cannot (ever hope to) excel or surpass.

'Aaye badra kare kare': Clouds approach, dark with rain.
'Ummeede-chashme-murowwat kahan rahi baqi / Zariya baaton ka jab
    sirf teleephon hua': What becomes of the gentle speech of the eyes,
    when the only communication is through the telephone? (One of
    Akbar's couplets.)

Chapter 13

farishtas: prophets, angels
rooh: soul
karkhanas: factories
thali: platter
cheez: brief musical composition
'Rakabiyon ne rapat likhwai hai ja ja ke thane mein / Ki Akbar naam leta
    hai Khuda ka is zamane mein!': My enemies have lodged complaints,
    running to the police station again and again, that this Akbar dares
    to utter the name of God in this day and age. (A couplet by Akbar.)
'Kiski jurrat ki Judge Sahib ko koi giraftar kare? Jinki zabaan se har
    daroga, har thanedar dare': Who dares to presume to arrest Judge
    Sahib, whose voice strikes terror in every (petty) police sub-inspector
    and inspector?
'Itwar ko dus baje aapke aane ki muhurat hai, Baiji Janki jinki door-door
    tak shohrat hai': Ten o'clock on Sunday is the hour of your coming,
    Madam Janki, whose name is applauded far and wide.
Diwan-e-Khaas and Diwan-e-Aam: The Mughal Emperor's two audience
    chambers, the former for the nobility, the latter for the common
    people. 'Aam' means mango. The usage employs a pun on the
    word 'aam'.
khaas and aam: For the elite and for the common reader
'Mere hal zaar ki ai buto tumhein kya kisi ko khabar nahin': Of my
    condition, O worshipped one, neither you nor anyone else has
    any idea.
'Chubh gayi jiyabeech pyari chhab tihari': To the depths of my heart has
    pierced your adorable image.
'Janeman jo nazara na hoga': Dearest, if I do not have a vision of you.
'Ram kare kahin naina na uljhe': God willing my eyes may not tangle
    with yours.

Dutt sultana, na Hindu na Mussalmana: The Dutta are kingly, neither Muslims nor Hindus.

kavya guru: master of poetry

'Gori sowai sej par / Mukh par daarey kes / Chal Khusrau ghar aapney / Raine bhayi chahundes': The beauty lies sleeping on her bed of roses, her face covered by her tresses. O Khusrau, it is time for you to return to your home, for night has fallen over the four corners of the land.

turushkapriya: inclined in favour of Muslims, Islamicate

bhajananandi: like Hindu hymn music

navarasas: composition demonstrating the nine emotional states

Chapter 14

sozkhwani: songs of lamentation mourning the death of Ali, Hassan and Hussain

majlis: Shia gathering during Mohorrum

tazia: model of the catafalque of the martyrs, carried in a funeral procession by Shias and ceremonially buried

'Mazhabi bahas mainey ki hi nahin / Faltu aql mujhmein thi hi nahin!': I never did engage in religious wrangling, I never had useless intelligence to waste. (A couplet by Akbar.)

kalma: Islamic declaration of submission to the only God, Allah, and His Prophet, Muhammad. Uttered during conversion to Islam.

likely to stand beneath this stole soon: reference to the Shia marriage ceremony

gopis: cowgirls

aswattha, nyagrodha, chuta, palash, bakula, bilva, kadamba: names of trees

lila: enchanted illusion

dharma: righteous law

bodhi: intelligence

batashas: sugar pellets offered as worship and as prasad

tapas: diligent effort

kriti: composition, creation, here a hymn

naada, the srutis, the jatis and the talas: sound, semitones, categories and rhythms

'Dheerey baho nadia': Flow softly, O river. (A medieval song.)

'Balam naiyya dagmag doley': O Beloved, my boat rocks this way and
    that. (A song.)
mazaar: monument over a tomb
naat: devotional song
'Raghubar aaj raho more pyare': Hindu devotional song
'Madina mein mor piya vala hai re': Islamic devotional song
'Balake ban mein jo sograka naamabar aaya': soz

Chapter 15

'Main kaise rakhoon praan shyam madhuban gailona': How should I
    hold on to my life, my Krishna has gone to the honey-bowers?
'Ab kaise jobna dikhaoongi': How should I now my blooming youth
    show?
'Rukh-e-gulshan ki dekhi bahar': I saw the flower garden of His face in
    springtime glory.
Pyare Ahmed-e-Mukhtar, Tumpar Allah Ka Hai Pyar: O beloved, lauded
    high one, on thee rests the favour of Allah.
'Ek Kaffir par tabiyat aa gayi': I am grown infatuated with an idolater
'Hamne to jaantak na pyari ki, Kanha na kar mosey raar': I didn't even
    seek to preserve my life, O Krishna, do not quarrel with me.
'Dar kharabat-e-mughan noor-e-Khuda mee beenam': Even in the tavern
    I behold the radiance of God.

'Ek Kaffir par tabiyat aa gayi.
Parsai par phir aafat aa gayi.
Humdum, isko dillagi samjha hai tu?
Dil nahin aaya, museebat aa gayi.
Yaad karke tumko ai jaan ro diye,
Saamne jab achchhi surat aa gayi.
Chupke-chupke ro rahe ho kyon samad,
Sach kaho kis par tabiyat aa gayi?'

I was taken with an idolater.
Then all hell descended on this purist-pretender.
Friend, do not imagine I am jesting,
It wasn't an infatuation, it was sheer misfortune.

Remembering you, O my life, I wept.
When your alluring face came before me.
Why do you weep in secret, O excellent one,
Tell me the truth, who is it you're taken with?

farmaish: request for a song
'Phadkan laagat mori ankhiyan': My eyelids begin fluttering (with a tic in
    the presence of the beloved).
'Mumkin nahin ke teri mohabbat ki bu nahin': It isn't possible that your
    love hasn't a (telltale) fragrance.
'Jabse us zaalim se ulfat ho gayi': Ever since I fell in love with that cruel one.
'Dil ek hi se laga, hazaron khade': The heart chose only one out of the
    thousands who vied.
'Kaffire ishkam Mussalmani mara darkar nist': My love has turned me
    into an infidel, I have nothing to do with being a believer.
'Tum hi kufr ho aur iman tumhi ho': You are my idolatry and you my
    honour.
'Gham raha jabtak ke dam mein dam raha': As long as there was grief,
    there was strength in my breath.
tat: bank
mehmil: women's tent on the camel's back
'Allah bachaey marz-e-ishq se dil ko, suntey hain ki yeh aariza achchha
    nahin hota': God save us from this illness called love, I hear this
    disease isn't good (for us). (One of Akbar's verses.)
'Bahut raha hai kabhi lutf-e-yaar hum par bhi, guzar chuki hai yeh fasl-
    e-bahar hum par bhi': The joy of loving someone has been with me
    once, over me has passed too the harvest season of spring. (A verse
    by Akbar.)
tokra: basket

Chapter 16

nok-jhonk: musical repartee
dangal: contest in singing
Fransisi: French
la haula wa la kuwate: exclamation of disgust. Literally 'There is no power
    except God!' (Presumably uttered to ward off evil.)

irshad: a conventional granting of assent to a poet to recite his verse

'Exhibition ki shaan anokhi / Har shai umda, har shai chokhi / Okhlidas ki naapi-jokhi / Man bhar sone ki laagat dekhi': The exhibition is uniquely grand, everything excellent, everything appropriate. Everything geometrically measured and mapped, Maunds of gold invested I saw. (A verse by Akbar.)

'Jab chhod chale Lucknow' and 'Babul mora naihar chhuto jaye': 'When we left Lucknow forever' and 'My father, my ancestral home is fast lost to me'. Two of Wajid Ali Shah's own compositions, mourning the loss of his kingdom.

gat: rhythm

mash-e-Allah: wonderful. Literally, may God protect from blight.

piya: beloved of. Used as pen name by ghazal writers in the nineteenth and early twentieth century.

Subhan Allah: Glory be to God!

'Gaye sharbat ke din yaaron ke aage ab toh ai Akbar / Kabhi soda, kabhi lemonade, kabhi whiskey, kabhi tea hai!': The days of sherbet are gone, friends, for in the days ahead, O Akbar, it'll be sometimes soda, sometimes lemonade, sometimes whiskey, sometimes tea! (A verse by Akbar.)

Thay cake ki fikr mein, so roti bhi gayi,
Chaahi thi shay badi, so chhoti bhi gayi,
Wayiz ki naseehatein na maneen aakhir,
Patloon ki taak mein langoti bhi gayi.

We hankered after cake and (in the process) lost our bread too,
We hankered after big things and (in the process) lost the small ones too,
We ignored the sermons of our teachers and finally,
In hankering after trousers lost our loincloths too!
(A verse by Akbar.)

Bepurdah kal jo aayeen nazar chand bibiyan,
Akbar zameen mein ghairat-qaumi sed gad gaya.
Poochha jo unse aapka purdah wo kya hua?
Kehne lageen ki aql pe mardon ki pad gaya.

When yesterday there appeared before the eyes some unveiled ladies
Akbar sank into the ground in utter confusion.
When he asked them: 'What's become of your veils?'
They answered: 'They now cover the wits of men!'

'Wah mutrib aur wah saaz, wah gaana badal gaya. Neendein badal gayeen,
    wah fasana badal gaya. / Rangey-rukhey-bahar ki zeenat hui nayee,
    gulshan mein bulbulon ka tarana badal gaya.': Those accompanists,
    that music, that song has changed. Our sleep has changed, and our
    story too. The look and colour of springtime has a different beauty.
    The song of the bulbuls in the garden has a different trill. (A verse
    by Akbar.)

Akbar's poem, 'Jalwa-e-Durbar-e-Dehli', on the Delhi Durbar:
Sar mein shauq ka sauda dekha,
Dehli ko humne ja dekha,
Jo kuchh dekha achchha dekha.
Jamunaji ke paat ko dekha,
Achchhe suthre ghat ko dekha,
Sab se unche laat ko dekha,
Hazrat Duke Canaat ko dekha.
Paltan aur risale dekhey,
Gore dekhey, kale dekhey,
Sangeeney aur bhaaley dekhey,
Band bajaney waaley dekhey.
Daali mein narangi dekhi,
Mehfil mein sarangi dekhi,
Bairangi baarangi dekhi,
Dahar ki ranga-rangi dekhi.
Achchhe-achchhon ko bhatka dekha,
Bheed mein khaatey jhhatka dekha,
Munh ko agarchey latka dekha,
Dil darbar se atka dekha.
Auj British Raj ka dekha
Partav takht-o-taj ka dekha,
Rangey zamana aaj ka dekha,
Rukh Curzon Maharaj ka dekha.

I saw the absolute peak of luxurious commerce.
I too went and beheld Delhi,
And everything I saw was grand.
I saw the river Yamuna's bank
And its clean, lofty embankments.
I saw the most exalted Lord,
His Highness the Duke of Connaught.
I saw processions and flags,
White skins and coloured,
Bayonets and lances,
And musicians of the bands.
I saw oranges on the boughs
And saarangis in the gatherings,
Things well matched and ill,
Brilliant temporary hues.
I saw sensible people strayed
Pushed and jostled by the crowds.
Although their faces seemed downcast (yet)
Drawn irresistibly to the Delhi Durbar.
I beheld the grandeur of the British Empire,
The shadow of the Mughal throne,
The colour of this present age,
The face of King Curzon.

'Sur kahan ke, saaz kaisa, kaisi bazm-e-saamai? Josh-e-dil kaafi hai,
    Akbar, taan udane ke liye': What (strange) tunes, what instruments,
    what a strange audience! O Akbar, the heart's enthusiasm is quite
    enough to let fly a few trills!

Akbar's poem 'Barq-e-Kilisa' (Lightning in church):
Zulf-e-penchan mein wah sajdhaj, ki balayein bhi mureed.
Qadey-rana mein wah chamkham ki qayamat bhi shaheed.
Ankhein wah fitnayey-dauran ki gunahgaar karein,
Gaal wah subahey-darakhshan ki malaq pyar karein,
Garm taqdeer jisey sunney ko shola lapkey . . .
Dilkash awaaz ki sunkar jisey bulbul jhhapkey . . .
Dilkash chaal mein aisi ki sitarey ruk jaayein

Sarkashi naaz mein aisi ki governor jhuk jaayein
Aatishey husn se taqwey ko jalaaney wali,
Bijliyan lutf-e-tabassum se giraney wali.

Her curled locks so ornamental as to entrap even the calamities,
Her attractive stature so regal that even the day of doom might be
    martyred,
Her eyes enough to vex the world, make sinners of us.
Her cheeks like the shining morn that angels might adore.
Fortunate destiny that embers might leap to know . . .
Her charming voice which might lull the bulbuls.
Her gait so attractive that stars might stop in their tracks
Her haughty affectation such that governors might bow . . .
She, the flame of whose beauty, can burn up (a man's) austerity.
Whose art of smiling can call down the lightning

'Khush naseeb aaj yahan kaun hai, Gauhar ke siwa? / Sab kuchh Allah
    ne de rakha hai shauhar ke siwa!': Who is fortunate here save
    only Gauhar? Whom God has granted everything save only a
    husband.
'Yun toh Gauhar ko mayassar hain hazaron shauhar / Par pasand
    usko nahin koi bhi Akbar ke siwa!': Although Gauhar can take
    her pick from thousands of husbands, she likes none save only
    Akbar.

Chapter 17

gusal-khana: bathroom
rok-token: gold coin gifted by the bride's family to the groom as a pact
    of engagement
muta marriage: a temporary marriage for a stipulated length of time as
    distinct from a nikah
'Yeh jalsa taajposhi ka, mubarak ho, mubarak ho!': On this coronation
    celebration, felicitations, felicitations!
Bachchon ki Parwarish: How to rear children
Hidayat Timardari: Suggestions on nursing
Tandarusti: Health

Chapter 18

walima: wedding reception at the groom's house to celebrate the coming
    of the bride
izzat: honour
'Hamare nabi aaj dulha bane': My Holy One is become a bridegroom
    today.
'Hari ka bhed na paayo Rama! Kudrat teri rang-birangi, tu kudrat ka
    wali!': No one has understood the mystery of God, O Rama. All
    nature (that Thou hast created) is varicoloured and Thou art the
    Master Artist.

Chapter 20

Assalaamoalaikum: Peace be with you
khankhwa: shelter
daira: place associated with a saint
sajjadanasheen: one who looks after a sufi daira, literally one who sits on
    the prayer mat
ganja: a form of cannabis

Chapter 21

mirasans: professional women singers specializing in folk songs at
    weddings and childbirths
kangan: heavy bangles
jhoomar: a sideways hanging forehead pendant
sahibzade: son of a sahib
bagiya: garden
'Sakhi-ri, main chali thi neer pachhore': Friend, I went trying to winnow
    the waters (of the river).
'Sri Ram kripalu': Lord Rama, the merciful.

Chapter 22

sakshi: witness
Usase kuchh mera bhi zikare dile nashad rahe: some mention of my
    unfortunate heart must be made to that one.

Jui ka fulva hathva lagat: the jasmine is within reach of my hand

swaras: notes

Jabki khamosh hui bulbul bustane husain: When in Hussain's garden the bulbul fell silent.

Hari bin morey kaun khabar le?: Who, other than God, comes asking after me?

Dil sahabe aulad se insaaf talab hai: The heart seeks justice from the Master, the Father.

Chapter 23

panchnama: legal procedure whereby five witnesses testify to the presence of a dead body

Scan QR code to access the
Penguin Random House India website